THEN
CRYSTALS

THE CRYSTAL CHRONICLES BOOK 1

R. DAWNRAVEN

CROSSED CLAYMORE PRESS

The Hidden Crystals by R. Dawnraven
Published by Crossed Claymore Press

Copyright © 2023 by R. Dawnraven
Map & Internal Images Copyright © 2023 by R. Dawnraven
Cover Art & Design by C. L. Simons
Author Photo by Justin C. E. Penner
Edited by Clare Marshall and Michaela Choi
Formatted in Atticus

All rights reserved.

No portion of this book may be reproduced in any form without written permission from the publisher or author, except as permitted by U.S. copyright law.

This book is a work of fiction and as such all characters and situations are fictitious. Any semblance to actual people, places, or events is coincidental.

ISBN 979-8-3632425-2-6 (paperback)
ISBN 979-8-3632438-3-7 (hardcover)

Contents

Dedication	V
Map	1
Part One	2
1. The Prophecy	3
2. The Elithar	10
3. Durme	17
4. Muddy Waters	26
5. Great Snapper	35
6. The Island	42
7. Sapphire	48
Part Two	54
8. Captain Anaril	60
9. Watcher	71
10. Gate	78
11. Mt. Hissan	85
12. Fire	93
13. Descent	104
14. The Crossing	112
Part Three	121

15.	Memory	125
16.	Sea of Gold	135
17.	Theft and Discovery	144
18.	Visit	150
19.	To Hide A Tree	156
Part Four		166
20.	Twisting Paths	173
21.	The Past	180
22.	Heated Clash	187
23.	Flight	198
24.	Taken	205
Part Five		212
25.	The Temple	223
26.	Reunion	229
27.	Revelations	237
28.	The Crystals	244
29.	Consequences	249
30.	Coming Out	257
Epilogue		261
Uhaan		262
Acknowledgments		263
About the Author		264

For all the queer kids.

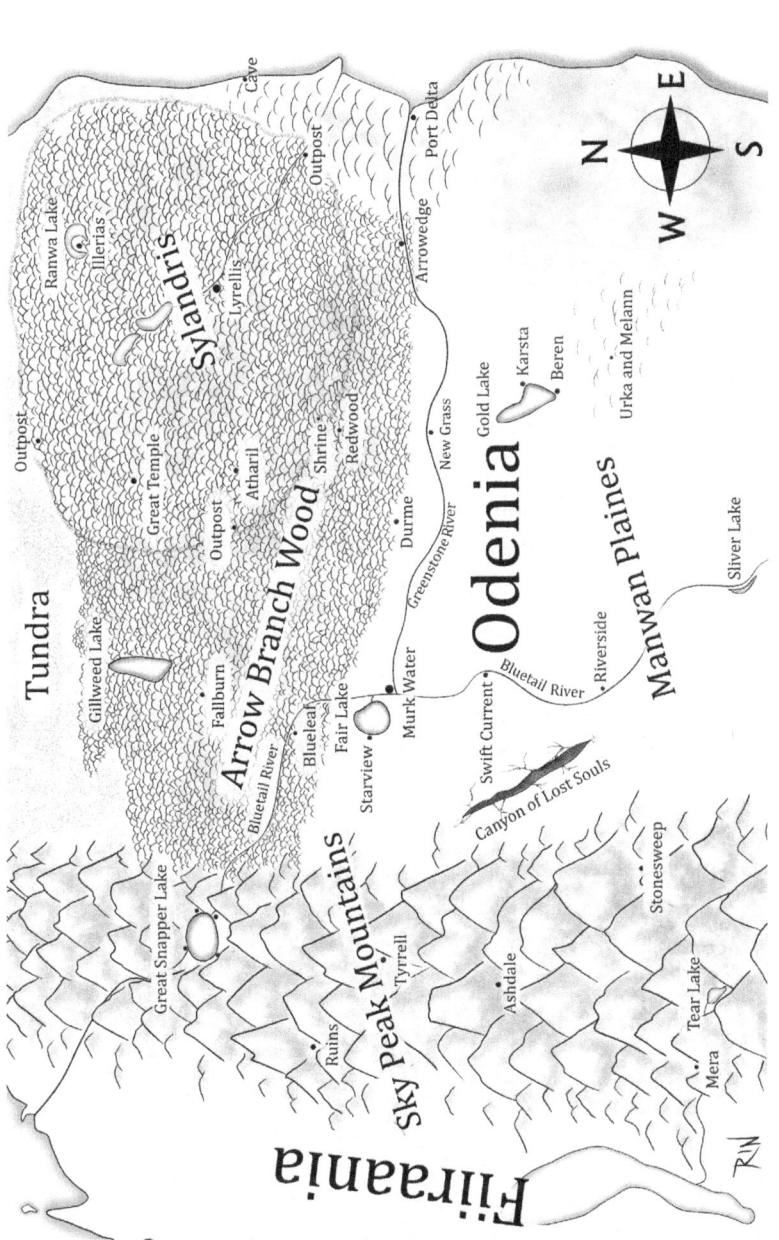

Part One

For nearly a decade they had been searching for the crystal and at last all their efforts were paying off. The dark-clad figure stood in a hidden chamber deep underground. The stone room was dimly lit by a few stubby candles which cast strange shadows on the walls. The figure ignored the shadows. These ones weren't dangerous, not like the ones they'd just had to face. The room was empty save for a carved stone box resting on a pedestal in the centre.

The seeker reached a pale hand into the box and pulled forth a pointed, dark purple crystal about half the length of their slender thumb. Their breath caught as the crystal's magic pulsed, sending a wave of shadowy energy rippling across the physical and aural planes, snuffing out the candles and plunging the chamber into darkness. But the crystal had done more than that; it had set into motion a series of events that would culminate with the fulfillment of their plans.

"It begins," they said softly, tucking the stone safely away inside an old dragonhide pouch, "the fall of the royal line."

One

The Prophecy

"You behave while I'm gone, Fae," said Cane, the master blacksmith of Redwood. "I should be back from Murk Water by the end of the summer. You know these guild seminars can be quite lengthy."

"Do you think they might run longer?" asked Fae, helping the dark-haired woman pack the last of her things.

"Unlikely," she replied. "Now, I know you want to search for your brother, but no more crossing the border into Sylandris, all right? They may be your people, but the elves aren't fond of non-magic users for whatever snooty reason. You know they don't take kindly to your presence, my boy."

He nodded, remembering how the border patrols had chased him through Sylandris' enormous trees, only ceasing their pursuit once he had crossed back into the human kingdom of Odenia. Apparently, leaving their forest was beneath them, but chasing down an elf with no *damis*—the source of an elf's magical ability—wasn't. While these incidents had shaken him up, they had not discouraged him from trying again.

Somewhere within the Elves' magical forest was his brother, his only remaining family—aside from Master Cane, of course. The stocky human blacksmith had found him many suncycles ago after his parents had been killed and his brother kidnapped. Though the incident had taken place at his childhood home, he remembered little of it; he and his brother had hardly been a decade old at the time. But the image of Ash being carried away by a stranger followed by a blinding flash had remained clear in his mind. Everything else was hazy chaos and noise, like looking out a window during a blizzard.

Fae passed Master Cane the last of her gear, which she strapped to her four-legged uhaan before swinging up into the saddle. "I've asked Gale to come check up on you, but I'm not too sure when she'll come through town," she said, her grey eyes meeting his brown ones.

Gale was coming? He didn't know Gale too well, but she was a good friend of Master Cane's. Her arrival meant Fae would have to act fast, for he fully intended to go against his master's wishes.

"I'll keep an eye out for her," he replied, rubbing her stocky uhaan between the two small horns that protruded above each of their eyes. "Have a safe trip, and don't let those old guys at the guild push you around."

Cane snorted. "As if that would ever happen. Stay safe, and don't burn the smithy down while I'm gone. See you in a few weeks, my boy." With that, she signalled to her mount and rode off, leaving Fae to do whatever he pleased. Except burn the smithy down or enter Sylandris.

• • • ● • • •

Fae strapped on his sword and tied up his long, oddly coloured hair—black at the roots fading to pure white at the tips. First, he would visit his childhood home near the royal city of Lyrellis, deep within the forest. He didn't expect to find Ash there, but perhaps he would find some clues as to why his family had been attacked all those decades ago. A chill that the setting summer sun could not drive away swept through him as he left the smithy.

Ducking between some houses, he slipped out of town, disappearing into the strip of trees that stretched between Redwood and the magical Sylandrian wards protecting the Elves' mysterious home. The setting sun cast strange shadows through the trees, making it difficult for him to find the old path that would guide him to the magical barrier. After a bit of poking around the undergrowth, he found the disused trail and soon stood before the wards. They wrapped around Sylandris, keeping unwanted creatures—namely bothersome humans—out of the realm. Due to his Elven heritage, Fae had no issues slipping through them.

He scooted behind a thick tree and waited, pointed ears straining to detect any sign of a patrol. Aside from the rustling leaves and chittering birds, the forest was quiet. But that didn't mean they weren't around. Last time, he hadn't realized the patrol had found him until they'd popped out of the bushes.

Convinced no one was in the immediate vicinity, Fae darted out from behind the tree and through the nearly invisible wards; only a strange shimmer distorting the air marked its presence. His vision flickered, his head spinning as he passed through it—just like last time.

Fae would never get used to how starkly different Sylandris was from Odenia. Taking a steadying breath of the sweet, pure air, he worked his way deeper into the trees. They were enormous, their trunks easily wider than he was tall. Their lowest branches were higher than the tops of the Arrow Branch Wood surrounding his home. Thick vines looped lazily through them, many thicker than his torso. Brightly coloured undergrowth made it difficult to walk, pulling at his clothes and snagging his hair. All his senses were on high alert as he pushed onwards.

The sun had just set when he came upon a decaying wooden structure covered in plant life. Fae slowly edged his way around the ruin, searching for its entrance under the light of the twin moons. It wasn't very big, and the fact it sat on the ground meant it couldn't be a house. As far as he knew, elves didn't build their homes on the forest floor; his family home had been high up off the ground. He rounded the corner and found the entrance, its sliding door partly open. He stepped towards it and nearly jumped out of his skin when something rustled in the broad-leafed bushes nearby.

Cursing silently, he ducked behind a tree, heart racing. There was one advantage to not having a damis: he gave off no aural energy that could be tracked. But that didn't mean he was invisible. And elves could see well in the dark.

The snapping of twigs grew louder. He thought he heard a voice but couldn't make out their words from his hiding place.

Fae tensed up, ready to bolt, his breathing steadied and ears strained. How many were there this time? If there were less than three, he might have a chance, but this didn't sound like a group of elves—perhaps only one or two at most. Strange.

"Blasted roots!"

The voice was young—too young to belong to one of the border guards. Fae's brow furrowed as a single elf pushed through the brush, cursing under their breath. The newcomer had to be around his age, give or take a decade. The thick underbrush snarled their refined silk clothing, leaving twigs caught in their long blond hair, foolishly worn loose. All in all, they looked extremely frazzled.

Fae debated staying hidden. The newcomer didn't seem to be a threat, and they were too close now not to see him. He sighed and stepped out from behind his tree, hands raised in a show of submission. *This better not be a mistake.*

"Who's there?" the blond elf demanded sharply, surprised and on edge. They—*he*—took a step back.

"Just another traveller passing though," Fae lied, his command of the Elven language, Illithen, rusty from disuse. If he could make it through this strange encounter, then he could continue with his mission. And it had to be quick; all the noise the other elf was making was bound to draw the attention of every living being in the forest.

Patrols weren't the only things Fae wanted to avoid. The citizens of Redwood called it the Untamed Forest for a good reason; many strange creatures lived in here, some of whom could use magic and wouldn't think twice about confronting an elf who had yet to finish his fifth decade of life.

The stranger narrowed his eyes and surveyed him for a moment, emerald gaze lingering on Fae's odd hair. Fae did likewise, but with less emphasis on the stranger's light locks. All Sylandrian elves had varying shades of blond hair—something he'd learned during his first attempt to sneak into their forest. The last patrol that found him mocked his strange colouring on top of ripping into him about being a *damisri*—someone without a damis.

A chill went down his spine. Magic-users could sense each other, which meant this elf knew he couldn't use magic.

Fae tensed up, ready for a fight, but the adolescent elf showed no signs of attacking. Fae gave him another quick once-over, noting that he carried a pack along with an out-of-place longsword at his hip; elves typically favoured magic over steel. At least when it came to beating up Fae.

"Where—"

"I don't like repeating myself. Who are you?" the other demanded again.

Fae blinked at the stranger's brash abruptness. If he kept this up, they were going to get caught. "Fae. And you are?" he said quietly and quickly, urging the other to catch on with a pointedly insistent look.

"You may call me Alysion," the traveller said just as loudly as before. His speech was different from that of the border guards. "What are you using to conceal your aura? I wasn't able to sense your presence at all and would like to hide my own."

"I'm not—" Fae froze at a noise in the forest.

"What is it?" Alysion demanded, still far too loud.

"Quiet!"

Alysion looked miffed but shut up, having heard the sound too.

"Patrol," Fae breathed, noticing that the other looked just as jumpy as he felt.

Snap!

He grabbed Alysion's wrist and pulled him towards the rotting door.

"Unhand me!" he yelped, struggling to wriggle free.

"Shh!" Fae hissed between his teeth, trying to squeeze past the sliding door. It wouldn't budge. "Help me."

"Not until you let go!" the other shouted.

Fae quickly released him.

Alysion took a moment to rub the spot like he was trying to remove a stubborn bit of dirt.

Bracing themselves, they heaved against the door, but to Fae's dismay, it still wouldn't move. *Come on!*

The resounding *crack* of a branch snapping close by redoubled their efforts. The rotting door suddenly gave, and the two fell into a heap inside. Fae blinked stupidly up at Alysion, who had landed on top of him, brown eyes meeting emerald. He was very grateful for the darkness that helped to conceal his burning face, the sudden proximity to the other elf stirring something deep inside him. A faint whiff of fruit followed Alysion as he scrambled off him, muttering something unintelligible.

"Do you live near Lyrellis?" Fae whispered as he regained his footing. He surveyed the shack. It was just as rotten on the inside as the outside, the air stale and musty. Dried leaves and twigs covered the dusty floor, piling up in dark corners. A pile of wood resembling an altar sat near the back wall, an abandoned shrine crumbling from decades of disuse.

"What? Why?" Alysion replied quickly but quietly.

"My family lived on the outskirts, and there were these berry bushes that—"

Bang!

The sliding door slammed shut, plunging them into pitch black so deep their keen Elven eyes couldn't see through it.

"What are you doing?" Alysion hissed somewhere off to Fae's right.

"I didn't do anything!" he whispered back. "I thought that was you!"

Alysion huffed loudly.

Rolling his eyes, Fae felt his way to the door. He bit back a yelp as his hand passed over something fuzzy on the wall. *Please let that be moss.*

"Hey—" Alysion whispered.

"I found the door."

"Turn around."

What now? Fae turned and froze.

Something small was glowing faintly in the centre of the decrepit shrine.

"What's that?" he breathed, squinting at the light. Was it the patrol?

The light pulsed and brightened. Fae threw up an arm to shield his eyes; he couldn't look away. The light grew, taking on the form of a tall elf dressed in long-sleeved robes.

Fae lowered his arm and stared at the apparition, his concerns about being found by a patrol momentarily forgotten. Beside him, Alysion did the same.

The glowing elf spoke, their musical voice sending a shiver down his spine:

Descendant, you have been assigned,
Seven crystalline powers you must find,
To protect the realm under the sun,
But be warned: darkness has taken one,
Power resides in the moon's lake,
Its sibling kept by a mountain's quake,
The golden sea protects another,
While the forgotten forest hides it's brother,
One is hidden where brilliance is cast,
And the heart will summon forth the last,
Unite them all to call power greater,
Else Sylandris shall fall at the hands of a traitor.

The apparition held out their hands as their words faded.

Fae's wrist started to itch, and he nearly jumped into Alysion when he saw it was glowing under his shirt. He pulled up his sleeve to reveal a strange glowing mark: a circle with six smaller dots around it. It faded to nothing before his eyes. Heart racing, he rubbed at the spot, but the mark did not reappear. He looked over to Alysion, staring at his own arm with a frown.

The apparition faded, and light along with it, plunging the shrine back into darkness. Fae, needing some fresh air, whirled around and slid the door open a crack. The faint light of the twin moons filtered in, restoring his sight. Taking a deep breath to calm himself, he turned and looked expectantly at Alysion. Was this a normal occurrence for magic users?

But Alysion ignored him, busy poking at his wrist.

"We should leave," said Fae quietly, wanting nothing more than to put as much distance between himself and the dilapidated shack. The glowing elf hadn't exactly been inconspicuous.

"But the Elithar are still out there," said Alysion, finishing his inspection and sitting down. He looked exhausted.

"After all that, the Eli-Elithar..." Fae stumbled over the new word, "are bound to find us. We need to move." He peeked out the door and scanned the area but couldn't see or hear anything. Whatever had been creeping around earlier must have been scared off by the glowing elf. "Besides, this isn't a very comfortable place to sleep."

Alysion reluctantly stood and started brushing dirt off himself like his life depended on it. "I suppose you're right."

Fae fought the urge to roll his eyes. This elf had to be the son of a noble. "My place isn't far. You're welcome to come with me if you have no place to go." As much as he hated to abandon his quest for tonight, it wasn't wise to keep going—not after all the light and noise.

Alysion opened his mouth to protest, then closed it. "Lead the way."

They would be safe in Redwood; the Sylandrians *never* crossed their border.

Two

The Elithar

Tensions were high as they moved through the trees, expecting the Elithar to be upon them at any moment.

"That was unexpected," Alysion whispered, a sound too loud in the quiet nighttime forest.

"Shh, we can talk when we get back to my place," Fae cut in. He had questions that needed answering, but right now, stealth was key.

But Alysion could not keep himself quiet as they passed through the Sylandrian wards. "Why are we crossing the border? I thought we were going to your place!" He stopped dead and glanced at the shimmering barrier over his shoulder.

"We are," Fae replied, turning to face him. It took all he had not to snap. At least they were safe in Odenia now. "I live in Redwood, near the edge of the Arrow Branch Wood."

"You live with humans?" Alysion asked, green eyes flashing. "I will *not* enter a human town! It's dirty, and smelly, and—"

"It's that or trying your luck with the Elithar," huffed Fae. He turned his back to his companion and continued through the trees, unbothered with leaving Alysion and his xenophobia behind. Reluctant footsteps followed behind him.

"What were you doing in the forest?" Alysion asked once they had put a considerable distance between themselves and Sylandris.

"I was looking for someone. We were separated a few decades ago."

Alysion's piercing emerald eyes suddenly met Fae's, and he shuddered under their intensity.

"Are you looking for a human? Is that why you're living amongst them? You won't find any humans in Sylandris."

Fae wasn't about to share his whole life story with someone he'd just met. "No, I'm looking for my brother. Redwood is...where my search led me." If Alysion was like the few Elithar he'd met, then Fae had no desire to tell Alysion the truth. Yet, despite his attitude, Fae had to admit part of him enjoyed being around an elf his age. The memory of Alysion landing on top of him in the shrine suddenly crossed his mind, and his cheeks flushed. He glanced at the ground, praying Alysion hadn't noticed.

"What were you doing so close to the border?" Fae asked, avoiding Alysion's gaze. "There aren't any Elven villages around here."

Alysion stiffened. "What I was doing isn't your concern."

"If you're a criminal on the run—" With all the excitement earlier, he hadn't considered that bringing home a stranger may be unwise.

"I'm not a criminal. I still have my damis."

Fae nearly tripped. *Still* had his damis? Damai could be lost? His mind raced with a million questions. As far as he knew, he'd never had a damis to begin with.

"What was the glowing elf all about?" he asked, dropping his voice. He rubbed his wrist. The mark hadn't shown up again.

Alysion didn't respond right away. "It's warning us about a traitor to the kingdom. *Seven crystalline powers you must find* is rather straightforward; there are magical crystals that must be found in order to stop whatever is coming."

"Are you going to do that?" He watched Alysion's face, but his expression was unreadable.

"I'd rather not. It sounds bothersome. But..." Fae the caught waver in his voice. "I can feel a pull. The magic of the prophecy was binding."

"A pull?"

"Yes, don't you feel it? You're bound as well."

Fae really did trip this time. "I'm *what*?"

"Maybe you can't. Your aura is feeble. I can't even sense it."

"That's because...because..." Fae scrambled for an excuse. "Because I'm wearing a talisman that blocks auras. It stops me from giving off an aura and from feeling them. When you're the only elf in town, you attract a lot of unwanted attention."

Alysion pondered that, then nodded. Fae let out a breath he was holding.

"I wouldn't want to be bothered by humans all day either, especially the few who *can* use magic," Alysion spoke as if he'd sucked on sour fruit.

"They're not all that bad."

"I suppose you would think that."

Fae decided against getting into an argument with him. "What was that about me being bound?"

"We were both present when the prophecy was delivered, so now we're a part of it whether we like it or not. The apparition marked both of us." He held up his wrist. Like Fae's, it showed no signs of the glowing mark.

"And what happens if we choose to ignore it?"

"As much as I'd love to, I'm quickly realizing I can't ignore the pull. It's tugging at my damis. I fear if I ignore it, it will only grow stronger and more painful. I wouldn't be surprised if it killed us in the end."

Fae's stomach dropped. Killed? Oh no, he couldn't let that happen. He needed to find Ash! Elves, he learned, matured much more slowly than humans due to their significantly longer lifespans. Although he was nearly half a century old, his mind and body were comparable to an adolescent human. Master Cane urged him to hold off his search for Ash until he was an adult, but Fae couldn't wait any longer. He would not allow himself to die now.

"Is there any way to undo it? I don't want to be bound to some weird glowing elf-thing."

"From what I've read, the only way to rid ourselves of it is to do what it's asking." Alysion looked just as thrilled as he felt about all this, which was to say, not at all. It was oddly comforting.

A thought occurred to him—one that might free him of this unwanted responsibility. "Have you read anything about non-magical people? For example, if someone didn't have a damis, like a human, could they be bound?"

Alysion gave him a strange look. "You've been spending too much time with humans."

"I'm just curious."

Alysion dropped his gaze, thinking. "I haven't read anything about that. But if you cast a spell on a non-magic user—set them on fire, for example, they'll still burn up. So I would safely assume they'd be obligated to fulfill the prophecy as well."

Fae's feet went cold. If Alysion were right, he would have to go through with this. He grit his teeth in frustration. Damn.

• • • ● • • •

"Hey Fae, who've you got there?" a woman's voice hollered as they made their way down Redwood's main road.

"Just a traveller I found in the forest," Fae replied, comfortably switching back to the Odenian tongue. It didn't go unnoticed by his companion, but Fae ignored his look, searching for the source of the voice instead—one of the carpenters Master Cane dealt with regularly, as carpentry resulted in many broken tools that needed repair. "It's those darn apprentices," the carpenter always complained whenever she came to the smithy, shaking her head. "They're so hard on things."

Right now, she sat on a stack of wood outside her workshop, sipping a mug of tea. Fae knew she liked stargazing, and tonight was a great night for it. Still, it was rather late for her to be out.

"Cat needed out, and when I saw the sky, I couldn't help myself," she said. "Anyway, he's quite the traveller; don't see elves too often, aside from yourself, of course." She eyed the newcomer from her seat. Alysion's hair shone silver in the moonlight, illuminating his Elven features.

"We don't have much need to leave our forest," Alysion replied, his grasp of the Odenian language much better than Fae expected.

"He's just passing through," Fae cut in before Alysion could say anything else. "We have to get going now. He's had a long journey."

"Looks like it," replied the carpenter. "Have a good night, you two!" She threw Fae a wink he hoped Alysion didn't see.

"Sorry about that," Fae apologized when they turned a corner. "Even though we're close to the border, people aren't used to elves coming to town." In all the decades he'd lived in Redwood, Fae had never encountered another elf. For whatever reason, they never left their forest.

Alysion sniffed. "At least she has good taste."

Fae coughed.

His companion furrowed his brow but stayed quiet until they reached the smithy.

To Fae's surprise, his guest didn't complain when Fae led him up to his room. Perhaps Alysion had been expecting a shack, and Fae's home was anything but; he lived on the upper level of the smithy with Master Cane. After a quick bath, for they were both dirty and smelly from their adventure, he showed Alysion to his room and then passed out in Master Cane's bed, not bothering to unpack his bag.

• • • ● • • •

Fae woke to the sound of movement. Groggy, he struck out at the shape near his bed.

"It's just me!" a voice hissed.

Thankfully, his fist hit empty air. Right. Alysion. His elven guest. What was he doing in here?

"Are you all right?" Alysion asked, looking more annoyed than anything, though he was already fully dressed and wearing his pack.

"I'm fine," said Fae.

"Good, because we have trouble. The Elithar are in town—I can sense them nearby. They've picked up my aura and know I'm here."

"So you're leaving?" Fae tried to shake himself from the stupor of sleep. The sun was barely up; they hadn't rested for long.

"*We're* leaving." Alysion glanced out the window at the dark street beyond. "We're both bound, remember?" He tapped his wrist. "We have to find the crystals."

The memory of their nighttime adventure came crashing back. Fae was suddenly wide awake. The prophecy.

"Right, and if I don't come and help, I'll be torn apart by the bond. I suppose I can't leave it all up to you, can I?" He leapt out of bed and swiftly changed his clothes. Alysion's eyes were on him, but he didn't care; it wasn't the first time someone had seen him undress.

"I don't want to do this anymore than you do," Alysion continued. "It will be easier if we work together, like when Gwynnestra Brightstar and Ruehnar Silverbrook created the Silverstar River to provide our kingdom with water. Had they tried to do it alone, they'd still be working to this day. Besides, you said we were looking for someone, no? Perhaps you'll find some clues as to their whereabouts on our journey."

If the journey took them into Sylandris, then that was a possibility.

Someone knocked on the door downstairs.

"They're here," Alysion whispered.

"We can escape down the outer stairway. It leads out back." Fae hastily belted on his sword and grabbed his pack.

Alysion shook his head. "Even if we did, they'd still catch us right away. They're tracking my aura."

"Then what do you suppose we do?"

The smithy door suddenly banged open, and footsteps pounded up the staircase.

"Leave it to me," Alysion whispered as a tall, heavily armoured elf strode into the room, flanked by two others.

"Prince Alysion, we've come to return you home."

Fae blinked stupidly. Prince...? *Oh.* The first line of the prophecy surfaced in his mind, clear as a sunny day. *Descendant, you have been assigned*—no wonder the glowing elf had come to them. Alysion was the direct descendant of the Divine Ancestors, the most important of all the Elven deities!

"That's rather unfortunate, Captain Anaril, as I won't be returning with you today," he replied calmly.

Though the captain's neutral expression remained, something in the air shifted. Fae's hand hovered above the handle of his sword, his senses on high alert. Though Master Cane had trained him in the art of the blade, he knew he was no match for three warriors armed to the teeth with magic and steel.

"We are under direct orders from the queen and king to escort you back to Lyrellis." The captain stepped forward. The two elves behind them entered the cramped room. Their armour was different from the border patrol, metal instead of leather, emblazoned with the mark of the royal family: a silver star. Fighting wasn't an option.

Alysion raised a hand, his palm facing the guards. "If you take another step, I'll attack."

The captain's eyes narrowed, but they didn't move any closer.

"Let us pass," he ordered, a spark igniting in his hand.

At some imperceptible signal, the other two elves backed out of the room. Captain Anaril stepped aside.

Alysion walked past them, his small flame flickering. The captain's hand twitched.

"Watch out!" Fae cried.

The prince's flame exploded in a burst of light and sound. Fae slammed into a wall, everything fading.

An incessant ringing in his ears and the smell of burned wood slowly brought him back to the world of the living. When he opened his eyes, everything was spotty and blurry; he could barely tell elf from furniture. He rose to his feet using the wall for support, legs threatening to give out, ribs aching from the impact.

Master Cane's bedroom was in ruins. One of the inner walls had been completely obliterated. Captain Anaril was slumped on the floor, having taken the full brunt of the spell. The two Elithar in the hall were buried under the ruined wall. They made no noise.

Fae's gaze met Alysion's; he looked equally shaken by the devastation.

"Are they d-dead?" Fae croaked, staring at the captain.

Alysion shook his head. "N-no. They'll be up soon. We need to g-go. The more distance we get, the more difficult my aura will be to track."

They pushed past the Elithar into the hall, and Fae led them down the exterior stairs. As soon as their feet hit the ground, they took off down the street, ducking into the nearest alley. The sun hadn't fully risen yet, which meant the roads were still empty—for now. But the early morning explosion had woken a good portion of the townsfolk, who were checking out the commotion.

Neither elf looked back as they dashed out Redwood's southern gate.

Three

Durme

They didn't stop running until they were deep into the Arrow Branch Wood, somewhere in the patch of trees which separated Redwood from the vast Manwan Plains to the south.

The elves avoided the central path weaving through the forest—they were too easily recognizable, and Fae didn't want to run into anyone who might report them to their pursuers.

"S-stop," Alysion gasped as they entered a small clearing, slowing to a walk. "I need a break."

Fae stopped, but he did not look happy about it. Alysion couldn't blame him; he had no desire to stop either. If not for his exhausted, shaking limbs, he would have kept moving.

"I don't know how long that spell will leave them out. I haven't had much practise with it," he said upon regaining his breath. Wrinkling his nose, he sat on the ground, doing his best to stay clean. Why was there so much dirt out here? He took a sip of water to soothe his sore throat before digging through his bag for something to eat.

Fae simply stared at the ground, his brown eyes unfocused.

"What's wrong? Too tired to speak?" Alysion asked before taking another sip from his waterskin. That *he'd* been the one to suggest taking a break rubbed him the wrong way. How was Fae's stamina better than his? He was the descendant of the Divine Ancestors! It was unthinkable for him to be bested by an elf of a lower family. If his mother ever found out about this, he would never hear the end of it—especially if she learned that Fae lived amongst humans. Doing so was utterly disgraceful.

"What's wrong? What's *wrong*?" Fae snapped his head up, eyes flashing. "You attacked the Elithar, you blew up my home, *and* you hid your identity!"

"Well," Alysion said stiffly, put off by Fae's aggressive tone, "I can't go around telling everyone who I am. I'd never get anywhere if I did."

"They're going to think I kidnapped you!" Fae went red in the face. "What am I going to tell Master Cane? It hasn't even been a full day since she left, and I've already burned the smithy down!"

Alysion suppressed the urge to roll his eyes at Fae's dramatics. "They won't think you kidnapped me; I'm the one who cast the spell. And I don't think the damage to the smithy is as bad as that. I only destroyed one room." He drew on his years of experience living in the court to keep his tone light and steady despite the circumstances.

Fae let out a groan, sinking to the ground. "Why didn't you just go with them?"

Alysion shook his head. He couldn't go back home. Not now. "If I went with the Elithar, it would...complicate things."

"Why not let them find the crystals? Neither of us wants to do it, and they have a whole army at their disposal."

"It doesn't work like that. We're bound to the prophecy, remember?" He tapped his wrist. "If someone else tried to take them, I don't think it would end well for us. There are records of chosen elves dying horrible deaths because others intervened."

Fae glared daggers at him.

"*But be warned: darkness has taken one,*" he recited. "Someone finding the first crystal has to be what started this whole thing. Whoever this traitor is, we can't let them get the rest. We have to do this, for our sakes and all of Sylandris."

Fae's glare did not soften.

Alysion sighed. "I'll have some gold sent along when we're done to repair your home."

"Fine," Fae said reluctantly, his face softening in a way Alysion couldn't decipher. "But you have to promise to help me find my brother when this is over."

"If we don't find him before then," Alysion conceded. *Right, he mentioned his brother before.* Though it wasn't unheard of for elves to have more than one child during their lifetime, it wasn't prevalent in this day and age. He figured at least a century separated the siblings in age, based on what he knew of the few nobles with two children.

Fae nodded, the movement drawing Alysion's attention to the way his dark hair shimmered in the sunlight. He'd never seen black hair on an elf before, never mind anything like Fae's strange fade. He had the sudden urge to reach out and touch it, wanting to know if it was as silky as it looked. Instead, he fiddled with his waterskin, his throat suddenly parched.

"He's somewhere in Sylandris," Fae said quietly as they resumed their march, albeit at a much slower pace. "I'm just not sure where."

"Then collecting the crystals is in your best interest. Sylandris will fall to the traitor if we don't."

Fae shot him another look he couldn't interpret. Annoyance? Disbelief? He wasn't used to being around elves his age, especially not other *nelim*—other males. His mother preferred he socialized with *belim*—elves who could eventually carry his heir.

A rustling nearby startled both of them. Heart racing, Alysion exchanged a panicked look with Fae, whose hand was on his sword, brown eyes wide. Neither moved until a fat, grey squirrel hopped out in front of them.

Fae let out a sigh of relief and started walking. "Do you have any idea where the crystals are?"

"Sort of," replied Alysion quietly, ears straining for signs that the elite warriors were nearby. Birdsong and animal scrabbling filled the forest, and he did not appreciate the noise one bit. "I can feel their auras, but they're very faint. I'm having a hard time pinpointing any because they're all in different directions."

Fae frowned. "Why can't they all be in one convenient place?" he muttered. "The apparition gave us hints, didn't it?"

Alysion nodded. "There are seven, though one has been found already, leaving six for us. We'll likely need the help of the others to take that one back. Whoever the traitor is, they must be incredibly powerful. Not only were they able to find the crystal, but they were able to hide its aura. I can't feel it." He gave Fae an accusatory look, but it went unnoticed as he dug through his pack.

"You wouldn't happen to have a map on you, would you?" Fae asked, coming up empty-handed.

"No, I didn't have time to pack one before—" he cut himself off. "No, I don't."

"We should probably get one. And maybe some mounts." They weren't foolish enough to believe they could outrun the Elithar on foot.

• • • ● • • •

They didn't speak much as they travelled, staying as quiet as possible. Even if they did, Fae didn't know what he would say. For all he knew, he was nothing but a commoner to him—one without a damis who had been raised by humans. From what he'd gleaned from the Elithar and Alysion, this made him the lowest of the low. Someone as important as the crown prince shouldn't even acknowledge his existence.

Not that Alysion knew he was a damisri; and Fae intended to keep it that way. If Alysion found out and abandoned him now, well, he didn't want to think about that. It was best to let the prince believe he was wearing an aura-suppressing talisman.

As to why he didn't have a damis, Fae hadn't the foggiest idea. He remembered his brother being praised for his magical abilities—Ash attended lessons in the Sylandrian capital of Lyrellis while Fae remained at their home on the outskirts, learning swordplay from their parents. He couldn't remember ever going into the city proper, but he now knew it was because his people wouldn't have accepted him.

They made it to the farming town of Durme without running into the Elithar, likely due to the distance they'd put between them making it hard for the warriors to track Alysion's aura.

But Alysion wasn't convinced. "Anaril isn't the captain of our warriors for no reason. Their tracking skills are among the best."

They stopped at the forest edge, the farming town visible on the Manwan Plains. Fae warily eyed the grassy expanse, disliking how exposed everything was. They would be spotted as soon as they left the trees, but they wouldn't be in the open for long—the northern gate of Durme wasn't too far from their hiding spot.

"We should disguise ourselves," said Fae. He'd been to the town a few times before and knew the passage of two elves would not go unnoticed.

"If you gave me your talisman, I could hide my aura and make it impossible for the Elithar to track us," Alysion grumped, his mood sour from sleeping in the woods without a proper bedroll. Fae suspected this was the longest Alysion had ever gone without sleeping in a bed, never mind a bedroll. "I thought I'd be sleeping in inns, not under trees!" he'd exclaimed earlier when Fae asked why he hadn't packed one. But Fae was tired too—both from Alysion's whining and the long trek—and looked forward to sleeping in a proper bed just as much as the prince.

"I already told you, I can't hand my talisman over. Master Cane said it's bound to me. It won't work for anyone else."

"Whatever," Alysion huffed. "If I try casting a spell to make myself look more human, it will leave an aural mark. It'd be like waving a flag for the Elithar. I may as well walk in wearing my own face."

Fae sighed and undid his hair tie. "That's not a good idea. Your face is too…distinct." He tied up his hair again, styling it to cover his pointed ears before rubbing some dirt on his face to make it look more rugged and human. "Would you like me to put some dirt on your face too? You won't have to cast the spell."

Alysion's horrified expression almost made up for all the whining.

"If you don't decide now, the Elithar will catch us."

"Fine. The dirt."

Alysion took a moment to adjust his hair to mimic Fae's style, his face hardened with focus.

"Looks good," Fae offered with an awkward smile.

Alysion scoffed and stuck his nose up. "Never mind the small talk. Get to it already."

Fae swallowed hard, willing the uncomfortable fluttering in his chest to settle. He cast a judgemental eye at Alysion's fidgeting limbs.

"I would if you'd stop moving," he said, straightening his back, attempting to look confident to try to shake off the weirdness settling in the small space between them. And that space only shrank in ever-narrowing circles as Fae set his trembling hands to work.

Alysion's eyes were an emerald threat, drawing him in. Nervously, he cleared his throat. "Y-you should close your eyes," he stammered. "Gods forbid I should get dirt in them." He laughed a little to avoid rousing any suspicions of an ulterior motive.

Alysion scowled down his nose, but then, much to Fae's relief, he closed his eyes with an annoyed sigh.

As he worked, Fae caught a whiff of something faint that pulled at his memories. He took a deep breath, and there it was again, entwined with the forest's verdant perfume of moss and foliage: the scent of lunaberries.

Emotions welled within him of an entirely different sort. Fae couldn't help feeling somewhat disjointed. One moment he'd been swirling in a confusing maelstrom of nerves and hormones; the next, dragged under the surface to the melancholy depths of his earliest memories.

Turning toward the road, he motioned to Alysion over his shoulder. "Let's go."

• • • ● • • •

The walk to the gate was every bit as unnerving as Fae expected. They could see the town guard watching the gate, or rather, watching them walk up the open, dusty road. Fae fought the urge to run. *They're not the Elithar. They're wearing the emblem of Odenia, not the star of Sylandris.*

Despite his worry, they reached the guards without incident, and after being asked what they were doing—"Resupplying and moving on," Fae said—they were let in. Only then did his breathing return to normal.

Shopping with the prince was a royal pain. Alysion wanted the best of everything, and his specifications were not something a small farming town could provide.

"Silk stands out too much," Fae told him. "You want to blend in."

After they had gotten everything they needed, like Alysion's bedroll and a map, they stopped for lunch, purchasing some fresh, mouth-watering meat buns from a stall. Though Fae was a decent hunter, he wasn't about to pass up an easy meal, especially since they'd be eating trail rations for the foreseeable future.

"What's wrong?" Fae asked Alysion, noticing his expression drop as the rather flustered boy running the stall bagged their buns. Was it his first day on the job? He'd handled the last customer with no issues.

"Nothing," Alysion grumped, avoiding his gaze.

Fae figured he was hungry and passed him one of the bags as they left the market searching for the uhaan seller one of the shop clerks had recommended. Hopefully, buying two of the hooved animals wouldn't completely deplete their store of coins.

Uhaan, the result of breeding unicorns and horses, had quickly proven to be far superior mounts, travelling further and longer than their predecessors. They were so hardy and efficient that no one kept horses anymore.

After a few wrong turns, they found the seller, who led out two large animals for their inspection. Fae thought these uhaan were powerfully built and ready for long days of travel, but Alysion turned up his nose at the sight of them, muttering something about unicorns and bloodlines. Fae ignored him and set to haggling.

Despite Alysion's misgivings, Fae thought he looked quite content to be sitting atop his red roan mare, no longer having to rely on his legs as they rode back out the town's northern gate towards the Arrow Branch Wood.

"Now then, we really need to figure out where we are going," said Fae. He stopped his mount, Sy-Sy, once they reached the shelter of the trees. Alysion pulled up close on Zen-Zen as Fae unfurled their new map.

"I think I know where one of the crystals is," he said, eyes scanning the parchment. "*Power resides in the moon's lake.* It's referring to a moon-shaped lake. Likely a full one, since magic is stronger under a full moon and strongest during those rare times when both are full." He pointed to a nearly perfect circle on the map labelled 'Great Snapper'. "It's this one; I can sense it."

"You can sense it?" Fae asked doubtfully. Great Snapper Lake was in the Sky Peak Mountains far to the west. It was no short trip.

"If you took your talisman off, you'd feel it too. When I follow the pull of aura in that direction, the energy grows stronger."

As they turned their uhaan towards the west, Alysion's eyes went wide. "Oh no," he whispered. "They're here."

"How many are there?" Fae whispered back, ears straining to detect signs of their pursuers over the pounding hoofbeats. His hand hovered over the hilt of his sword. How hard was it to fight from uhaan-back? He'd never been trained in mounted combat.

"Captain Anaril and a few others, maybe five in total? It seems like they're using a smaller force so they can move without alerting the humans."

"Do you think we can take them? You can use magic against them."

"Maybe," Alysion said slowly. "You saw how—run!" He suddenly urged his mount into a gallop. Fae quickly followed suit, a wave of fear washing over him.

A flash of white lit up the forest behind them.

"What was that?" Fae hollered over the sound of hooves.

"A spell to knock us out! Don't let them hit you!"

They tore through the trees, urging their uhaan to run as fast as they could. It was reckless—one bad step and one of their steeds could break a leg. Yet neither he nor Alysion slowed.

He cursed under his breath as a spell crashed into a tree in front of him, sending stinging splinters of wood into his face.

"We aren't going to make it!" he shouted, but Alysion ignored him. The prince had something in his hand.

"Brace yourself," Alysion hollered. He turned in the saddle and let loose a wild blast of heat towards their pursuers—to no effect. He cursed his botched spell, then cursed again as Captain Anaril's uhaan came charging up the path ahead of them. They pulled up their mounts and prepared to fight.

"Psst, Fae."

Fae jumped in the saddle and looked around frantically. Who was calling his name out here? Another enemy? But wait—they hadn't spoken Illithen. He glimpsed something moving between the trees beside them.

"Fae, get your friend and come with me!"

He recognized that voice: Gale. Master Cane's friend.

"Alysion, follow me!" He turned Sy-Sy to where he'd seen her and rode into the bushes.

"Keep goin'!" she said as they rode past her hiding place, switching to a heavily accented Illithen. "I've got a trick for them elfies!"

They did as they were told, but Fae couldn't resist turning as Gale hurled something through the trees at the Elithar. It exploded like a flash of lightning.

Sy-Sy and Zen-Zen quicked their pace, startled by the noise. Fae blinked as spots formed in front of his eyes, ears ringing.

"What was that?" Alysion asked as Gale rode up to them on a sizeable dun-coloured uhaan.

"Special somethin' we watchers use in case we ever run into somethin' nasty. Scrambles auras while causin' momentary blindness and deafness. Won't stop 'em for long, but should be enough for us to get the heck outta here!"

Four

Muddy Waters

They rode swiftly through the trees, fearing the Elithar would catch up. Fae eyed the darker-skinned woman riding beside them. She wore light leather armour well suited to long-distance travelling, a sword sheathed at her hip, and a hunting bow slung across her back. Her locs, streaked through with brilliant red, were tied back, revealing round human ears.

"So Fae, who's your elfie friend?" she asked in accented Illithen.

"You may call me Alysion," he said, riding up between them with a sour expression; apparently, he didn't think highly of humans speaking his tongue.

"Oho! A noble perhaps?" she said as she put a closed fist over her heart in some kind of greeting. Fae thought he recognized it from his childhood in Sylandris.

"Put your fist higher," Alysion corrected in a haughty tone that rubbed Fae the wrong way. Gale simply smiled and tried again.

"Better."

"Alysion, this is Gale. She's a Dragon Watcher," said Fae.

"What is a Dragon Watcher?" Alysion raised a perfectly shaped brow.

"I patrol the lands for dragons," explained the human, "and report back to Murk Water if I hear of anythin' strange. Only those who can use magic are allowed to be watchers. Need it in case there's trouble."

"You do realize that dragons are forbidden from crossing the Sky Peak Mountains. It's part of treaties that were drawn up at the end of the Syl-Raanian War," Alysion said as if he were speaking to a child. "There are wards in place to stop them if they try."

"Phhft. 'Course I know that," Gale answered. "I had to take watcher trainin', and they taught us all sorts of borin' things like that. But just 'cause the dragons agreed to it doesn't mean they won't *try* to sneak across every now and then. Hear they liked eatin' the big, hairy *nuu* that live on the Manwan Plains. But enough about me. What're two young elfies doin' out here aside from gettin' into trouble?" She gave Alysion a jovial slap on the shoulder.

Alysion flashed Fae a panicked look—partially due to his inability to handle Gale's forwardness (though Fae thought he deserved it for being rude), but with a wariness that matched Fae's own. Had Gale realized they were being attacked by the Elithar? She may be a friend of Master Cane's, but ultimately she was loyal to the monarch of Odenia. It wouldn't be wise to tell her about their mission. Who knew what she would do with that kind of information—likely report it right back to her ruler, causing a whole heap of problems.

"There's always trouble to get into when you wander around the woods," Fae said, earning a bark of laughter from Gale.

"Ain't that the truth!" she said. "But really, where're you off to?"

"We're on our way to visit one of my family's secret summer homes," said the prince, saving Fae from having to come up with something.

"Jus' the two of you?"

Fae's face flushed.

"For now," said Alysion.

"He's asked me to show him through the forest," Fae added quickly.

"Hmm, Cane asked me to keep an eye on you while she's gone," Gale said, scanning the trees. "Might be best if I come along; Cane'll tan my hide if anything happens to you! I'm just on patrol anyways."

The elves exchanged a look, but neither could come up with an excuse to shake her off.

Travelling with Gale did have its advantages. They had another person to take watch at night—much to Fae's relief, as the broken-up sleep was making Alysion very moody—and she was a much more efficient hunter. Gale even offered to spar with them when they made camp each night, which Fae eagerly agreed to, curious as to what he could learn from a Dragon Watcher. Alysion was less enthusiastic and practised swordsmanship on his own, keeping his distance. Fae figured he couldn't bear the thought of sparring with a human, yet he couldn't convince the other elf to spar with him either.

At least Alysion conceded to teach him about Sylandrian culture to help pass the time. In fact, Fae would say he was delighted to show off his knowledge, though he was careful not to reveal anything too important about the court in case Gale overheard. Surprisingly, Alysion didn't talk much about the Divine Ancestors. Being one of their descendants, Fae thought he would natter on non-stop about them. He didn't press the prince about it, not caring much for the Elven deities who had decided he was a lesser being.

"So, how far're you two goin' to get to your fancy summer home?" Gale asked as they rode beside the Bluetail River a few days after their encounter with the Elithar; there had been no sign of them since. Alysion assured Fae they had managed to throw them off with Gale's surprise, since he could no longer sense their auras. As much as Fae wanted to believe him, something in his gut told him not to let his guard down.

"We plan on stopping at Great Snapper Lake for a short rest," replied Alysion, to Fae's surprise. Even though Gale was a close friend of Master Cane's, Fae wasn't sure if they should trust her with any information. "We'll have to part ways there."

"Don't you have watcher duties to attend to?" Fae asked.

"Sure do, but lucky for you two, the Great Snapper fishing villages are due for a visit from us," she explained. "Since they're so close to Fiiraania—and therefore dragons—we have to check on 'em regularly."

"Wouldn't it be smarter to station someone there permanently?" Alysion asked as if it were the most obvious solution in the world.

"We tried, but people complained that winter is too cold and long, so they stopped," Gale explained, oblivious to Alysion's rudeness. "Think the real complaint is that it's just too borin'." She threw Fae a wink.

• • • ● • • •

The Bluetail River slowly curved to the north-west, snaking its way through the Sky Peak Mountains and flowing into Great Snapper Lake. They kept close to it, not wanting to accidentally stray too deep into the Arrow Branch Wood; they were well beyond familiar territory.

"Is it just me, or does the river seem strange?" Alysion asked, staring at it intently.

They were a few days into the Sky Peak range, the tall mountains rising around them like jagged teeth. Fae had been impressed by the foothills, having spent all his life in the forest, but they were nothing compared to the snow-capped peaks kissing the sky.

Fae peered at the water—it was muddier than usual and giving off a swampy smell.

"Feelin' weird energy," said Gale.

Fae frowned. The *water* had an aura? That wasn't fair.

Concern flashed across Alysion's perfect face, but he didn't say anything more.

By the time they stopped to make camp for the evening, the water had turned completely opaque, the distinct scent of decay wafting from its surface. They kept away from it to avoid the stench, but soon it became so strong it was inescapable.

"We're running out of water," Fae stated when they stopped. His waterskin was nearly empty, and the uhaan refused to drink from the river. Alysion insisted on a quick pace, hoping to reach Great Snapper a day early—he'd confided to Fae that he'd sensed the Elithar's auras not long after they crossed the river near the town of Blueleaf—but they couldn't do that without water.

Leaving a rabbit to cook over their fire, Gale wandered over to the far side of their camp and started to dig a hole. Both elves watched her, confused.

"You can get water from the ground," she explained. Sure enough, as she dug deeper, water began to well up at the bottom, clear and stink-free.

"We're going to need more than that," observed Alysion.

"Here's where you come in, blondie. You can use magic to pull up more!" she said triumphantly.

A flash of panic briefly crossed Alysion's face as Gale went back to tending to their dinner.

"If they're already onto us," Fae whispered, the sizzling of juices rolling off the rabbit helping to cover his voice, "then it doesn't matter if you use magic now. We might not make it to Great Snapper if you don't."

Alysion sat on a rock, his gaze dropping to the ground.

"What's wrong?" Fae asked, taking a seat near him.

The prince played with a lock of his golden hair. Fae couldn't help but notice how the fire added a pleasant orange hue to it, like the setting sun.

"I'm not sure about this..." Alysion trailed off, bringing his knees to his chest and wrapping his arms around them as if trying to hide.

"Are you not able to do it?" Fae didn't believe that. Alysion was the crown prince—his family were the most powerful magic users in Sylandris!

"You saw what happened to your home," he said so quietly that Fae almost didn't catch it. "I didn't mean to blow it up."

Fae was taken aback by his confession and didn't respond right away, not until he realized he needed to say *something*. "Well, um, it's good to know that," he said lamely. "Back then, you were under a lot of pressure and—"

"Being under pressure is no excuse!" Alysion growled. "I should be able to control a spell like that without any issues; I'm the—" he cut himself off.

Fae shot a worried look at Gale, but she was preoccupied with taking the rabbit off the fire. So far, she hadn't done anything overly suspicious, but the other night while she'd been on watch, Fae had gotten up to relieve himself and hadn't been able to find her anywhere. He'd taken up her post until she had returned—which hadn't been long—not wanting to leave the camp vulnerable.

"Food's ready," she said.

"Come on. Maybe you'll feel better once you eat." Fae dared to pat him on the shoulder as he stood.

• • • ● • • •

Alysion's mood didn't improve much after eating, but he reluctantly agreed to Gale's plan. He approached the hole and felt for that part inside him—his damis—that allowed him to access magical energies. Closing his eyes, he focused on what he wanted to happen: for the moisture in the ground to rise up and fill the hole. Energy rushed through him, and before he could gain any control, it overwhelmed him, doing as it pleased. His companions shouted, breaking his focus.

He opened his eyes, shocked to find himself soaking wet. Before him was not the small pool he'd intended but a roaring geyser shooting past the treetops, soaking the camp in cold water as it rained down. Alysion severed the connection, and the geyser collapsed, drenching them all.

Fae spluttered and pushed his dripping hair out of his face. "What was that?"

"What you asked for—water," he replied defensively, trying not to notice Fae's wet clothes clinging to his frame, outlining his body. The tips of his ears started to itch.

"Well, we all needed a bath," said Gale, wringing out her soggy hair. "I'll see to dryin' our gear."

Alysion sensed her aura shift as she summoned a gust of hot air to dry their bedrolls and frowned at the strangeness of it. Was this what Odenian magic was like? It was different from that of his people, more rugged, maybe? Wild? It was incredibly unusual for a human to be born with a damis, and how those few came to be was beyond him. Some said it came from humans and elves mingling generations ago, a thought that made Alysion's lip curl with disgust. His people had inherited their damai from their Divine Ancestors; they weren't a gift to be shared!

He felt a hand on his shoulder and instinctively tensed up, waiting to be reprimanded for another failure. Instead, Fae stood next to him, shirtless.

"You'll get it next time," was all the elf said.

Alysion's stomach fluttered, and his tongue turned to stone. All concerns about his abysmal spellcasting instantly evaporated as emotions he didn't understand surged through him. He simply nodded, relieved that Fae hadn't noticed his racing pulse.

• • • ● • • •

The Bluetail River eventually became a roaring waterfall, emptying into Great Snapper Lake. It continued out the northwest edge of the lake, flowing through the mountains into Fiiraania, the land of the dragons, and then into the distant ocean.

The trio stood atop a rocky cliff, studying the murky water far below, noses crinkled in disgust from the foul reek of the spray. Fishing villages ringed the lake, and snow-capped mountains surrounded those. There wasn't much space for agriculture, but some small fields were crammed between the towns and the mountains, likely producing just enough to keep everyone fed. Each town appeared to grow a different crop, for the fields were different colours.

"The lake looks just as bad as the river," said Fae.

"Lake used to fill the whole valley," said Gale. "Gotten smaller over time, allowin' those villages to pop up."

Boats moved across the lake, circumventing an island at its centre. Though large enough to house a village or two, it appeared to be uninhabited, but it was difficult to tell through the dense covering of foliage.

"The villages do lots of tradin' with each other since they're so secluded," Gale continued. "Hard to get supplies this far north, 'specially when winter hits and makes the trails impassible."

The elves disguised their ears as they approached the nearest village: a mishmash of wooden houses jammed tightly together at the lake's edge.

Earlier, Alysion had tried to assure Fae that the crystal's aura was strong enough to hide his own from the Elithar. "They'll know we came down here, but they won't know which village we are in," he'd whispered when Gale was distracted. "It'll give us a bit of time to search."

But Fae's ever-growing worries hadn't been eased. If the villagers discovered they were elves, news of their appearance would spread like wildfire during a drought, and the Elithar would be upon them even faster. They also had Gale to deal with; they hadn't had a private moment to figure out how they were going to shake her off.

Alysion was excited to sleep in a real bed, but that only lasted until they set foot inside the village's only inn, the Golden Carp. The overwhelming smell of fish and filthy lake water hit them like a hammer as they walked through the door. Alysion looked like he was going to be sick.

"It's this or sleep outside," Fae told him as they trudged up the stairs to their room.

The room, whose walls may have been white at some point, had two small beds, meaning someone would have to sleep on the floor. Fae had hoped Gale would get her own room, but she'd insisted on staying with them since it was cheaper. He couldn't argue against that—they needed to be as stingy as possible with their gold.

"Right boys, I'm heading down for some grub and ale. Join me when you want!" Gale said with a wink that neither elf could interpret.

Fae waited for Gale's footsteps to fade before speaking. "So, how are we going to get rid of her?"

"I'm not sure," said Alysion. "I've been busy trying to pinpoint the *thing*'s exact location." He was wise to avoid particular words; for their safety, they had decided to use the Odenian tongue while they were in town, even in the confines of their room.

"And what have you felt?" Fae asked quietly, leaning closer to be sure they weren't overheard. "Do you think it's in this village?"

A pang of disappointment struck him as Alysion moved away to start airing out his gear. "No. It feels like it's on the other side of the lake."

That figures. "You mentioned its aura will hide yours; doesn't that mean the Elithar can sense it too? And Gale?"

Alysion nodded. "I don't think they can feel it as strongly as I can due to the prophecy's bond. The Elithar will still sense it, but I hope to find it before they get a chance to investigate. And Gale already knows something is here. I saw it on her face when we were on that cliff."

Though they had done their best to hide the fact the Elithar was hunting them down, Fae didn't believe Gale hadn't noticed *something* was amiss. Their pace had been too quick for two elves who were supposedly on their way to a summer home, and they had stayed away from well-travelled areas. Not to mention Gale's timing when she ran into them in the Arrow Branch wood—it was too good.

Fae's stomach twisted. How much did he *really* know about Gale? She travelled around looking for trouble to report, and she came to the smithy now and then to visit Master Cane and have her weapons repaired—that was it. He frowned.

"Fae?" Alysion said, now seated on one of the beds, arms crossed, frustrated by how many times he'd had to call his name.

"Ah, sorry. What were you saying?"

"I think what we're after is on that island."

Fae stood at the window, gazing at the island across the mud-coloured lake. It didn't look special, but if Alysion said the crystal was there, Fae was unlikely to doubt him. If only he could sense auras...

"We need to get a boat," said Alysion.

"And shake off Gale." She would find it suspicious if they took a boat out to the island, no matter their excuse.

The prince looked uncomfortable.

"What is it?" Fae asked, taking a seat on the other bed. It felt divine, and he couldn't wait to sleep in it, terrible smells aside.

"I don't know if I want to leave Gale."

"What? Why?"

"She's been very helpful for a human. She hunts and takes watch at night so I don't have to."

Ah, that's why he wants to keep her around. She must remind him of the palace servants.

"She has been helpful," Fae conceded, "but how are we going to collect *it* if she's with us? We would have to tell her about the prophecy, and I don't think that's a good idea. What if Odenia decides to join the hunt? Or to strike at Sylandris? There's too much at risk."

Alysion sighed. Fae felt a tinge of guilt, but he refused to jeopardize their quest for the sake of his comfort. If Sylandris fell, then Ash would be in danger. Fae wouldn't allow that to happen; he couldn't bear the thought of losing his only remaining family.

Five

Great Snapper

Unable to come up with a good plan for dealing with the friendly watcher, they gave up and went down to the tavern on the main floor. Fae made sure his ears were well hidden while Alysion used magic to disguise his features.

Gale sat at a crowded, rowdy table across from a rather large, hairy man. They each had an elbow on the table, their hands clasped together, locked in a struggle. "Gimme a moment, boys," she said, straining. As the elves closed in, they noted the empty mugs of ale all around the combatants.

"Let's get a table," Fae suggested just as Gale slammed her opponent's fist down with a triumphant cry. The lineup of fisherfolk waiting to challenge her applauded the victory.

They found a free spot away from the excitement and sat, ordering some tea. Fae debated ordering ale to blend in with the crowd but would rather keep his mind clear. He didn't think he'd be able to stomach it anyway; the smell in here was terrible. Besides, no amount of ale would hide the blotchy green hair Alysion had accidentally given himself. It attracted more attention than either of them would like, and Fae had half a mind to send him back to their room.

Fae discreetly surveyed the dingy taproom. There wasn't much to it: rough cobblestone floors beneath simple wooden tables and chairs, a crowded bar beside the single staircase, and an unlit fireplace beside that. The decor was minimal; some old fishing gear hung on the walls along with one giant preserved fish. It was a hideous thing: pale grey and covered in bony protrusions. A plaque beneath honoured whoever had caught the massive specimen, but Fae couldn't read it from where he sat, nor did he care to.

The mood wasn't as lively as he expected. Usually, evening was when taverns were the rowdiest, but this place was oddly quiet—save for Gale's corner—and a bit depressing. Fae tried to get a better read on the room while Alysion discreetly counted their remaining funds under the table.

"Don't have many coins left," he muttered.

"So, no fancy meal tonight. We need to hire a boat tomorrow."

Alysion sighed but didn't protest. Fae figured he was lamenting their would-be dinner of bony fish from the foul lake. *He certainly was. Bet the food in the palace is delicious.*

"Bah, another one's gone missin'," Fae overheard a grizzled voice say just as the server delivered their tea. It didn't smell funny as Fae worried it might; Alysion wouldn't drink it if it did, but by the way he eyed it with his nose scrunched up, he may not touch it regardless. *Spoiled prince.* Fae turned his attention back to the speaker, an old fisherman sitting nearby, conversing with two others.

"That's the third boat in the past few days," the other man responded in a sombre tone. "Weather's been good, water's as high as ever, Spirit's island is as green as it is every summer. Whatta you think's gettin' 'em, Jin?"

"Hard te say," Jin, the first speaker, responded. "Never seen anything like it before."

"D'you think the spirit's mad?" asked the third person, a middle-aged woman.

"Could be, but what we do to make it mad? That's the real question."

Fae shifted his chair to hear them more clearly. He didn't quite understand what they were talking about—it sounded like boats were disappearing. Alysion looked up at him, but he shook his head, not wanting to miss something.

"Well, not much we can do about it right now," said the woman dejectedly.

"Tomorrow, we'll be sendin' boats out as usual, but if somethin' else happens, then I dunno what we'll do. Gotta fish to eat, gotta fish to survive," said Jin. All three nodded sagely.

"Speakin' of fish," began the other man, "you noticed how the waters looks these days, all dark-like and smelly. Net I hauled up the other day was all sickly lookin'. Had to toss most of 'em back! Think it's the same thing?"

"Sick fish, sick lake, lost boats. Gotta be the Spirit doing this," said the woman. Their conversation ended as the server dropped off a round of ale, then quickly drifted to mundane fishing matters.

Fae glanced at Alysion, who seemed to have clued in. "Did you hear that?" he asked quietly.

"All the more reason to get to the island," the prince responded with an uneasy grimace.

Fae didn't fancy a potential trip to the bottom of the lake either. "I don't think we'll be in any danger. Unlike the fisherfolk, we have magic."

Alysion wasn't reassured.

"Good news, boys—I won!" Gale sauntered over and plopped herself down in a vacant chair, pocketing a hefty bag of coins. "Dinner's on me!"

Gale had won a fair amount of silver at the impromptu arm-wrestling tournament, and when they returned to their room after their evening meal, she divided the coins amongst them.

"I won't use all this, and you seem to need it more than I do."

"But we're meeting up with Alysion's family soon. We don't need money," Fae lied.

"Well, you never know what could happen! By the way, what happened to your hair, blondie?"

• • ● ● ● • •

Gale was still asleep when Fae woke the next morning. Judging by how things went last night, he figured she would have a wicked hangover and would be out for a while longer. Slipping away wasn't his favourite plan, but they didn't have many options. They pulled their hoods up, grabbed some food from the woman minding the counter downstairs, and set out for the docks.

They had barely made it down the front street before they heard an all-too-familiar voice hollering after them. "Oi! Where are you two sneaking off to?"

Fae closed his eyes and took a slow breath to calm his racing heart.

"We told you, we're going to see my family. I can't be giving away our secret location, can I?" said Alysion, turning to face her, his hair colour back to normal.

"Hah! Like I believe that!" Gale huffed as she caught up. "Come on. You two are going to tell me exactly what's going on."

Much to their surprise, she led them to the docks. Had she figured them out? Impossible—she'd been too busy arm-wrestling with the fisher-folk.

The docks were nothing fancy—rough, weathered wood that had seen better days. Most of the boats were already out, so they were alone.

Gale walked out onto the creaking wood and sat on a post, unconcerned by how unstable it seemed. "You boys are after whatever's out on the lake, aren't you?" She looked between them, her tone more serious than usual.

Alysion said nothing. Fae wasn't sure if it was due to guilt or his efforts not to gag from the sickly smell of the lake. His own nose begged him to chop it off.

Gale rolled her eyes and cast a spell to shield them from the stench. A faint blue half-sphere covered them, reminding Fae of the barrier around Alysion's home. He immediately took a deep breath of clean air.

"It'll also stop others from listenin' in on us," the watcher explained, switching to Illithen to show them it was safe. "Now, go on—and don't think I haven't noticed those elfies who're after us."

Fae let Alysion take the lead on this one, unsure how much he wanted to reveal to her.

"It's as you said. We're after what's on the island," he said, glancing nervously at Fae.

"What's out there? Somethin' those other elfies aren't allowed to have?"

Fae hated how insightful Gale was. "Just tell her everything," he said with a resigned sigh.

Alysion relayed the prophecy to her, the bond having imprinted it into their memory.

Gale didn't reply right away, taking in everything they had revealed. "Phew...You boys sure are into somethin' crazy! But findin' magic rocks, that's gonna be tricky!" Surprisingly, she took everything well. Perhaps too well.

"Of course, now I can't just let you two younguns' traipse off on yer own; it's too dangerous! I'd be a sorry excuse for an adult if I did that," she said with a nod. "And Cane'll tan my hide if you got hurt."

Fae and Alysion exchanged a worried glance.

"But—" Fae started.

"I know these lands better than either of you. Especially *you*, mister fancy," she jabbed a finger at Alysion. "Care to tell me who you are?"

"I'm the Prince of Sylandris."

"Humph, figures. No wonder those elfies are after you; I'd recognize that star crest on 'em anywhere. Bet they're not too pleased about you runnin' all over the place. Do they know what you're doin'?"

"They're unaware," answered Alysion.

Gale went silent for a moment. "That's probably for the best."

As much as Fae didn't trust her, having Gale come along meant he could keep an eye on her. After all, he didn't want her wandering off to collect the crystals for Odenia. His wrist twinged; he pulled up his sleeve, surprised to see the mark—faint but visible, like an old scar.

"We should get going," he said, stepping forward. "We need to hire a boat to take us to the island."

Gale's eyes gleamed with excitement as she hopped up from the post. "I can paddle us wherever. This lake ain't so big." She pointed to a shape on the beach. "There's a sampan we can use. Just gotta get 'er in the water!"

The flat boat was in rough shape: it was incredibly weather-beaten, and Fae wasn't confident it could support all three of them. Not only that, but the only way to steer it was for someone at the back to push it along with a tall wooden pole. It wasn't the sort of boat Fae would trust out on a lake half this size.

When they pushed it out onto the lake, the sampan showed off its sole redeeming feature: it didn't fill up with water as soon as they got it afloat.

Gale hopped in with an excited smile on her face and took up the pole. Awkwardly she manoeuvred the sampan over to the dock. "Watch your step, don't need you two capsizin' 'er before we even get anywhere," she chuckled.

The elves stashed most of their gear near the dock, not wanting to risk it if the sampan did capsize, and reluctantly climbed aboard.

It was slow going. Gale's sampaning skills weren't spectacular, but they were enough to keep moving in the correct direction. Sadly, she had to let her smell-repelling barrier fade, wanting to conserve her abilities. Both elves held their hoods in front of their noses to help block it; no one would notice their ears out on the lake.

"The villagers say it's a spirit's island. Do you really think a spirit lives there?" Fae asked.

Alysion shrugged. "Perhaps, but it's likely just human superstition."

"They said boats are disappearing."

"Sounds like spirits to me!" Gale hollered from behind. "You gotta start givin' us humans more credit. Just cause we ain't got as much magic as you elfies doesn't mean we don't recognize it."

Luckily, she didn't see Alysion roll his eyes.

As they approached the island, they scanned the rocky shore; no one was moving about, nor could they see any moored boats. Whether the emptiness was out of respect or fear, Fae couldn't be sure.

Gale glanced at the sky and frowned. The day had been clear when they'd left the docks, but it was getting cloudier and darker by the moment. The wind picked up, making the water churn. "Think a storm's comin'," she warned.

"Can you take us as close as possible?" Fae asked. They had already come so far; it'd be a shame to turn back now.

"I don't think I want to. The water could bash us into those rocks." She jutted her chin at the large, dark shapes ringing the shore. It was hard to see a safe route to shore through the choppy waters.

"Do you know any wind spells that could help us?" Fae hollered to Alysion.

"I could try…"

"Be worth a shot!" Gale shouted over the howling gust, struggling to keep the sampan pointed in the right direction. "Might not make it at this rate!"

"O-okay," Alysion's hands shook as he lifted them.

Fae gripped the sampan's sides and braced himself, praying they weren't about to take a trip to the bottom of the disgusting lake.

The wind shifted at Alysion's command. The boat immediately took off, blasting towards the island as if it had a sail. Alysion skidded back across the wood and smacked into Fae, who just managed to stop them from tumbling into Gale. Somehow, she managed to keep her footing.

"Alysion, control this!" Fae yelled over the roar of rushing air, eyeing the sharp rocks ahead.

"I'm trying!" replied Alysion, peeling himself off Fae and starting up another spell. The clouds let loose, raindrops stinging their skin.

The jagged rocks loomed closer. If the sampan hit them at this speed, they'd be done for. Whatever Alysion was trying to do wasn't having any effect.

Fae swallowed his panic. "Just cut the wind—we're close enough!" he called out desperately, hoping the prince could hear him over the storm.

The sampan lurched as white caps crashed all around them. Fae's stomach threatened to empty itself as they ramped off a massive wave, catching air before slamming down into choppy waters that threatened to toss them all overboard.

"Make a big wave! One moving towards the island!" Gale hollered from the back.

"What? Why?!" cried Alysion, his voice laced with frustration and fear.

"Just do it!" she insisted. Alysion's wind had died off, but they were still hurtling towards the island at a dangerous speed.

Fae didn't know if he should feel relief or fear as a giant wave rose before them. Gale confidently pushed them right for it.

"Hold on, boys!"

"What're you doing?!" Alysion cried.

Fae gripped the edge of the sampan as tightly as he could.

The sampan shot up the back of the wave and sailed over the rocks.

Six

The Island

Alysion thought his heart would burst from his chest when the rickety sampan cleared the deadly ring of stone in one piece. When the sampan bottomed out after passing the threshold, the wind and rain abated, and sunlight pierced through the clouds. Unlike the rest of the lake, the water inside the rocks was calm, and Gale gently pushed them to shore.

Alysion pried his white-knuckled hands from the edge of the boat and staggered to shore, leaving the other two to haul the sampan onto the beach. He plopped himself down on the rocky sand, taking a much-needed breather.

"Had me a little worried there, Princey, but you pulled it off! Good work!" said Gale.

He could only nod, his stomach roiling.

There were no paths on the island, just dense undergrowth that snagged their hair and pulled at their clothes. Alysion led the way, following the call of the crystal. Unfortunately, this meant he was the one breaking trail, which did little to brighten his foul mood.

They'd reached the island in one piece, but he'd come close to killing them all. It was beyond humiliating! Why did he always have such a hard time with magic? Though he'd technically succeeded out on the lake, he knew his mother would never approve of his abysmal performance. At least she hadn't been around to see it; he didn't need another lecture about how he was a disappointment to the Ancestors' line.

He pushed past a branch, and there was a sudden yelp behind him. He whirled around, ready for a fight, and found Fae rubbing a red spot on his face.

"Maybe I'll lead for a bit," the other elf said.

Alysion's mood plummeted even deeper as he stepped aside to let Fae pass, careful not to whack him with another branch.

"My apologies," he mumbled as the other elf took up the lead.

"Just have to be careful," was all Fae said.

The undergrowth grew denser as they walked. Fae drew his sword and used it to carefully hack away at the brush.

"Neither of you know any earth spells, do you?" Alysion asked as Fae chopped away, noticing his occasional winces. Right, Fae was an apprentice blacksmith; it couldn't be good to misuse his blade like this. He'd get him a new one someday. Something nicer.

"No, I don't," Fae replied. "I've never been very good at magic. I prefer working with my hands in the forge."

"Right," Alysion grumped. *I guess he can't use it with that talisman—what a waste.*

"Hey now, not everyone's good at magic," said Gale. "Some folks just find it harder to use than others. Wish I could command the earth, but I use wind magic. It's hard for us humans to learn more than one or two types of magic, unlike you elfies who can dabble in all types."

"Even the lowest born elf can learn all types of magic because of our damai. Each individual has an affinity for certain types, making them easier to master than the others," Alysion explained.

"Are there ever any elves born without a damis?" Fae asked.

He snorted. "Of course not; they're a gift from the Ancestors. The only elves without damai are those who have had them destroyed as punishment for desecrating the Ancestors' gift. After having their damis destroyed—witnessed by a representative of the Ancestors—they're banished from Sylandris forever and will be put to death if they return. They are marked, so the wards do not let them pass back through."

"When was the last time you elfies did *that*?" Gale asked from behind.

"We haven't had to perform the *Silias* for decades, maybe even centuries," he replied, rubbing his wrist. The mark was reappearing. "I've never witnessed it."

"What's your affinity?" Fae asked.

"Fire. Stop, we need to turn here."

Alysion corrected their path a few more times before emerging onto the rocky shore of a small round pond—a miniature Great Snapper. They stopped near the water's edge, eyeing it warily. It was pitch black; not even the sun's rays could penetrate it. Fae didn't need to sense auras to know something was wrong. His wrist tinged; the mark glowed faintly.

"Ah, so this is the source of the funky water," muttered Gale.

The smell was unbelievable, like a carcass that had been rotting in the sun for days. It took everything Fae had not to retch.

"The crystal is somewhere in there," said Alysion, coming to stand beside him.

Of course it was.

"We should've brought the sampan," Fae lamented.

"Hah! You think we could have hauled that through the trees?" said Gale. "Looks like you might be goin' for a swim, Princey." She began to walk the perimeter of the lake.

Alysion tried a summoning spell—that's what Fae thought he was doing, anyway—with his face scrunched in concentration and one hand outstretched. But after a strained moment, nothing happened.

He took a step forward, and Fae's hand shot out like a viper to stop him from walking into the filth.

Alysion jumped at the touch, one of his feet splashing into the pond. The calm surface immediately erupted, dark shapes thrashing across the water and latching onto him with slimy tendrils.

"Get it off!" Alysion screamed, tugging frantically at his leg.

Fae raised his battered sword and slashed down at the thing—a snake?—where it emerged from the water, severing it. There was no expected spray of blood.

"It's just a vine!" he hollered. More shot out towards Alysion, who turned tail and darted towards the trees. Fae hacked at the vines, but there were just too many. Another scream rent the air—Fae whirled around to see Alysion tangled up on the ground, the plants dragging him towards the water.

"Gale!" Fae cried, but the watcher was battling her own mess of the writhing things. He dashed over to help Alysion, noticing the vines were ignoring him. *They're drawn to auras!* Fae was invisible to them.

But that didn't help the prince, and he couldn't find a better way to get rid of the slimy plants; every time he swung his blade, more vines converged, covering Alysion's face and pulling him ever closer to the putrid water. Fae needed to come up with something quick.

Wait a minute, plants…

"Alysion, hit it with fire!" he screamed, praying the prince would hear it beneath his bindings.

A vine coiled around his sword—he pulled against it frantically but couldn't free it. *No, no, no!* He couldn't lose his blade now; he would be completely helpless without it!

"Come on, Alysion! Fire!"

Light flickered through Alysion's vine prison, and Fae turned away as a wave of heat washed over him. When he spun back around, Alysion was free, surrounded by charred bits of vegetation. He sat up, gasping for air.

Fae helped him to his feet. "Are you all right?"

But Alysion was too busy trying to suck air back in his lungs, as foul as it was.

"Oi, you two survive?"

Gale had held her own against the vines, the tendrils she hacked away slipping back into the calm water.

"I think so," Fae hollered as she hurried back to them.

"The crystal…" Alysion whispered, drawing Fae's attention.

"The crystal?"

"The crystal is controlling the vines. I felt it when they had me," he stammered, trembling. "The villagers are correct. There is a spirit here. The crystal is making it go berserk."

Fae glanced around, expecting something to appear before them.

Alysion shook his head. "We don't need to look for it; the spirit has been with us the whole time."

"What?" The back of Fae's neck prickled.

"This island doesn't belong to a spirit," he said carefully, "it *is* the spirit."

The island was a spirit? *How?* Fae shifted his feet nervously as if the ground would open up and swallow him whole.

Alysion stepped to the water's edge, careful not to touch it. "I have to go down there," he said resolutely. "Retrieving the crystal is the only way to calm the island spirit and save the valley."

"You can't!" exclaimed Fae, heart racing as panic surged through him. If something happened and Alysion didn't make it back…"The vines—"

"I know, but I don't have a choice!" Alysion snapped. "We need the crystal. There's no other way to get it."

Fae looked at Gale, hoping the watcher had a better idea, but she shrugged helplessly.

"Nothin' I can do except offer support up here," she said.

Fae produced a length of rope. "At the very least, let's keep you connected to us."

"I'm not a fish," muttered Alysion, though he made no effort to shoo him away.

Fae fumbled with the rope, his hands feeling big and clumsy as he looped it around Alysion's narrow waist. He bowed his head, cheeks flushing as his fingers brushed against the prince's clothes. He gave the knot a good tug and slowly backed up a few steps, needing to put space between them.

"There, a royal catch," he said awkwardly, avoiding Alysion's gaze.

Without another word, Alysion turned and waded into the water.

• • • ● • • •

His ears burned until the vines dragged him under. He hardly had the chance to take a deep breath before his world went dark, the foul water stealing his sight and filling his nose. All thoughts of Fae quickly fled his mind.

If he hadn't touched the crystal's aura once before, he never would have let the lake take him. But when the vines held him, his aura brushed against the crystal's, and the stone had hesitated.

He struggled against the vines as they dragged him deeper. It didn't seem to matter that he'd been chosen by the prophecy—the crystal still saw him as a threat. Before long, his lungs craved air. He cursed himself for not knowing any spells to allow him to breathe underwater. But what if he made his own air?

Reaching into his damis, he unleashed a mighty gust of wind. A burst of bubbles exploded in his face, rapidly shooting up to the surface before he could suck in a breath. Damn. Burning the vines away likely wasn't going to work either. He stamped down his rising panic, a difficult task when he needed to breathe. Think, *think*.

The crystal was trying to protect itself against those who would use it for evil. Fighting the vines meant fighting the crystal, thus triggering its defences. Alysion needed to remain calm, prove he harboured no ill intentions. Battling against his instincts, he stopped straining and let the vines drag him down.

Don't lose yourself, don't forget why you're here. He had to be nearing the crystal; the small pond couldn't be that deep, could it? Reaching out with his aura, he tried to feel the stone, but all he could sense was the oppressive energy of the tainted water. His wrist burned as if someone had pressed a red-hot brand to it.

His mind began to blur; all he could think about was how badly he needed air. Maybe he had messed up. Maybe the crystal was going to kill him after all.

Maybe he was going to die.

Panic flitted through his sluggish mind, but he had no energy to act on it. *No...I can't...*

Lost in the fog, he opened his mouth, choking as the dark water filled his lungs.

Fae—

Seven

Sapphire

Alysion floated in a dark, quiet place. It *felt* like he was still underwater, but he could breathe—unless breathing wasn't necessary here. Either way, his chest no longer hurt.

Alysion turned around, trying to see through the murk, but it was useless; the strange water was too thick. His panic began to rise when a flash caught his eye: a faint beam of light emanated from the mark on his wrist, pointing somewhere below. At least, he thought it was below him. Alysion twisted his wrist, but the beam did not move. *That must be where the crystal is.*

Swimming here was a strange experience, like squirming through mud. The beam of light remained constant, as did the pressing darkness; he couldn't tell if he was making any progress

Alysion pressed on, clumsy and heavy against the sludge, his limbs slowing with each movement. He thrashed wildly against the pressure, but all it did was sap his strength. Soon he was too exhausted to move and had no choice but to surrender himself to the murky void.

Come on. I need you, Sylandris needs you, he projected to the crystal, imagining his message travelling along the beam of light. *There's something terrible coming that I need your help to stop.*

The mark flashed, and Alysion saw something ahead. He forced his leaden limbs into motion. The beam of light grew brighter as he advanced, relieving him of the endless darkness.

The object was within reach now: a stone box with wave-shaped cutouts. Inside, he glanced a mud-coloured rock a bit smaller than his thumb.

This ugly thing is the crystal? He reached into the box and grasped it.

Alysion screamed. He thrashed about in the water, clawing opposite his heart where his damis resided as white-hot pain shot along his arm and into his chest. The crystal's aura was bonding with his, but it was tainted—it wanted to consume him.

Bringing forth all of his willpower could barely keep the malevolent aura at bay. But Alysion was exhausted. All he wanted was to lay down and rest...

A sharp tug around his waist reminded him of Fae's hands, calloused from working in the smithy, tying the rope around him. What would it be like for those hands to touch him? Fae had touched his face once before—

Alysion's ears burned. Fae was counting on him. All of Sylandris was counting on him.

I won't give in, not now! He was the Crown Prince, and he wouldn't let a silly crystal beat him!

Steeling himself, he pushed back against the strange aura, forcing it back into the crystal. Blue light filtered through his fingers as he opened his hand. The dark staining faded, revealing a dazzling blue that nearly blinded him in the darkness. Sapphire.

The pain in his chest eased as the Sapphire's true colours shone through. Soon only a tiny spot of dirt remained, and with one final push, it disappeared.

Alysion's legs hit solid ground and he collapsed, coughing up mouthfuls of water.

• • • ● • • •

"Alysion!" Fae cried as he appeared out of thin air onto the rocky shore. Fae made it just in time to catch him, alarmed as he was. Was Alysion all right? Was he dying?

"Lay him down," said Gale. "He needs rest."

Fae did as he was told, sitting down and laying the prince's head across his lap. Gale knelt beside him, holding a red-limned hand over him. "Hmm."

"What? What's wrong?"

"His aura's taken a beating, but he'll be fine. Looks like he found your rock; his aura's changed."

Alysion clutched something in his hand. Fae carefully tried to pry it open, but his grip was stronger than iron. Giving up, he stroked Alysion's damp golden locks, heart fluttering. One day he'd know what they felt like when they were dry.

Fae's legs were almost completely numb when Alysion came around, but he kept his complaints to himself as he opened his eyes.

"Hey, how are you feeling?" Fae asked softly.

Alysion mumbled something unintelligible.

"Sorry, I didn't catch that." Had the gross water caused some kind of permanent damage?

"I said, 'hey' is not an acceptable way to address royalty," he said hoarsely.

Fae snorted, his entire body relaxing. Alysion was fine. "If that's how it is, then you must be feeling well enough to stand." As nice as it had been to have the prince's head cradled on his knees, an experience he wouldn't mind repeating under less stressful circumstances, he needed to stretch his legs.

Gale barked out a laugh as they climbed to their feet, realizing they must have looked ridiculous, shaky and unsteady like newborn uhaan. Fae rubbed his legs to bring back some sensation.

"Thank you."

Fae looked up; Alysion was studiously examining something in his hand, but he caught the redness tipping the prince's ears.

"You're welcome," he replied as he came closer to get a look. "That's the crystal?"

Alysion nodded. A translucent blue stone glowed faintly in his hand.

"I suppose it's a water crystal."

"Yes, the Water Sapphire."

"Oi," hollered Gale. "If you're feelin' well enough to chat, then you're well enough to walk back. I don't want to spend the night out here—and you both reek."

Alysion was quiet for a good part of the journey, busy examining the blue stone he'd scooped up out of the lake. Fae tried his best to leave him be, but eventually, his curiosity got the better of him.

"How did you manage to get the crystal?" he asked.

"After the vines pulled me under, I had to prove myself to the Sapphire. I had to convince it that I wanted to use it to protect Sylandris. After that, my bond mark led me to it."

Fae's brow furrowed. "You speak as if the Sapphire is alive."

"It is. Sort of. It doesn't have thoughts, but through its aura, I can feel...sensations? I suppose they are emotions, in a primal sense. I'm not sure how to explain it." Alysion shivered. His clothes were still damp and muddy from his dive despite Gale's attempts to magically dry them.

"Only the most powerful magical doodads are like that," she piped up, leading the way back through the trees. "That's what makes some so dangerous; they can start to influence your thoughts."

"Can the Sapphire influence your thoughts?" Fae asked.

Alysion looked troubled. "It's possible, but I don't believe it will. When I found it, it was in a very sorry state. As we suspected, it's the cause of the sickly lake. From what I have been able to glean from it so far, its aura tried to bond with that of the island spirit, but they weren't a good match, so both their auras became distorted."

Fae nodded. "But the crystal's been here for a long time, hasn't it? Why did it act up now?"

"That's easy," said Gale. "It started when you two saw your glowing elfie. Your prophecy musta poked the Sapphire awake."

Alysion nodded. "Now that I have the Sapphire, I can feel some of the other crystals more clearly—the ones we are physically closer to. And they too are no longer dormant."

"Great," said Fae, not looking forward to fighting for six more shiny rocks. But he would do it for Ash. And maybe he would do it for Alysion too.

• • • ● • • •

The scent of burning incense permeated the small wooden room, thick and heavy in the air. Most would have found the smell stifling, but it did not bother the half-nude elf kneeling in front of the altar, eyes closed with hands cupped atop his knees. The younger nelim sat still as stone, each breath slow and controlled, for he was deep into his daily meditation. His aura pulsed, strengthening as he breathed in, fading as he breathed out.

As he exhaled again, a disturbance brushed his consciousness. Something across the aural plane had shifted. He focused on it, wanting to know what had caused such a change. His eyes suddenly snapped open.

"A crystal has been taken?"

Taking a breath, he focused on detecting which one had been found. But the aural ripples were faint—the crystal was far away. The elf persisted, pushing his aural consciousness as far as he could. It was difficult; many other pulses of energy got in his way, confusing him. He feared he'd lost the trail, but eventually, he found the source. *The Sapphire!*

He sprang up and grabbed his embroidered white robes from where they hung, quickly pulling them on—the slamming of the heavy wooden door startled the two attendants waiting outside.

"Summon the *ayel* immediately," he barked, still adjusting layers of robes and fixing his long white hair.

Both of them silently scurried off to carry out their orders, not wanting to get between their *isidyll* and whatever had angered him.

Within minutes, the ayel had gathered in the Verdant Hall, a large room formed in the trunk of an enormous tree, its walls well-polished and carved with forest motifs. The ayel knelt in two rows along the sides of the hall, leaving the centre walkway open. They wore identical outfits: robes of silver, black, and violet, almost as ornate as the isidyll's. Their unnaturally white hair was cut short. The white-clad elf took his place at the head of the hall.

"The Water Sapphire has been taken, and we must retrieve it." A shocked muttering arose from amongst the gathered.

"Isidyll Navir, how do you—"

"Silence!" the isidyll snapped. They had no time for questions—he'd only been able to track the Sapphire to its hiding spot, and whoever had it wouldn't remain there for long. The thief would have a few days' start on them even if they sent the *konn* out immediately.

"I want you to select a few of your best disciples to send out on a retrieval team. They leave immediately for Great Snapper Lake. Dismissed."

The ayel left, save for one clad in black robes. He alone, aside from the isidyll, wore his hair long; unlike the others, it retained some traces of colour. "Would it be better if I went personally, Isidyll Navir?"

"No, Drath-ayel, the senior konn can handle this. I'd prefer if you kept working to locate the other crystals."

"Whoever took the stone must be extremely powerful. Reclaiming it is no simple task. Are you sure the konn will be able to handle it? Sending the more skilled ayel might be better," the older elf suggested, his voice full of concern.

"Not many know what the crystals truly are. There's a good chance the Sapphire was picked up by some idiot human who doesn't understand what they've found."

"And if not? If it *was* found by someone who knows its true nature?"

"That's not possible," Navir snapped. "Only the king and queen know of their existence, and our spies tell me that they weren't alerted when we acquired the Amethyst."

"Very well. I shall take my leave then." The dark-robed ayel bowed and left the hall.

Navir ran a hand through his hair. Who had taken the Sapphire, and just what were they after?

Part Two

It was a chilly winter day; the sun shone through the bare trees, turning the small, snowy clearing into a sparkling wonderland. Tarathiel sat astride his grey uhaan, his breath coming out as puffs as he waited. The snow crunched behind him, and his heart leapt in anticipation.

"Hail and well met, dear Tarathiel!" the approaching elf called out, the sun outlining his long hair in rays of gold.

Tarathiel sighed, taking in Illuven's beauty as he rode into the clearing. He had always been good-looking; Tarathiel had been enamoured with him since they were young, but now that adulthood was nearly upon them, Illuven was absolutely breathtaking.

"What is it?" asked Illuven.

"Nothing, my good Illuven. Nothing at all."

Illuven raised a perfectly shaped eyebrow. "Then why have you called me all the way out here? This wasn't an easy place to find."

Tarathiel only now noticed the twigs caught in Illuven's silky hair. "I don't want others intruding on us. Nobles can be quite nosey."

Illuven smiled. "That they are. I can't do anything without an audience."

"Yes, I suppose that's how it is when you're to be joined with Princess Lymsia."

Illuven's face immediately fell. "So...you've heard?"

"Is there anyone in Sylandris who hasn't?" replied Tarathiel.

"I suppose not." Illuven stared at the reins in his hands. "I—"

"Congratulations," said Tarathiel, smiling.

"Stop. Both of us know I don't want this." Illuven looked up, meeting his green eyes.

Tarathiel let the facade of happiness slide from his face, frustration and anger replacing it. "How...how could this have happened?"

But they both knew the answer to that. The princess was wholly infatuated with Illuven, and of all the proposed candidates, he was the most suitable. He had the correct noble standing, proper upbringing, and powerful lineage; Illuven's family was an offshoot of the royal line from ancient days when royals could have more than one child. They had kept themselves as high-bred as possible, their magical prowess bested only by the royals themselves.

And Illuven was no exception: his abilities far surpassed those of all the other young elves and even some of their instructors. Tarathiel cursed Illuven's radiant appearance for having drawn the princess' eye.

"And they didn't listen when you told them you were interested in someone else?"

"It doesn't matter. I've been chosen by the royal family. I'm supposed to break off any connections to others."

Tarathiel's hands involuntarily balled into fists around his uhaan's reins. This was utterly unacceptable; Illuven was *his*.

"There has to be something we can do."

Illuven shook his head. "This decision is beyond either of us."

"You don't get a say in it at all?"

"No. I'm expected to graciously accept and appreciate such an honour. Declining isn't an option."

"This isn't an offer. It's a demand!" Tarathiel nearly shouted.

Illuven gazed upon his love, eyes filled with sorrow. "I'm sorry. I wish I had the option to decline. I truly do. Anyone else in my position would be overjoyed; it's a great honour."

Tarathiel huffed and loosened his grip on his reins. "We will figure something out." There had to be a way around this; he just needed time to think.

• • • ● • • •

Despite Illuven's impending union with Lymsia, he and Tarathiel continued to meet secretly in the hideout they had built as children. Over the decades, their meeting spot had transformed from a haphazard shack leaning up against the base of a thick tree to a small cottage high in the safety of its branches. The cottage's interior was fully furnished—it lacked a proper kitchen, but they had no need for one, as the magical flame in the fire pit was more than enough to suit their needs. Aside from improving the hut, they spent most of their time there relaxing and enjoying each other's company.

One late spring afternoon, they met up in the cottage as usual. However, their visits were becoming less frequent, much to Tarathiels' annoyance. Illuven's union was scheduled for summer, not long after the *Striiya*, the coming-of-age ceremony. Because of the extra lessons Illuven had been forced to take in preparation, they had fewer opportunities to meet. Though he was a high-bred noble, there was still much for him to learn about culture and etiquette if he was going to be crowned the next king.

"My tutors have me studying the royal lineage and the Divine Ancestors," he said with a sigh, lounging on the bed occupying a whole corner of the cottage. Tarathiel lounged beside him, a book open on his lap. "It's things we already know, but they want to be sure I have it all memorized."

"Why? When are you ever going to need that information?" asked Tarathiel, his irritation evident.

"It's not about using it, dear Tarathiel; it's simply about knowing." He reached up and brushed a stray pale hair from Tarathiel's eyes. As he crept closer to adulthood, Tarathiel's hair had turned almost pure white, a rare and striking colour.

The pale elf snorted. "There are more useful things you could be learning about, like how to kill a dragon."

"Not everything is about dragons."

"Well, it should be! For decades I've been researching how they treated our people during the Syl-Raanian War, yet I have never found anything pertaining to any punishment for their crimes," he explained, becoming heated. "We just let them fly away after nearly ruining us! The peace treaties and agreements signed between our peoples don't make up for all the lives lost, all the cities reduced to ash."

"I understand where you're coming from, but let's not waste this precious time together discussing this."

Under normal circumstances, his words would have angered Tarathiel, but since their time was limited, neither of them wanted to waste it. Instead, they sat in peaceful silence, simply enjoying each other's company.

"Have you come up with any ideas for—" Tarathiel stopped, feeling an intimidating aural presence on the forest floor below.

They exchanged a glance. Tarathiel rose and peeked out one of the windows to see who was out there. The cottage wasn't far from Lyrellis, but it was still a trek to get out there. And though Illuven didn't know it, or pretended not to, Tarathiel had cast wards around the cottage to hide it. He was confident that whoever was down there hadn't found the hut nor felt their auras. Through the leaves, Tarathiel couldn't see anyone on the forest floor. The aura faded.

"Just someone passing through," he said, returning to the bed. He didn't like the worry on Illuven's face.

Illuven nodded and relaxed.

"As I was saying," said Tarathiel, "have you come up with any ideas for getting out of the arrangement? I haven't been able to come up with anything good." Ever since he'd found out about the union, Tarathiel had put his research on dragons and the war aside.

The mood in the cottage plummeted. "No, I haven't," Illuven responded slowly.

Tarathiel felt a pang of disappointment but wasn't terribly surprised. "Well, we'll figure something out. We still have some time."

Bang!

The cottage door flew open. A great aura flowed in, followed by an angry elf and a moment of stunned silence.

"How dare you!" the newcomer snapped. "I've been searching for you all afternoon, and this is what I find?"

Neither of the elves on the bed moved, in complete shock over the appearance of Princess Lymsia herself.

"Well?" she prompted, eyes blazing, arms crossed.

"We're just visiting," said Illuven weakly.

"Is that so?" she said, her green eyes darting to Tarathiel. "You can't afford to ruin your reputation by spending it with lower-born nobles. You're wasting time."

Rude, thought Tarathiel, biting his tongue. He didn't want to get Illuven into any more trouble.

Illuven climbed over him and reluctantly stood. "What do you need to see me about?"

"I'll inform you once we're someplace more private," she said, her voice softening.

"It doesn't get any more private than this," Tarathiel huffed, tired of her snotty attitude.

"You are to remain quiet unless spoken to," Lymsia snapped. "I should have you punished for leading the future king astray, but today I'll let it slide as I have more pressing matters to attend to."

Tarathiel ground his teeth, his expression tightening as his irritation returned. He forcefully swung his legs over the edge of the bed and rose to his feet, glaring at the princess. "Punish me? For what? I haven't done anything wrong. As Illuven explained, we were simply relaxing. That isn't a crime."

"Tarathiel, don't," said Illuven, giving him a pleading look that he ignored.

"Don't argue with me," she hissed. "I can change my mind if I wish. Illuven is to join the royal family; he can't be seen gallivanting around with the likes of *you*. It'll cause too much unrest in the court."

Something inside Tarathiel snapped. "The likes of me? What's *that* supposed to mean?" Unrest in the court? Hmph. The court needed some unrest. "Everything is about you royals, isn't it? *Your* union, *your* noble image. Has it ever crossed your *divine* mind to ask Illuven what he wants?"

Princess Lymsia's eyes flashed. "Silence! Don't talk about things you don't understand. Starting now, you are forbidden from seeing each other!"

Tarathiel resisted the urge to set her on fire. "Forbidden?" His lips curled in a snarl. "You can't dictate what we choose to do!"

"As heir to the throne, I can," she said coldly. "If you're caught together again, you will be severely punished." Her tone made it clear that Tarathiel would be the one taking the punishment. "Come, Illuven. We're leaving."

Illuven mouthed an apology to Tarathiel and glumly followed her out.

Tarathiel flopped back on the bed, blood boiling. *Damn them!* One of the few days he had left with Illuven was ruined—and by the very thing they were both dreading. *The princess doesn't even love him; she just likes how he looks!* He threw a pillow and punched the wall, imagining Lymsia's face beneath his fist. *They won't get away with this!*

Eight

Captain Anaril

Fae, Alysion, and Gale returned to the inn, still damp and reeking of lakewater. The first thing they did was grab some clean clothes and make their way to the local bathhouse, despite any worries that their antics on the island had attracted the Elithar's attention.

"I'm not leaving until I'm properly clean," Alysion said stubbornly. "Besides, it's getting late. We can leave tomorrow."

If Alysion wasn't concerned about the Elithar's whereabouts, then Fae wouldn't be either. They were filthy from their trek and smelled something awful. Besides, who knew when their next bath could be?

The bathhouse was nicer than they anticipated: artful wooden carvings of leaves and animals decorated the entrance, and to their pleasant surprise, the pools were not tubs of lukewarm water but outdoor hot springs. Alysion went straight for the men's bath, making a point to ignore the mixed one. Fae shrugged at Gale and followed him, not wanting to leave him unsupervised.

"Well, girls' bath for me, then!" Gale didn't seem disappointed at all.

At this time of day, the springs were empty. Most of the villagers were out fishing, and with it being summer, soaking in the pools was more enjoyable when they cooled off in the evening. So Fae and Alysion had the bath all to themselves; they didn't have to worry about the fisherfolk discovering their true heritage.

Fae removed his towel and stepped into the water, sinking until it covered his collar bones. He closed his eyes and leaned back against the stone of the pool, letting out a sigh of relief as the hot water soothed his weary body.

Alysion remained standing on the edge, his towel around his waist.

"Are you coming in?" he asked.

"I am," was the huffed response he got.

Fae couldn't help but stare. It was the first time he'd gotten the chance to see so much of him. Usually, he hid behind a tree or kicked Fae out of the room when he was changing. The prince's body was more defined than he expected, seeing as Alysion rarely used his sword. Perhaps magic helped him maintain his physique? Regardless of the reason, the sight set his heart aflutter. Catching Alysion's hard look, Fae reluctantly pulled his gaze away.

Alysion was still on the edge.

"Is something wrong?"

"No," he said moodily, finally dropping his towel and stepping into the pool when Fae looked away again.

Fae noticed that his ears were red. What did that mean? Did he...? No, it couldn't be. He was just being shy.

"Is it too hot for you? I think they said there's a cooler pool down the hall."

"It's fine," came a stiff reply.

"All right then." Fae closed his eyes and let Alysion do his thing, not wanting to get on his bad side. After waiting a bit, he cracked one open, curious to see if Alysion had relaxed. Gods knew they needed it.

Alysion was submerged in the water up to his neck, his hair floating like a fine noodle soup around him. Fae bit his lip in an effort not to laugh.

"What?" Alysion asked sharply.

"Nothing," he replied, looking up at the clear blue sky. Alysion stared at him suspiciously in his periphery, but Fae had no desire to tell him off.

"Tell me where we're going next," Fae asked the sky.

"South," he replied. "I can feel one almost due south of here."

"In the mountains?"

Alysion nodded. "Yes, but I'm not sure how far we have to go."

"The prophecy must have a clue." He moved closer to Alysion, who became very interested in the water as he quietly recited the prophecy.

Being so close made Fae's whole body feel light as air. Alysion smelled like the floral soap they'd used to clean themselves before entering the pool. Though different from the forest and lunaberry scent he was used to, it was still appealing.

He edged closer, eyes on his perfect lips, wishing Alysion would turn to face him so that he could—

"What are you doing?" Alysion asked suddenly.

Heart hammering, Fae backed away, glad the heat of the water hid how his face burned. "Nothing."

They sat in awkward silence for a moment before Alysion cleared his throat and continued reciting the prophecy as if nothing had happened. Fae wasn't sure if he was relieved or hurt, but he pushed away his hormonal emotions as they considered the prophecy's riddles. Unfortunately, neither of them could figure anything else out.

Reluctantly, they left the bath. Fae went first so Alysion could have his privacy. As much as he wanted to turn and get one last glimpse, he diligently kept his eyes forward as he strode back into the changing room. Hopefully, there would be more opportunities to be alone with Alysion—opportunities where clothing wasn't necessary.

• • • ● • • •

Alysion's ears burned hotter than dragonfire—and it wasn't because of the hot spring. Why had Fae gotten so close? It was as if he—no, it couldn't be. Fae was nelim; he wouldn't have thoughts like that about him, *another* nelim. And the crown prince to boot. Then again, the nobles were allowed to take whoever they wished to be their mate, regardless of gender. Only the royal family didn't have that freedom; they had to pick a mate who could help them pass on the Ancestors' divine lineage.

Alysion frowned. Which family did Fae belong to? He never spoke about his parents, only about the human blacksmith who'd raised him. Just how long had Fae been living in Redwood?

Alysion sunk into the water until it was just below his nose. Despite all the mystery surrounding him, Alysion couldn't deny that he felt much more comfortable with Fae than with any of the *belim* his mother constantly set him up with. *He's not bad looking either...* The image of water rolling off Fae's toned back when he'd left the bath filled his thoughts. The heat from his ears crept along his face. *Oh no.* The prince dunked his head underwater to clear his mind—it wasn't as effective as he'd hoped.

That night, Alysion awoke in a hazy place. Startled, he quickly got to his feet and peered around; where was he, and who had brought him here? But even his keen eyes couldn't make anything out through the fog, only meaningless vague shapes. Then there were voices—angry voices. His instinct told him to avoid them, but curiosity ruled.

Silently he crept through the mist, trying to find whoever was out there. *In here?* This was a dream, wasn't it? It had to be. Because the last thing he remembered was trying to fall asleep in their room at the Golden Carp.

Focus.

He pressed on, and the voices got louder. They were just in front of him, but he still couldn't see through the mist. He stepped forward again, the hair on the back of his neck prickling.

Someone sighed loudly next to him, making him jump.

"I'm sorry!" he exclaimed, whirling around. But he was only met with formless shapes.

"I've told you this before. Your plans are too harsh. The royal family will never go for it." said a youthful nelim voice.

He cocked his head. The voice, while somewhat distorted like everything else, was strangely familiar.

"They are not!" responded another. Like the first speaker, they had the lower tone of a nelim. "My plans are as harsh as they need to be. Look at what they've done to us! Our cities are gone, and our people have been reduced to a mere shadow of our former glory. We have the power to strike back at them, to make those beasts…" The voice trailed off, and there was silence.

The first voice spoke. "I understand where you're coming from. You're not the only one who feels that way. But like you said, we have no resources. Even if the royal family agreed with your ideas, we don't have the means to fulfill them."

"Ah, but that's where you're wrong." The second voice became hushed, almost too quiet for Alysion to hear. "I snuck into the library's secret room, and there I learned about a set of crystals that would—"

"Oi! Turn off that light! We're trying to sleep," grumped another voice, this one familiar and female. Gale.

The dream haze disappeared, and Alysion found himself staring up at the ceiling of the inn. A faint blue glow shone from the small leather pouch around his neck. He grasped at it, and the light slowly dimmed. Despite how hot it was in the room, Alysion pulled his blanket up higher to cover it.

Had that strange dream come from the Sapphire? And if it had, what did it mean?

• • • ● • • •

They set out before dawn the following day, climbing the cliffs that would take them out of the Great Snapper region and into the Sky Peak range. Alysion was still shaken up from everything that happened yesterday, but thankfully his companions had the sense not to bother him. He couldn't tell them about the dream just yet. Who did the voices belong to? Was one of them the traitor? They had mentioned the crystals—

The Sapphire's energy flared, and with it came a handful of auras.

"Oh no," he said, turning in the saddle.

"What is it?" Fae asked from behind him.

"The Elithar have found me. They're coming."

They urged their mounts to climb faster, but the cliff trail loose stones that could break an uhaan's leg littered the cliff trail. They had to go slow.

"How close are they?" Fae glanced over his shoulder.

Alysion focused on the approaching auras. "They're still on the far side of the lake, but they're moving fast."

"Have you always been able to feel 'em from so far away, Princey?" asked Gale from the head of the group.

"No, the Sapphire is helping. Usually, when their aura feels this strong, it means they are very, very close."

"Then it's good we have the Sapphire to help watch our backs," said Fae.

They managed to keep ahead of the Elithar over the next few days, their journey taking them straight south through the heart of the mountains. Though they pushed their mounts as fast as possible, the winding paths made the going frustratingly slow. Their only solace was that the terrain also hampered the Elithar's pursuit.

Now that Alysion had bonded with the Sapphire, his aura was much easier to track. Shaking the Elithar off would be impossible, but he would make the most of the situation: alongside Gale and Fae's sparring, Alysion practised magic every night.

It felt good to use magic again, even if he still had very little control over it. And practising without his tutors hovering around him was...freeing. He could mess up all he wanted, and no one would yell at him. When something went awry, he had only himself to worry about—and sometimes his companions if a stray spell went their way. Thankfully, Gale was quick to divert any of his mishaps with a gust of wind.

Even through the mistakes, his companions were supportive. Out here he didn't have to see his mother's disappointed expression when she inquired about his progress, nor his father's troubled but watchful eye. Without the extra pressure, he thought he was actually starting to improve.

After a few evenings of consistent practise, his curiosity got the better of him, and he decided to add the Sapphire's power into the mix. Using the Sapphire was very different from relying solely on his aura. The stone wasn't just an inanimate object that provided him with extra aural energy; it had a consciousness of its own that exuded an air of tranquillity and coolness. He got the feeling the blue crystal wanted to please him.

Alysion called upon the Sapphire's power and nearly doubled over as a wave of aura crashed into him like a tsunami. The sheer volume of energy the Sapphire held was staggering—he could easily lose himself in it if he weren't careful. *It's no wonder the crystals were hidden away. This kind of power in the wrong hands could be disastrous!* He had to get the stolen crystal back and collect the others before anyone else caught on.

It worried him that the other hidden crystals were also emitting strong auras; they shone like beacons. And it didn't help that he still had no idea who the traitor could be or what they planned on doing. That strange dream was trying to tell him something, but was it a vision of the past or the future? Maybe it hadn't been a vision at all, just a dream born from his own worries.

• • • ● • • •

Fae studied the map as they wound their way south, trying to figure out just where they were headed. Nothing was jumping out at him, save for an unlabelled dot to the west.

"What do you think this is?" he asked, holding up the map to Alysion. He scanned the page. Fae narrowed his eyes and peered through the trees ahead for any sign of the watcher's dun uhaan—Gale had ridden ahead to scout the terrain, though she should have returned by now.

"That's *Shidrakos*, an old outpost from the Syl-Raanian War. Because it's so close to Fiiraania, we used it to report any dragon sightings back to Lyrellis. It was destroyed during the war. Apparently, the top of one of the nearby mountains was shaved clean off during a fight."

Indeed, one of the mountains had been drawn with a flat peak. "Have the dragons always lived on the other side of the mountains?" Fae asked.

"Fiiraania has always been their territory, but before the war, some lived in these lands. After the war, the Sky Peak wards were set up to keep them out. Our people barely survived—even now our population is still a fraction of what it used to be."

"Can you tell me about the war?" Fae asked eagerly. He'd heard a few stories from travelling human bards, but it wasn't the same. Alysion could give him a more detailed—if perhaps biased—account.

Alysion puffed out his chest, pleased to have another opportunity to educate his lesser. Fae hid his smile.

"Centuries ago, before the humans came and founded their kingdom of Odenia, some dragons killed a *thelim*, inciting hostility between our people. Not long after that—"

"Why did they kill a small child?" Fae asked, eyes glowing with curiosity.

"Don't interrupt me," grumped Alysion. "No one knows why. Anyway, the *vorais*—the ruler of the dragons—was willing to make amends for the crime, but before anything was settled, a new vorais overthrew them. He refused to hand over the culprits, stating the thelim had been in the wrong for crossing into their lands. Things quickly went downhill from there; not long after, they threw our emissaries out and attacked and elf that entered Fiiraania. We stopped sending emissaries over but then elves of all bloodlines started to disappear from the villages we used to have in the Sky Peak Mountains. A patrol managed to catch a dragon near Shidrakos and from them we learned that the dragons were killing and eating any elves that strayed too far from home. They even admitted to some twisted dragons keeping elves as slaves."

"What? Why?" A chill went up Fae's back. Slavery was outlawed in Odenia, but it was difficult to enforce in the rural and border communities. Fae had heard disturbing stories of adolescents going missing, only to turn up moons or suncycles later nearly starved and beaten to death. It chilled him to think of Alysion, someone with great magical prowess, being captured and forced to submit to anyone.

Alysion frowned. "I told you not to interrupt me."

"Sorry, go on."

"They began to burn our villages, slowly creeping out of the mountains and closer to Lyrellis. And though we tried to convince them to stop, we realized we could no longer rely on peaceful means. It's not easy to parley with a savage beast."

Fae didn't know any dragons, but hearing Alysion call them 'savage beasts' didn't sit well with him. *But they'd razed entire villages to the ground...*

"So, Sylandris declared war on the dragons. The fighting lasted about a century, and during that time, our great cities were decimated, our people reduced to almost nothing. We retreated into the forest, casting the Sylandrian ward around the sole intact part of our territory. My grandfather, the king, died from the wounds he'd sustained not long after it ended. The dragons were ruthless in their assaults. The dwarves living on the plains suffered too, but I don't know much about it. In the end, we managed to kill the vorais with the help of some powerful magic, and a new vorais—the current one—was chosen with the approval of the Sylandrian court. Then treaties and agreements were drawn up and signed with blood, our realms forever separated by these very mountains. You can feel the magic of the great wards west of here working to keep them out."

Fae didn't bother to remind the prince that his 'talisman' prevented him from feeling the wards. It was best to avoid that topic altogether; else he risked Alysion figuring out the truth. And that wasn't something Fae could afford—for Ash's sake and his own. He shifted in his seat, suddenly restless.

• • • ● • • •

Fae was shaken awake one morning with Alysion's finger pressed against his lips. He crawled from his bedroll and hastily belted on his sword, which lay within reach on the ground beside him.

Elithar, Alysion mouthed. They quickly packed their few things and mounted up.

No one spoke as they rode, the tension in the air palpable. Even their uhaan kept quiet, picking up on their rider's urgency.

Every snap of a twig, every rustle of leaves set Fae on edge; he expected the Elithar to pop out with their blades drawn, hurling spells at them. His hand hovered over the new sword he'd gotten before they'd left Great Snapper, even though it wouldn't be of much use against sorcerers. Ugh, if only he could use magic!

"They're here," muttered Alysion.

Fae's pulse quickened.

Riders suddenly materialized around them as if they were part of the trees themselves.

The trio brought their uhaan to a halt, the animals snorting and throwing their heads.

One rider approached. Fae recognized the tall captain who had cornered them back home in Redwood—Captain Anaril. He kept silent, hand still at his sword, as they addressed Alysion.

"My prince, it's time for you to return home with us."

Alysion met the captain's piercing gaze, one that Fae couldn't hold. "No. Instead, you'll deliver a message to my parents: I will return when I feel like it."

Captain Anaril's expression didn't change, but every nerve in Fae's body tensed. Though Alysion outranked them, he was playing a dangerous game.

"Unfortunately, we are under direct orders from Her Majesty the Queen. Your words have no weight here, my prince," the captain replied, their tone suggesting they would cut Alysion down without batting an eye if the queen had ordered it.

Fae studied Captain Anaril's stoic expression. Their face was youthful; if they'd been human, Fae would guess they were approaching their third decade.

But their eyes told another story: the captain had seen the passing of the centuries, maybe even millennia, and had witnessed countless deaths. There was no doubt in Fae's mind they had fought in the Syl-Raanian War.

Despite the warm summer sunlight streaming through the trees, Fae shivered. The surrounding elves prepared to attack.

"You will be returning with us to Lyrellis, and if..." Captain Anaril glanced at Gale as if she were nothing. But when their cold grey gaze turned to Fae, he froze, realizing that the captain knew he had no damis. *Of course they know!* his mind screamed at him. *They're the best aural tracker Sylandris has ever seen!*

Captain Anaril's gaze returned to Alysion. "If you want your companions to survive, I suggest surrendering now."

Even if Alysion went with them, Fae wouldn't be walking away with his life. The moment their eyes had met, Fae knew the captain had already made up their mind to rid the world of a damis-less blight.

"I will not return with you," he said firmly.

"Then do not mourn them."

The Elithar launched their spells. Colourful beams of magic streaked towards Fae and Gale, hissing and crackling.

Sy-Sy reared with a cry, nearly throwing Fae from his back. As a streak of fire lit up the ground in front of them, Fae clung desperately to the saddle. The shot barely missed.

"Easy boy!" Fae called, but his voice was lost in the confusion of the fight. Out of the corner of his eye, something glimmered. He pulled his frightened uhaan around, Sy-Sy narrowly avoiding an arrow made of ice.

"Fae, Gale, get behind me!" Alysion hollered.

Fae reluctantly moved to follow his instructions, hoping Alysion knew what he was doing—grouping together would only make them an easier target. Sy-Sy barely got two steps in before Fae dove from his back, a dart of yellow light crackling through the air. He managed to break his fall with a roll, scrambling to his feet. Sy-Sy thundered off into the trees, leaving him alone against two mounted warriors. Their hands glowed.

Fae drew his sword. If only he had magic of his own, then maybe he would stand a chance! He ducked as an arc of blue fire whooshed overhead, the heat singing the hairs on the back of his neck. As he straightened up, something hit him square in the chest, throwing him to the ground. He landed hard on his back, winded.

"Fae!"

He gasped, desperately trying to fill his lungs. Dark shapes loomed over him. *Get up, get up!* He tried to push himself upright, but his shaking limbs wouldn't respond. *Damn it!* This couldn't be the end—he hadn't found Ash!

Entirely at the Elithar's mercy, Fae did the only thing he could think of and curled up defensively. Something howled through the air above him, and something wet splattered across his face.

"Fae!"

Hands grabbed him and hauled him to his feet. A glint of gold flashed before him—Alysion.

Still wheezing, Fae turned to find his attackers lying stunned in a puddle. He wiped his face, relieved it was just water. As he did, he caught sight of the Sapphire hanging around Alysion's neck.

"Where's Gale?" he asked.

"Dealing with Anaril and the other two," replied Alysion.

Gale was still astride her uhaan, throwing bursts of air at the Elithar—invisible until they struck their targets. The warriors tried to break away, but she wasn't giving them a chance. It was impressive; Fae had to wonder how a human could hold her own against three of Sylandris' best.

Alysion helped him onto Zen-Zen, waiting nearby, undisturbed by the commotion, and climbed up behind him. "You steer," he ordered. "I'll get them if they come after us."

Fae picked up the reins, managing not to flinch as Alysion wrapped an arm around him. If only they could be this close when their lives weren't in danger...

"What about Gale?" he asked.

"She has a plan. We just need to get out of here."

"But—" As skilled as Gale was, Fae didn't think she'd be able to escape the elite warriors. Especially not Captain Anaril.

"Just go!"

A pang of guilt struck him as he spurred Zen-Zen away from the fight, leaving Gale and Sy-Sy behind.

Nine

Watcher

Zen-Zen ran for as long as she could, but the uhaan tired quickly with two passengers. So both elves dismounted and continued on foot, putting as much distance as possible between themselves and the Elithar. But eventually, the stubborn uhaan dug in her hooves and refused to budge, making it clear it was time for a break.

Alysion pulled some water from the ground for her, pleased that he could do it without creating another geyser. Did the Sapphire have something to do with his success? His control over water was better when he used it, though it didn't help with other types of magic. His fire, in particular, was still unpredictable. He'd thought about asking Gale for help but couldn't yet bring himself to stoop to that level.

"Do you think Gale's okay?" Fae asked after they'd sat down, tossing some dried jerky to him.

"Yes," said Alysion stiffly, still tense from the fight as he tried to relax on a tree stump. "She told me she had a plan. Said she'd find us later."

"Did she say what her plan was?"

"No, just that we should trust her." And Alysion did, but judging by the look on Fae's face, the feeling was not mutual. "What?"

Fae stood to brush Zen-Zen. "Can we trust her?"

"Why wouldn't we? She's done nothing but help us out."

"That may be true...but something's off. When we first ran into her, she never asked about the Elithar, even though she would've sensed who they were. She also didn't ask about you or our mission until it came up. I know some people like respecting others' privacy, but given how strange it is for two elves to be wandering around Odenia in the first place, she must have an ulterior motive. Especially now that she knows about the crystals and the prophecy."

"Maybe humans are just that simple," said Alysion.

Fae shot him a dark look. "I've lived with them for decades; they're not."

Decades? That was a good chunk of time, especially for an elf who only now approaching adulthood.

"We can't forget that she's working for the monarch of Odenia," Fae continued. "She's probably told the crown about the crystals and the prophecy—it's literally her job to report strange things. I wouldn't be surprised if she's been secretly asked to hunt the crystals. Gale did become rather insistent about staying with us once she learned of their existence."

Alysion snorted. "I think she's just worried about your mentor chastising her for letting you get hurt." While he couldn't see the cheerful watcher betraying them, he did know of a handful of smiling Elven nobles in the royal court who promised one thing and did another, so the concept wasn't unfamiliar.

"There's been a few nights where she's disappeared during her watch," Fae continued. "And sometimes she takes a really long time scouting."

"She was probably relieving herself," he said, crossing his arms.

"And how is a single human, with limited magic, supposed to fight off the captain of the Elithar and two of their best warriors?"

"All right, I get it," said Alysion, holding up a hand in defeat. He hadn't thought about what Gale was planning for the Elithar, and now that he had, it *was* suspicious. However, he didn't doubt for a minute that she would return, despite the odds stacked against her. "What should we do when she comes back? Question her?"

Fae put the brush away, the grazing uhaan looking pleased. "No. If she comes back, we'll keep a closer eye on her and keep the important information to ourselves."

Ah, this was why Fae didn't want to discuss the prophecy's riddles with Gale—he didn't want her to figure out where the other crystals were and report them back to Murk Water.

• • • ● • • •

Gale caught up to them as the sun began to set. "Boy, Princey," she said, throwing a set of reins to Fae, "yer aura sure is easy to track. It's like you're wavin' a big 'ol flag."

To Fae's surprise and joy, she had found Sy-Sy. He immediately wrapped his arms around the uhaan's neck. "No more running off," he whispered.

Sy-Sy flicked his ears.

As they made camp, Fae tried to read Gale. Aside from looking worn out, which did little to dampen her spirits, she escaped the Elithar unscathed. But how was that possible? She couldn't have done it alone—unless she possessed powers far beyond what she claimed.

His stomach suddenly plummeted. The glowing elf had told them one of the crystals had already been taken. Had Gale done it? He shot Alysion a glance but didn't dare speak to him now.

"So, how did you escape?" Fae asked as they sat around the fire, waiting for their meal to cook.

Gale's face lit up. "Not gonna lie, it was tricky. Didn't know if I'd make it. That crusty old captain is one tough nut."

Alysion coughed.

"Pretty much exhausted all my magic for the week trying to get away from 'em, but I had a few watcher tricks up my sleeve." She pulled a cracked wooden talisman from her pocket. "In case we ever do run into a dragon. Freezes enemies for a bit, but you can only use it once. Used another that messed up their auras to throw 'em off the trail. Won't last long."

"Why would you expect to run into a dragon?" said Alysion, frowning. "You know they can't cross the mountains because of the wards."

Gale shrugged. "Just a precaution. Have a few others for nasty spots."

"Well, we're glad to have you back," Fae said with a forced smile. Gale's bag of surprises did nothing to assuage his worries; if anything, it made her all the more dangerous.

• • • ● • • •

They rode as fast as they could to keep ahead of the Elithar. Bypassing their supply stop in the town of Tyrrell, they aimed further south for Ashdale, a town sitting at the base of an old volcano. Traffic increased as the volcano loomed closer, forcing them to disguise their speech and ears.

"The crystal is close," Alysion whispered.

Fae nodded, wrist starting to prickle. He looked up at the darkening sky and frowned—despite the cloud cover, it didn't smell like rain.

"Hey boys," said Gale from the head of the group. "I think Mt. Hissan is waking up."

Fae's stomach knotted, and he exchanged a worried glance with Alysion. *A volcano?* They urged their mounts faster.

When Ashdale came into view, the sky was black with smoke and soot. Far above them, the top of the mountain glowed an angry orange. The trickle of people fleeing the village turned into a thick stream; it was easier to stay off the road than fight the flow.

"*Its sibling kept by a mountain's quake,*" recited Alysion, staring up at the orange-topped mountain.

Fae looked up at the glowing cone, fiddling nervously with the reins as the mountain belched out flaming rocks, sending them crashing into the trees on its northern slope. He'd rather fight the vines again than deal with an angry volcano.

"Mm, usually Ashdale is a nice place if you can stand the tourists. The volcanic hot springs are its main attraction—much nicer than the ones around Great Snapper. Many of Murk Water's nobles visit them," said Gale. "I have a friend here; we should find her."

"Won't she be in the middle of evacuating?" asked Fae.

"Pah, she'll be too busy helping others evacuate to worry about her own safety. And—oh, there she is!"

"Gale!" a voice called out. "I was getting worried you wouldn't make it!"

The human elbowing her way through the throng had a soft face and shoulder-length wavy brown hair that matched her eyes. Fae was shocked by how ordinary she looked; he'd expected to see another hardy watcher.

"Yes, sorry Mitchy, the trails are full," said Gale, waving.

Mitchy had been expecting them? Fae raised an eyebrow at Alysion.

"Let's get you all to my place," said the human, taking Gale's hand and swinging up behind her on the watcher's uhaan.

Mitchy lived in a simple two-storey house on the edge of town. When they stepped through the front gate, Fae's vision flickered.

"Mitchy trained with me to be a watcher. She has wards around the house just in case. They'll help to hide our auras."

"They stop people from snooping where they shouldn't," added Mitchy.

They hitched their mounts around back and followed Mitchy into the kitchen.

"Can't stay for long. Apparently, we've got business around here," said Gale.

"You're going up the volcano?" Mitchy asked, raising an eyebrow. "You and your two...friends?"

"She's safe, boys; you don't have to hide."

Fae lowered his hood reluctantly, not appreciating being backed into a corner; he didn't want to reveal his identity to a complete stranger.

Alysion slowly did the same beside him, more concerned with taking in the tiny kitchen.

Mitchy let out a low whistle. "It's been a long time since I've seen any elves. You're just as pretty as I remember."

"You've seen elves before?" Fae asked.

"Met some during our training," she said. "Now, tell me why you three are going up Mt. Hissan."

"My apologies, but we can't. It's personal business," said Alysion.

Mitchy crossed her arms and leaned back against the counter, surveying them. "Then your names?"

Fae's skin prickled uncomfortably as her eyes moved from Alysion to him. If she could use magic, she could sense his lack of damis. But wait—could she also sense the crystal? Would her protective wards shield their secrets?

"I'm Alysion, and this is Fae," said the prince, wise enough not to reveal his entire identity.

"How long has the mountain been acting up?" Gale asked.

"Started smoking about a moon or so ago, but the fireballs started flying two days ago. That's when the evacuations began." Mitchy shook her head and sighed. "Well, you're welcome to stay here for as long as you like, though I don't expect this place to be around much longer."

Alysion opened his mouth to speak, but Gale cut him off.

"We'd love to. The sun's going to set soon; we don't want to be caught on the mountain at night."

Mitchy nodded. "I'll need to grab some stuff from the market if I'm cooking for all of us. Won't be able to find much, mind you. You go ahead and settle in—feel free to run the bath." She wrinkled her nose at them as she headed out.

After a bath and a scrumptious meal that left everyone full and sleepy, the elves went up to the spare room. Fae figured Gale would like some time to catch up with her friend, and he wanted to figure out their plan for the volcano.

But Alysion had other ideas. He lay on the bed, having claimed it for himself, while Fae was given some extra bedding to make himself a nice nest on the floor. "Sorry, it's this or convincing your friend to share," Mitchy had said. The look on Alysion's face had been worth spending the night on the floor.

"If you don't mind me asking, where is your family?" the prince asked once Fae finished laying out his bed.

Fae lay down on his back and let out a comfortable sigh. Even though he was on the floor, it was still a nice break from sleeping outside. "My parents are dead."

There was a pregnant pause.

"I'm sorry," said Alysion quietly.

"It's fine." No, it wasn't fine. Fae didn't remember much of the fight. All he could recall was Ash disappearing into the trees and the flash of light that had left him outside the Sylandrian wards, the memory tinted by intense feelings of fear and confusion.

Alysion eyed him expectantly.

"There was a fight at my home, and they were killed." His throat tightened up. Even after all these years, it was still hard to talk about. Though he couldn't remember exactly how they died, there was no doubt in his mind they were gone.

"Is that when your brother went missing?"

"Yes, he was taken by the ones who attacked us."

They fell into an uneasy silence, broken only by Alysion's snoring. How could he sleep so easily when they were going to scale an active volcano tomorrow morning?

Restless, Fae decided to crash the Dragon Watcher reunion. He needed some cheering up and figured they had some fascinating stories to tell.

Halfway down the stairs, his pointed ears picked up hushed voices that stopped him midstep. He shouldn't listen in (Gale and Mitchy were probably reminiscing about the past), but something about their tone gave him pause. When Gale mentioned the name of the royal Sylandrian family, Brightstar, the staircase swayed beneath him as his concerns about her came rushing back. It took all his willpower not to barge in there and demand to know what they were up to, but Fae restrained himself. If the Dragon Watchers turned on them now, they would have nowhere to run.

He strained to hear, Mitchy's wards muddling their conversation. Gale didn't seem to be telling Mitchy the true reason behind the volcano's activity, but he couldn't be sure.

Not daring to breathe, he went down another step, listening intently.

"If it was, then we should inform our—"

"Not yet, not until we know more," Gale interrupted. "Don't want to stir up trouble until we have some evidence."

"Hmph, I suppose you're right," replied Mitchy, unimpressed.

"I'll send a report once we know more, but for now—"

Fae took another step, the wood beneath letting out a loud squeak. Both women went quiet.

Fae took the rest of the stairs as if nothing had happened, turning into the kitchen. "Sorry to interrupt, just want a drink."

"Help yourself; glasses are in the upper cupboard," Mitchy replied nonchalantly. Gale just smiled at him.

"Thank you." Fae fetched a glass of water and quickly returned to their room, trying to keep his shaking hands steady. He set the glass down on the nightstand before nearly falling into his bed-nest.

Gale *was* sending reports of their journey to the queen in Murk Water, and the human monarch was concerned about the elves. Was she the traitor the prophecy warned them about? Had she once had an alliance with the elves that she broke? That meant Odenia had the first crystal. The more Fae thought about it, the more it seemed to add up. The queen had spies everywhere; one could be travelling with them right now. *Watcher*.

Ten

Gate

"Boys." Fae grunted and rolled over, having drifted off not too long ago.

"Boys!" Gale hissed in the human tongue. "Get up."

He slowly sat up, rubbing his eyes, but he could barely see in the pitch-black room. "Wha—?"

"Quiet," she whispered. "We need to leave."

Alysion stirred in bed, thumping around as he untangled himself from the blankets.

Gale shushed him. "The Elithar are onto us. We need to go *now*."

Fae scrambled to his feet, suddenly wide awake. "I thought Mitchy had wards up?" Had she betrayed them?

"They're up, but I think Alysion's aura is too strong for them to cloak—especially with that rock giving him a boost. She isn't a fancy Sylandrian sorcerer, after all."

"Will she be all right?" Fae whispered, gathering the last of his things. They'd been expecting an early departure, just not this early.

"She'll be fine. I told her trouble might find us."

Fae's gut twisted. What if it was a trap? What if it wasn't Elithar out there but a legion of Odenia's soldiers ready to take the Sapphire?

They descended the stairs and stopped at the front door. Fae peeked through the curtain of the front window.

"I don't see anything, but they could be hiding anywhere." The dark gaps between houses would be perfect for setting up an ambush.

"We'll go out the back," said Gale. "Hopefully, we can make it out of town before anything too crazy happens."

That was far from a perfect plan, but neither elf had anything better to offer. So they slipped out of the house and roused their sleeping mounts, saddling them as quickly as they could. Fae wished they hadn't untacked the uhaan, but the animals had needed the break.

Fae eyed every shadow with suspicion as they carefully made their way onto the front street. Every muscle in his body tensed, his heart beating so loudly he was sure everyone else could hear it. Alysion sat stiff as a board atop Zen-Zen. Only Gale looked relaxed, but he knew she was on high alert—but for friends or foes, he could not say. His only solace was that her human eyes were weaker in the dark.

Time dragged on as they rode, the uhaan's hooves much too loud in the silence of the night. Of course, it didn't help that the town was nearly deserted due to the evacuation.

As soon as they could, they left the front road, sticking to the slower, narrower side streets. Fae detested the feeling of being hunted—part of him wanted to remain cautious, but the other part wanted to throw it all to the wind and rush out of there as fast as they could.

The silence stretched on, broken now and then by the cries of early morning birds. *Something doesn't feel right.*

They were nearly to the gate; he could see it in the distance. Perhaps they would make it. Perhaps they had managed to slip past all the Elithar.

"They've found us!" Alysion suddenly hissed in Illithen, startling Fae and Gale.

"What, how?" Fae whispered back, breaking out in a cold sweat.

A bird cried out close behind them.

"The Elithar learn the sounds of local fauna and use them to communicate—it's the pattern that gave it away," Alysion shouted as they raced towards the northern gate. "They must have masked their auras and snuck in."

"Less talkin', more ridin'," Gale hollered back at him.

"Faster!" Fae cried as figures darted towards the gate. They weren't mounted, but one was preparing a spell.

"Don't slow down!" shouted Gale as Alysion's uhaan dropped her frantic pace. "Run right through 'em if you have to!"

Despite his alarm, Alysion urged Zen-Zen onwards.

"They've surrounded us!" Fae called out. The captain and two others had fallen in place behind them, filtering in from the side streets.

"What do we do?" Alysion cried.

"On my mark, jump and conjure a gust of wind," said Gale. "Ready? Three..."

Fae wasn't ready; he couldn't cast a spell! "I—" A flash of blue fire shot towards them. They swerved sharply to avoid it.

"Two!" she continued as they regrouped, bearing down on the Elithar at the gate.

"One..."

Fae instinctively ducked down as he heard the familiar surge of air—it blew past over his head.

"Now!" Gale cried just as the Elithar at the gate launched another attack.

Their mounts shot off the ground as a gust of wind blasted behind them, sending them flying straight over the Elithar.

Fae landed with a jolt and nearly slid off Sy-Sy, barely managing to hold on as they thundered down the open road. He shook all over.

Something too bright streaked across his vision and crashed into the ground. Sy-Sy stumbled.

"Mountain's tryin' to help us, let's go, boys!" hollered Gale.

Fae glanced back at the red-hot chunk of rock—it was nearly as large as he was. No, the angry mountain wasn't trying to help them, but they would use it to their advantage.

The ground became steeper as they rode up the mountain, slowing their progress. When the sun finally peeked over the horizon, they let their tired uhaan slow to a walk.

"Are they gone?" Fae asked, his instincts urging him to keep running.

"Hard to tell," said Alysion, voice strained. "The crystal's very angry. It's making it difficult to sense anything. We might be able to lose them in these trees." Lush green trees covered the mountainside, the rich volcanic soil allowing them to grow thick and tall. Hopefully, they would provide cover from the Elithar along with the flaming fireballs raining down from the sky.

"Few more moments, then break's over," said Gale.

The entire mountain suddenly quaked, making the uhaan roll their eyes and stamp their feet.

"Nevermind!" said Gale, urging her uhaan onwards.

"You know," said Fae, staring up at the glowing peak far above them, "I bet there's a quick way to the top. I seriously doubt someone hiked all the way up there to hide the crystal." He couldn't picture Alysion or any of the court scaling the mountain without magical aid. "And someone has to check up on it now and then."

The mountain rumbled again, and they pushed their mounts into a fast, bouncy trot.

"Think Fae's onto somethin'. There's gotta be a hidden gate that takes you right to the top!" said Gale. "But I don't feel anythin'."

Alysion closed his eyes, clutching the pouch around his neck.

"Talisman doesn't let me feel auras," Fae reminded her with a pang of guilt. He didn't enjoy lying to his companions, even the untrustworthy watcher, and desperately wished it were safe to tell them the truth. But he couldn't risk losing Alysion's trust—not when finding Ash was on the line.

"It's fine," she said. "It'd be good for Princey to master picking out specific auras amongst others. No better place to do it than here!"

Fae watched Alysion, mesmerized by the volcano's glow bathing his golden hair in fiery orange. A wave of heat that had nothing to do with the volcano washed over him, and he was transported back to that moment in the bathhouse where he had almost kissed him. What would Alysion taste like? Fire? It was the type of magic he was most connected to—

Fae shook the thoughts from his head. This wasn't the time to fantasize!

"I feel something!" Alysion said, his emerald eyes snapping open.

"The gate?" Fae asked.

"I think so. I'm not sure what else it could be. It's not too far from here." Alysion led them into the bush, the trees becoming more sparse as they rode.

"Hmm, there's somethin' here," said Gale, coming to a stop. "Look at the trees; that ain't natural." She rode up to one and ran a gloved hand over its gnarled trunk.

Fae touched one and blinked in surprise. A slight vibration hummed through it. Was this what it felt like to sense auras?

"Somethin' magical did this," observed Gale. "Gate must be here. We just gotta pull it out of whatever plane it's hidin' in. Another job for Princey!" Gale looked much more excited about that prospect than Alysion did.

"You've never tried a summonin' spell?" Gale raised an eyebrow.

"I have. They've just never worked."

"You can do it!"

Fae nodded along to Gale's words, trying to boost Alysion's confidence. They needed him to succeed. If not, they had a long walk ahead of them.

But his expression was troubled. "It won't be that easy, and it'll probably put up a fight."

The mountain suddenly shook, throwing more flaming rocks into the sky. They crashed down somewhere on the far side.

• • • ● • • •

Alysion closed his eyes and pulled out the Sapphire out of the pouch. He hung it from his neck by the leather cord he'd painstakingly wrapped around it one night, stuffing it down his shirt so the cool crystal touched his skin—it was easier to use when he was in direct contact with it. The crystal glowed faintly as he tapped into its power, focusing on the residual aura he had noticed before. A roiling sea of red and orange flared up, bombarding his senses. *No, not you!*

Jaw clenched, he dismounted and began pacing between the trees, seeking out anything other than the angry aura surrounding him. The Sapphire pulsed, sending out a calming wave to clear his mind. Within the tumultuous aura of the furious crystal bent on destroying the region, he felt something else. He reached for it.

The mountain rumbled, and his concentration slipped; only the Sapphire's steadily flowing power prevented him from losing it.

Stopping between two trees, Alysion finally connected with the feeble flow of energy. Immediately, he met resistance; it wanted to push him away, to convince him that he'd been mistaken. That there was nothing there. This trick might have succeeded on a lesser sorcerer or someone who hadn't already known what was at the other end. But not Alysion.

Alysion pushed back against the force, harmonizing his energy with the flow. He wouldn't have been able to handle this, even with the Sapphire's help, if he hadn't been practising magic every night.

Drawing on more of the Sapphire's power, he pushed past the block and slipped into a stream of aural energy. It pulled his consciousness as if he were merely another part of it. Alysion floundered for control—it was like swimming through rapids.

So he gave himself up to the current.

A mass of bright aura loomed ahead, and Alysion was swept right into it. The aura rejected him, pushing him back up the flow. Thrashing in the swift current, he fought against it, harnessing the Sapphire's power to keep him anchored.

The mass was the gate; he was sure of it. But how was he supposed to bring it back into his world? Keeping his rising panic under wraps, he imagined himself grabbing it like a herdbeast by the horns, physically dragging it out of the aural current.

But the gate didn't want to leave. The bright aura slammed into him, trying to knock him back into the physical world. Alysion dug in and took the hit. He wouldn't let a silly gate push him around!

Come on! Maximizing his draw on the Sapphire, he forced his will upon the gate, demanding its return. In his mind's eye, the aura bucked and thrashed, desperate to free itself from his grasp. Gritting his teeth, he yanked hard—

And found himself beneath a fiery sky.

"Success!" Gale cried. "You alive, Princey?"

Alysion lay flat on his back, panting as if he'd just run a lap around Sylandris. "Just...need a moment."

A hand reached out to him, and he gladly took it.

"Good job," said Fae, hauling him to his feet.

Alysion nodded and slipped the Sapphire back in its pouch, admiring his handiwork: a mass of bright yellow energy swirled between the two trees. He was unable see what lay on the other side of it.

"It could disappear at any moment," warned Gale.

Alysion leaned against a tree, catching his breath, while Fae tied their uhaan's reins around their necks so they didn't drag free. They didn't dare bring the animals up to the crater with them.

"You wait here for us, all right?" Fae said to them. "Unless things get bad, then run."

"Who's first?" asked Gale cheerfully; apparently, she had no qualms against being the first to go.

"We should go together. If something happens, we can handle it as a group," said Alysion, straightening up.

"Right then. On three," she said.

They stepped through the gate and into the unknown.

Eleven

Mt. Hissan

The trio found themselves overlooking a lava-filled crater. Had it not been for the heat-shielding charms Gale had given them, the intense heat assailing them would have been unbearable. Unfortunately, the charms did nothing against the terrible sulphuric smell.

"Watch out for toxic gas," Gale hollered, barely audible over the hissing of steam and rumbling of the mountain.

"See anything?" Alysion called, relieved that the gate still swirled behind them.

Neither Fae nor Gale had.

"Right, let's split up and find it quick!" said Gale over the noise.

"I think I'll go with you," Fae said, stepping close to him. "Might need two pairs of hands when we find it."

Alysion nodded, heart suddenly racing.

The mountain rumbled again, the tremor nearly knocking them over as more firebombs flew from the crater in a burst of steam; Alysion watched the burning rocks crash to the ground somewhere near Ashdale. The blood drained from his face. *By the Ancestors, what are we doing here?*

"Well, let's get going," Fae muttered as Gale hurried off around one side of the crater.

Alysion stood rooted to the spot, senses overwhelmed by the heat, noise, and chaotic aura. A hand grabbed his, the contact snapping him back to the present.

"I can walk on my own," he huffed, quickly pulling away, the tips of his ears burning with a different heat. "I think it's this way." He stepped closer to the boiling crater and followed the lip around.

Alysion searched as quickly as he could for the crystal, but the hazy air and the overpowering aura made it difficult to pinpoint its exact location, even with the Sapphire's help. He and Fae had long since lost sight of the gate, and he prayed it was still open. He longed to be back in the lake, floating in the void of the Sapphire's peaceful aura. It'd been quiet there, and he hadn't risked being burned, squashed or poisoned—not that drowning would have been pleasant.

At least he wasn't alone this time.

Whoever hid the crystal would have kept it close to the gate.

The volcano shook again. Alysion wished it would settle. Each fiery ball that spewed from the crater left its own aural signature, confusing his senses. If they couldn't find the crystal in time, the mountain would erupt, wiping out Ashdale along with anyone still in the area.

Even though the lives at stake belonged to humans, the thought of them dying didn't sit right with him. They hadn't done anything to earn such a fate. If anything, the elf who had hidden the crystal here was to blame for endangering them like this. Alysion felt a flash of annoyance towards whichever of his forebearers had made this decision.

Taking a breath, he eyed the angry crater and took a few hesitant steps closer. He hoped the crystal's aura wouldn't get any stronger this way; climbing down there would ruin more than just his treasured hair. But that was exactly what happened, the crystal's aura pulsing as his wrist twinged. He let out a slow sigh. *Of course it's in there.* Where else would someone hide a powerful artifact steeped in fire magic?

Alysion crept closer to the crater's rim, noting the roiling mass of lava licking the edges.

"Hey, is your wrist doing this too?" Fae asked, his mark glowing brightly.

"Yes." His answer was little more than a squeak. "It means we're close."

Alysion resisted the urge to close his eyes as he stepped right up to the lip. He ignored his screaming survival instincts and cautiously peered over the edge, staring down the center of the cavity. Not far from where he was, yet conveniently out of reach, was a stone box seamlessly merged to the crater's wall.

"Of course..." Fae said beside him, peering down at the box. Alysion had a sudden urge to push him back away from the edge, away from danger.

A stream of gas hissed up towards them. Alysion grabbed Fae's arm and yanked them both back before their faces were scalded off. They stumbled backward, Fae nearly landing on top of him.

"Th-thanks," Fae stammered.

"No problem," he replied, heart hammering against his ribs as they regained their legs.

Alysion turned his attention back to the crystal. How was he going to get down there without suffocating or being burned to a crisp? He had a feeling Gale's charm could only withstand so much heat; swimming through lava likely exceeded that threshold.

"I have an idea," said Fae, who had been silently watching him think. "It's not ideal, but it might be our only option."

Alysion narrowed his eyes at the implication. "Go on."

Fae carefully approached the edge and pointed. "There are enough handholds for me to climb down. You stay up here and blast away anything the volcano spits at me."

Alysion's chest tightened. "Absolutely not. What if I accidentally blow you off the wall? You saw what happened with my wind magic out on the lake!"

"You've been practising, and I know you've improved."

Alysion frowned.

"Sometimes I check on you when me and Gale take a break from sparring," Fae said, looking intently into the crater.

Alysion wasn't sure if it was just the heat of the erupting volcano, but Fae's face looked a bit redder than before. His own ears were undoubtedly warm.

"You've...?" Fae's been watching him practise magic?

"Think of this as another session for practising control."

This was a terrible time to practise control! "I'm the prince; I should do the climbing."

Fae shook his head, the lava's glow reflecting off the white tips of his hair, tinting them orange. "It's *because* you're the prince that you have to stay up here. Your magic is much stronger than mine. Plus, you have the Sapphire to help you out. We can't have the crown prince falling to his death, can we?"

As much as he hated to admit it, Fae was right. "Isn't there a better way?"

"We don't have time." The mountain shook again.

Alysion closed his eyes, breathing deeply through his nose to clear his mind. "Fine."

• • • ● • • •

Fae eyed the crater, calculating the best route down. The wall was rough and uneven, with a myriad of little nooks and crannies for his hands and feet. He took as deep of a breath as he could, given the poor quality of the air, then dangled his legs over the edge.

"Okay, here we go," he said nervously, flipping onto his stomach and easing himself over, feet feeling for the holds he saw before.

Alysion stood off to the side, ready to blast anything that came near him. Aside from a full-on eruption, Fae was certain the prince could handle anything the crystal threw at them.

He kept his eyes on the wall, searching for holds as he cautiously descended. The rock was warm beneath his hands and likely would have burned them to a crisp had it not been for Gale's charm. Now, if only it could help filter out all the ash and smoke—Alysion's occasional spells helped, but it was still difficult to breathe down there.

A rush of air slammed him from above, hitting him like a cart. Fae lost his grip, his body twisting sideways, away from the wall. Heart in his throat, he tried to pull himself flush against the stone, but Alysion's wild spell was too strong. Fae clung on for dear life with one hand, the other dangling uselessly.

Come on, Alysion! His fingers slipped. Gritting his teeth, he focused on his grip, terror threatening to swallow him. If he gave in, his strength would fail, and he would be lost to the volcano.

The wind died down. Fae twisted back into position, his free hand quickly finding a secure hold. Taking a moment to slow his heartbeat, Fae resumed his descent with trembling limbs.

Soon his foot came into contact with something flat and solid, and much-needed relief flooded through him. *Thank the gods!*

Carefully, Fae eased himself around the box until it was beside him. Dancing flames decorated its sides, and through the gaps between them, Fae could see the crystal resting safely inside, blazing red.

He snaked his hand between two carved flames and closed it around the translucent red stone. The instant his skin touched the crystal, red hot pain tore through him, the mark on his wrist blazing with the light of the sun. It was like burning up from the inside. Fae clenched his teeth, pained tears leaking from his eyes as he mustered his strength—if he couldn't, he would fall to his death.

Fae didn't let go. Slowly, the pain subsided; he pulled the crystal from its cage and slipped it into a bag on his sash. Drawing in a breath, he started his ascent.

Hand, hand, foot. Hand, hand, other foot. Hand, hand fo—

He was nearing the top when the mountain shook more violently than before, nearly dislodging him. An upward gust of hot air from the crater was the sole thing that prevented him from falling to his death. But that couldn't be a good sign. Fae risked a glance below—lava shot up beneath him in plumes. He had to get out of here.

But he wasn't alone. Alysion threw fistfuls of air at the rising plumes, preventing them from scorching him as Fae climbed, pushing himself beyond his limits. And as soon as Fae was within reach, Alysion knelt and reached out a hand, hauling him up.

Fae flopped over the lip like a fish out of water.

"Crystal, in bag," he panted, sitting up.

"No time. The mountain's about to blow," Alysion said, helping him to his feet. For once, he didn't care that he was filthy.

Fae leaned heavily on him, exhausted. They stumbled over to the gate, a difficult task thanks to the mountain's incessant shaking. Or maybe it was just his legs.

"Not your legs," muttered Alysion. Had he said that out loud?

"Hey boys!" Gale hollered. "We gotta go!"

They hurried through the gate just as Mt. Hissan erupted.

• • • ● • • •

The isidyll paced across the polished floor of the Verdant Hall, fists clenched and teeth bared at nothing. *How* dare *they?!* Another crystal had been taken; he'd felt the aural shift. Who dared to hunt the crystals and delay his plans? No one should even know of the crystals' existence. Yet another had been found!

Had only the Sapphire been taken, Navir would have believed it mere chance, but now the Ruby had been claimed. There was no denying it: someone was consciously seeking out the stones.

He hissed through his teeth, wanting to lash out at something. They needed to find the other crystals as quickly as possible; they couldn't risk losing any to whoever this hunter was. Navir closed his eyes and steadied his breathing. *Think: who could they be, and what are they after?*

The team of konn he'd sent to the Great Snapper region hadn't discovered the thief's identity, but they had found traces of Elven magic. While helpful to know, it hadn't narrowed down Navir's extensive list of suspects by much. But they had reported something else unusual. The Elithar were on the move in Odenia, and their presence had been noted at Great Snapper. Strangely, they hadn't been the ones to take the Sapphire, and the konn confirmed they were hunting a fugitive. Usually, Navir wouldn't care about fugitives, but the timing was too perfect. Whoever the Elithar were after was the same elf who had taken the Sapphire—and likely the Ruby.

As the ayel began to stream into the hall, he took a few more calming breaths.

"Another crystal has been taken!" he announced once they had taken their spots.

Murmuring broke out amongst them.

"Quiet!" Navir warned, and the gathered elves slowly fell silent. "The Fire Ruby was found on Mt. Hissan. Have your konn make for the mountain immediately. If this is the same thief, then tracking the auras of two crystals should be no trouble for them. Not only do I want the crystals brought here, but the thief as well. From the konn's report, we know it was an elf who took the Sapphire—an elf on the run from the Sylandrian Guard. They may or may not have accomplices."

The isidyll looked at each ayel in turn.

"The fact the konn have been unable to properly identify—never mind apprehend—the thief thus far is completely unacceptable. This is their last chance." He let the threat hang in the air as the ayel bowed and hurried out.

Navir returned to his private meditation hall, wondering if he should send some of the ayel to track down the crystal snatcher instead of letting the konn do it. They were much more capable than their disciples, but he couldn't afford to send any of them after the thief at the moment. There were too many things to do to prepare, plus there was an entire temple complex to run. But if the konn didn't produce any decent results soon, Navir would have no choice but to send them out. If it came to that, he hoped the other four crystals would already be in hand.

He reached into the collar of his robes and pulled out a dark crystal hanging on a silver chain around his neck. *Soon the stones will all be mine, and I will use them to punish those who have done wrong—*

"Isidyll Navir," a voice spoke behind him.

Navir's robes billowed as he whirled around, quickly tucking the crystal away.

"What is it, Drath-ayel?" the isidyll said, eyeing the darkly-clad elf who had followed him into his private room.

If Drath hadn't already been occupied with other tasks, Navir might have sent him after the thief instead. But Drath had been the one to approach him with this plan, so Navir wasn't about to bother him with extra tasks.

"I think we agree that someone is specifically targeting the crystals," said the ayel.

Navir nodded.

"As you know, that is rather problematic for us. But having someone else retrieve the crystals can work in our favour."

Navir cocked his head. What was he getting at?

"It might be wise to let the thief continue collecting the crystals. Once they have all been accounted for, we can swoop in and take them. It would save us much time and effort—it's much easier to track the aura of a crystal that has already been found, and we wouldn't have to defeat the crystal's magical defences."

Drath had been the one to tell him about the crystals and their power, and he had helped Navir ascend to the rank of isidyll: the spiritual leader of the temple, the elf closest to the Ancestors. Not that either of them cared about the Ancestors; it was all a facade. No one would question strange aural outbursts coming from the Great Temple, and the temple was protected by extra wards that hid such things. It was the perfect place for them to execute their plans.

"I change my orders," said the isidyll. "The konn will retrieve the Sapphire and Ruby and continue to trail the thief."

Drath nodded. "If it turns out the thief isn't targeting the crystals, would you like us to bring them here for questioning? We don't want threats running around."

"Yes. Tell the konn they must move swiftly; we can't risk the crystals falling into the hands of the Elithar. Relay the new orders at once."

If the Elithar got a hold of them, he didn't know what they would do. As powerful as the ayel and konn were, they couldn't take on the full might of the Sylandrian guard—not until they had all the crystals. Then the guard and the Brightstars would pay.

"A wise decision," said Drath with a small bow. "But before I leave, I have good news."

Navir raised a white brow.

"I have determined the location of a crystal."

Twelve

Fire

The gate spat them out where they had left the uhaan before blinking out of existence. The animals huddled together, snorting and stamping the ground, their fear evident. Alysion kept an eye on Fae as he hobbled over to Sy-Sy and awkwardly mounted him, calming him with soft whispers and pats. Alysion did the same with Zen-Zen, and she soon stopped snorting.

"What kind of crystal is it?" asked Gale.

"Fire," replied Fae. "Nearly scorched me to death when I took it." He fiddled with the bag at his waist and produced a brilliant red stone, passing it to Alysion. "You should hold onto it since your affinity is fire."

Alysion had more than a few questions but didn't get the chance to ask them as a searing heat filled his body, centring around his damis. He gasped and nearly dropped the Ruby, clutching at his burning chest.

"Alysion!"

"Princey!"

He raised a shaking hand. "It's fine; it's just bonding with me. The Sapphire did the same thing." Minus the sensation of being scorched from the inside out. The crystal brushed against his consciousness, blazing with a fiery passion—it was a stark contrast to the calm coolness of the Sapphire.

"Mm, don't suppose a fiery rock can help us here. We've got enough of those already!" said the watcher. The volcano rumbled in agreement, lava spewing over the edge of the crater and running down the mountainside towards them, burning everything in its path. "All right Princey," said Gale, swinging up onto her dun-coloured steed. "Ready to make a gate of your own to get us outta here? We can't outrun that."

The blood drained from his face. Make a gate? He couldn't possibly do that! Only the most skilled and powerful sorcerers of the court were capable of such a feat. As he went on fretting, part of the mountainside blew apart, sending debris flying through the air as molten rock and toxic gas burst forth.

"I don't have a choice, do I?" he said, fidgeting with his reins.

"We'll help where we can," replied Gale.

Maybe he didn't have to make something from nothing—he could reroute the existing gate. Alysion steered Zen-Zen over to where the portal had been. Clutching the stones' pouch through his shirt, he felt for the gate's aural signature. This time, when he entered the stream, it let him drift as he pleased. As he floated, the image of a nearby mountain they had passed on their way to town came to mind, and he willed the stream to accept a new course. Though it didn't pull him along, it didn't want to yield to his demands, either. Drawing on the Sapphire's power, he began to force his will upon it; but Alysion was tired—from witnessing Fae risk his life and bonding with the Ruby.

Come on, he pleaded. *We didn't come all this way just to die!*

Somewhere far away, his companions called to him, urging him to hurry. He couldn't fail Fae again, not after nearly blowing him into the crater.

A bright power suddenly surged through him, filling him with warmth and vigour—the Ruby. Letting the crystals guide him, he combined their energy and bent the gate's stream. Its aura shifted—he'd succeeded! As he returned to his body, the remade gate opened before them.

It was the last thing Alysion saw before darkness took him.

• • • ● • • •

Fae kept watch over the sleeping prince while Gale cooked up something to eat, safe inside the barrier she'd summoned to keep them from being buried in hot ash.

Nearby, Mt. Hissan was still spewing the earth's innards, covering the land in molten lava and filling the sky with dark ash and smoke. One side of the mountain had completely collapsed.

"He's just wiped out from usin' so much magic," she said, looking up from the delicious-smelling pot she stirred.

Fae could only nod; he was exhausted but wouldn't dare to sleep. What if Alysion woke up screaming in agony? What if Gale tried to take their crystals? With the prince out cold, she could easily overpower them.

He was on high alert for any danger. The Elithar were bound to catch them soon, especially now that Alysion had two crystals. And that wasn't all—there were magical wild cats in these mountains known to prey on travellers.

Please wake up soon. Chest tight, Fae looked down at Alysion's sleeping face, gaze resting on his delicate lips. Were they as soft as they appeared? Fae wanted—no—*needed* to know. Gale was busy with cooking; Alysion was dead to the world. No one would know if he...

Fae leaned in close and Alysion suddenly fidgeted. He hastily pulled back, heart racing, grateful the prince hadn't woken. What was he doing? It wasn't like him to behave like this! And yet, Fae couldn't deny that he wanted to kiss him, to claim those soft looking lips with his own. There was something different about Alysion, and it lit a fire within Fae that he'd never felt before.

But that wouldn't excuse his behaviour. He couldn't take advantage of him like that; he would never forgive himself if he did.

Fae closed his eyes and breathed in deep through his nose. He caught a whiff of Alysion's scent, unmistakable even when buried beneath smoke and ash. The familiar lunaberry smell had long since faded, but that was all right. He didn't want to be reminded of his childhood home right now.

How did Alysion feel about him? Was he even interested in the same gender? Given his position, it wasn't likely.

I'm an idiot.

The last embers burning inside him cooled, and Fae's mind cleared. On the off chance that Alysion did feel something for him, they could never be together. It wouldn't be long before he learned Fae didn't have a damis and completely rejected him. Besides, the court would never allow it; they would execute him for being an auraless outcast—Captain Anaril had made that very clear. No, he could never have Alysion unless he figured out a way to gain a damis of his own. All he could do for now was keep a tight lid on his feelings so Alysion never found out the truth. Besides, once they had collected the crystals and found Ash, they would part ways.

Fae sat back to continue his watch when the pouch resting on Alysion's chest caught his attention. Really, that should be tucked away, not out in the open where anyone could take it!

With a shaking hand, he tucked it beneath Alysion's top, his fingers tingling where they touched skin. He quickly pulled his hand back and sighed, mind drifting to how it felt when he'd grabbed the Ruby. His brow furrowed. It'd been like a lesser version of what Alysion experienced when the crystals bonded to him. Had the Ruby tried to bond with him but failed because he didn't have a damis? Fae rested his chin in hand. If it had tried, that meant there was hope, right?

He watched the rhythmic rise and fall of Alysion's chest, an idea slowly coming to him. Was it possible to create a damis? Were the crystals powerful enough to do something like that? Damai had originally come from the Divine Ancestors, but perhaps when they had all seven crystals…

Doubt crept in. Maybe it only tried to bond with him because he'd been the one to collect it; because the glowing elf's prophecy had marked him. It likely had nothing to do with whether or not he could acquire a damis. Unless it could only bond with the royals—but no, the first crystal wouldn't have been stolen if it was useless to anyone but the Brightstars.

Fae's thoughts continued in circles until Gale called him over for food.

• • • ● • • •

Alysion had another confusing dream.

He was showing Fae around his home when he suddenly disappeared and found himself in the hazy nothingness he'd seen after bonding with the Sapphire. This time the fog was thinner; he could make out the general shape of the elf near him but couldn't distinguish much else.

"Hello?" he called out nervously, but like last time, he was ignored—a small relief.

The elf spoke, and Alysion recognized the speaker from the last dream. This was the elf who had been fighting for *something*, only to have his plans rejected by another seemingly familiar voice; though Alysion hadn't been able to place it.

The elf spoke quietly and quickly, as if he were talking to himself. Alysion turned on the spot but couldn't see anyone else.

"How dare they! They're the ones who defied their own treaty, and for that, they will pay..." There was some unintelligible muttering as the elf moved through the fog.

Where were they? The minimal light shone in strips, like the shadows of trees cast across a forest path. He jumped when two ghostly elves walked up behind him.

"We're here to escort you. Your sentence has been decided."

Alysion blinked. Was that Captain Anaril? It sounded a lot like them. He squinted at the hazy figure—the right height and shape. He thought he could make out the captain's sword at their side. Was this a memory? A look into the future?

Before he could decide, the dream slipped away.

Alysion woke to a soothing warmth on his chest—the Ruby. He lay quietly for a moment, not wanting his companions to know he was awake. Uneasiness crept over him, and he pondered the dream, thoughts slotting into place. But Alysion hoped he was wrong about them.

To confirm his suspicions, he needed to find the identity of the elf from his dreams. And he knew just who to ask.

• • • ● • • •

They departed camp during the latter part of the day when Alysion felt well enough to ride. Fae dozed off and on in the saddle, catching up on lost sleep. The prince didn't speak a word as they left Ashdale and the now quiet Mt. Hissan behind.

The volcano had utterly obliterated the town, burying portions of it beneath rock and cooling lava. Entire neighbourhoods had gone up in flames. The destruction weighed heavily on Alysion's mind, judging by the pained expressions that kept flitting across his face throughout the day.

"Don't worry," Gale told him, "Mitchy was helpin' organize the evacuation. By the time we arrived, there was hardly anyone left."

"But we still failed! Collecting the crystal was supposed to stop the volcano, like removing the Sapphire helped clear the lake. But it didn't."

"Like I said up there, there's nothin' we could've done. Nature had to run its course."

Despite his sombre mood (it didn't help that everything around them was coated in a layer of grey ash), Alysion filled Fae in on his latest dream when Gale wandered off that evening to find them some fresh dinner. Once Alysion was done, Fae told him what he'd overheard at Mitchy's. But whether or not Alysion was bothered by the Dragon Watchers and Odenia possibly plotting to get the crystals, Fae couldn't say. Alysion's expression remained unchanged.

So Fae switched topics. "Where are we headed next?" he asked.

"The other crystals are east of here," Alysion said, his voice devoid of emotion.

• • • ● • • •

They were eating a quick breakfast the following day when Alysion suddenly gasped and dropped his plate of food.

"Princey, what's wrong?"

Fae moved to help him when his wrist suddenly seared like he'd pressed hot coal to it. The shock was enough to make him sick.

"What's wrong with both of you?" asked Gale, alarmed.

Fae, doubled over in pain, waved her off, urging her to deal with Alysion instead.

"Hey, Princey, can you hear me?" he heard her asking.

Alysion, breathing heavily, did not respond.

"Hmm, his aura feels off," said the watcher.

"I-I see a golden hill. At the bottom is a box," Alysion stammered, his eyes vacant and unfocused. "It's a crystal. Someone's there. They're taking it."

"What else do you see, Princey?"

Alysion fell silent, his breathing slowly returning to normal.

The burning in Fae's wrist ebbed to a dull throb. He straightened, covered in a light sweat.

"Wh-what happened?" he asked, looking between Gale and Alysion.

"Think Princey had a vision," replied Gale, supporting Alysion until he could sit up on his own. "Sounds like you saw someone takin' a crystal."

"I wasn't myself," Alysion said weakly. "It was like I was seeing through someone else's eyes."

"Do you think it was the person who took the first crystal?" Fae asked, feeling antsy. If this was going to happen every time someone else found a crystal, they needed to hurry up. It was bad enough that two had been found already.

"Maybe. I did feel a sense of triumph. They knew exactly what it was they found," replied Alysion.

"Best we assume it's your traitor," said Gale, "or someone workin' for 'em."

Fae, rubbing the reminder of the pain out of his wrist, shot a suspicious look at her back.

They mounted up as soon as they could, eager to get going. Fae kept a close watch on Alysion, worried about his health. Between all the visions and the events in Ashdale, Fae was impressed that Alysion had the energy to ride.

"I can't feel the stolen one as strongly now," he said, closing his eyes as he honed in on it. "Its aura is fading quickly."

"I wouldn't expect the thief to linger," said Fae. "If they're targeting the crystals, then they must be working on finding the next." But hopefully, the three of them would get to it first. Already four of the seven had been found. "Can you still feel the others?"

"Yes. We need to leave the mountains and go to the Manwan Plains."

"You boys wanna get to the plains fast or slow?" asked Gale from the back.

"What kind of question is that? Of course we want to get there as quickly as possible," huffed Alysion.

"Well, it's just that the Canyon of Lost Souls stands between us and them."

"The what?" asked Fae, turning to face her.

"Big ol' canyon filled with souls of the departed. They're trapped down there. Dunno why."

Fae gave her an incredulous look.

"A demon keeps them there," said Alysion, deathly serious. "It feeds off them."

Gale snorted. "Ain't no demons down there, but can't deny something creepy calls that place home. Not many who go in come out again. Though, a few claimed they encountered a being that granted them a wish—for a price."

That piqued Fae's curiosity. "What did they wish for?"

"Didn't ask. But anyways, we can go around the canyon, but it'll take us days, maybe even weeks. Or, we can brave goin' right through it. Shouldn't take more than a day."

"There isn't a bridge across it?" Fae asked hopefully.

Gale shook her head. "Every time someone tries to build a bridge, it falls apart."

Fae frowned. "And you think we should go into his place?"

"It's that or walk around and risk losin' the thief."

"Catching the thief is too important," Alysion replied flatly. And despite his misgivings, Fae had to agree.

• • • ● • • •

"Someone's following us," whispered Alysion as they neared the eastern edge of the Sky Peak range. The snow-capped peaks gradually gave way to rolling foothills thick with pine trees covered in windblown ash.

So far, they hadn't had another run-in with the Elithar, but Alysion assured them the warriors were hot on their trail. Though why they hadn't made a move since Ashdale was beyond Fae's understanding. Did they fear Alysion's new power? He had an affinity for fire magic, so acquiring the Ruby had made him that much more powerful. So powerful that he'd accidentally sent one of their camps ablaze, to everyone's annoyance.

"Well, if them snotty elfies didn't know how far ahead we were before, they do now," Gale had grumped at his outburst, kicking dirt over burning clumps of grass while Alysion doused the flames with water.

Of course, the incident had done little to lift his mood.

"Someone aside from the Elithar?" Fae asked quietly.

Alysion nodded. "I feel auras, but I don't recognize them."

"A band of human sorcerers?"

"Nah, those ain't human auras," said Gale.

Dark figures materialized from the forest, instantly encircling them and cutting off any escape routes.

"Damn," she cursed, her uhaan coming to a stop.

The newcomers wore dark, hooded outfits with light leather armour intended for travelling—or ambushing. They didn't need heavy armour if they could use magic.

"Who are you?" Alysion demanded, sounding every bit the royal he was.

One of the figures blocking their progress responded by drawing a sword with blinding speed, lunging at him.

"No you don't, you tricky bastard!" Gale knocked the incoming blade aside with her own. The strangers sprang into action.

Since the fight with the Elithar, Fae made sure he and Gale practised mounted combat when space permitted. But he very quickly realized he was far outmatched, as his unmounted opponents were more agile than he was. They darted, stabbing and slashing, confusing him and making Sy-Sy antsy. A blade came for him, and he dove out of the saddle—it swung harmlessly towards the uhaan's rear.

Fae drew his blade and stabbed at his attacker's legs, reaching under Sy-Sy's belly. A pained grunt told him that he'd connected. *Good.* He slapped Sy-Sy on the haunches, urging the uhaan to escape. But the animal didn't need telling twice. He reared up, letting out a fierce cry, and charged forward, trampling one of the dark figures as he hurried away.

Fae didn't watch him go; the one he'd stabbed in the leg was still after him. They lunged, sword pointed straight at his chest as they closed the distance. Fae parried and retreated a few steps, careful not to get too close to Gale or Alysion, still mounted. It would do him no good to get trampled.

Fae dodged another strike, the assailant's leg wound slowing him down. Side-stepping, Fae swung his sword up, connected with the attacker's, and sent it flying. Perfect. Both of them leapt to grab it: Fae snatched it out of the air and sheathed it upon landing; he didn't know how to fight with two swords and wasn't about to try now.

Disarming his opponent didn't scare them off as he'd hoped. Instead, they raised a hand and barked a quick spell. Fae let out a small gasp as a violet blast of energy struck him in the chest, knocking him onto the ground. He lay there stunned, wheezing, and helpless.

Damn, if only he could use magic!

Move, move! But his body was too sluggish and heavy to obey, leaving him entirely at his opponent's mercy.

The hooded figure loomed over him, pale hair glinting under their dark hood. Fae's ragged breath caught in his chest, his skin growing cold.

His opponent grinned.

All thoughts fled Fae's mind as his pulse raced, eyes fixed on their pale hair. Try as he might, he couldn't bring himself to move, no matter how loudly his mind screamed.

• • • ● • • •

Alysion saw Fae go down but couldn't get to him—two ambushers were doing their best to unseat him, blocking the way. He snarled, trying to push through, but their swords were more than enough to keep him back.

That only added fuel to his flames.

He stole another glance at Fae, praying to the Ancestors that the other was back on his feet. But, to his horror, Fae was still on the ground. A dark shape loomed over him.

His blood turned to ice. He drew on the Ruby's energy, and the crystal eagerly connected with his consciousness, urging him to unleash its power. Alysion was more than willing to give in to its call, harnessing the fiery aura which melded so nicely with his own. He wouldn't let anyone else get hurt for these crystals. Especially not Fae—he'd burn everything to protect him.

But before he could unleash the magical energy blazing within him, a new foe burst forth from the trees.

The Elithar had caught up.

• • • ● • • •

Fae blinked stupidly—in an instant, his hooded assailant had disappeared. Now free, he staggered to his feet, blade held loosely at his side; his muscles still weren't properly responding. There were more bodies amongst the trees, chasing the hooded ones away. For a fleeting moment, he felt a bit of relief. But it evaporated when he recognized their saviours.

Fae let out a loud whistle, calling for Sy-Sy to return. Four Elithar warriors were busy pursuing the dark-clothed strangers, and Gale stood with Alysion, staring down the approaching captain. Fae didn't think Alysion would win that contest.

Thankfully no one paid him any attention, save for Sy-Sy who ambled up behind him. Fae quickly checked the uhaan for any wounds before swinging up into the saddle. They plodded over to the prince, keeping their distance from Captain Anaril, who would gladly fulfil their promise of killing him.

But before they could get too close, Alysion caught his eye and shook his head, mouthing one word: *Run*.

Fae turned Sy-Sy and urged him into a rough gallop just as a raging firestorm swallowed everything behind him.

Thirteen

Descent

"That won't delay them for long," panted Alysion. He and Gale had caught up with Fae not too long after the fiery blast. Alysion looked haggard after using the Ruby's power—the scene reminded Fae of the ruined smithy.

"I'd be surprised if the captain falls for that trick again," Fae said, still shaken up from the encounter, his opponent's horrible grin looming in his mind.

"They'll hang back to put out the fire," replied Alysion. "They don't want anyone to know they were there."

"Who do they think is going to find them?" asked Fae. "We're in the middle of nowhere, and the closest towns belong to the humans."

"That's not the point. The Elithar demand perfection and discipline at all times, which means they'll also track down those hooded elves. Those strangers attacked me—the Crown Prince! Captain Anaril will *not* tolerate that."

Fae got a sudden chill, very out of place on a warm summer day. So they *had* been elves. He'd suspected as much from their movements; they were nowhere near as nimble as the elf who had bested him. Fae tensed, eyes darting from tree to tree as if expecting someone to burst forth. *Calm down. The Elithar are chasing them off.* Why had he frozen up like that? He hadn't felt fear like this running into border patrols. Or even when facing down Captain Anaril.

"Did you recognize those elves?" Fae asked, stomach in knots.

Alysion shook his head. "I've never seen anyone dressed like that. Their auras were unfamiliar."

"They're bad news," muttered Gale, speaking for the first time since they had regrouped. "Those elfies had strange auras."

"Have you encountered them before?" Fae asked her.

Gale shook her head. "Never seen the likes of 'em before now, and I hope not to see 'em again. Likely wanted Princey here. Or your magic rocks."

"No one knows about the crystals," Alysion said quickly, bristling.

"You sure about that? Do you know what them rocks are supposed to do?"

"They're to stop a traitor, someone who wants revenge against the kingdom," said Alysion.

"Maybe...maybe they were working for the traitor," suggested Fae.

Out of the corner of his eye, Gale nodded along.

"There have been many traitors throughout history. To single out one who's still living isn't easy," said Alysion.

"I suppose we'll just have to keep an eye out for those spooky elfies in case your captain doesn't get 'em all," Gale said, but her unspoken words hung in the summer air:

There could be more of them out there.

• • • ● • • •

They crested the top of the last foothill a few mornings later, finally leaving the Sky Peak Mountains behind them. Neither the Elithar nor the hooded elves had snuck up on them again, but Alysion said the elite warriors weren't to far off.

"Is that...?" Fae started, looking at the land ahead of them. It was primarily an open field, but about half a day's ride away, a dark gash split the earth, extending north and south as far as he could see. He couldn't see beyond it, though he knew the vast Manwan Plains were out there somewhere.

"Yup, that's the Canyon of Lost Souls," said Gale. "Take us about a day to cross it since we gotta climb on foot with the uhaan. It'll be slow goin', but still faster than goin' around."

Alysion muttered something, his expression dark, but all Fae caught was the word *demon*.

"Well, no use in standin' here and lettin' that crusty old captain catch up—let's go!" Gale urged her uhaan forward, and the three of them left the foothills.

As they neared the canyon, the ash-covered grass died off; soon, there was nothing beneath their feet but bare earth and rock. A distinct chill clung to the air despite the heat of the sun. The uhaan snorted nervously as they approached, unwilling to get any closer. The group's mood quickly dropped as if the ominous tear in the land were feeding off their anxiety.

When they reached the lip of the canyon, Fae did not want to go anywhere near it; he had half a mind to ask if they could go around it instead despite the time loss.

He tried to coax Sy-Sy to the edge, but the uhaan threw his head and dug his hooves into the dirt. "All right, I'll take a look first."

Fae dismounted—Gale and Alysion did the same—and peered over the side. The sensation that came over him was strange: as if he were dragging his body towards the canyon's edge like a sack of rocks.

An eerie swirling grey mist filled the gaping maw, preventing them from seeing the bottom. Fae looked across to the far side but still couldn't make out any details. No trails, no stairs. Maybe coming here wasn't a good idea.

"Path's over there," muttered Gale, nodding towards a thin trail roughly hewn from the stone. It zigzagged down along the canyon wall, disappearing into the mist.

Fae wasn't sure what unnerved him more: the precarious path or the threatening air billowing out of the canyon. He kicked a rock over the edge, waiting for a *thump* as it hit the bottom, but the sound never came. *Just how deep is this stupid thing?*

"Don't suppose you know any spells to fly us across?" he asked.

Alysion snorted. "Of course not."

"Only way across is to walk." Gale led her uhaan to the start of the path. "So, who's first?"

"I'll go," the prince said flatly, and Fae couldn't help but be surprised—he thought he'd want to be in the middle where it was safest. "I have the strongest magical capabilities of anyone here." Alysion squared his shoulders and led a very reluctant Zen-Zen onto the path.

It took Fae some persuading to get Sy-Sy to follow them, but eventually, the uhaan conceded. Fae kept a reassuring hand on Sy-Sy's neck—for himself just as much as the animal. Gale followed with her mount right after him.

Fae's heart pounded with each step, his eyes fixated on the grey fog below. What would happen once they entered it? He looked back at Gale but couldn't read her expression.

As he and Sy-Sy entered the mist, a chill crept up his body, and before long, he couldn't see his surroundings—not the sun above with its feeble light, nor Alysion ahead of him. He couldn't even see Sy-Sy; if not for his hand on the uhaan's neck and the clip-clop of hooves, he wouldn't have known he was there.

"Alysion?" Fae called out, hoping his voice sounded steadier than it felt.

"I'm here," he answered, sounding further away than Fae anticipated. He swallowed his growing panic and resisted the urge to pick up the pace. It was too dangerous to move faster while leading Sy-Sy along the narrow ledge. He could only hope they would reach the bottom soon.

Alone with his thoughts, Fae's mind raced. What if the mist blocked aura? If it did, then Alysion would be powerless. *And Gale would be free to take the crystals.* The sunlight got dimmer as he descended, which did little to ease his growing worries.

He didn't know how much time had passed, but eventually, the prince came into view, only about an uhaan-length ahead of him.

"Alysion!" he called out, relieved to be clear of the mist. Unfortunately, the air down here wasn't any warmer. If anything, it was colder, the sun's rays unable to pierce the strange swirling blanket above them. It wasn't pitch black, but it was very dim—a gloomy twilight.

"Oh good, you're safe," he said, relief written all over his face. "And Gale?"

They waited.

Then, "I'm comin', I'm comin'," she said, slowly materializing. "Just had to go slow."

They resumed their descent.

"Is everyone all right?" asked Fae, peeking over the edge of the path. To his dismay, he still couldn't see the bottom due to another thick layer of mist. He wasn't sure if his nerves could handle another trek through that.

"I'm fine," replied Alysion.

"Me too," said Gale flatly, though she looked a bit peaky.

Was the canyon affecting her more because she was human? Or was it was because she was plotting something?

What Fae saw wasn't another cloud of mist but a gloomy fog that filled the bottom of the canyon.

"Great, just what we need," Alysion huffed when they finally reached flat ground. "How are we supposed to navigate through this?"

Fae strained his eyes but could not see to the other side.

Alysion tried to summon a flame, but all that appeared was a sad puff of smoke that was quickly lost in the fog. He furrowed his brow and tried again. A small flame sprang to life then flickered out. "I can't use magic!" he hissed, drained by the simple task.

"Figured this would be the case," said Gale.

"And you didn't think to warn me sooner?" he asked, sounding rather offended.

"I wasn't sure, so I didn't want you two to worry. That spooky cloud's what's done it. Seems like it knocked out anything magical, both people and artifacts."

Fae frowned, his fears becoming reality. Gale definitely should have warned them. He'd keep a close eye on her just in case she tried anything.

Something moved through the gloom ahead of them.

Fae's hand flew to his sword, senses on high alert. They weren't alone.

Transparent white figures slipped effortlessly in and out of the fog. One drifted close enough for Fae to get a good look at, clad in ghostly armour with pointed ears.

Elves.

"Who are they?" he breathed, keeping his voice down so as not to disturb them.

"Dunno," said Gale loudly.

Fae flinched. What if the souls attacked? *Could* they attack? One had a sword hanging off their hip.

"They look like fallen warriors," murmured Alysion, "but I don't recognize that armour."

"Styles change," said Gale, more quietly this time. "And who knows how long they've been down here—longer than my lifetime, that's for sure."

The spectres paid them no notice, silent as death itself.

"Do they even know we're here?" asked Alysion.

Fae had no answers, but if the wandering souls weren't aware of their presence, that was fine by him.

"Should get a move on if we want to stay ahead of those royal pains in the ass," said Gale, mounting up. "This place is hidin' your aura and those of your rocks, so we'll be able to shake 'em off down here. Might take us a while to find the trail up the other side."

She urged her mount along, the fog threatening to swallow her up. The elves quickly followed.

Great, just great. Not only was magic useless down here, but they were also completely hidden from the outside world—if something were to happen to them, no one would ever know. It was the perfect spot to ambush Alysion and take the crystals.

Fae kept his eyes on the watcher as they rode along. He was alert for any signs of trouble, muscles tensed and jaw clenched in his focus. Despite his growing anxiety, he couldn't deny that he preferred navigating the canyon over fighting Captain Anaril. The captain was set on killing him, while the canyon just might let him live. He could only pray that Gale didn't have an ulterior motive for bringing them here.

After riding in silence for some time, Fae noticed Sy-Sy slowing. His large hooves dragged on the ground, and his neck drooped low. Fae didn't want to fall behind and leave Alysion alone with Gale, nor did he want to be left alone with the souls.

"Hey, guys," he called out. "We need to stop for a moment. I think Sy-Sy has something stuck in his hoof."

Fae hopped out of the saddle, knees buckling as a wave of exhaustion washed over him. He let out a yawn he couldn't repress. They hadn't been riding for all that long; he shouldn't be this tired. Perhaps traversing the upper layer of mist had been more taxing than he'd realized.

He checked each of Sy-Sy's hooves but didn't find anything. Perplexed, he climbed back into the saddle. Sy-Sy grunted at the added weight.

"Sorry boy, we're going as fast as we can."

"All good?" Gale called.

"I think so. He's just tired."

"We all are," said Alysion stiffly. "So hurry up."

Gale rolled her eyes when he turned his back.

"Do you know how much further?" Fae asked her, trying hard to keep his tone light.

"Sorry boy, I don't." She looked towards the hidden sky, expression betraying nothing.

"What's that?" Alysion asked sometime later, staring at something dark on the rocky floor ahead of them and coming to a sudden stop.

Fae's fear spiked as he pulled up beside him, ready to draw his blade. A giant black shape—a serpent?—stretched out parallel to the walls. "An animal?"

"Don't think so," said Gale, squinting through the gloom. "Won't know till we get closer."

Fae did *not* want to get closer, nor did he want Alysion approaching that thing. What if it attacked him? What if Gale was colluding with it?

"C'mon, you elfie weenies."

Fae felt a short-lived flicker of amusement before the oppressive air sucked it away. *Wait a minute...*

"Oh, interestin'—it's a river!"

As it materialized through the fog, the darkness moved, flowing along a channel.

"That's not water," said Fae. Sy-Sy snorted and shook his massive head, distrusting the strange river just as much as his rider did.

Something resembling dense, black smoke filled the riverbed, wisps of darkness rolling off and dissipating into the surrounding fog.

"Whatever you do, don't touch that," said Gale, warily eyeing the flowing blackness.

"Can we go around it?" Fae scanned the river, but it was impossible to see through the fog.

"Don't think so," she replied. "Heard there's a bridge somewhere down here. Think we might find it if we follow the river down that way." She pointed into the fog.

He frowned. "You seem to know an awful lot about this place."

"Hear lots of stories in my line of work. It was mentioned in part of our trainin' incase we ever ended up down here," Gale said, shrugging.

Fae wasn't sure he believed that; this place was too good a spot to stage an ambush. With two crystals in hand, he figured it wouldn't be too hard for her to find the others. She was undoubtedly clever enough to do it.

Alysion huffed loudly. "Let's just find the bridge."

They followed the river north. Fae had a sneaking suspicion that the canyon was responsible for more than their sinking mood—the less time they spent down here, the better.

Unless keeping them here was part of Gale's plan.

"Bridge should be just ahead," the watcher said, her voice devoid of emotion.

"Finally!" exclaimed Alysion, digging his heels into Zen-Zen's sides when the crossing began to emerge through the fog.

"Oi, Princey, don't go runnin' off!"

Fae's heart stopped cold as a pale spectre drifted into the prince's path.

Fourteen

The Crossing

Zen-Zen swerved around the phantom warrior, the uhaan's footwork nimble enough to earn her a place in the royal stables.

Alysion let out the breath he hadn't realized he was holding. What would happen if he touched a lost soul? He didn't want to find out.

"Princey, slow down!" Gale hollered after him.

Alysion *did* slow, but for a different reason. When the crossing fully materialized out of the fog, he found himself frozen. *By the Ancestors, we have to cross that?*

The ancient wooden bridge spanned the bizarre river, its rickety boards just above the flowing darkness. Skulls and bones decorated the wood; they were primarily humanoid, but some belonged to dragons. Others were unidentifiable. Alysion shuddered when he realized they were real.

"This looks promising," Fae mumbled moodily, stopping beside him.

"Better than swimming," said Gale sharply.

The canyon was taking its toll on all of them. Alysion wanted out as quickly as possible.

"It's just a bridge," he grumped, urging Zen-Zen to step out on it. "Nothing to—" He hardly heard the dull thump of her hoof hitting the wood as the world started to spin.

He was alone. Confused, he spun around but couldn't see either his companions or their uhaan. Even Zen-Zen, who he'd just been astride, was gone.

"Hello?" he whispered, afraid to attract the attention of the fallen elven warriors. Wait—where were they? He couldn't see the pale spectres drifting around either.

His ears picked up a sound, like a low murmur.

"Is someone there?" he asked a little louder, whipping around as he tried to determine the source of the noise. But he found nothing.

His hand habitually went to the pouch around his neck. His connection to the crystals was still incredibly weak.

All right, relax, he told himself, taking a few deep breaths. *Maybe everyone's already on the far side of the river.*

Alysion started to walk, frequently glancing over his shoulder. The whispering grew louder.

He caught his name on the wind.

"Fae, is that you?"

No answer.

Alysion's hand drifted from the pouch to the hilt of his relatively unused sword. "Fae, Gale, this isn't funny."

Still, no one responded, yet the whispering continued, resonating all around him, even from below. Cautiously he approached the side of the bridge and gripped the guard rail—also made of bones—vertebrae by the looks of it—as he peered over the edge and bit back a scream.

Hundreds of faces stared up at him, formed and carried by the black smoke, their eyes hollow pits of darkness. Their mouths moved, whispering.

Then the faces moved, too, rising out of the river. Alysion moved to flee, but his hands stuck to the guard rail.

All rational thought flew from his mind as he struggled to free himself, trying to draw on the crystals' powers to help. But he could no longer feel their auras. He let out a scream of pure terror as the faces floated up onto the bridge.

Alysion thrashed against whatever was binding him to the rail and broke free. Not that it did him much good—by now, he was surrounded.

He drew his sword, hands shaking.

"Wh-What do you want?"

The ones closest to him were all human, and as they loomed nearer, he noticed they looked disfigured—perhaps melted or burned. He caught a few whispered words, and all strength left his hands, his sword clattering onto the wooden planks below. Alysion knew who these people were: the villagers who had perished in Ashdale when he'd failed to stop the volcano.

"N-No, I tried!" he cried. "I tried to stop it! I thought getting the Ruby would..."

The floating faces remained unchanged and continued to level their accusations, their voices growing louder, turning into a chant.

Inadequate. Failure. Useless.

Alysion sunk to his knees, each word piercing deep. How many times had he heard these exact words from his mother?

I know! I know! He squeezed his eyes shut and covered his ears to block out the noise. *I failed you; I failed all of you!*

Something touched him—Alysion flinched, expecting the cold finger of death. But it was neither cold nor warm.

"Get up," said a familiar voice, cutting through the horrible chanting.

He looked up as the spectral form of his mother bent over him, a hand resting atop his head.

His breath caught. "Wh-what are you doing here?" His mother wasn't dead. She was safe at home in Lyrellis, probably complaining to his father that it was taking too long to find him.

His eyes met hers, and to his short-lived relief, he saw they were not black voids like those of the faces around them, but they were cold, filled with disappointment.

The queen's fingers curled painfully into Alysion's hair and pulled him up.

"What're you doing!?" he cried, eyes watering.

"A useless heir like you has no place among us."

Alysion went limp, her words sucking all the remaining fight out of him. It was true. He was a useless heir. He couldn't control the simplest of spells, never mind stop a volcano. And then there was the matter of finding a belim mate...

There was a flash of silver and a searing pain in his neck. He caught a glimpse of a red blade, and his mother's phantom figure shimmered, transforming into something else. Something dark. But before he could make any sense of it, the world spun again.

• • • ● • •

"Alysion?" Fae called out, wondering why the prince had stopped. Was there something on the bridge?

He urged Sy-Sy forward as Alysion spun around, frantic.

"What's wrong? Is something coming?" Fae asked, panic rising in his chest. Alysion's worries about demons echoed in his head.

"I thought I saw..." he started. "No, never mind." He rubbed his neck and urged Zen-Zen to continue, Gale riding up beside him. Fae took up the rear.

"Oi Princey, you're bleedin'," said the watcher.

When Alysion pulled his hand away from his neck, it was covered in blood.

"Did that spook get you after all?" she asked, handing him a strip of cloth from one of her saddlebags.

"Maybe it did," replied Alysion, avoiding her gaze by cleaning his hand.

"Or maybe it was you," Fae said, glaring at her back.

"'Scuse me?" said Gale, turning in her saddle to look at him, her expression blank, unpleasantly reminding him of Captain Anaril.

"Maybe you cut him with something to weaken him. Something you could pass off as the canyon's effect!" he hissed.

"Fae, what are you going on about? It wasn't her. Stop it," snapped Alysion. He pressed a bandage against his neck.

But Fae couldn't contain his worries any longer. He needed to know the truth.

"Why did you really lead us down here?" he demanded, not bothering to mask his accusatory tone.

"It's the shortest way to the plains," replied Gale, stopping her mount. The elves followed suit.

"I know you're plotting something with your queen. You want the crystals for Odenia! I've noticed you disappearing at night when you're on watch."

He saw a flicker of something cross Gale's face. It looked like amusement.

Gale let out a sigh, her features relaxing. "I can assure you I ain't plotting anythin' with the Queen of Odenia. Only thing I want is to help you two stop whatever's comin'."

"I overheard you talking to Mitchy. You two have plans for the Brightstars." He glanced at Alysion, who did not look nearly as concerned as Fae thought he should.

"I don't know what you heard, but we weren't only talkin' about them."

"So Mitchy knows about the crystals and the prophecy?"

"Yeah, she does," Gale said carefully. "What happens if we fail will affect everyone, not just you elfies."

"Do you know what's coming?" asked Alysion before Fae could say anything else.

"I have guesses, but nothin' solid yet."

Fae briefly wondered if Alysion should tell Gale about his strange dreams with the disembodied voices. He shook the thought away. No, they couldn't trust her yet.

"I can promise I don't want any harm to come to you or your prince. Or anyone, for that matter! Except maybe this traitor we've gotta stop."

Heat rose to Fae's cheeks when he heard 'your prince', but he ignored it. There were more important things at stake here.

Was Gale telling the truth? Was she lying? In his heart, he wanted to believe her. She was Master Cane's friend, after all.

"If I get us outta this canyon in one piece, will you trust me?" she asked.

"I don't know," he answered, shooting her a glare.

"Then what can I do?"

"At this point, nothing."

"All right, this place is getting to our heads," said Alysion before they could go on. "We can deal with this later." He urged Zen-Zen across the bridge.

• • • ● • • •

As the dim sunlight faded, Fae found it harder to stay awake and, more concerning, harder to breathe. It was like he'd been running all day despite being in the saddle; Sy-Sy was doing all the work, and the uhaan was exhausted. Fae worried that Sy-Sy wouldn't have the strength to make the climb once they found the path up.

Gale dropped back from the front, Alysion taking the lead. "You all right? You don't look so good."

"I'm fine, just sleepy," he replied, trying and failing not to sound irritable.

"Hmm," was all she said.

They soon came to a curve in the dark river, leading it along the cave wall before veering back towards the canyon's centre. A plain wooden bridge spanned the entire u-shaped curve. It was nothing like the impressive yet disturbing bone structure they had crossed earlier. The new bridge was small; they would have to dismount and walk their uhaan across single file.

Fae did not want to set foot on the thing.

"We have to cross it," said Alysion as if reading Fae's mind. His voice was steady, but his eyes betrayed his anxiety.

"I'll go first," volunteered Gale as they slid off their mounts.

Before either elf could stop her, she stepped onto the wooden planks and shifted her weight, checking to see if the wood would hold. "Solid," she concluded before moving forward, her dun uhaan following calmly.

Alysion went next, also testing the boards before venturing out.

Fae didn't waste time with the boards and followed Zen-Zen closely, not wanting to be left alone. He kept looking back over his shoulder just in case the souls, or anything else, tried to sneak up on them.

"Watch yourselves, boys. There's some rotten planks up here," Gale called back to them.

His companions had cleared the bridge when Fae's world tilted. He let out a startled yelp as one foot broke through a rotten plank, bits of wood plunging into the smokey river below. He hastily yanked his foot back up before it touched the swirling stuff.

"You good?" Gale called from the bank, concern plastered all over her face.

Alysion looked just as worried.

"I'm fine!" he hollered, carefully leading Sy-Sy the rest of the way across.

"You sure you're fine?" Gale asked, eyeing him up once he reached the bank.

"I didn't touch the...water."

"Good," said Alysion. "Let's keep going. I think I see the way out."

A path slowly appeared through the gloom. Unlike the way they had come down, which zigzagged back and forth down the wall, this one was a single steep angle.

"Let's get outta here," said Gale.

Dismounting to fit on the narrow pathway, they started their ascent with Alysion in the lead.

Despite his exhaustion, the climb seemed to be going well. It felt much shorter than their descent, likely because they weren't weaving back and forth. In no time at all, they reached the halfway point, the strange magic-nullifying cloud close above them.

Alysion suddenly cursed.

"What's—" The words died on Fae's lips as he looked down where the prince was pointing. The fog filling the canyon had receded, and the river below was rising. Already it had overflowed its banks and covered the canyon floor. The pale souls were nowhere to be seen.

"Better get a move on!" hollered Gale from the middle of the line.

They picked up the pace, moving as quickly as they dared on the narrow ledge.

By the time Alysion disappeared into the mist, the dark smoke was more than halfway up the canyon walls and still rising.

Gale soon reached the cloud. She paused. "Are you all right?" she called down to Fae, worried. He was falling behind.

"I'm fine," Fae wheezed. But he wasn't. The canyon was weakening him, and his foot—the one that had gone through the bridge—prickled with a painful chill. Perhaps that was just a side effect of being so tired; his mind was playing tricks on him, fuelled by his stress. Awkwardly he tied Sy-Sy's reins together around the uhaan's neck. "Go to Gale!" he commanded, tapping his rear. Sy-Sy trotted off without him.

"You sure?" Gale called.

"Yes, take Sy-Sy and go!" Not having to worry about his trusty steed was a weight off his mind.

Gale gave him one last look before disappearing into the mist.

Don't look back, don't look down. It was difficult to resist the urge to check on the stormcloud-like vapour rising up to swallow him. But if he did, his pace would falter, and he wouldn't recover. It was hard enough to run as it was.

The cloud above him was nearing. Would it stop the river? Fae couldn't count on it. He'd be dead if he did. Forcing his heavy legs to move, he darted into the mist.

Running uphill was challenging in itself, but running uphill through the mist was almost impossible. His strength drained even faster, his exhausted muscles leaden. Though Fae tried to keep his eyes on the path ahead, the visibility was close to zero. His vision swam—or maybe that was just the mist swirling around him.

But just as he felt he was going to collapse, he cleared the mist, nearly blinded by the setting summer sun.

Almost there. Alysion peered down from the top of the canyon, and Gale was ahead with the two uhaan. He would make it!

A quick glance down caused him to stumble. The dark river rushed up to meet him.

• • • ● • • •

"He's going to make it!" Alysion said, trying to keep a lid on his rising panic. By the Ancestors, he couldn't bear the thought of losing Fae; he was the first elf to treat him as something more than a prince.

He pulled out the crystals, wracking his mind for a way to help Fae. "We need wind magic!" he cried, cursing himself for not practising more wind spells. He'd been too distracted by the Ruby. *Damn that thief. If only I had the wind crystal, then I could fly down there!*

"Can't you try something, Gale? Anything?"

"Canyon sucked everythin' outta me. Can't even produce a sneeze right now." She watched Fae intensely, jaw clenched. "C'mon, boy. You can do it!"

"Don't you have a talisman or something?" he asked desperately.

Gale shook her head. "Not anything that can help."

"He's clear of the mist. He should cast a spell of his own—" A sudden, horrible thought hit him. No, it couldn't be! Though his magic had been dulled by the canyon, his ability to sense auras hadn't, thanks to the crystals. Gale had said magical artifacts—including talismans—didn't work. Yet he'd still felt nothing from Fae.

The watcher didn't respond, her hard expression confirming his suspicions as the mist steadily gained on Fae.

"We have to do something!" Alysion cried, pacing frantically along the edge.

"Might be able to squeeze out a spell, but nothin' that'll help," muttered Gale.

Alysion's breath caught as Fae lost his footing and landed hard on the stone path.

Get up!

Fae didn't move.

Alysion threw himself over the edge.

• • • ● • • •

Navir paced across the polished wood floors of the Verdant Hall, angry and impatient. The konn he'd sent out after the stone-snatchers had been wiped out. They were the best of their class, next in line to be promoted to ayel—once there were openings, of course. Their failure had been unexpected until he learned the Elithar had a hand in their demise.

He bared his teeth. The entire situation was beyond frustrating. But, some good that had come of it. The Elithar hadn't gotten their hands on the crystals, and the thief's identity had been revealed: the Crown Prince of Sylandris and two human lackeys, one of whom was a Dragon Watcher from Murk Water. Why the prince was travelling with two humans, specifically one connected to the crown, Navir could not say, but the thought of another force going after the crystals made him want to lash out. At Drath-ayel's arrival, Navir's anger evaporated like water on hot stone.

"You have it?" he asked, not needing or expecting an answer; he'd felt the crystal's aura as soon as the gate had returned Drath to their realm.

Without a word, the ayel knelt on one knee and offered up an embroidered silk bag.

Navir, unable to contain his excitement, accepted it and carefully removed the crystal. He turned the orange crystal over, examining it. The Wind Citrine was his!

"I trust you had no issues?" he said.

"None at all, Isidyll. I didn't encounter the stone-snatchers, nor the Elithar for that matter. The Citrine was well hidden. It would have been impossible for anyone unaware of its existence to find it."

"Good. Go rest. Tomorrow we will discuss the next step."

Part Three

Today was the day all young elves looked forward to, and Tarathiel was more excited about it than most because he would see his beloved Illuven again. It had been a while since he'd last beheld his love, as they had been forbidden from visiting each other by that blasted princess. A handful of times, Illuven managed to slip away unnoticed for brief visits, but they hadn't returned to their cottage. Doing so was too risky.

This bright and glorious day was an exception to the rule, for they were about to undertake a special mission that all elves took before the *Striiya*—the coming of age ceremony. Even the princess couldn't keep them apart.

Tarathiel and two others waited with their uhaan near the magical barrier separating their realm from Odenia. As usual, Illuven was running late, but that didn't matter. The four of them had waited their whole lives for this moment to come, so a little bit longer wouldn't kill them. Soon, the rhythmic sound of hooves approached, and Illuven came around a bend.

"Are you ready to go?" Ylana asked as he rode up, the only belim in their group.

"I am. My apologies for being late," said Illuven.

Tiriel reached over and clapped him on the shoulder. "It's fine. We understand."

"Let's go!" said Tarathiel.

They took off, the uhaan throwing their heads as they picked up on their riders' excitement. Their destination on the eastern shore lay beyond the kingdom's borders, and for each of them, this would be their first time leaving Sylandris.

Elves who had not yet reached adulthood were forbidden from leaving the safety of the wards; this ride was considered a rite of passage for those on the cusp. When they returned, the *Striiya* would take place, and they would receive the tattoos that marked them as adults.

Tarathiel stayed close to Illuven, content to simply be in his presence. Though the ceremony joining him to Princess Lymsia wasn't for a few more moons, Illuven had already been moved to the palace. Tarathiel wasn't going to let this precious time together go to waste.

They rode all day, reaching their destination just before nightfall. The ground before them suddenly fell away, giving way to the thin band of the beach and the endless expanse of the ocean below. They pulled up their mounts, awestruck by its sheer vastness and raw, untamed power.

"It's amazing," Illuven breathed.

"I never could have imagined anything like this. It's breathtaking," Tarathiel agreed.

The four of them rode down the cliff, setting up camp in a cave on the beach. Each time, the same cave was used for the rite because it possessed enchantments to keep the tide at bay. The uhaan roamed freely along the beach, grazing on tall grasses near the cliffs. The elves ate the meal they had brought along before laying out on the sand to watch the sunset. Brilliant colours streaked the sky above: reds, oranges, and pinks mirrored by the churning waters beneath. They watched as the sun, a bright fiery ball, slowly slipped into the sea.

"I hope it's not too bright for the fish," joked Illuven.

Tarathiel rolled his eyes, but the corners of his lips quirked.

They sat close, Tarathiel's hand slowly moving nearer to his love's. On a night like this, he could throw caution to the wind; try to forget—even for a moment—that Illuven was already spoken for. As the dark ocean swallowed the last rays of light, he gently took Illuven's hand and gave him a small smile, which the other elf returned. Ah, how he wished every night could be like this one, but it was hard to ignore the sadness lurking in the depths of Illuven's golden eyes.

"Do you want to go for a walk?" Illuven asked him. Something in his tone told Tarathiel that this wouldn't be a leisurely stroll.

"All right." He stood and brushed the sand from his legs. "We'll be back in a bit," he said to their companions.

They walked beside each other along the beach, ankle-deep in the warm, salty water. Tarathiel resisted the urge to reach out and hold Illuven's hand. Now wasn't the right time for that.

Only once they were a reasonable distance away from the others did Illuven stop.

"I spoke with the queen about us. I wanted her to understand our relationship."

Tarathiel froze.

"As you can imagine, it didn't go well..."

"Did you expect it to?" he stammered, regaining control of himself. Why had Illuven done that?

"I'm not too sure what I expected, but she was not pleased. Princess Lymsia hadn't told her about us."

"No, I can't imagine that she was impressed." Strange, why hadn't she told her mother? She'd made such a huge fuss about it.

"The queen..." Illuven stopped, his expression falling.

"The queen?" Tarathiel's heart drummed violently against his chest. "What did she say?" He needed to know, even if he didn't *want* to.

"Princess Lymsia was present when I spoke with the queen. She told her mother how she'd forbidden us from seeing each other. The queen agreed with her. At first, I thought it was only until the union took place, and that after that we could have friendly visits..."

Friendly visits? As if that would be enough!

Illuven was silent for a moment. "The queen said it's not in my best interest to keep seeing you. As a member of the royal family, I have an image to uphold."

Yes, the princess had already made that clear when she caught them in the cottage!

"They don't want me to see you again. Ever. For any reason."

No. Tarathiel hadn't realized his fists were clenched until his nails broke skin. "They can't do this!" he hissed, turning his gaze down to the sand as tears blurred his vision.

"I'm sorry," Illuven said quietly, his voice choked. "Tonight—"

"Don't—"

"Tonight will be our last night together."

• • • ● • • •

When Tarathiel woke the next morning, the first thing he saw was Illuven sleeping soundly near him. The sight set his heart aflutter, though he desperately wished they'd been able to sleep together, curled in each other's embrace. But they couldn't—not with Ylana and Tiriel sharing the cave with them, not with the threat of the royal family hanging over their heads. Though Ylana and Tiriel would never tell anyone about them being together, they would be compelled to tell the truth if the royals questioned them, else risk severe punishment. Tarathiel wouldn't jeopardize Illuven's standing like that, nor theirs.

Everyone else was still asleep, and though he knew he should wake them, Tarathiel couldn't bring himself to do it just yet. Not when the morning light reached into the cave and struck Illuven's hair, and it shone brighter than the most luxurious of golds. He sighed, wanting nothing more than to bury his face in the silky strands. It was difficult to resist the temptation, especially when Illuven's face looked so peaceful. But Tarathiel didn't want to disturb him; he didn't want to bring his love back to the waking world where a harsh reality awaited.

If only there were something he could do. He knew Illuven wouldn't be happy in the palace, stuck by the princess's side night and day. Illuven preferred the outdoors, to ride wherever he pleased.

But how can I reverse a royal decision? He had no idea, and time was quickly running out. Tarathiel sighed, determined to make the most of their day together—it would likely be their last.

Fifteen

Memory

Fae played with Ash in the small garden on the forest floor below their home. It wasn't much of a garden, just a hodgepodge of plants and herbs their parents grew—but it was appealing to the eye without looking terribly out of place amongst the other colourful forest flora. His favourite was the wild lunaberry bushes that grew all around; they were such a tasty treat!

The house itself blended with the surrounding foliage, high up in the canopy of the trees. If Fae hadn't known it was there, he would've had difficulty spotting it. Dada was nearby, tending to some plants and keeping a watchful eye on his rambunctious boys. Fae chased after his twin brother, both giggling as they ran around the base of their tree, its trunk many times wider than the thickest elf they knew. Neither Ama's nor Dada's arms could reach around it, making it a most impressive tree—perfect for their home.

"Fae, Ash, come here!" Dada called. Still laughing, they hurried back around, stopping as their father came into view.

"Time to go inside," he told them, much to their disappointment.

"But we don't wanna!" Fae protested.

"There will be other chances to play, but right now, we should go in." He herded the two young elves towards the rope ladder. They were still too small to leap from branch to branch to climb up.

"No!" Fae fussed, scooting around their dada, running as fast as his little legs could take him.

"Faeranduil, come back here!" their dada shouted.

"Fae!" Ash called as well, but his brother did not return.

Fae ran blindly into the trees and hit something solid. He fell to the ground, glancing up in confusion. The hooded face of a stranger greeted him.

"Hello?" he said. The stranger's dark clothes and suspicious expression made him uneasy.

Without a word, they roughly scooped him up, tucked him under their arm, and carried him back towards his home.

"Put me down!" he fussed, squirming and kicking, but the stranger had a firm hold on him.

"Who are you? What are you doing with my son?" his dada demanded as they made it back to the garden.

"We're here to correct the wrong," the stranger said, his voice reminding Fae of the massive feathered serpents that lived deep in the forest. They could easily swallow a young elf whole.

More dark-clad elves materialized through the trees around them. Fae quivered in fear.

"Nylian!" his dada hollered.

Fae heard a noise far above and saw his ama leaping deftly down from branch to branch, longsword at her hip. She landed near the ladder beside Ash and walked over to Dada. The harsh look in her eye unsettled Fae even more; Ama was always gentle.

Ash began to cry loudly, but Fae couldn't see him—the strangers had closed in, forming a semi-circle around his parents. Terrified, he started to cry too, wanting the stranger to put him down. Dada would protect them, wouldn't he? Ama was here to help too! No one could beat them when they were together, not even the royal family!

"Fae, don't be scared. You'll be all right." While Dada spoke, Ama sprang into action, drawing her sword and leaping at the hooded strangers.

Fae's world suddenly filled with blaring noises and bursts of bright light. He had no idea what was happening, being jostled around by his captor as he darted through the chaos.

"Dada, Ama!" he cried, searching for his parents, tears blurring his vision. He was just able to make out their familiar shapes.

Ama fought with sword and magic against a group of dark strangers. Too many. But they were dropping quickly, thanks to her blade. Dada, casting what looked to be every spell at once, was in a similar situation. He caught Fae's eye and said something he couldn't hear, but Fae understood. Dada was on his way! His flash of relief quickly evaporated when a victorious cry sounded. A fiery blast of magic struck Ama, sending her crumpling to the ground. She didn't get up.

"Ama!" he screamed, thrashing wildly. His flailing earned him was a sharp smack.

"Shut up," the stranger hissed. They suddenly leapt back as his dada came charging forward, letting out a vicious cry, teeth bared. Fae had never seen him like this before.

"Dada!"

His captor whirled away, dodging bright flashes of magic. He led Dada on a short a chase before suddenly stopping and holding Fae up. His dada immediately came to a stop, panting hard, one hand raised in preparation for a spell.

"Surrender if you want to live," the stranger said.

"Release my sons!" Dada growled back.

"You're in no position to negotiate." The remaining intruders encircled them. One held Ash, sobbing and magically bound.

His dada glanced around. Fae thought he was getting ready to unleash some crazy magic, but then, he lowered his hand. What was he doing?

Movement caught Fae's eye—the stranger holding Ash slipped away into the trees. But Dada didn't notice. "Da—"

"Bind him," Fae's captor said to the others. Some of the strangers approached Dada, but a shockwave of brilliant magic slammed into them, knocking them to the ground. Fae's captor stumbled and lost their grip. He wiggled free.

"Dada!" he cried, hurrying past the stunned intruders.

"Fae!" his dada called, reaching out for him. His expression shifted to a look of pain as something splattered across Fae's face. The point of a sword protruded from his chest.

Dada?

Everything went white.

• • • ● • • •

Alysion nearly dropped Fae as he pulled the elf's limp form from Sy-Sy's back. *Humph, he deserves to be dropped!* Despite his emotional turmoil, Alysion's ears burned hotter than Mt. Hissan as he half dragged Fae to the bedroll laid out near the fire. He tried not to think about the muscles he could feel through Fae's clothing.

"An elf with no damis? That's impossible," he hissed as he tucked Fae into the blankets, nearly dropping him again in the process.

"Nothin's impossible. Think about it; it explains a lot about him. Have you ever even seen him use magic?" said Gale, sitting under a scraggly tree near the fire.

No, not even when their lives had been on the line. "Why didn't he tell us he was a damisri?" *Why didn't he tell me?* He placed a hand on Fae's forehead and frowned at how cold it was. Gale said he would be fine after some much-needed rest, but Alysion wasn't convinced. The river's wispy tendrils of darkness had their hold on Fae when Alysion reached him. Had he saved Fae in time?

"Well, that's pretty obvious. He must've been scared of how you'd react. Don't think either of us hasn't noticed how you treat non-magic users, Princey. I might be able to handle your snippy comments—which I admit you've gotten better about—but this is somethin' different, and you know it." Gale crossed her arms.

"Are you saying this is my fault?" Alysion said quietly, failing to curtail his accusatory tone. He plopped himself down on his bedroll beside her; they sat opposite Fae to leave him undisturbed.

Gale let out a low sigh. "What happened in the canyon was just unfortunate. No one's to blame. Don't beat yourself up for not noticin'."

Perhaps he had noticed it. Perhaps he had chosen to believe Fae despite it. Perhaps he only wanted to continue fantasizing about being together. Now it would never happen. Ever.

"How...how does something like this happen? How can an elf exist without a damis? We are the direct descendants of the gods. Our magical ability is a gift from them!" It didn't make any sense! It was fine for humans not to have them—they had been created from the earth, perhaps shaped by the gods, but not born of their lineage.

"Well, I don't know much about you and your Ancestors or any of your other lesser deities for that matter, but is it that important?" asked Gale.

Alysion's mouth hung open, eyes wide. "Punishment for the most heinous of crimes is the destruction of one's damis. Those criminals have forfeited their divine heritage and are forever banished from our realm. It would make sense if Fae had undergone the Silias, but he hasn't. We haven't had to perform it in ages, and he's too young for it anyway." Alysion put his head in his hands and rubbed his temples. "For him to be without a damis...I don't know what it means."

Gale snorted. "You elfies are too damn dramatic for your own good."

Alysion ignored the comment. "His hair is strange. At home, everyone has hair like mine. I've never seen hair that dark on an elf, and certainly not with that odd fade."

"Well, what *do* you know about him? Maybe there's a hint in whatever he's told you."

His gut twisted. He'd been meaning to ask Fae more about himself, but he hadn't had the chance. Or maybe he'd just felt too awkward. "He spent his early years near Lyrellis until his parents were killed. Now he's searching for his brother. Somehow, he ended up living with that blacksmith." An elf with no aura and no family—was Fae cursed? Perhaps, but Alysion had never sensed the lingering energy of a curse on him. Just like he'd never sensed his aura.

"Did he say why he was livin' in Redwood?" Gale asked.

Alysion looked over at Fae's still form, his brow wrinkling. "He said his search for his brother had brought him there. Since he's convinced his brother is still in Sylandris, Fae must have been staying there because it's as close to Sylandris as he can get as a damisri. But he'd be killed if he was caught crossing the border."

Gale huffed her disapproval.

Alysion agreed. The thought of anyone hurting Fae made him sick. *Wait a moment. The attack on his home—did it have something to do with his lack of damis?*

• • • ● • • •

Fae couldn't recall falling asleep again, nor at what point he'd stopped listening to their conversation. When he awoke next, the morning sunlight greeted him—a good sign. Grunting, he slowly sat up, checking if anything was broken. There were no sudden stabbing pains, just a dull ache all over his body. He blinked a few times, clearing his vision.

"Ah good, you're awake! Princey'll be happy. How're you feelin'?" Gale came over with a bowl of rabbit stew, steaming and fragrant.

Alysion would...? But all thought was pushed aside as he ravenously dug into the stew. With each mouthful, he felt more alive.

"Easy there. Don't need you chokin' or gettin' sick. Take it slow."

Reluctantly, Fae did as he was told, not speaking until the bowl was empty. "I'm fine. Sore all over, but that's about it." His head hurt, which wasn't a surprise. Between the horrible memory and the canyon's aura, it was a wonder he was even awake. He set the empty bowl down and took a look around.

Their camp was tucked in a small copse of trees not too far from the dreadful canyon. It made sense—they couldn't travel far with him in such a state. He caught sight of Alysion, who surprisingly had his sword out, practising various forms. Fae couldn't help but admire the way he flowed through them, each movement perfectly controlled. It was a shame Alysion wouldn't spar with him; they could learn a lot from each other.

Fae dropped his gaze. He would never be worthy of someone like that.

"You want to try standin'?" Gale asked, oblivious to what was going on inside him. "Here, I'll help you." She held out a steady arm.

Nodding, he took hold of her proffered arm. And he was glad he did—his legs weren't cooperating. "How long was I out for?"

"About two days. Princey scooped you out of there while I held back the mist. Almost got both of you."

Alysion glanced over at the sound of his nickname. He quickly looked away when their gazes accidentally met.

Fae's innards lurched when he caught the prince's pained expression. *Great.* He couldn't bear the thought of seeing the same cold, hard look Captain Anaril gave him mirrored on the one he had come to desire. He faced Gale instead.

"Thank you for saving me. I don't deserve it after what I said to you in the canyon."

Something crossed Gale's face, disappearing before he could figure out what it was. "The canyon brought out all your worries and fears. It preyed on *all* of our good feelins'. I understand why you don't feel you can trust me, but I hope to earn that trust. And like I told you at the beginnin', Cane'll tan my hide if anything happens to you."

Fae hung his head. "I'm sorry, I didn't mean for it to come out like that."

Gale gave him a kind smile. "Better out than in."

He nodded. "Are the uhaan all right?"

Gale pointed to where all three were grazing in the short prairie grass just beyond the trees.

Fae's spirits rose at the sight of Sy-Sy. He released Gale's arm and hobbled over to the animal, his stiff legs slowly loosening. Sy-Sy grunted when Fae wrapped his arms around him, burying his face in his furry neck.

"You're in no shape to be ridin'," the watcher said a bit later, scowling.

"We don't have time," he argued, saddling up Sy-Sy. They needed to get back on track, and he didn't want to lay around with his head threatening to explode with disturbing visions of the past. Riding would help clear his mind.

But as they rode east towards the Bluetail River and the Manwan Plains, Fae's consciousness was clouded.

He spent the first portion of the ride mulling over the memory that had resurfaced. His insides grew cold as he replayed the scene, lingering on what the attacker had said: *We're here to correct the wrong.* He tried to digest those words, his stomach churning in the process. He thought he might vomit. *I'm the reason they died. They died protecting me from those elves who wanted to eliminate the damis-less blight.*

It was no wonder his young mind had blocked this out. The tragedy of that day was a lot for anyone to handle, never mind a small child. It didn't help that his thoughts kept straying to the last thing he'd seen; light fading from his dada's eyes as the sword pierced through him. *A sword he could have avoided if he hadn't been distracted by me. If they hadn't come for me.*

Guilt pressed heavily upon him. Fae took a few deep, steadying breaths. *Dada must've been the one who sent me away. Somehow, he cast a spell as—as he died.* But only Fae had been caught by it. The strangers had taken Ash. The strangers…

Fae pushed aside his mounting remorse as he went through the memory again, focusing on the assailants. Black outfits and precise movements. His stomach twisted unpleasantly as fear tried to take hold of him. Fear he had felt very recently.

By the gods! These are the same elves that ambushed us in the mountains! A faint spark of excitement pushed away the seeds of terror trying to take root. Finally, a clue!

But what had become of Ash?

He looked up at Alysion, wanting to share what he'd learned, but when he saw how stiff his posture was, he faltered. The prince hadn't said a word to him since he'd woken up, and Fae wasn't in the mood to discuss his damis. Nor was he prepared to share the memory with them. His existence had led to his parents' deaths; Alysion would only despise him all the more for it.

Well, if they were going to get into it, they may as well try to start on the best foot.

Steeling himself, he rode up beside Alysion. "I haven't had a chance to thank you for saving me back in the canyon."

"No, you haven't," he said tersely, staring at the grass ahead, "but it doesn't matter." He urged Zen-Zen forward, leaving Fae behind before he could speak.

Gale rode up beside him.

"How did you guys save me?" Fae asked her, deflating. He needed a distraction.

"Must've blacked out from exhaustion. 'Cuz you're what them elfies call a damisri, the canyon drained you faster. Scared the crap out of us," she said, nodding towards Alysion. "Well, Princey didn't waste any time and jumped down the cliff towards you, usin' my wind to help. Thankfully you were already through that unmagic cloud; otherwise, who knows what might've happened. He grabbed you, and both of us flew you out. It was tricky, but we managed. Didn't think I had enough magic left in me."

"I'm surprised he did that for me."

"Bah, he likes you," said Gale, making Fae's pulse quicken.

Surely she didn't mean *that* kind of like. Alysion must like him as a friend. He probably didn't have many, being royalty and all.

"But now it's your turn, mister. You've some explainin' to do," said Gale.

And here it was, the moment he'd been dreading since this all started.

Alysion slowed in front of him. He turned in the saddle, and Fae caught his stoney expression as he looked back at them, waiting for his explanation. Fae's heart plummeted at the sight, his gaze falling to the reins in his hands. How to begin?

"As you now know, I don't have a damis," he started, feeling oddly disconnected from himself. "For as long as I can remember, I've never been able to sense auras—my own or someone else's, nor have I ever cast a spell of any kind. As a child, I remember being taught the sword, but not magic. My brother was the one who studied magic." His words died, and silence filled the air.

Alysion *tsked* impatiently. "That's it? You don't know why you don't have a damis?" His harsh, judgmental tone pierced Fae like an arrow.

"I wish I knew," Fae didn't look up.

Alysion dropped back, now riding beside him.

"Elves aren't born without damai. All of us have them. They're a gift from our Divine Ancestors! The only damisri in existence are criminals who've had them destroyed. You're not telling us something," Alysion hissed.

"I don't remember anything like that happening! What kind of crime could a young child commit to earn such a punishment? The only people who might've known are my parents, and they're not around!"

"Maybe your parents did something, and their punishment was the destruction of your—"

Fae's fist collided with his face. Alysion blinked in shock, slowly raising a hand to his swelling cheek.

"Cool it, you knuckleheads!" said Gale, forcing her steed between them.

Fae, panting as if he'd just run up the canyon, dropped his fist and urged Sy-Sy into a gallop.

"Oi, get back here!" Gale called after him, but he ignored her. He needed to get away. Now.

Fae let Sy-Sy run blindly, not caring where they went. *Stupid, idiotic prince!* He knew Alysion wouldn't take the news well, but he'd gone too far. How *dare* he say such things about his parents! They weren't criminals!

His parents had been good. Not once could he ever recall them complaining about his lack of magic. Though thinking back on it, they had only trained deep in the forest where no one would find them, and he couldn't recall having any friends aside from his brother. Perhaps he'd been too young? His parents had always encouraged—no, urged him to stay in the house and read when he wasn't practising with his wooden sword.

He hadn't even been allowed to leave for important occasions, like when the old queen regnant—Alysion's grandmother, he realized—had passed. A damisri wouldn't have been well received at the funeral. *They'd tried to keep me safe by hiding my existence.* His heart twisted.

Sy-Sy slowed, tired from their frantic race across the plains. Fae didn't press him to keep going. The tall grass swished behind him—Gale. Good. He didn't want to deal with Alysion right now; his rotten mood would only be worse after the punch. *He deserved it.*

Sixteen

Sea of Gold

By the Ancestors! Why had he said that to Fae? Why? Now that he'd cooled off, Alysion knew better. *Of all things, I had to go after his parents!* He wished there was a tree around so he could bash his thick head into it, but sadly, there were none to be found out here in the stretching grasslands between the canyon and the Bluetail.

He dismounted and sat in the grass, Zen-Zen nosing him while they waited for Gale and Fae to return. He should have gone along with her, but he just couldn't bring himself to do it. He couldn't face him yet.

He'd overheard what Gale had said, that he liked Fae. Well, Alysion couldn't deny it. He did like Fae. And more intimately than the watcher implied. But Fae was someone he could never have. A damisri would never be accepted by his people, no matter how good their bloodline.

Alysion buried his face in his hands. *I'm such a fool.* Perhaps he'd said that to Fae to try and drive him away and protect his own fragile heart.

Well, it worked.

After this, Fae would never forgive him, his throbbing face a testament to the other's hurt and anger. What he hadn't realized was just how much it would hurt his own heart, how much his feelings for Fae had grown. He'd been called a disappointment all his life, berated by his mother and instructors. Yet all their scolding hadn't hurt as much as the fury in Fae's eyes as he'd run off. He'd take a hundred more punches.

Alysion flopped back in the grass, hands still covering his face, wishing Gale would hurry up so he wouldn't have to be alone with himself any longer.

But what if they didn't come back? What if Fae decided he'd finally had enough and left? No, of course they would come back. They needed to. *He* needed them to.

He took a deep breath to loosen the growing tightness in his chest. Fae was bound to the prophecy like he was, and without a damis, Fae didn't stand a chance of finding the crystals or his brother. Fae needed him.

Alysion heard the muted thudding of hoofbeats in the distance. *See, they're already close.* Rising to his feet, he was about to mount Zen-Zen when he suddenly frowned. The sound was coming from the wrong direction. From the canyon.

Damn, it's Anaril. So caught up in himself, he'd failed to notice the Elithars' auras growing stronger.

Letting out a breath, Alysion hopped onto Zen-Zen's back and readied himself for a fight. He'd already evaded the captain a few times now. Things were only going to get messier. At least his companions weren't here, but he knew the captain could sense Gale's aura and would go after her next. *Which will lead them right to Fae.* Alysion quickly came up with a plan, vowing to do whatever it took to prevent the captain from reaching his companions.

"Your highness," said the captain, nodding their head at him from atop their mount—the barest show of respect.

Alysion watched the captain carefully. The other four Elithar fanned out to surround him. "I was just thinking about you," he started. "I have something to ask, actually."

The captain narrowed their eyes but did not speak.

"Recently, I had a vision you were a part of. There was another elf involved, one who despised dragons." He carefully studied the captain's face as he spoke, but it didn't change. "They were arrested for treason—wrongfully, they claimed. I'd like to know who this elf was. I suspect this was a more recent occurrence."

Captain Anaril had lived a long life, longer than any elf he knew. They'd seen many criminals and traitors in their time.

The captain's nostrils flared. "The one you speak of claimed to be plotting revenge against the dragons for how they treated our people during the

Syl-Raanian War. But this was a lie. Instead, they devised a terrible plan to debase the royal family and were caught when it failed."

Alysion did his best to look wholly absorbed with what Anaril was telling him as he slowly began to draw on the Ruby's power with as much stealth as he could muster. It wasn't easy; the Ruby wanted nothing more than to consume everything in a raging inferno.

"They underwent the Silias to have their damis destroyed?" he asked.

"That was their sentence."

Alysion thought he saw something flicker behind the captain's eyes. *Are they hiding something?* The surrounding auras shifted—the Elithar were ready to attack. *Just a bit more...* The Ruby's power burned within him; it took everything he had to keep it reined in.

"What was their plan for the dragons?" Alysion asked, stalling.

"Pardon me, my prince, I'm curious as to why you are inquiring about a traitor who's been on the run for a few centuries."

On the run? When an elf was exiled and had their damis destroyed, they were left alone unless they tried to sneak back into Sylandris. "What's their name?"

"They are called Drath."

That wasn't a Sylandrian name.

At some invisible signal from the captain, the Elithar unleashed their magic

Alysion let loose the power he'd been building, throwing up a roaring wall of flame that burst outwards.

The Elithars' battle-hardened steeds shied away from the intense heat. He turned Zen-Zen and raced off in the direction Fae and Gale had gone. Yet he soon heard the rhythmic sound of hooves pounding after him. The Elithar had recovered their wits faster than he'd anticipated.

Turning in the saddle, he threw streaks of fire at them, trying to unseat the warriors gaining on him. But they were tenacious, and Zen-Zen couldn't hope to outrun the high-bred steeds.

• • ● • •

"You hear somethin'?" asked the watcher. Fae and Gale were making their way back towards Alysion when they suddenly stopped to listen.

"I think so," replied Fae. He couldn't see anything besides the golden grass shining in the bright sunlight. By the gods, did he ever hate how exposed it was out here. And they weren't even in the heart of Manwan Plains yet.

"Better hurry up and get back to Princey."

"Yeah." Fae didn't want to deal with the prince, but he didn't have a choice. He needed Alysion to find Ash. Besides, the prince had probably fallen into a hole or something while they were gone.

"Is that him riding towards us?" Fae asked, a dark spot appearing on the horizon, getting steadily larger.

"You're the one with the elfie eyes."

True. He squinted, recognizing those long golden locks. "Yeah, that's him, and he's waving."

"Mmm, that can't be good. Ain't much of a waver."

They both pulled up their uhaan and waited, ready to run in either direction. Alysion was yelling something, but it wasn't until he was nearly upon them that they understood his message.

"Elithar!"

Neither Fae nor Gale needed telling twice as they wheeled their mounts around and urged them into a gallop, matching Alysion's frantic pace. From the amount of sweat on Zen-Zen, they must have been running for a while.

"Are they close?" Gale hollered, pulling up beside him as he raced on.

"Yes! We need to lose them!"

"If we can beat 'em to the river..." she said before trailing off.

Fae hoped she had something in mind because the nearest crossing was in one of the towns to the north—too far away.

But the river was close, and they reached it much sooner than he expected. Fae hadn't realized how far he'd ridden earlier. "What do we do now?" he hollered, their pace slowing as they neared the riverbank.

"I have an idea," said Alysion. Stopping at the edge of the bank, he pulled out the Sapphire and closed his eyes. The blue stone glowed in his hands.

Fae watched, fidgeting in the saddle. Whatever Alysion was planning, it needed to be quick.

A ripple cut across the water to the opposite shore. Sy-Sy shifted his weight, picking up on Fae's nerves.

"Oooh, look, boy! The water's risin'."

Fae gasped. The water was indeed rising, but it wasn't overflowing the banks. It held its shape and stayed its course, flowing onwards as if nothing were amiss.

"What the—" he started.

The water formed an arc in the air in front of them. They could easily ride under it.

"Go!" Alysion grunted.

They hurried across the exposed riverbed as quickly as they could, but the rocky bottom was wet and slippery, forcing their steeds to walk. It stank of muck and musty plants.

Fae couldn't help but marvel at the water above them. The sunlight pierced through it, illuminating fish that swam on by as if nothing strange was happening. The entire riverbed sparkled with rainbow dots of refracted light.

He glanced back at Alysion, but he still had his eyes scrunched closed in concentration. *A shame.*

They made it across without incident, though Alysion accidentally gave them all a good soak when he sent the water crashing down into the channel with a mighty splash.

"Good trick," said Gale approvingly as they rode on.

"Bit more than a trick," said Fae, wringing his hair out, still in awe of the floating water bridge. "It was amazing."

"It worked. That's what's important," Alysion replied, exhausted.

"Be hard for them elfies to catch us now!" said Gale.

"We'd better not stick around," said Alysion, leading the way onto the vast Manwan Plains.

Fae had been impressed by the stretch of rocky grassland between the canyon and the river, but it was nothing compared to what lay before them. *It's like an ocean.*

Golden grass stretched out endlessly across the horizon, stalks shimmering as they swayed in the gentle summer breeze. The sky was a brilliant shade of blue, a few clouds floating lazily along.

As they rode, the grass grew taller, reaching up to tickle the bellies of their uhaan. The thick ground cover slowed their progress—they couldn't risk one of the animals stepping in a hidden hole and injuring a leg, and anything they accidentally dropped from the saddle was lost to the ages. But, this meant the Elithar would be slowed as well, or so they hoped.

Camp that night was an awkward affair, not just because they had to stamp down the grass to make a usable space.

"Right, you two figure this out," said Gale, going to catch them something to eat. Neither of them expected her to find much.

Fae, brushing Sy-Sy, looked over his shoulder at Alysion, who used his magic to start the fire. He prayed the prince wouldn't set the entire plains ablaze. But Alysion worked carefully, and Fae couldn't see any glow indicating he was using the Ruby to help. *Some prince he'd be if he couldn't even light a fire on his own.* He almost smiled. Almost.

They hadn't said a word to each other since they'd left the river, riding on in brooding silence, and Fae didn't know what to say to him now. He certainly felt no remorse for hitting him; Alysion deserved it.

"I'm sorry for what I said."

Fae blinked stupidly, taken aback, wondering if he'd misheard or imagined it. With Gale gone, Fae figured he'd use the opportunity to berate him for being a damisri and for running off.

Say something!

Alysion looked at him expectantly. His apology seemed genuine, but Fae wasn't sure if he was ready to accept it. He was still processing the circumstances around his parents' deaths, and Alysion's words had only rubbed salt in the wound.

"Thank you," he said awkwardly.

Something like relief flashed across the prince's face before he cleared his throat. "I was able to ask the captain about the elf who keeps popping up in my dreams. They confirmed that what I saw was from the past. His name is Drath."

"Drath? That's not an elven name."

"He was exiled and underwent the Silias. Apparently, he's on the run, which is odd. We don't chase down exiles once they've left Sylandris."

Fae nodded.

"Anaril said Drath claimed to want revenge on the dragons for how they treated us during the Syl-Raanian War but used that as a cover to plot against my family. I didn't get too many details. I was busy trying to get away."

"Shame, but we can't risk running into the captain again to ask," said Fae. "At least now we have an idea of what the traitor's—Drath's—goal is. He must want to use the crystals to usurp your family or start another war with the dragons." He didn't think it wise to rule out the possibility that Drath hadn't been lying about the dragons all along.

"Then we need to hurry up and get the next crystal," said Alysion, "before he finds another."

• • • ● • • •

It only took a day or two of travel before the Elithar began to catch up to them. As they crossed the grassy plains, Alysion could sense their approaching auras. They needed to hurry.

"How far is the next crystal?" Fae asked.

"It's further from us than the Elithar, somewhere east across the plains," he replied.

"Not much we can do out here to lose 'em," said Gale, surveying the endless grass. "Does get a bit hillier further in, makin' it harder for 'em to catch up. Just gotta keep ridin' and hope we stay ahead of 'em long enough."

They took off across the plains, pushing their mounts faster than they had dared to before, and after a few more boring yet tense days of riding, they made it into the gently rolling hills.

It was around midday when Alysion called for them to stop.

"What's goin' on, Princey?"

"I feel something."

"Elithar?" Fae asked.

"Yes, but not them. There's something else." There was another aura nearby, but it was faint. Without a word, he rode Zen-Zen up a gentle hill, then stopped, his breath catching as he gazed into the small valley nestled below.

"I know this place," he whispered. This was it! This was the place from his dream—the wind crystal had been hidden here. Without waiting for his companions to catch up, he rode down the hill, spotting a familiar box.

"Oi, Princey, wait up!"

He ignored Gale's call, focusing on the auras around him. He could feel the crystal, its aura stale, but it wasn't the only lingering energy here. Judging by the overlapping auras and trampled grass, the crystal had put up a great fight.

He rode up to the empty box and dismounted. A visual examination didn't yield much: it was made of polished wood and decorated with motifs of grass blowing in the wind. Closing his eyes, he tried to pick out the thief's aura amongst the mess. If he could find the thief, they could find the wind crystal. But aside from the crystal's aura, he couldn't tell the mingling energies apart.

Frowning, Alysion called on the Sapphire's power, using it as he had on Mt. Hissan to find the gate. His connection with the Sapphire had grown thanks to his training, making the stone's abilities stronger.

One life force stood out from the rest. Concentrating, he tried to find the thief's trail, but even with the Sapphire's help, it wasn't easy. It was as if the thief had tried to cover their tracks.

Idiot, just follow the crystal's aura!

Within moments he was walking up the slope of the northern hill.

"Alysion!" Fae called.

But he ignored him. Alysion came to a sudden stop and cursed, detecting another familiar aura nearby. Opening his eyes, he turned back to his companions. "The wind crystal was here. The thief took it and disappeared through a gate." Wherever the thief had gone, it was either magically shielded or too far for him to sense the crystal. He huffed.

"Was wonderin' what happened here," said Gale as she and Fae rode up the slope. "Looks like someone fought a herd of nuu."

"So then, what do we do?" asked Fae. "Do we try to follow the thief? Can you reopen the gate they used?"

Alysion shook his head. "The gate on Mt. Hissan was special. Normally, gates fade once they close. We would have to open a new one, and I don't know how to do that, not even with the crystals' help. It takes a team to open a new gate." It wasn't something just anyone could do, save for perhaps his parents.

"So we'll continue tracking the current crystal?" Fae asked.

Alysion nodded. As much as he hated the thought of the thief having one of the crystals, he couldn't risk them getting their hands on another and handing it over to Drath. Better to collect as many as they could before they challenged someone strong enough to claim a crystal. Someone with a grudge against the royal family.

Seventeen

Theft and Discovery

Alysion tossed and turned in his bedroll, caught in the usual nightmare of fighting with his mother while his father silently watched. Partway through, a brilliant light filled the area, blinding him and obliterating the forms of his parents. His blood ran cold when he opened his eyes.

No! he shouted, but the thief approaching the stone box couldn't hear him. Unable to stop them, Alysion tried to take in every detail, but he could only see what the thief saw, which wasn't much, for the intensity of the overwhelming light was blinding.

He switched tactics, calling on the Sapphire, but he couldn't properly connect to the stone.

The thief reached into the box and recovered a dazzling yellow gem. Before Alysion could get a good glimpse of it, there was another burst of light and nothing else.

"Come back!" He woke in a panic and sat bolt upright, startling Gale, who was on watch. Fae was already awake, concern and pain twisting on his face as he rubbed at the mark on his wrist.

"What's wrong, boyo?" asked Gale, looking up from the stick she was whittling.

"Another crystal was taken!" Alysion said in a rush, starting to get up. "It was the same thief!"

Gale came over and pushed him back down. "Easy there. Take some deep breaths, nice and slow, then tell us what you saw."

Alysion did as he was told, his panic subsiding enough to form coherent sentences.

"This gives us even less to go on than the last dream," said Fae.

"Sounds like they got a light-magic crystal," mused Gale.

"It was," replied Alysion. "There's no mistaking that type of magic. I haven't been able to produce any light magic yet—only fire-based spells that happen to be bright. Only the most powerful nobles use it back home, and even they spend decades learning it. It's incredibly rare for anyone to have a natural affinity for it, and shadow magic even more so. Of course, anyone with an affinity for shadow magic would hide it; it was outlawed centuries ago."

"Why's shadow magic banned?" asked Gale.

"Those who could wield it caused a lot of harm to our people," he said. Now wasn't the time to discuss it.

"Where could the light crystal have been hidden?" asked Fae. "I would have guessed somewhere out here, but this is where the wind crystal was."

"I have no idea," said Alysion. He'd felt the aura of the light crystal, the Topaz, disappear, but now that it was gone, he wasn't sure which direction it came from. Maybe to the north? Ugh, if only he'd been able to see where they were! At least he could still sense the current crystal they were chasing.

"Maybe it was inside a dragon's mouth," suggested Gale, chuckling. "Would be very bright in there when they're breathin' fire!"

Alysion did not share her amusement but appreciated her attempt to lighten the mood.

"There are two crystals left unaccounted for: the one we are currently after and the mystery one. For some reason, I still can't feel its aura..." Alysion hated that fact. Was it because it was so far away? That was a scary thought since the crystals' auras were so strong. He hoped that his inability to sense it was simply part of its defences.

"One of these crystals is earth-based," he continued. "I still don't know what kind of magic the other will hold. Some spells exist outside of the six major elements, like summoning spells, but they don't have a collective element of their own that I know of."

"Summonin' spells use a mix of elements. Water and light, I think," said the watcher. "They tried explainin' it to us young watchers, but it didn't make much sense to me!"

"Let's get back to sleep. We can figure this out when we're more awake," said Fae, yawning and lying back down.

Gale nodded, returning to her post.

Alysion settled into his bedroll, rolling onto his side to stare into the darkness beyond the camp. But with how his thoughts raced, sleep was not coming anytime soon.

• • • ● • • •

The next few days passed uneventfully. The Elithar remained on their tail but hadn't managed to catch up.

"Are we losing them?" Fae asked as they rode.

"No," replied Alysion. "Anaril won't let us get away again."

"How much further to the crystal?"

"Its aura is much stronger, but it's likely a few days out."

Fae nodded, wishing they could get there faster. He hated how open the plains were, even with the scattered hills. And they were all quickly growing tired of the winds that blew across the sea of golden grass, chapping their lips and watering their eyes. Sometimes they blew so strongly it was hard to make any conversation at all. Night was no better. At least it hadn't rained—there was no shelter from summer storms in the grasslands.

"So the crystal is likely on the other side of these hills," said Fae, unfurling their map, curious to see what lay ahead. He frowned. "That region seems to be unmarked. And there aren't many towns between here and there. We'll lose a few days detouring north to hit one." That wasn't good; they needed to resupply soon.

"Then we don't have time to stop in town," Alysion said sharply. "We can't let the thief get this crystal. Besides, I'm sure we can find food out here." He sounded more confident than Fae felt, but he wasn't the one hunting and foraging. "We can't let the them reach the forest before us!"

"We'll be worse off if we don't," argued Gale. "We have just enough food to make it to one of the towns—"

"Forest?" Fae cut in. "What forest?"

Alysion suddenly became very interested in his reins.

"What forest?" Fae repeated. "The map doesn't show a forest."

Alysion sighed, taking a moment to collect his thoughts. "There is an old legend about a hidden forest somewhere in these lands," he began. "It's called the Glimmering Forest. Supposedly, thelim are sent there as a punishment for misbehaving. I think it's where we're going."

Fae held in his laugh out of respect for Alysion, but hearing Gale's cries of mirth, he allowed himself to smile.

"Really? A place for bad elfie children?"

"It's a legend! I think it's where the crystal is hidden. The prophecy mentioned a forgotten forest, and it's the only strange forest I know of. I've eliminated the lines about the crystals that have been found, and with only two crystals left—"

"And your stories don't give us any hints as to where it is?" asked the watcher.

"Well, no, they don't want others to stumble across a forest full of delinquents," Alysion said, sitting stiffly in the saddle.

"You mean a forest with a hidden crystal in it. *While the forgotten forest hides it's brother*," Fae recited. He wondered if his parents had told him and Ash the tale of the Glimmering Forest. The thought made his heart ache.

"So what happens to those who get sent there?" Gale asked, not bothering to hide her amusement.

"Misbehaving thelim suffer unspeakable punishments until the sentence is up—if it has an end. They claim that most die before they are eventually released."

Gale lost herself to another round of laughter.

Fae just shook his head. What in the name of the gods were Elven nobles teaching their offspring? Usually, cautionary stories were scary, but not like this. This was too traumatizing.

"I don't want to lose another crystal," said Alysion, his delicate face clouded with worry.

"We won't," said Fae, riding up beside him to clap him on the shoulder, wishing he could offer more. But just because Alysion apologized and tolerated his presence, it didn't mean the elf *wanted* him. But he did look a little less gloomy afterwards.

• • • ● • • •

"Hey, boys, come check this out!" Gale hollered from where she sat astride her uhaan atop a hill.

The elves quickly rode up to meet her.

"What are we—?" Alysion started.

A strange looking house rested at the bottom of the hill, partly recessed into the ground with earthen steps leading down to the entrance. The walls were layered sod with long, thick wooden poles lying across their tops, creating a frame for the sod-covered roof. The home blended in nicely against the hills, but a ready-to-harvest garden dug into the slope made it stand out. Colourful fowl pecked around the side of the house, and a small area around the back had been fenced off for livestock. There were a few animals there now, including a pair of the smallest uhaan Fae had ever seen.

"Might've found a solution to our supply problem—if they have any to spare," said Gale gleefully.

Fae's spirits rose, and a quick look at Alysion showed him he felt the same way.

Without another word, the prince rode down the slope.

"Oi! Wait up, Princey, you can't just barge in!" Gale hollered, she and Fae quickly following him.

Fae's vision flickered with the unmistakable sensation of passing through a ward. He glanced at his companions—had they felt it too? Nerves gripped him as they descended the slope, sincerely hoping the occupants of the house were friendly.

The door opened as if on cue, and two individuals stepped out, both carrying polearms. The house's inhabitants were short—very short, and both bearded.

Dwarves! Fae tried not to stare as they approached. He'd never seen dwarves before. They never came through Redwood.

"Who are you?" the taller one demanded in Odenian. They sported a long, braided black beard, and to Fae's surprise, their voice did not have the low tone of a man.

Dwarven women have beards too?

The short woman pointed her weapon at them.

They slowed, and Gale pushed to the front—a wise move. They had no idea how Alysion would handle dwarves, and they couldn't risk bungling this.

"We're travelling across the plains in search of—" both elves glanced at her quickly "—rare medicinal plants. Heard phoenix grass can be found out this way."

"Never heard of it," said the shorter one, who appeared to be the taller dwarf's daughter. She, too, had a black beard, but it was heavily braided and not nearly as long. Fae thought she appeared to be close to adulthood but wasn't too sure. The tip of her weapon was casually pointed towards the sky, but her muscles were tense, ready to spring into action at a moment's notice.

"Careful," he muttered to Alysion, switching back to Odenian. Speaking Illithen would give them away, even if the dwarves couldn't understand it.

"That's all right!" said Gale cheerfully. "We just want to stop for a short rest if you don't mind. Maybe purchase some food?" Her eyes drifted towards the fowl pecking at the ground.

Both dwarves exchanged a look, neither dropping their guard.

"We have no room for guests," said the woman.

"We don't need to spend the night," said Fae. Sy-Sy stepped closer but stopped outside the polearm's reach. Their hard stares lingered on his oddly coloured hair.

"Elves!" said the older one, taking a step back but keeping her weapon up.

Damn, they'd forgotten to cover his ears.

The dwarves went silent, taking in this revelation. The three travellers waited patiently, their uhaan swishing their tails.

Eventually, the older dwarf lowered her polearm. She looked them all up and down—her gaze lingering on Gale—before she spoke. "Not everyday you see Sylandrians outside the forest. Since your people conjured the wards to keep the dragons at bay, I suppose you may rest here for a bit. What do you need?"

Eighteen

Visit

Alysion watched as Gale bent low to avoid hitting her head on the low door frame, following Melann, the older dwarf, inside.

They literally don't have room for us in there, he thought with mild amusement. The house hadn't been built with taller people in mind.

He and Fae untacked their uhaan, finally letting the animals take a proper break. He knew they should leave them saddled in case the Elithar or the hooded elves showed up, but their mounts deserved a good rest. The Elithar wouldn't catch up to them tonight—not unless they opened a gate, which was beyond their abilities.

He glanced over at Fae, who had already tended to Gale's mount and was checking Sy-Sy's back for saddle sores while brushing him out.

"He's a beautiful animal."

Alysion jumped and spun around to see the younger dwarf approaching Fae. He frowned.

"Thank you. His name is Sy-Sy, and mine's Fae."

"I'm Urka." She sat on a large rock, dark eyes never leaving Fae as he finished tending to his mount.

Alysion hastily laid down Zen-Zen's sweaty tack where it wouldn't get stepped on and approached the dwarf. "I'm Alysion."

Urka hardly spared him a nod. Alysion bit back the urge to snap at her. How dare she brush him off!

"This is the first time I've ever seen any elves," she said. "How long have you been travelling for?"

Fae gave Sy-Sy one last pat, then left the uhaan to graze. He sat in the grass near the rock. Alysion did the same.

"You should finish brushing Zen-Zen," Fae said.

Alysion stared at him, nostrils flaring, then got up and stomped back over to his uhaan. *Who's he to tell me what to do! I'm not a child!* He huffed and started brushing Zen-Zen's coat, making sure to stay within earshot.

"We've been travelling since the early summer," Fae explained, "searching all over for different plants and herbs. But, I will admit, this is my first time meeting a dwarf. We don't usually see you up north."

We sure don't!

"Well, you elves don't let anyone into your forest," Urka said. "Have you found anything good so far?"

"We've found a few things, but the phoenix grass is our main target. It's used a lot in Sylandris, but it's hard to come by. Doesn't like the shade of the forest, I guess."

Urka nodded, eyes gleaming. Alysion scowled.

"What about you and your mother? How do you manage out here?" Fae gestured to the rippling grass.

"It's not bad. There are roaming tribes around part of the year, so we do a lot of trading with them. They head south when the cold drives away the nuu. Winters are the hardest, but we manage."

"Are there no other dwarves around here?" he asked.

"We live all over these plains, but everyone is hidden like us. Most live underground in the tunnels."

"Tunnels?" Fae asked, curious.

Urka slid off the rock onto the grass beside him. "We have tunnels running underneath the entire plain. Our people think it's safer underground. They still worry about dragons even though they left these lands long before I was born."

It was easy to see that the dwarf enjoyed having someone else to talk to. Alysion desired nothing more than to barge in and tell her off, but he held himself back. He'd just apologized to Fae and couldn't risk jeopardizing their relationship again. He moved to Zen-Zen's other side, casting dark looks over his shoulder, hating how comfortable they were with each other.

"Do you ever see the other dwarves?"

Urka shrugged. "Sometimes. Usually during emergencies, and for certain celebrations."

"Why do you two live on the surface? If you don't mind me asking."

I mind you asking! Alysion gripped the brush tightly as he quickly finished grooming his uhaan, knuckles white.

"Mam doesn't like living down there. She was born up here and found it too depressing. She prefers running the farm. I've never spent more than a few days down there at a time, and I don't like it either. A few others live up here, scattered between the hills. They run larger farms and help feed the cities."

"There are entire cities under here?" Fae gave the dirt a quizzical look.

"Nothing fancy, but cities all the same." Urka moved closer to him. "I can draw—"

Alysion, blood boiling, closed his eyes and pressed his face against Zen-Zen's neck like he'd seen Fae do when he was stressed. The low rumbling of the large animal muted their voices, taking him to a quiet, calming place.

• • • ● • • •

Dinner that evening was delicious. None of them could remember when they had last eaten like this; weeks on the road had skewed their sense of time—and taste. For all Alysion knew, this could be the blandest meal ever, but to him, it was bursting with flavour. Not to say that Gale's trail cooking was terrible, but it was nice to eat something other than game meat and foraged berries. And he didn't ever want to see a stick of dried rations again.

They ate their fill, talking little at first as they savoured the meal. Then Urka, seated across from Fae, began asking questions about his life. Too many questions. And when Fae explained that he'd been raised by humans and didn't know much about elves, that Alysion was the expert in that area, she asked about life in Redwood instead.

Alysion stabbed at the remnants of his food.

"We dwarves are similar to humans," explained Melann. "We aren't all born with magic like you elves are. Dwarves who can use magic are revered, gaining prestigious positions within our communities. The city councils are primarily made up of magic-users."

She and Urka apologized profusely for the lack of space, but the sod house did not have room for guests. It was divided into two parts: the smaller front area for the dwarves and the larger back portion for the animals.

"We can leave the animals out overnight," Melann offered, a bit embarrassed. "You can sleep back there if you want."

"It's all right," said Gale, "We're used to sleeping under the stars!"

Gale and Melann cleaned up while the elves spread their bedrolls beneath a sparse tree nearby. Alysion suspected the two women had an ulterior motive, given some of the glances they'd exchanged over dinner, but left them to it.

An approaching aura, soon followed by footsteps, drew his gaze. It was Urka. He frowned.

"Do you want to go for a short walk?" she asked Fae, pointedly ignoring Alysion.

Rude.

"We'll stay in sight of the house."

"Sure, give me a moment," Fae said, quickly fluffing up his bedroll before they strolled up the hillside together.

Alysion watched them go, eyes narrowed. Why was she so interested in Fae? He had half a mind to follow them, but Urka would surely notice his aura. Still, he couldn't just sit here; he needed to know what was going on. If he strained his ears, he could hear their voices but couldn't make out anything more. Concentrating, he called forth a gentle breeze, one that would carry their words down to him.

"Nice night, isn't it?" he heard Fae say. Alysion positioned his bedroll so he could see them stop halfway up the slope.

"Oh, yes it is," the dwarf replied, distracted.

Their conversation was clear as day, thanks to his spell. Alysion's lips quirked, pleased that it hadn't gone awry for once.

"I'm always amazed by how many stars you can see out here. Back home, the trees hide most of them. Same with the mountains." Fae sat in the grass, laying back to stargaze. "The vastness of the void could swallow me up."

Urka fidgeted and sat beside him.

Alysion clenched his jaw, wishing he were in her place.

"What's the matter?" Fae asked, sitting back up. But Urka said nothing.

Come on, get to it.

"Living like this is hard. While I do prefer living up here, it gets very lonely. The Council of Hardstone, the city closest to us, is upset that Mam won't join them. Since she's a magic-user and all."

Fae nodded, the moonlight shimmering on his hair.

"Since I can use magic too, they want me to step up and do what she won't."

Everyone could feel the 'but' coming.

"I'm not as skilled as she is, nor do I think I ever will be. It doesn't bother me, but the council is being pushy." She let out a slow breath. "They keep sending potential partners my way, but I have no interest in having one. Not yet anyway. I know they're doing it because they want more magic users around. We're useful."

Alysion nodded along. *I know that feeling.*

"What does your mother say about it?" Fae asked carefully.

"That it's my choice, and she will support me either way. I know she'd prefer it if I didn't give in."

"Why does she dislike the council so much?"

"She used to be part of it, but the politics were too much for her—plus she didn't like living below ground. Every year, each city sends a handful of council representatives to attend a large meeting to discuss how everyone is faring. Mam was selected to attend once, and it didn't go well. She proposed building a new city above ground—the first in centuries. Only a handful of the gathered dwarves would even consider her idea; everyone was too afraid of moving to the surface."

"Afraid of what? The dragons?"

"Yes. We used to have small cities scattered all over the plains. The dragons would destroy them while out hunting nuu, so they never had a chance to flourish. Eventually, most surface dwarves moved underground and never came out again. When my mother made her proposal, the dragons had already been banished from these lands. Neither of us understands why they're still afraid; no one's seen a dragon since the war. So there's no reason for us not to try building again."

Humph, this dwarf has some sense. Now, if only she would get to the real reason why she'd brought Fae up here.

"I would love to see a city built on the surface," said Urka. "I wouldn't mind joining the council if they were open to it, but when I approached them, they had the gall to tell me to focus on finding a partner." She snorted. "They think finding a partner is easy, that you can grab just any dwarf and go from there. I did meet some of the boys they presented, but none of them felt right. Eventually, I started tossing out their letters."

"Probably a wise decision," Fae said.

Alysion agreed. Why couldn't those in power see others as more than just tools? He'd never be like that once he was king.

The dwarf sighed and flopped back onto the grass, staring up at the twinkling stars. "I—" she started, slowly sitting up. She tugged at her beard.

Alysion's heart began to race, and he broke out in a cold sweat. It took everything he had not to run up the hill.

"I think I like you," she said quickly, burying her face in her hands.

The pause between them lasted an eternity.

Say something! Alysion had his blanket in a death grip, his entire existence hinging on Fae's response.

"Um, thank you," Fae stammered awkwardly.

"I'm sorry!" Urka quickly stood, but Fae grabbed her wrist to stop her. She looked at him, eyes glistening.

"Hang on," he said. "You don't need to apologize."

Yes, she does! You're not for her!

Urka slowly sat back down, deflated and miserable. Fae let go.

"But I'm afraid I can't return your feelings. We only just met, and I have other things I need to take care of."

"You like him, don't you?" Both elves froze. "It's not hard to see. From the way you look at him, I can tell you really care about him," she continued. "I shouldn't have butted in. I'm sorry."

The conversation faded with the breeze.

Fae *liked* him?

Nineteen

To Hide A Tree

"I asked Urka if she knew anything about Drath, but she didn't. But she did teach me about the Earthen Mother who gave life to their people ages ago." Fae had found Urka's story about the dwarven goddess fascinating, but judging by Alysion's expression, he couldn't have cared less. At least his mood had improved since leaving the dwarves.

As they travelled through the hills, it was evident their bright summer was coming to an end. The sparse vegetation interspersed throughout the grasses turned brown, and the nights were getting cooler. The new northern winds had bite to them—a taste of what the changing seasons could bring.

"Gotta finish this up before winter," said Gale. "Be hard to travel once the snows come."

When the sun was high on a clear day, they finally reached the unmarked spot on the map. Alysion was confident that once they crested the final hill, they would find a sprawling forest. At this point, Fae didn't care what was on the other side so long as it was something other than endless grass.

Alysion's shout from atop the hill had him urging Sy-Sy to move faster. When he reached the top, he let out a sigh.

He'd gotten his wish. The grass was gone, but so was everything else. What greeted them was not a lush forest but a bleak wasteland of dried, cracked earth. The swirling wind kicked up puffs of dust.

Ah, the map isn't blank; there truly isn't anything here.

"This can't be it!" said Alysion, the frustration evident on his face. "There has to be more. There has to be a forest. I can feel the crystal!"

"Well, then it's here somewhere," said Gale, riding up beside him. "Might not be a forest, but that doesn't matter. If it's an earth crystal, then I bet we gotta dig it up!"

Alysion glared at the grey earth as he rode down the hill. By the time he reached the bottom, the last of the tall grass had disappeared.

"Wait up!" Fae quickly followed, concerned. The flat wasteland was even more exposed than the heart of the plains.

Alysion dismounted and looked for clues.

"Is it close by?" Fae asked when he caught up. His wrist started to itch.

"Its aura is both strong and weak, like it's nearby but also very far away. It's like the hidden gate on Mt. Hissan." He crossed his arms.

"Do you sense the our thief?" Fae dared to ask.

"No, I don't sense any other auras at all." Well, that was one bit of good news.

"Why don't we take a quick break?" Gale suggested from the top of the hill. "Food might help us think. The crystal's safe for now."

Alysion looked like he wanted to do anything but take a break, but Fae was already riding back up the hill as Gale rummaged through her saddlebags for the last of the food the dwarves had given them.

"Why don't you try delving into one of the crystals to see if they can dig up another memory?" he suggested when Alysion joined them. Fae wasn't sure if this would work—since the last memories came to Alysion in dreams—but they had nothing else.

The prince gave a reluctant nod and dumped both crystals into his hand. He sat in silence for a few moments, eyes closed, brow furrowed in concentration. Alysion let out a harsh breath as the crystals flashed and his eyes shot open.

"They showed me something, but it was hazier than the dreams," he said. "I couldn't make out what anyone was saying. One of the voices sounded like my father's. And he wasn't happy."

"Seems like they showed you something out of your own dreams," said Fae.

Alysion's troubled expression deepened. "Maybe."

"Perhaps being asleep is the key," he suggested.

At that, Alysion cocked his head in thought. "Oh! That's it! I've heard that shadow magic has a connection to the realm of sleep and dreams. Drath has the shadow crystal, so our crystals must be connected to it."

Fae nodded. "But doesn't that mean Drath can see into your dreams?"

The tips of Alysion's ears went red. "I-I don't believe so. The Ruby and Sapphire wouldn't allow that. I can sense it."

"You've been havin' other weird dreams, Princey?" said Gale, eyeing each elf as she handed them some food. "And you didn't think to tell me?"

Both averted their gaze.

"We weren't sure if we could trust you, and then we just forgot," Fae mumbled.

"Humph, guess I can't fault you for that," she said.

After exchanging a quick glance with Fae, Alysion filled her in.

"And that crusty captain thinks it might be some elfie named Drath? That's a weird name."

"I wonder if the captain could tell us anything more about Drath," said Fae.

"We're not going anywhere near Anaril," said Alysion, eyes narrowed. "We barely manage to escape them each time. And now that we know the truth about your damis," his emerald eyes flicked towards Fae, spiking his heart rate, "I won't let you anywhere near them. They won't hesitate to cut you down, despite what I say."

"I'm with Princey on this one," said Gale. "That captain won't fall for any more tricks. I'm fresh out anyways."

The high noon sun beat down, warming the barren land. They finished their meal, each lost in thought. Fae debated telling them about the dark-clothed elves from his past. He would have to; there was no getting around it.

"The elves that—"

"The crystal!" exclaimed Alysion, jumping up, hand going to the pouch around his neck. He pulled out the Ruby and Sapphire, and both were lit up like beacons, nearly blinding them. "The crystal is calling us, only it can't let us in until the sun is at it's zenith."

"Well, if that crusty captain didn't know where we were before, they do now," grumbled Gale, hastily repacking their things. "Fae, grab the uhaan. I think we're about to find our next shiny rock."

Fae, wrist prickling, quickly did as she asked. *I'll tell them later.* He led the uhaan to where Alysion stood with the crystals held against his chest, eyes closed. Neither he nor Gale spoke, not wanting to break his concentration.

At the bottom of the slope, where scraggly grass turned to hard-packed dirt, something flickered. Slowly, a gate appeared, similar to the one on Mt. Hissan, save it was a vibrant green.

"Good work, Princey! You sure are improvin'!" said Gale.

They mounted up and rode into the swirling green mass, the wasteland vanishing behind them.

• • • ● • • •

It was as if they'd been transported to another world.

Dense forest surrounded them—or what appeared to be a forest. Massive trees made entirely of crystal reached for the sky, each leaf just as detailed as their organic counterparts. A single branch was composed of enough gemstone to feed a city for years. Bushes of minerals covered in diamond berries lined the forest floor alongside a few soft plants—primarily the squishy moss underfoot—but their dazzling counterparts vastly outnumbered them.

Despite its beauty, the forest was eerie. The air was still and quiet: no rustling of leaves, no sounds of animals. The faint glow from the crystalline plants was the strangest of all, the only source of light in an otherwise pitch-black forest; the midday sun had disappeared.

Alysion peered through the glowing leaves to search for any recognizable constellations, but the dark sky was devoid of celestial bodies—no stars, no twin moons. They weren't on the plains anymore. But where were they?

"Oh, my—" breathed Gale, awestruck.

"Looks like we're in the right place," said Fae. "To hide a tree, use a forest; to hide a crystal, use a crystal forest."

They were so taken in by the spectacle that they didn't notice the gate fading away until it had disappeared entirely.

"Can you reopen it?" asked Fae warily.

"I'm not sure," replied Alysion. "Perhaps with the Sapphire's help..."

"So, where do we start?" asked Fae. "*Everything* is crystal."

He turned Zen-Zen about, but felt the same aura no matter which direction he faced. "This isn't good," he huffed. "Everything is giving off magical energy; I can't pinpoint it."

"Try touching a tree," Fae suggested. "A forest like this isn't natural. It has to be connected to the crystal."

Alysion rode up to the nearest tree and placed his hand on its trunk. The pink and blue stone was smooth as glass beneath his fingers.

"Oh!" he exclaimed. It resonated with magic—the magic that had given it form, the magic of life.

Both Gale and Fae put their hands on their weapons and closed in.

"No, it's okay. The forest is still alive."

"How is that possible? It's all gemstones," said Fae.

Eyes closed, Alysion concentrated on the aura circulating within the tree. He followed the energy to the ground, where the tree's roots mingled with others. He searched further, following the aural flow from plant to plant. One bush he couldn't feel the entirety of, and when he opened his eyes to look, he saw that parts remained soft and green.

His curiosity soon got the better of him. Alysion pulled back, trying to feel the entire system as a whole. The incoming energy nearly knocked him from Zen-Zen's back.

The forest was one vast consciousness. Alysion could feel every plant in their immediate vicinity: every tree, every bush, every bit of undergrowth. The information was staggering. If he pulled back even further, he would feel more of the forest, but the sheer volume of plant life around them was overwhelming enough. He'd go mad if he tried.

Instead, he focused on the aura circulating through the gemstone plants. There was no doubt in his mind that it was the earth crystal, but his wrist wasn't acting up any more than usual. Wherever the crystal was, it wasn't around here. He pulled himself out and turned to his companions.

"The forest wasn't originally like this," he began. "It was once a normal forest. When the crystal was hidden here, it changed things to protect itself." He pointed to the spiky plant he hadn't been able to feel the entirety of. "See how the bases of the leaves have turned to gemstone while the tops are still normal?"

"Are you saying this entire forest is the crystal?" asked Fae, eyes wide. Alysion knew what he was thinking: how could they transport an *entire* forest?

"Yes and no," he said. "Everything is connected to the crystal, similar to how the branches of a tree are connected to the trunk." He touched the tree again and focused on the aura within. "Which means I should be able to follow the aura to its source. But it's difficult; the aura is twisted like a gnarled root, and I can feel all the other plants. I'll start to follow the flow in this tree and end up in that bush over there." He nodded to one nearby, covered in translucent blue leaves.

"Ah, so this is how the crystal is defendin' itself," said Gale. "No angry volcano or stormy lakes. Just like Fae here said: to hide a tree, use a forest."

"We have a problem," said Fae. "There isn't enough real plant life for the uhaan to eat, and we have yet to find a stream." There was no trickling of water, only pressing silence.

"Princey here can probably pull up some water. The ground is still plain old dirt."

"Can the Sapphire help locate the crystal?" Fae asked.

Alysion was already hanging the smooth blue stone around his neck, tucking it beneath his shirt. "I don't have any choice but to use it. I can't make any progress like this."

Tink.

Both elves whipped around in their saddles.

"Oop, sorry, boys. Just wanted to see somethin'." Gale held a translucent pink leaf plucked from a plant. Its glow slowly faded, but it didn't revert to its organic state.

Alysion glanced around, checking to see if the forest would retaliate. Nothing happened.

Gale played with the leaf for a moment, tapping it and holding it up to a glowing tree so she could peer through it. Satisfied with whatever she gleaned, she wrapped it and placed it in her bag.

Alysion rode off between the trees. Standing around wasn't getting him anywhere, and without food for their mounts, they couldn't afford to dawdle.

The sky didn't change with the passage of time, making it impossible to determine how long they'd been in the forest. Eventually, they convinced Alysion to stop for the night; he was strained and worn out despite the Sapphire's help.

They ate a small meal and then settled down to sleep, Fae and taking turns Gale keeping watch. So far, they hadn't encountered any other living things, but it was better to be safe than sorry. Perhaps the crystal would have a change of heart and attack them while they slept.

• • • ● • • •

Fae took the first shift. He sat at the base of an amethyst tree, carefully plucking some leaves off a nearby bush and packing them away for later. He'd use them to help rebuild Master Cane's smithy. It wouldn't be long before she returned from Murk Water, and he couldn't bear the thought of her coming home to ruins. And to find him missing. Guilt gnawed at him. *I should've left a note or something*. But with the Elithar chasing them down, that hadn't been possible.

Fae searched the dark sky for a way to ease the mountain of guilt inside him. He still hadn't talked to Alysion and Gale about his parents' deaths or the elves responsible, but now that they were so close to another crystal, Fae didn't want to distract him with his troubles.

They needed to focus on finding the crystal and stopping whatever Drath was planning. When they finished—*when*, not if, he would tell Alysion about his memory; it would likely help them find Ash.

Fae jumped at a faint rustling behind him, senses on high alert. But it was only Alysion. He stepped out of the gloom and took a seat beside Fae, playing with a lock of golden hair.

"Is something wrong?" Fae asked quietly, not wanting to disturb Gale, who slept nearby.

Alysion didn't respond right away, and Fae didn't press him. He was exhausted from trying to stay on the correct course. One slip up could have them wandering for days—time they couldn't afford to lose. There had to be a good reason for him to be awake now.

"Are you cold? Would you like a blanket?" Fae asked, but Alysion shook his head. The forest remained pleasantly warm despite autumn's approach.

Alysion sighed softly next to him but still didn't speak.

"Do—?"

"I'm sorry," Alysion said, burying his face in his hands.

Fae wasn't sure what to say. Sorry for what?

"All of this, it's been a lot," Alysion continued, slowly raising his head. "I never could have imagined the hardships we've had to overcome. My life in Sylandris was far more sheltered than I realized. I don't get along with my parents. Nothing I do is ever good enough for them, regardless of how much I study or practise. I mean, you saw how disastrous my magic was when we first met."

Something must have crept onto Fae's face because Alysion quickly said, "I'll take care of the smithy, don't worry. No one'll ever know it was damaged."

"Thank you," Fae said more stiffly than he intended.

"At first, looking for the crystals was just an excuse to avoid going home. But then we found the Sapphire, and I realized how dangerous they could be, how important it is for us to find them. When the thief stole the wind crystal, I didn't know what to do. I felt horrible about Ashdale, then to add that on..." He sighed. "Fulfilling the prophecy was supposed to be my chance to redeem myself, but we've only got two crystals, and things are going wrong already."

Alysion drew his knees up, holding them close to his chest.

"I want to go after Drath, and it drives me mad that I can't. But we have to find the remaining crystals first."

Fae nodded. "We're all frustrated."

Alysion shook his head. "My mother thinks I'm a failure—she's right. I'm supposed to be the next king of Sylandris, yet I can't even collect a few crystals! And when we do find one, bad things still happen!"

"Ashdale wasn't your fault. It's Drath's for starting all this. Had he not decided to seize the crystals, Mt. Hissan wouldn't have been woken by the Ruby."

Fae could feel him shaking and saw a tear roll down his smooth cheek. He resisted the urge to brush it away, placing his hand on Alysion's shoulder instead.

"It was never going to be easy," Fae started. "Personally, I'm impressed we've managed to collect two—and soon to be three—so quickly. It's frustrating that some were taken, but we'll figure it out. Remember, you're not alone. I'm bound just as you are, and Gale is helping however she can. And some good has come out of this: we saved Great Snapper, and you rescued me from the canyon."

Alysion stopped shaking, staring glumly at the ground instead. "Gale helped at the canyon."

"There's nothing wrong with being helped. Your mother is being too hard on you. I highly doubt she governs Sylandris all by herself."

Alysion nodded. "I suppose that's true."

"We'll retrieve the crystal that's here, then set out to find Drath. If he happens to find the last crystal before we do, then it's one less thing for us to track down."

Alysion mumbled something. Fae caught the word 'mother'.

"You need to care less about what your parents think. I understand that they're the queen and king and that there's a lot of responsibility on you, but your worry is holding you back. Your magical abilities have improved a lot."

"That's because I rely on the crystals. It's not my own ability."

"Of course it is. You don't use the Sapphire when getting water for us—and it's been a while since you've soaked me." He flashed a small, supportive smile. "Now, what are you apologizing for?" Alysion had already apologized for his behaviour near the canyon.

"I..." he started, losing confidence.

"You?" Fae prompted.

Alysion looked up, his face red. "Um..."

Fae waited. Something important was coming. Was this about his lack of damis?

"I like you."

• • • ● • • •

Navir knelt before the wooden statue of the Divine Ancestors in the Sacred Hall, eyes closed. The scent of sandalwood imbued the surrounding air, the sticks of incense burning in a clay pot filled with sand at the statue's feet. Deep in meditation, he didn't move even as footsteps approached. Whoever it was could wait until he was finished.

"They have entered the forest, Isidyll," said the only voice that would dare disturb him. "And the Elithar are not far behind them."

"Good. Have all the konn returned?" he said without turning around.

"Yes. They are ready to move out at your command," said Drath.

"They're no longer needed. The prince and his companions will soon be backed by the power of another crystal, and the blasted Elithar have proven to be formidable foes. This situation calls for someone more capable."

Navir stood and stared Drath down. The ayel was down on one knee, head bent in subservience. "It is time to collect the remaining crystals. Please assist Kara-ayel in preparing to retrieve them and the prince. Do remind her that we need him alive."

The ayel nodded. "And his companions?"

"They and the Elithar are expendable."

"Very well."

Part Four

Tarathiel and Illuven spent most of the morning lounging on the beach just outside the cave while Tiriel and Ylana collected shells nearby. They sat on the dry sand, surrounded on three sides by an invisible ward that shielded them from the water—which was well above their heads—with the rocky cliff to their backs. Above them was an open blue sky; it would be another sunny day.

If they wanted to, they could pass through the barrier and swim up to the top of the cliffs, but they were content to wait for the tide to go out, watching as schools of colourful fish swam by. No one was in a hurry to return home, especially not Tarathiel.

By midday, the water had dropped enough that they could wade to the trail that took them back up the cliff. With a heavy heart, Tarathiel reluctantly followed his friends, holding Illuven's hand.

As they began to ride back, Tarathiel entertained the thought of him and Illuven taking off, leaving Sylandris behind forever. They would be free—free of the joining, free of the royal family, free of everything. Of course, they might have to live with humans, but he thought that was a reasonable tradeoff for being together the rest of their days. Sadly, Illuven would never agree to it. Though Illuven hated the engagement as much as he did, he wouldn't dare break it off in such an improper manner. He was too damned polite.

They were halfway to the Sylandrian wards when Illuven's uhaan stopped in her tracks.

"Come along, Illuven!" called Tarathiel. He and the others halted their mounts.

He narrowed his eyes as Illuven's steed began to act up, stamping the ground nervously and throwing her head. What was going on?

The uhaan suddenly reared up and let out a shriek of terror. Tarathiel's heart dropped, but Illuven's quick reflexes kept him in the saddle.

"Easy there, girl!" Illuven called out as the frightened uhaan bolted towards their group. The rest of the animals were startled into a run, but the elves managed to keep them under control.

They all looked around to see what had spooked Illuven's mount.

"What's that?" asked Ylana, gesturing to one of the massive rocks littering the ground, her eyes alarmingly wide.

Something enormous crawled out from behind the enormous pale stone: a dull copper beast with four legs, a pair of leathery wings, and a long tail ending in a mass of spikes.

"By the Ancestors, it's a dragon!" exclaimed Tiriel.

The dragon roared, displaying a mouth full of dagger-like teeth before lunging at Illuven and his terrified mount.

"Don't touch him!" screamed Tarathiel, a crackling sphere of magic leaving his hand before he knew what he was doing. It hit the dragon square between the eyes.

The beast snorted and came to a stop. It looked more angry than hurt, but the spell had distracted it long enough for Illuven to rejoin the group.

A deep roar filled the air as the dragon pumped its wings, furious. The uhaan reared and bucked, flailing wildly to escape the danger and the riders that encumbered them. Tiriel was thrown to the ground, and his steed took off.

"Come back!" he called, but the terrified animal didn't stop, for the dragon was charging straight for them.

"I think their wing is broken!" Illuven hollered. "Their movement isn't right."

"Good, that means it can't fly," replied Tarathiel, preparing another potent blast of magic. His blood boiled. How dare a dragon breach the Sky Peak wards! A broken wing meant it would be easier to kill; Tarathiel had no desire to let the foul thing live.

But why didn't it speak? Dragons were fully capable of speech and—though he hated to admit it—were nearly as intelligent as elves. Instead, this dragon behaved like a wild beast, displaying no discernable conscious thought in its rolling eyes.

"We should flee," shouted Ylana, helping Tiriel onto her uhaan's back.

"Absolutely not. We need to end it before it hurts anyone else!" Tarathiel threw a crackling spell at the charging beast, which struck a rock as his uhaan reared up beneath him. Without a second thought, he slid from the animal's back and drew his thin sword.

The dragon was nearly upon them, closing the distance with surprising speed for a creature more suited to flight.

Without warning, it opened its mouth and let out a white-hot stream of flame. Tarathiel and Illuven dodged it, but Ylana's uhaan, laden with two riders, wasn't quick enough. Flames licked its hindquarters, drawing a pained wail from the beast. It collapsed to the ground—Tiriel jumped free, but Ylana was pinned, one of her legs trapped under the animal's bulk.

"Help me!" she cried, desperately trying to pull herself free. Her uhaan tried to stand, but its rear legs gave out. The flesh had burned away, leaving bloody, exposed muscle. As the uhaan flailed above her, Ylana slid out and crawled away, her leg crushed. The dragon's fire struck again.

And Ylana was in its path.

Tarathiel would never forget her horrible screams as she burned alive. Tiriel, on his way to help her, froze in shock.

A rain of ice shards suddenly clattered against the dragon's neck, unable to pierce through the rock-hard scales. Illuven had dismounted and threw everything he had at the dragon, aiming for its damaged wing.

Tarathiel let out a howl and quickly joined him. A burst of light nearby told him that Tiriel had also rejoined the fight. Tiriel and Ylana had been close—they would have been mates.

One of Illuven's spells hit its target. The dragon roared in pain as ice embedded itself into the tender wing membrane.

But the dragon caught on, moving to protect its weak spot. Tarathiel's and Tiriel's next spells missed their mark.

"Surround them!" Tiriel shouted over the noise. "They can't avoid attacks from all sides!"

Tarathiel and Illuven nodded and split up, running to opposite sides. In the corner of his eye, Tarathiel caught a flash—Tiriel hit the dragon with a bolt of lightning, momentarily stunning it to clear their path.

Once in position, they unleashed a barrage of magic; the beast twisted and turned as it tried to avoid their attacks. It reached out with tooth and claw, but the nimble elves kept out of reach. Roaring in frustration, the copper beast whipped its head around and let loose another stream of flame at Tarathiel, who narrowly avoided it. But the attack allowed Illuven to strike with a fiery blast of his own. The flame sped along the dragon's good side to no effect. Even the leathery wing appeared to be unharmed.

"Did you expect fire to work?" Tiriel called out.

"It was worth trying," was all Illuven said.

Neither side seemed to gain an advantage over the other. The dragon's scales were nearly impenetrable, and the dragon couldn't risk going for one of the elves and leaving their injured wing exposed.

In an unexpected move, the copper dragon suddenly lunged towards Tiriel, who hadn't fully recovered after delivering his latest bolt of lightning—perhaps the dragon was more clever than Tarathiel thought. Panicked, Tiriel sent a spray of sparks towards the incoming beast as he darted out its path.

But it was already too late.

Time slowed as its great maw closed around Tiriel's torso with a loud, sickening crunch, crushing the life out of him in an instant.

Tarathiel's vision went red with Tiriel's spilled blood. "No!" he roared, gathering everything he had for a spell to end the horrible beast.

"Tarathiel, don't!" Illuven called from somewhere far off, but Tarathiel ignored him. He ignored the dragon, too, as it turned towards him with its mouth open and glowing. Nothing could disturb his focus.

"Distract it!" he yelled, a bright blur signalling that Illuven was already moving, sword drawn, rushing towards the dragon to strike at the weak wing. Tarathiel nearly broke concentration as the dragon's tail unexpectedly whipped towards Illuven, smashing into his shoulder and knocking him aside. Illuven let out a cry of pain as he hit the ground, losing his grip on his glowing sword as he rolled across the rocky grass. He didn't get up.

Tarathiel roared, unleashing his charged spell upon the beast. A dark burst of raw energy rushed towards the dragon just as it belched another jet of flame. The beam of darkness cut through the fire to hit its target head-on.

Tarathiel fell to his knees, drained. As the shadow magic faded, he looked up and let out an anguished cry.

The dragon was still on its feet.

How? He tried to stand, but his legs wouldn't cooperate. *Is this it?* He closed his eyes, expecting death to descend upon him in a fiery rage, but nothing happened. Carefully, he looked up. The dragon hadn't moved. *What?*

Slowly, it collapsed with a tremulous sigh, the ground shaking with its dead weight.

Breathing hard, Tarathiel forced himself to his feet, swaying from exhaustion, his legs limp as he approached with one hand on the hilt of his sword. Was it dead, or was this a ruse to lure him in?

The dragon was still. So he drew his sword and jabbed it in the shoulder. No response. *Good.* Carefully lifting a wing, he checked for the rise and fall of its lungs, but the beast was utterly silent. Trembling, he let go and took a step back. He'd killed it.

With forbidden shadow magic.

His legs nearly gave out. He could use shadow magic? How? Since when? At least no one had been around to see it; otherwise, there would be trouble—more trouble than the strange appearance of a rogue dragon.

Illuven groaned from where he lay on the grass, pulling Tarathiel from his spiralling thoughts.

"Illuven!" He hurried over to his fallen lover. Illuven clutched his arm, curled up on his side.

"What's wrong? he asked, kneeling beside him.

"Arm—broken," Illuven gasped, his face damp with pained sweat.

Tarathiel cursed himself. He wasn't very good with healing spells, and mending broken bones was far beyond his abilities.

"I can't fully heal it, but I can help reduce the pain."

Illuven uncurled so Tarathiel could access his arm, making a distressed noise that pierced his heart like an arrow.

"Easy, my love, easy." Tarathiel got to work. He held one hand over Illuven's injured arm, gathering the remnants of his aural energy. For once, he prayed to the Ancestors, asking for their help. As he did, a faint blue light limned his hand, spreading along Illuven's arm. If the Ancestors heard him, they gave no sign, which didn't surprise him. Rarely did they intervene—if they even existed.

"How does it feel?" he asked, removing his hand. The light faded.

"It's not great, but I'll survive."

"We'll get someone to fix it properly once we're home." Tarathiel stood and scanned the scene, eyes resting on Tiriel's mutilated body. Fighting back revulsion, he approached and tore a strip of blood-free fabric from the fallen elf's outer robe.

"A sling. For your arm," he said, holding out the fabric to Illuven. "Now that the dragon is gone, the uhaan will return. Are you able to ride?"

"I believe I can." Carefully, Illuven slid his arm into the makeshift sling.

Tarathiel whistled, calling their wayward steeds, the magic infused in the sound compelling them to return.

While they waited, they examined the dragon's corpse. Neither could stomach investigating their fallen companions just yet.

Besides, they had never seen a dragon in the flesh before. Tarathiel had to admit the beast was impressive; it was nothing like the wolves and feathered serpents of the forest, which were unique in their own ways. This was different, with rock-hard scales, tough yet pliable wing membranes, and lethal teeth and claws.

But for all their searching, they didn't find any clues as to why the dragon was here and why it had mindlessly attacked them.

"Still feels warm," Illuven muttered, running his hand over the copper scales.

"Do you want a fang?" Tarathiel asked, deciding to take one as a trophy. Not many living elves could claim they were dragonslayers, not even those who had fought in the Great War. "You helped kill it."

Illuven shook his head. "I don't want another reminder of this day."

Tarathiel nodded and set to work removing one of the dragon's large canines. It was a difficult task, but he finally managed to cut it out with a spell. He carefully tucked it into the pouch on his waist. Perhaps he would have it fashioned into a dagger.

The three surviving uhaan returned, which meant they could no longer put off dealing with the bodies of Ylana and Tiriel.

Holding Illuven's good hand, they approached the spot where Ylana had been.

Very little survived the dragon's fire; all they could collect were some melted pieces of jewellery and ash. Neither of them spoke as Tarathiel scooped the ashes into a small pouch that had been strapped to her uhaan—the pouch containing the seashells she'd collected that morning. It was like a knife to his heart.

The smell of blood surrounding Tiriel's body was overwhelming; Tarathiel fought hard to keep the contents of his stomach down.

"Should we take him back with us?" asked Illuven, sounding just as queasy.

"No, I'll clip some of his hair." Doing his best not to look, he deftly severed a handful of Tiriel's golden locks with his sword. He tied a few around his wrist and helped Illuven do the same.

Illuven was shaken—he wore a look of weary horror mingled with pain from the state of his arm, and Tarathiel wondered if he really could manage to ride home.

"If you want to mount up, I'll collect his things," said Tarathiel, taking Tiriel's sword and several small items that were still intact. Leaving Tiriel's body there didn't feel right, but they had no way of bringing him back with them, not in this state.

"I'm sorry, my friend," Tarathiel said, weaving a spell. The ground beneath Tiriel churned, slowly pulling his body into it. All that remained was a patch of disturbed earth. Tarathiel cast another spell, moving a rock onto the spot and shaping it into a marker—two birds with their wings raised towards the sky.

They left the dragon's corpse to rot.

Twenty

Twisting Paths

Fae couldn't sleep. After the confession, Alysion had fled to bed. Not too long after, Gale had relieved him of his shift. He hadn't said anything to her. Laying in his bedroll was even worse than being on watch because he had nothing to distract him from his thoughts.

I like you.

What? *How?* Never had Alysion given him any indication that he was interested in him, leading Fae to believe his feelings were one-sided. Gale had been right about him after all. He should have trusted her intuition.

The memory of the first time someone had confessed their feelings to him came back—it had been a few decades ago, back when he'd been around the same age as the adolescent humans in Redwood. One of the girls had come up to him and blurted out her love, shocking him into silence. She had been the first of many; all wanted to 'marry' an elf. But this time, it wasn't someone he hardly knew. This was Alysion, someone he'd come to know fairly well over the past few moons.

Or had he?

He's not just Alysion. He's the Crown Prince of Sylandris.

And despite Alysion's ramblings disguised as lectures, Fae knew very little about Sylandris.

Well, what do *I know about him? He's a prince who doesn't get along with his parents, and he has powerful aural abilities.*

And that was it.

His heart sank.

But no, that couldn't be all of it. Perhaps Fae didn't know much about Alysion's home life, but he knew his personality. He could sense when Alysion's frustration stemmed from his self-deprecating thoughts towards his magical prowess as opposed to his hunger.

Yet he'd never noticed Alysion's desire. Was he that bad at reading the signs, or did elves show affection differently from humans? Fae wasn't sure. Every interaction they'd ever had took on a new meaning—but he'd go nuts if he tried to analyze everything Alysion had ever said to him. Fae was glad no one could see his face burning—the same way Alysion's ears sometimes turned red. *By the gods, I've been an idiot.*

There had to be some way to get this off his mind. He rolled over, using a meditation technique his master had taught him to help clear his thoughts before starting a new metalworking project.

It worked, but his sleep was restless.

To his dismay, he was treated to that memory again, rising with a start just as the sword thrust through his father's chest, warm blood splattering across his face. He sat up and touched his cheek, letting out a slow breath when he realized it was dry.

"You all right?" Gale asked softly from where she sat at the base of a tree.

"Yeah, just a dream." Now wasn't the time to tell her.

• • • ● • • •

"We'll find the crystal today," stated the prince, his confidence surprising Fae.

Had he had another prophetic dream? No, Alysion had the Sapphire in his hands and was circling the area. He made no mention of his confession.

Fae's head ached, and he wanted nothing more than to have some alone time. Between the confession and reliving his parents' deaths, his entire body was stiff and tight like someone had strapped lead armour to it.

He left Alysion to his aural tracking and went off to help Sy-Sy find something to eat, seeking a distraction from his violent visions. He touched his face, unable to shake off the feeling of blood. Even scrubbing his cheek with his sleeve did nothing to alleviate the sensation. *Damnit.*

He caught a glimpse of Alysion through the glittering trees and this thoughts swung the other way. Alysion *liked* him. What would happen if they were together? How would the Sylandrian court handle it? The captain wanted him dead; that was no secret. There was no way the rest of the nobles would accept him. He was simply too far down the pecking order. Not to mention that he couldn't give the royal family any heirs.

Fae let out a long sigh. Perhaps if he knew where his family had fit in, he could make a case for himself. They'd lived somewhere outside Lyrellis, far enough away that no one would accidentally find him. His parents hadn't ever let him go anywhere or interact with anyone. Fae had no idea if they'd been members of the court, warriors, or peasants. Could elves even be peasants? Perhaps it wouldn't matter. Being a damisri was enough to have him officially branded an outcast, regardless of his heritage. And if Alysion really was on such bad terms with his parents, he couldn't expect any aid from the prince since no one would give him their ear. Not until he was crowned king, which was a long way off.

Ugh, all this made his head throb. And his heart.

Sy-Sy bopped his shoulder with his muzzle, grunting in concern.

"It's all right, I'll be fine," he said, giving the uhaan's velvety cheek a good rub.

Sy-Sy lowered his head and sniffed the ground, searching for something to graze on.

"Right, let's try to find you something to eat, and some for the others too."

Despite Fae's optimism, they didn't have much luck and soon returned to the empty campsite. Fae was about to sit down when a voice rang out through the trees:

"I've found the trail!"

• • • ● • • •

Once Alysion had discovered its aural signature, he figured the crystal was no more than a day's ride away. They wasted no time setting out.

"I can't believe elves think this is a place to send thelim who misbehave. This forest is amazing," Fae said, breaking a bout of silence.

"I don't think anyone's been here since the crystal was hidden. The stories were meant to frighten the young, as a tactic to get them to behave," Alysion replied.

"And to keep people out of the forest," added Gale.

"But which came first, the stories, or the crystal?" asked Fae, trying to catch his eye.

Alysion shrugged and looked away, heart racing. Being so close to Fae made it hard to focus. His mind kept wandering to what he had said last night, the memory making his ears feel like they were burning off. Thank the Ancestors he was leading the way.

Why had he confessed last night? It was too soon! He needed to develop a solid plan to make his parents accept Fae first! Because if Fae liked him back, he had to find a way to make this work.

And it wouldn't be easy.

"As heir, it is your duty to carry on the royal line," his mother had reminded him thousands of times. At first, he'd agreed, but once his parents started introducing him to potential partners, he'd found that he had no interest in belim. While he understood the purpose and importance of carrying on the royal line, having a belim mate felt wrong.

Once, he'd tried to explain it to them; his mother ended up scolding him for half the day while his father merely watched. He didn't know what had been worse: her lecture or his father's pained expression.

"But other nobles can choose partners of any gender! Why can't I?"

"You're not like other nobles," was the only thing his father had said.

"As a direct descendant of the Ancestors, you are obligated to put aside your foolish desires and fulfill your duty," his mother had explained coldly. "How can our lineage survive if you do not produce an heir of your own? And you do have some choice in the matter—you may choose any of the noble daughters."

In the end, he'd fled the palace, wishing he had a sibling who could take this responsibility off of his shoulders. Royal couples were only able to have one child. Kings and queens of the distant past had been able to until a certain point; it had something to do with the Ancestors wishing to prevent a succession crisis.

For now, Alysion had to act like he hadn't said anything to Fae for the sake of this quest and his own sanity. *Once we have all the crystals, I'll figure this out.*

They passed a patch of soft grass growing between the colourful, tangled tree roots and stopped to let the uhaan feed. Unfortunately, it was nowhere near enough to sate the hungry animals.

Alysion took a few deep breaths. These distractions were only making it harder to focus on the crystal. The stone was doing everything it could to send him off course, and he could only sort out the false trails from the truth with the Sapphire's help.

As crystalline roots and vines crowded the path and threatened to trip them up, they dismounted, knowing the ground was too treacherous for the animals to pass while burdened with riders.

Alysion didn't like walking. It was slow and sharp; jagged bits of vegetation dug into his feet as he led his uhaan down the trail.

It wasn't until past sundown—judging by how sore and hungry they were—that Alysion told them to stop.

"It's around here somewhere. I can feel it." He handed Zen-Zen's reins off to Fae. With his wrist throbbing and giving off its telltale dim glow, he started poking around the area.

"Its box is likely made of crystal," Fae called out to him as he moved further from the group.

Alysion wasn't so sure. *From what we've seen, the earth crystal can manipulate both plants and stone.* He didn't believe that the crystal would be content with sitting in a box—not when it could create something more. He skirted some pastel trees, and his vision went green.

"I found it!" he hollered back at his companions. A massive tree of glowing emerald stood before him, branching out above with leaves so dark green they were nearly black. The tree's immense canopy covered the entire forest, blocking out the sky. Unlike the other crystalline flora, it provided no light.

"Aha! That's why it's so dark!" exclaimed Gale as she and Fae joined him, marvelling at the emerald tree.

"So," said Fae, eyeing the enormous trunk, "how are we going to take this back with us?"

"We're not," said Alysion. "This tree is the box." He touched the glass-like surface. "The emerald itself is contained within it."

"I don't suppose any of us brought a pickaxe? I'd rather not lose another sword to plants, especially not crystal plants," said Fae humorlessly.

"Pickaxe'd be no good," said Gale. "It can only be removed by magic."

Fae shrugged. The dots on his wrist flashed under his sleeve.

"This is going to be difficult," said Alysion, hand still on the trunk. "When I try to make any kind of connection with the tree, it pushes me out." He couldn't sense its roots, its branches, or the individual leaves far above them. The tree wasn't willing to let him in, not even when he used the Sapphire and Ruby—it didn't react at all to the other crystals' auras. He pulled back, frowning. How was he supposed to get the Emerald if he couldn't connect to it?

Fae pulled him from his spiralling thoughts. "Sometimes, when I'm working on a tricky piece for Master Cane, I can't go at it with the hammer like I normally would because it would ruin it. I have to be gentle."

Alysion stared at him blankly.

"What I'm saying is maybe there's a better way than trying to force it. Remember how you got the Sapphire? You had to be, uh, *nice* to it."

Alysion took a step back and looked up at the dark leaves, taking a few moments to relieve the tension building within him. "So I should try talking to it? What should I say?"

"Just ask if it wants to come with us!" Gale suggested.

"Wouldn't hurt to try," Fae shrugged.

Alysion didn't share their confidence, but he placed his hand on the tree again and closed his eyes. *Would you like to come with me?* he thought, imagining the question flowing down his arm and into the emerald giant. The tree's energy shifted, and his eyes snapped open.

"What'd it say?" Gale asked quickly. He must have made a noise.

"Sorry, I don't know yet. It caught me by surprise."

"But it responded to you?" Fae asked.

"I think so. Let me try again." He sent his question to the Emerald, and this time the tree responded almost immediately. The aural language—if it could be called such—was not easy to understand. The Emerald didn't speak only for itself; it spoke for the entire forest. After some time, Alysion deciphered what the Emerald was saying. He stepped away, drained.

"That's not a good face you're makin'," said Gale.

"It's a complicated answer. The Emerald isn't completely opposed to joining us. It seems to know that we aren't trying to steal it for nefarious purposes."

"Can it sense the other crystals?" asked Fae. Alysion nodded.

"That's good," said Gale.

"Yes, but if the Emerald is removed, this forest will lose its source of power. Since all the plants are connected to it..."

"Will everything die?" Fae asked after a moment.

"I can't be sure," said Alysion, flicking some hair over his shoulder, noticing how Fae's eyes caught the movement. "The Emerald isn't sure what will happen. That's why it's hesitant to join us."

Gale bent over to prod at some of the gemstone plants.

"Worst case is that everything dies," said Fae, thinking out loud, "and best case is they either stay the same or revert to their non-crystal forms."

"The Emerald likes this place, doesn't it?" said Gale, still poking around the plants.

"Yes, it's been here for so long. It'd be sad if the forest died."

"The Emerald would feel sad?" asked Fae.

"In a sense, yes," replied Alysion. "The Ruby has intense emotions sometimes." He often sensed something akin to jealousy from the burning crystal when he used the Sapphire; he made a mental note to use the Ruby more often.

"Easy, girl!" Fae called as Zen-Zen nearly pulled him over. She had her muzzle to the ground and was trying to eat a plant that hadn't fully crystallized.

"Wait a minute..." said Fae, falling silent for a moment.

Alysion and Gale exchanged a look.

"The forest has been here longer than the Emerald has," he explained. "The Emerald altered what already existed. Can it try slowly withdrawing its power? I'm sure if it's careful, everything will be fine.

"Won't hurt to try," agreed Gale.

Alysion reached out to the Emerald.

Twenty-One

The Past

"It's working!" Fae called out. A tinkling sound came from nearby, like two glasses tapping together.

Alysion turned towards the sound and saw the translucent pink leaves on a bush slowly fade to solid green. He touched the soft leaves and felt nothing—the Emerald's aura had gone.

A large snout pushed him aside as all three uhaan converged on the bush. Aside from the animals quickly consuming it, the bush appeared healthy; it didn't wilt or curl as the Emerald's aura faded.

Alysion let out a sigh of relief.

The Emerald continued, the tinkling growing as its aura slipped from the vegetation. Delicate crystal leaves slowly reverted to their natural forms, becoming soft, supple, and green. Branches and trunks lost their translucency, growing dark and opaque. The permeating glow slowly dimmed, plunging the forest into darkness.

"Looks like we're gonna be waitin' a while," said Gale. She broke out their kitchen set and prepared to cook something up. "You two go find some deadfall for the fire."

Fae motioned to Alysion to follow him into the forest. "Come on." It was exactly what he dreaded.

"So about last night..." said Fae as soon as they were out of earshot. A jolt of panic shot through him. He wasn't ready for this.

Ears burning, Alysion busied himself with picking up sticks the Emerald had released, mentally bracing himself for the worst. His heart pounded loudly against his chest; he feared Fae could hear it over the crackling sound of the changing forest. What if Fae wasn't interested in him? What if he had misunderstood what he'd overheard? What a fool he'd be!

"You're not the first to confess to me. Many of the girls back home have, and some of the boys," Fae said as he collected fallen twigs.

Well, that wasn't a bad start, though Alysion felt a lick of jealousy. Just how many human adolescents *had* confessed to him?

"At first, I was flattered. I finally felt like I was starting to fit in in the village. So I tried going out with a few of them, but it never worked out. The confessions eventually stopped once they noticed I was ageing more slowly than they were."

Alysion gave a disapproving sniff. He knew from his studies that relationships with shorter-lived races never ended well. Humans died centuries before elves did, leaving behind broken hearts.

"Being with them didn't feel right. It wasn't solely because they were human," Fae continued.

Alysion sensed eyes on his back, but he didn't turn around.

"But because I realized that they weren't attracted to *me*. Even though Sylandris is so close to Redwood, elves are still viewed as mysterious and exotic, just as they are throughout Odenia. If anything, the sentiment is stronger among the people of Redwood because they get rare glimpses through the barrier. In some places, elves are nothing but a fantasy. People will live their entire life without ever seeing one. We are something untouchable."

The fire in his ears had subsided, so he dared to look up at Fae. The other elf gave him a small, sad smile.

"The stories the humans tell of your home...I think even you would be amazed by how they describe it."

Alysion nodded, unsure of what to say. He fumbled with the sticks in his hands, but luckily for him, Fae was too caught up in his tale to notice.

"So when I became available, a living legend—" he snorted "—everyone jumped at the chance. I figure their families pressured many of the girls into it. Who wouldn't want children with elven blood? It would raise their social standing quite a bit even though I have none." Fae's humorous laugh rippled down Alysion's spine. "If only they knew what our people think of me."

Rage flared inside him—rage at his people and their stuck-up ways. Once he was crowned king, he would ensure Fae was accepted. No, he would start now. It was the least he could do for someone who had suffered so much.

"As for the nelim—the boys—well, I like to think their intentions might have been a bit purer. But by then, I'd given up on taking humans seriously."

Alysion's gut twisted. Had Fae taken *his* confession seriously?

"But then I met you and ended up on this crazy journey. Not once have I felt any doubt about you, not even when Urka confessed to me."

Alysion froze, not daring to believe what he was hearing.

"Ever since I met you, things have felt right. We've had our ups and downs, but never have my emotions wavered. I will admit, I never expected you to confess, especially since you're the crown prince and I'm just a damisri. I thought I would take my feelings to the grave. But now that I know how you feel, how can I?"

Time came to a standstill. Alysion didn't dare breathe.

Fae sighed. "But regardless of what I feel, I can never stand by your side. Your parents and your court will never accept me. We both know it. Among our people, I am someone—no—some*thing* to be ridiculed."

Alysion's heart was breaking. The sticks he'd collected clattered to the ground. Bringing Fae back to Sylandris would be, well, complicated. But he would do it. He would find a way. And he would make sure no one laid a hand on him.

"You don't know that," Alysion said, voice sounding steadier than he felt, hands balled into fists at his sides.

Fae blinked. "Excuse me?"

"You don't know it won't work. We haven't tried."

"In case you've forgotten, the captain has made it very clear they want my blood."

"I'm well aware of the risks," he snapped. "I know my people much better than you do. But there are ways." If his people wouldn't accept Fae, he didn't need them!

"You're not abandoning the throne for me. Besides, the Elithar would hunt us down for the rest of our lives if we ran away. It's no life to live."

Alysion fell silent, hating that Fae was right.

"Ash is still missing. I can't do anything to jeopardize my chances of finding him."

Ah right, his brother. They'd been so caught up with seeking out the crystals and avoiding everyone that he hadn't put much thought into the missing elf.

"Have you thought about where he might be now?" he asked cautiously.

Fae sat on a jutting root, and Alysion moved to sit next to him. When he spoke, it was slow and reluctant.

"While I was recovering from the effects of the canyon, I regained the memory of the day my parents were killed—the day I was found by Master Cane and taken to Redwood."

"You—" Alysion stopped himself. *He hadn't remembered how they'd died? No wonder he's been so off lately.* Alysion had certainly deserved that punch.

He listened intently as Fae recounted the memory, his voice occasionally cracking.

"My father tried to save me from their leader who had me in their grasp, but my cries distracted him, and a sword ended his life just as he completed the spell that sent me to Redwood." Fae shuddered, tearing up as his voice dropped to a whisper. "I can still feel his blood on my face."

Alysion's body moved of its own accord, his arms wrapping around Fae and squeezing him tightly. By the look on his face, it had been a long time since anyone had held him like this.

"I'm sorry," Alysion whispered close to his ear. He could have stayed that way forever, but eventually, he had to let go.

Fae wiped his misty eyes. "The elves who killed them and took Ash—I'm certain they're the same elves we encountered near Mt. Hissan."

Alysion opened his mouth, then closed it. It was possible; only a few decades had passed, hardly the blink of an eye for an elf.

"When we were ambushed, and the one elf had me pinned, I felt fear like I never had before. Back then, I didn't know why I reacted like that, but after seeing the memory, I realized they were part of the same group, if not the same individuals."

"Do...do you know why those elves came for your family?"

Fae's face twisted with discomfort as if he were about to be sick.

Alysion put a hand on his back and stroked it gently. It was hard to ignore the spark between them; he wanted to slip under Fae's shirt to feel the toned muscles of his back. *By the Ancestors, now isn't the time for this!*

"They came for me," Fae said, voice hardly more than a whisper. "They came to *correct the wrong*, to eliminate the elf who shouldn't exist."

Alysion sat in shock. How could anyone ever think about killing Fae? *Easily. The Ancestors don't favour him for whatever reason. Being a damisri is reason enough to send someone to deal with it.* But then he frowned, brow furrowing.

Something didn't add up. When the hooded elves had attacked them weeks ago, they hadn't recognized Fae. *Perhaps they'd been too focused on getting the crystals?*

Was there a connection between their attempt to kill Fae as a child and their desire to collect the crystals now? Based on their actions, they seemed to be a group of radicals trying to take Sylandrian law into their own hands. Alysion couldn't recall reading or hearing of a group like that, at least not one that had survived into more recent times. But there was one criminal who had been arrested for plotting against the court, for trying to take things into their own hands.

"I think the hooded elves might be working for Drath," Fae said quietly.

• • • ● • • •

"There you are. I was startin' to wonder if somethin' happened." Gale sat before her pot, waiting for them to return with kindling so she could start cooking. "You boys okay? You look like you've seen a ghost."

"We're fine," replied Fae, piling the wood beside the fire pit she'd made. He didn't have enough energy left to tell her about his memories. But he would soon.

"'Kay," she said, unconvinced. She didn't press for answers.

As they ate, the forest darkened. Some trees still glowed faintly, but the light was patchy and inconsistent. Upon close inspection, Gale declared it was a type of bioluminescent moss. When they had finished eating, the only magical lights remaining were the massive tree housing the Emerald and their glowing wrists.

"Think the Emerald's ready," said Gale. She got up and stood near the immense tree, watching as its green glow slowly dimmed like the setting sun. Both elves hurried to join her.

The tips of the tree's branches far above them began to revert as the crystal recalled the last tendrils of its power. The tree darkened, gemstone giving way to leaf and bark, its glassy surface becoming rough.

"It's getting smaller," said Fae, watching the branches retract in on themselves. The massive canopy shrank, allowing the sun's rays to shine through, passing the thinning trunk to the empty depression it left on the forest floor. An ordinary tree stood before them, a green stone resting at its base.

Alysion picked it up and staggered as their auras connected.

Fae was instantly at his side, catching him as he slumped over. "Alysion?" he asked, worry flooding his face.

"I'm fine," Alysion mumbled, making a weak attempt to shake him off.

Fae hid a smile and helped him back to the campsite.

"So, how do we get out of here?" asked Gale once Alysion had rested. Fae had taken the opportunity to fill her in on his memory.

"It will guide us," said Alysion, the green crystal in his hand. "Follow me and stay alert. The forest is no longer veiled."

"So, you're sayin' a forest suddenly popped up in that wasteland?"

"Yes."

Gale humphed. "So much for bein' discrete."

"I don't think there's anything we could've done to avoid that," said Fae, coming to Alysion's defence.

Gale shrugged. "Suppose the real issue is how we're gonna find Drath if you can't feel his crystals."

"I don't know yet, but if they want the crystals, then he or his elves may find us first," replied Alysion.

They wound their way back through the forest, amazed by its transformation. Though it no longer sparkled and glowed, it was still beautiful. Sunlight filtered through the trees, dappling the ground. Gone was the deathly stillness of the air; a cool breeze rustled the leaves, reminding them that autumn was on its way.

It didn't take them long to reach the edge of the forest, confirming that the Emerald had led them all over the place to confuse them. When they emerged, night had fallen over the rolling hills of the Manwan Plains, the grasses shimmering silver in the moonlight.

"Hold up, gotta make sure it's safe," said Gale. "Never know who might've—"

A sharp *twang* cut her off, followed by a dull *thud*. An arrow protruded from the tree beside her.

A horn sounded, followed by the pounding of hooves.

Beside Fae, Alysion went white. "Captain Anaril brought reinforcements."

Twenty-Two

Heated Clash

"We have you surrounded. Come out of the trees!"

"Who's that?" Gale asked, but Alysion merely shook his head.

"We'll shoot if you don't comply!" Bowstrings creaked behind them.

"What do we do?" asked Fae, trying to push down his panic.

"Just do as they say for now," said Alysion, tapping Zen-Zen's side with his heels. Fae and Gale followed him out of the trees. The elves behind them moved to cut off their potential escape.

Alysion was right: Captain Anaril had called in reinforcements. At least a dozen warriors surrounded them, some heavily armoured for battle, others dressed lightly for faster riding. He would have been impressed if not for how eyes flicked to him, expressions dark. They wanted him dead.

The circle opened to let Captain Anaril through on their sleek uhaan. If the chase over the past few moons had frustrated them, their face did not show it, but the reinforcements said it all.

"Dismount and step away from your uhaan, then drop your weapons," they said, giving Gale a cold look that would have frozen anyone else to the spot. The watcher wasn't bothered and hopped off her steed, pulling weapons out of places Fae would have never thought possible.

How had her uhaan carried all that weight? he wondered as the pile beside her grew. Some of the weapons he was certain he'd never seen before, like the small dagger she removed from her boot with a ruby embedded in its pommel. Maybe it was magical. She carefully laid the dagger atop the expanding pile. *At least she was prepared.*

Catching a chilling look from one of the warriors, Fae slid off Sy-Sy's back and slowly unbuckled his sword belt, glancing at Alysion, who nodded back.

Just go along with it, he seemed to say.

Fae placed his sword on the ground, Alysion doing the same. Next went the hunting bow Gale had given him, along with his dwindling supply of arrows. Unlike Gale, it didn't take long for the two elves to disarm.

"Enchanted artifacts next," ordered the captain.

Fae only had the heat-repelling talisman Gale had given them back on Mt. Hissan and readily dropped it. He couldn't help but wonder how many trinkets Gale was carrying—likely her body's weight worth if her weapon stash was any indication. He wasn't disappointed when she started dropping things to the ground: rings, pendants on cords, her leather bracers, and more.

"Think that's all," she said, giving herself a final once-over.

Alysion only dropped the heat-repelling talisman. He wasn't foolish enough to hand over the crystals, even if the Elithar were technically their allies.

To Fae's surprise, Captain Anaril didn't question it. Were they trying to keep the crystals a secret?

Several warriors moved forward to pat them down and check the gear still strapped to their saddles. They didn't find anything else.

After their inspection, the soldiers slapped metal bracelets inlaid with moonstones onto Gale and Alysion's wrists.

"The bands block aura. Any attempts to use magic will result in some unpleasantness," explained Captain Anaril, giving Alysion a pointed look as the prince tried to pull it off. "Mount up," they commanded.

Their hands were left unbound, but without magic at their disposal, the Elithar had nothing to fear from their captives. They rode in close formation around the trio, keeping them separated.

They were taken to the Elithar's camp, nestled between the hills to protect them from the elements. The tents—the same colour as the dying grass—were difficult to spot from a distance. The soldiers led their captives to the largest tent, forcing them to dismount their uhaan as they led the animals away. A pang of despair struck Fae at the thought of never seeing Sy-Sy again.

Fae looked over at Alysion, but his face was devoid of emotion. Gale's face was uncharacteristically blank. But Fae knew she was likely studying the camp's layout as they marched through it, searching for escape routes. Neither of them touched the silver bands on their wrists.

Most of the escort had left by now, with a mere pair of warriors accompanying them inside, positioning themselves before the door. Fae thought the tent was smaller than expected before noting the panels dividing it into sections. Captain Anaril stood at the back of the room, surveying them.

"So," started Captain Anaril, "the prince has decided to keep the company of an outcast and a supposed Dragon Watcher." Their eyes drifted from Fae to Gale as they spoke, passing over Alysion, who stood between them.

Fae remained silent, afraid that speaking would provoke the captain into killing him. His throat had gone parched.

"You," Captain Anaril said to Gale, their cold, sharp eyes fixed on her. "Who are you, and why are you travelling with the prince?"

Gale cleared her throat. "Name's Gale. Like you said, I'm a Dragon Watcher. Found these boys lost in the woods one day and decided to help 'em out."

The captain frowned; it was the first time Fae had seen them with an expression other than stoicism. "A likely story from a lackey of Murk Water—if that is indeed where you are from. You are after what Prince Alysion carries."

"Pah, if I wanted what he has, I could have taken it long ago. Yet here I am."

"We both know there are others out there. It would make sense to wait until more had been found before striking."

Gale snorted. Captain Anaril's eyes narrowed, and Fae suppressed a frightened shudder.

"I'm just doing my job of watchin' out for dragons and other nasties around Odenia."

"As a watcher, you should be aware that dragons are forbidden from crossing the Sky Peak range. There are wards in place to prevent this," stated the captain sternly, repeating what Alysion had told her many times.

"'Course I am, but better safe than sorry. Besides, dragons ain't the only danger out there."

Captain Anaril stared at her as if trying to reach her thoughts. Gale returned the look, unfazed.

Something unpleasant crept down Fae's spine as the captain turned their attention to him. He resisted the urge to look to his companions; he needed to appear strong even if he didn't believe it.

"Tell me, what is a damisri doing in the presence of the crown prince?" They spoke calmly, but Fae could detect the underlying threat.

Swallowing, he opened his dry mouth, praying his voice didn't crack. "I ran into Prince Alysion near Redwood, and now I am accompanying him across the lands."

The captain's eyes narrowed. "I don't have time for games. What is your true purpose? Who sent you to follow him? To earn his trust?"

Fae blinked stupidly. Who? "I-I'm not working for anyone," he stammered. Who could he possibly be working for? The hooded elves, maybe? Other damisri?

"Lying will get you nowhere," Captain Anaril said cooly, eyes narrowed.

A jolt of pain shot through his body, forcing a strangled cry of pain from his lips. He fell to his knees, staring wide-eyed at the tent floor.

"He's not working for anyone!" Alysion shouted. "Leave him alone!"

"Those without damai are exiles. You are well aware of this, my prince."

"He hasn't undergone the Silias. Look at him! He's my age!"

The captain ignored him, their attention back on Fae. Fae tried to suppress his trembling; he had to stay strong if he was going to convince the captain of his innocence.

"I will not ask again. Why are you travelling with the prince?"

"I'm helping him find what he seeks," Fae began. "I've been bound to this quest just as he has. Once we're done, we're going to find my missing brother." Fae raised his wrist, but the mark had faded once they'd collected the Emerald. Another blast of pain ripped through him. He fell forward, catching himself on his hands, hissing through his teeth, refusing to cry out.

"Captain Anaril! If you do that again, I will have you dismissed," Alysion threatened.

The captain ignored him. "Who are you working for?"

Shaking in agony, Fae braced himself for another jolt. He wasn't sure if he could handle it; his trembling limbs could hardly hold him up.

"I believe someone is plotting to overthrow the court," he said, daring to raise his head, expecting more pain. "A traitor."

The shock didn't come.

"A traitor? Like yourself?" asked the captain, their icy gaze boring through him as if trying to detect a lie. They snapped their fingers, and Fae's body froze. He tried not to panic as they turned their attention to Alysion. "Hand over what you have collected."

"No," he said firmly.

"You have no idea what you're dealing with—"

"I know he isn't a traitor!" Alysion cut in, ignoring the look Anaril gave him. "We were both marked by the prophecy. It wouldn't have chosen Fae if he was part of the problem. Instead of harassing him, you should be *helping* us figure out what Drath is planning! He's already taken a few of the others."

A distressed cry erupted from outside.

Captain Anaril nodded to one of the guards by the door. The guard hardly made it out before another came hurrying in.

"My apologies captain, but we're under attack."

"Who dares to attack us?" the captain asked.

"The ones you encountered in the Sky Peak Mountains."

Fae's stomach dropped; the hooded elves were back. He struggled against his invisible bonds.

"Mind freein' us? We can help you fight them," said Gale, holding out her cuffed wrist.

The captain gave her a stern look.

"At least let Fae go!" Alysion demanded, but Captain Anaril and the other guard were already striding from the tent.

"Don't worry, Princey, I got him." Gale pulled a slim packet of shimmery powder from her pocket and sprinkled some into her hand before blowing it over Fae. The instant it hit him, he could move.

"What was that?" he stammered.

"Special powder that helps with magical paralysis. It's undetectable 'cause it's just a ground-up plant. A mighty rare one, mind you."

"Thank you." Fae didn't want to know where she had gotten something like that; she had far too many tricks up her sleeve.

Two armoured Elithar pushed their way through the sides of the rear room panel.

"You are to remain with us," said one, sword drawn. The other didn't say a word, but she brandished her blade.

"Wouldn't you two be better off helpin' subdue the attackers?" asked Gale.

"Quiet," said the first one, taking a threatening step closer to the watcher.

"All right, keep your helmet on," said Gale, rolling her eyes and stepping to the side just as Alysion shot a dart of flame towards them.

"Get our stuff, I'll hold them off," he called out, launching another fiery blast to keep them occupied. Apparently, he could still use the crystals' magic even with the band on.

Fae and Gale rushed around the Elithar and pushed through the rear panel. Fae was alone in one small section and as Gale moved about in another beside him. Travelling gear cluttered the room, but none of it was theirs. He rifled through it, glancing up nervously, anticipating the Elithar would burst in. A whiff of burning fabric drew his attention to the flap he'd come through. Smoke was seeping in. *Please let that be Alysion's magic.*

"Found some stuff!" Gale called from across the divider. A blade poked through the flimsy wall; with a grunt, the watcher sliced through it. "Here you go!" She passed Fae his sword.

"Is our travel gear in there too?" he asked as he buckled it on. It was reassuring to have his sword back, even if it wouldn't do much good against sorcerous elves.

"Yeah, but we can't carry it on our own. Gonna have to leave it here and get more later." She tucked away various amulets and talismans as she spoke. Fae strapped on his pack. "Let's get Princey and get outta here!"

He followed Gale to the tent's main compartment, coughing as smoke filled his nose. The fabric walls burned quickly, the structure threatening to collapse. Fae's eyes watered as he searched for Alysion.

He had the Elithar backed against a burning panel, pinned down by streams of flame.

"Hang on, I got somethin' for 'em!" shouted Gale. She pulled out another packet of powder and tossed it at the warriors. It exploded in a shimmering cloud—the soldiers collapsed, unconscious.

"Let's go!" Fae hollered, tugging Alysion's arm.

"We can't just leave them!" he protested.

They dragged the Elithar outside—a difficult task as their armour made them heavy and awkward—and deposited them a safe distance from the burning tent.

"It'll wear off soon. Let's go!" Gale called above the sounds of battle.

The camp was in complete chaos. Even though the sun had set, everything was well lit; the captain's tent wasn't the only one ablaze. Elithar ran to and fro after the attacking elves, who were nowhere to be seen. But they were here, the blasts of magic hitting the camp signalling their concealed presence.

"This way," said Alysion, "I saw them put our uhaan with the rest."

"Can you get the bands off us first, Princey? Or at least yours?"

Alysion lay his other hand over the band and screwed up his face in concentration. The band began to glow, first yellow, then orange.

"What are you—?" Fae started to ask, but all he got in return was a harsh hiss. He winced once he realized what Alysion was up to; the smell of burning flesh was difficult to ignore.

Within moments, Alysion shook the band off, the magic inside it burned away. Fae tried not to look at his wrist—which now sported a horrible, blistering red mark—nor at the smouldering grass beneath the cooling metal.

"That's gonna scar," said Gale.

Alysion shrugged and pressed his hand—blue with the Sapphire's power—to the mark, soothing it. "Let's just get out of here," he said, his voice strained.

Slowly, they wove their way over to where the uhaan were tethered at the edge of the camp. But getting there was no easy task—they were forced to duck behind burning tents whenever the Elithar got too close or when a colourful bolt of magic came shooting towards them. The hooded elves were putting up quite the fight.

As they rounded a corner, Fae nearly ran into an Elithar's polearm before Alysion stunned the soldier with a burst of magic. He pushed his way to the front.

"I'm the only one who can sense auras at the moment," he said, keeping Fae behind him. Fae suspected he had another motive but didn't argue.

The fighting hadn't reached the uhaan, but the animals were restless, bothered by the clamour of battle.

"You keep watch. I'll grab them," said Fae.

"But—" started Alysion

"No buts. I don't have magic—they won't sense me. And I'm better with animals."

Alysion wasn't happy, but didn't stop Fae as he worked his way over to their tethered uhaan. He didn't think twice as he pushed through the masses of furry bodies, clicking his tongue as he went to make sure they knew he was there. The last thing he needed was to spook one and end up on the receiving end of a bone-shattering kick.

"Sy-Sy," he called out as he neared the uhaan. Sy-Sy flicked an ear in his direction. Fae called again, and the uhaan turned towards him.

"Hey boy," he said, giving Sy-Sy's thick neck a good rub. He happily bobbed his head.

"I know. I was worried about you too. Let's get you and the others untied, okay? Gale and Alysion are waiting for us." He untied all three of them and checked their tack, noticing the pages had left them saddled. It was more than he could have hoped for; riding bareback through the fighting would have been a challenge.

As he turned to lead them back to his companions, a bright light flared, followed by a raging cry.

That can't be good. He mounted Sy-Sy, steering the uhaan around the herd with the other two in tow, heart pounding as he rejoined his companions.

Alysion glowed a fiery red, summoning a massive fireball and hurling it at the approaching elves.

Fae shielded his eyes as it exploded, turning night to day. But not even that could deter them. They continued their approach a little more singed than before.

"I have them!" Fae hollered.

"Great!" said Gale, swinging onto her dun uhaan. "C'mon Princey, get yer royal butt up here."

"Give me a moment!"

"Now!" said Gale, reaching down and grabbing him by the scruff. "You can blow up people later, you crazy pyromaniac!"

Alysion looked abashed but mounted up, the glow around him fading to a charming pink. It wasn't a bad colour on him.

"Better shut off that light; we'll be too easy to follow," said Gale as they took off into the night, not caring which way they went as long as it took them away from the camp. The pink glow faded to nothing. "Those elfies and the Elithar'll be on us soon enough."

• • • ● • • •

The trio didn't stop until their panting, sweat-soaked steeds demanded it. When they reached the far side of the hill, they dismounted, walking the animals beside them to recover their strength. Since they didn't have any of their gear, there was no camp to set up, nor any food to cook. They would hunt at some point, but for now, all they had were the few snacks in Fae's bag.

"Sleep for a bit. I'll keep watch," said Gale.

"Don't you need to rest?" asked Fae.

"I'll be fine. Part of watcher trainin' was to go without sleep. Never know what could happen while you're out and about in the wilds!"

Fae wasn't convinced but was too exhausted to argue. All the fear and anxiety coursing through his system had worn off, leaving him utterly drained. He flattened a patch of dying grass and curled up. He'd just shut his eyes when soft footsteps approached. Alysion.

"Hey," he said, quietly enough that Gale wouldn't overhear.

"I thought 'hey' was no way to greet anyone," said Fae, sitting up.

"I don't think our relationship has progressed enough for me to call you 'beloved'," retorted the prince, sitting close enough for their shoulders to touch. Neither moved away.

Fae let out a shaky breath, feeling wide awake again. *Beloved?* "No, it hasn't. You confessed then left me in the dust."

"I just...got scared." Alysion's shoulder trembled next to Fae's. He let out a slow breath. "But, it's something I've been feeling for a while. I just didn't know what it was right away. It took you falling into the canyon for me to figure it out."

"That's why you were so angry. Not because of my lack of a damis, but because you were worried about me."

Alysion nodded, the moonlight turning his hair a silvery white. "Part of me was disappointed to learn you didn't have a damis—another part of me was terrified. We both know getting the court to accept us will be difficult, but it's my parents who will be the hardest to deal with. They've told me time and again that part of my duty as future king is to produce an heir, which means I have to find someone to be queen. When I explained to them that I have no interest in belim, they didn't take it well, especially my mother. So I ran away and eventually met you by the barrier."

Fae blinked. He'd thought Alysion had run away for something trivial, but this was something else. As royalty, he didn't have to worry about day-to-day survival, but the pressure and emotional demands of being the prince were harsh. Add in parents who wouldn't even hear you out, who treated you like a thing instead of a living, breathing elf, and you had the makings of a disaster. "I see why you left."

"My parents are always on my back about everything. This journey has been a blessing. If we can find all the crystals and stop whatever is coming, they may listen to me. Maybe they will see that I'm not useless." Alysion stared at the ground.

Fae hadn't known his parents all that well, and having been raised by the master blacksmith, he couldn't relate at all to Alysion's situation. For the most part, he'd been happy living with Cane. He put a reassuring hand on his back, a touch that Alysion leaned into.

"Knowing how hard things will be," Alysion said slowly, staring at the ground, "I understand if you don't want to be with me."

"I'd appreciate it if you looked at me when saying those kinds of things," said Fae, a hint of annoyance creeping into his tone. "As for us, here's what I think about it."

Alysion looked up, and Fae gently claimed his mouth with his own. Alysion's lips were even softer than he ever could have imagined. He closed his eyes and breathed in deep through his nose, taking in the other's familiar foresty scent, his heart racing. To his delight, Alysion groaned quietly, opening his mouth to him, trying to give as much as he was receiving. His mouth grew hotter, and their kiss became rougher, messier. It didn't bother him that Alysion didn't seem to know what he was doing; he would teach him.

Alysion made a noise that sent a spark of heat straight through him, fanning the flames of desire. The prince's hands were on his back, pulling him down. Fae eagerly obliged; they fell into the grass, limbs entangled. As he explored Alysion's body, feeling every dip and curve, he desperately wished their bothersome clothing wasn't between them. But that would have to wait until things weren't so dire. *We will get through this,* he vowed, never wanting to give up his prince.

Eventually, they fell asleep in each other's embrace, their heated bodies keeping each other warm in the cool late-summer night.

The sun was beginning to peek over the horizon when Gale woke them.

"All right, you two, enough of your smoochin'. Them elfies are catchin' up!"

Twenty-Three

Flight

"I sense the Elithar and the hooded elves. The latter is quickly catching up to us," said Alysion as they galloped across the prairie. "I sense another aura, but I'm not sure what it is. I think it's coming from their mounts."

"Prolly using somethin' to give their steeds a boost," mused Gale. "Not good news for us. Can't shake 'em off out here."

They were back out on the open prairie, having left the hills during their frantic escape the previous night, leaving them exposed.

Fae's spirits sank. They couldn't outrun their pursuers; they would have to fight.

"I'm sure that with the crystals we've collected, we can handle them, or at least buy ourselves enough time to come up with a better plan," said Alysion, trying to ease the mood as they pushed their mounts to the limit across the endless sea of dying grass.

"Unless they have some crystals too," said Fae.

Alysion shook his head. "I don't sense any with them."

That was only a minor relief. Fae hoped it wouldn't come to fighting—the prince was the only one who stood a chance against them since Gale still had the aura-suppressing band on. Or did she? Fae glanced at her wrist, but their gait was too rough for him to see.

The sun was barely above the horizon when Gale called out for them to slow to a walk.

"All right, boys, the uhaan need a break. They haven't recovered from our run last night." She was right—their steeds' sides heaved beneath them from the strain of galloping for hours.

Gale looked over her shoulder and frowned. The elves followed her gaze to the dark blot of riders in the distance. And they were gaining speed.

"Whatever those guys are ridin' ain't natural," she said. "We've got two options: we run until they catch us, or we confront 'em on our terms."

"How far away are the Elithar?" Fae asked Alysion.

He concentrated, picking their auras from the others. "They're behind the dark riders, but I'm not sure how far."

"So we can't expect the captain to help us."

Alysion shook his head. "Likely not." He scanned the flat terrain around them. "But I have an idea. You two keep going."

Fae gave him a worried look but nodded when he saw a faint green emanating from the crystal pouch. Hopefully, Alysion knew what he was doing; Fae had never seen him use earth spells before.

"Be safe," he said as he rode past. As powerful as Alysion was, Fae didn't like leaving him alone.

• • • ● • • •

When Fae and Gale were a reasonable distance away—and their pursuers closer—Alysion dug the Emerald out of his pouch.

It was a shame he hadn't gotten the opportunity to practise using the Emerald's power, but if he could handle the other two crystals, he should have no problem using it; it had willingly joined them, after all.

Closing his eyes, he focused on the green gem, strengthening their bond and willing it to do as he wished. The Emerald brushed against his consciousness—calm like the Sapphire but with a rougher edge. Opening his eyes, he leapt from the saddle and pressed it to the ground.

Alysion nearly collapsed as a massive shock wave of green light rippled across the plains, heading straight for their pursuers, widening as it went. As it swept over the grass, the ground quaked and rumbled, splitting apart as jagged rocks burst from the earth. Their sharp tips pointed towards the sky, each one about as tall as a pine tree and closely resembling them in shape. Within moments the entire section of flat prairie between him and the riders had been turned into a forest of impassible stone, stretching far to either side. Alysion could hardly see them through the new wasteland of rock.

Hah, let's see them get past that. They'll have to go around! The Emerald pulsed, pleased with their accomplishment. "Not quite a crystal forest but close enough, eh?" he said, swelling with pride. "Let's catch up to the others!" Zen-Zen, stamping the ground uneasily, needed little encouragement.

"Nice work, Princey," said Gale when he caught up, clapping him on the back.

Her praise pleased him, but Fae's appreciative smile pleased him more. His ears warmed as memories of last night came flooding back.

"They'll have to blast their way through those rocks or go around," he explained. "Either way, it's going to take some time."

"That's one way to solve the problem," said Fae, twisting around in the saddle to survey Alysion's work. His heart skipped a beat.

"Don't get too comfortable just yet," warned Gale. "Dunno if that trick'll hold 'em as long as we'd like. Them elfies are pretty skilled and darned determined. So's the crusty captain."

"I could use the Emerald to build us a protective shelter," he suggested.

Gale shook her head. "Can't hide in it forever, and we've got no supplies. We're not prepared for a siege."

Alysion used the Sapphire to track the riders' auras throughout the day. The elves had gone north around the stones instead of pushing through. Hopefully, it would be enough for them to escape; they couldn't rely on Anaril to help them now.

The sun eventually gave up the sky to the twin moons. Both were nearly full—a rare occurrence, their light bathing the landscape in silver. According to his studies, magic was strongest beneath two full moons. He had yet to experience the phenomenon, for it only happened once every few millennia. The next would occur on the coming winter solstice.

But he had more pressing matters to deal with now.

"They're catching up," he said.

"How long until they reach us?" Fae asked, turning to face him.

As he moved, the moonlight danced across his hair, drawing the prince's attention. When Alysion first met him, Fae's hair had been black with white tips, but now, white came in at the roots. Did it always grow like that, one colour to the next? Was it a side effect of not having a damis?

"Alysion?" Fae prompted.

Alysion prayed Fae didn't see the red in his cheeks. "Sorry, I'm just trying to figure it out. It's hard to get a proper feel, given how quickly they can move." *Good save.* Even though their relationship was out in the open, some things were still too embarrassing to say. "They'll be upon us shortly, so if we want to plan something, we'd best do it now."

"May as well stop then. No sense in tirin' ourselves out more if we don't have to. Shame we don't have any more snacks. Melann's buns were delicious," Gale stopped her uhaan and dismounted.

Alysion's stomach reminded him it was indeed a shame they had no snacks. "I could put up a wall of rock around the riders," he suggested, dismounting.

"That might hold 'em for a few moments, but not much more," said Gale. "After that stunt you pulled, they'll know we have the Emerald and be ready for another trick. Think the Emerald can even do something like that again after just usin' it?"

"Yes," he replied, never doubting the crystal's power. But whether or not *he* could was another story. The strain of the day was catching up to him, and he reluctantly let out a yawn.

"Right, I think you need some proper rest, Princey," said the watcher. "You two may have gotten cozy last night, but it wasn't much of a break. Try to get some sleep for now, and I'll wake you when they're closer."

"Don't you want to sleep? You stayed up all last night," said Fae.

"I told you, I'll be fine." The edge to her tone told them it wasn't up for discussion.

Alysion shrugged and went off to make himself comfortable on the ground. Fae soon joined him in the tamped-down grass nest. He had no idea how he managed to fall asleep while so wound up, but when it did eventually claim him, he wished it hadn't.

He was holding Fae's hand, showing him around the palace. They stepped through the doorway of his bedroom, and Alysion found himself standing alone in a dark void.

"Fae?" he called out in panic. *It's just another memory, probably from the Emerald.*

But it didn't feel like a shared memory. No, it was more like the visions he'd received of the thief taking the crystals. Alarm shot through him. Had the thief found the last crystal? The back of his neck prickled—he was being watched.

"Is someone there?" he asked, his voice steady and confident as the crown prince's should be. His hand instinctively went for the pouch around his neck. The leather felt soft and real in his palm—too real for an ordinary dream—but his connection to the crystals was oddly diminished.

The darkness shifted. Alysion wasn't in a lightless void—murky clouds swirled around him, reminiscent of the Canyon of Lost Souls and its river of black smoke.

A violet light beamed straight down from the swirling masses above him, continuing past his feet and disappearing into the nothingness below. Carefully, Alysion shifted his weight, confirming something solid but invisible beneath him. It did little to ease the growing unease gnawing at his innards.

Something dark appeared within the beam, emanating a threatening aura. The shape took on an elven form—the thief reaching out to him? But that idea was quickly squashed when the elf emerged from the light.

Though nothing more than a dark shadow, Alysion knew they weren't the thief. They were shorter, for starters, and bulkier, as if clothed in many layers.

"Who are you? Are you Drath?" Alysion demanded as the figure stepped towards him.

They held up a glowing purple crystal—the Shadow Amethyst. The hood pulled low over their face meant the violet light wasn't bright enough to illuminate their features.

"I am the one who seeks what you possess." Alysion couldn't tell if the elf spoke aloud or in his head.

"And what might that be?" He prayed he sounded confident.

"I thought by now it would be obvious," said the voice.

Whoever this was, they couldn't be much older than him. Their voice lacked the depth of age and experience that Gale's and Anaril's had. But it was distinctly male. Hearing it made him think of Fae; he hadn't heard many voices belonging to nelim his age. Which meant his elf couldn't be Drath, since Drath was at least a few centuries old. But then, who were they and why did they have the Amethyst?

"I'm not giving anything to you," Alysion said firmly.

"That's not up for debate."

"It certainly isn't. I'll keep what I have, and you'll continue on your way." Alysion no longer had to fight to keep his voice steady.

The robed nelim raised an empty hand. The prince didn't have a chance to prepare himself before something slammed into him, sending him spinning into the void. He smacked into the invisible floor, rudely reminded of its existence. Damn, this dream hurt.

"All right," he muttered to himself, getting up, "have it your way." He called on the Ruby, its power trickling into him. But before he could gather enough for an attack, he was struck again.

This time, everything went dark.

• • • ● • • •

"Gale, he's not waking up," Fae leaned over Alysion, who'd been tossing until a moment ago when he'd suddenly gone still. It took everything Fae had to remain calm.

"Is he breathin'?" Gale asked, eyes on the rapidly approaching riders nearly within firing range.

"Yes, but that's about it."

"'Kay," was all she said. All their plans relied on Alysion's magic; without him, they were powerless.

"Should we—?"

"Fae, do you trust me?"

Fae met her eyes and nodded.

"Good. Get him on Sy-Sy and flee. I'll hold them off while you wake him up."

It wasn't much of a plan. Fae didn't want Gale to sacrifice herself, but if it allowed him to save Alysion...

Without a word, Fae mounted his uhaan. Gale slung the unconscious prince across his lap, who flopped in a very undignified way. Had he been awake, Alysion would have been mortified by such treatment.

"Will you be all right?" he asked, part of him wishing he could stay and confront his parents' killers with her.

"Don't worry about me. I have a surprise for 'em." She passed him a bag of medicinal herbs before securing her own to Sy-Sy's saddle. "Snagged 'em off one of those snotty elfies. They might wake him."

"Thank you."

"Now go!" She slapped Sy-Sy's rear, and the uhaan shot forward, Zen-Zen loyally galloping alongside them. "And don't look back!"

Twenty-Four

Taken

Fae couldn't look back even if he wanted to. It took everything he had to keep Sy-Sy's mad dash under some semblance of control, all while preventing Alysion from slipping off. And somehow, he was supposed to wake him up.

He tied Sy-Sy's reins together, letting the uhaan run free. Using one hand to hold the limp prince in place, he used the other to dig through the medicinal pouch he'd clasped in his teeth, pulling out all kinds of dried plant bits and vials of powder. He held each one to Alysion's nose as he'd seen the herbalist back in Redwood do. None had any effect. *Bet I need that phoenix grass for this,* he thought with exasperation. Or maybe Alysion had to ingest them, which meant they would have to stop. That wasn't going to happen.

A tremor shook the ground; the uhaan kept running. Fae looked back, but the ride was too rough to make out anything, even with the twin moons in the sky. All he could discern was a large blurry, dark shape where Gale had been. Guilt washed over him; he shouldn't have left her alone. As amazing as she was, her chances of surviving were slim. Hopefully, whatever had shaken the earth was the surprise Gale had mentioned.

Fae tried the herbs again. "Come on, wake up," he mumbled around the fabric in his mouth.

A brilliant light flashed behind him, followed by a terrible roar. Both uhaan sped up, their eyes rolling and mouths foaming with effort. Fae's heart sank. *Gale.* Whatever was happening did not bode well for her.

Slipping the bag of herbs around his wrist, he made no attempt to stop or slow the animals. He would deal with Alysion once they had put more distance between them and the fight.

The uhaan only started to slow once their adrenaline wore off. Sy-Sy's sides trembled beneath him; they were already beyond their limit.

"You're doing great," he murmured, giving Sy-Sy a comforting pat on the head.

Since the herbs weren't working, Fae had another idea. He awkwardly eased his hand down the front of Alysion's shirt, feeling for the leather pouch. To his dismay, it was sandwiched between him and the saddle.

Don't drop them, don't drop them. He slid the small bag out of Alysion's shirt and poked a finger inside just as Sy-Sy stumbled from exhaustion. Time stood still as the Sapphire slipped from the pouch, bounced off Sy-Sy's leg, and disappeared into the grassy void.

Gods be damned!

Fae snatched the reins and gave them a sharp tug, trying to turn the uhaan around. "Whoa there, boy, we have to stop!" Sy-Sy slowed, too tired to resist. The uhaan was still moving when Fae slipped out from under Alysion and half fell to the ground. He raced across the grass to where he thought he'd seen the blue crystal fall.

No no no no! He frantically searched the tall grass on hands and knees, finding nothing. If only he could *sense* auras! But he couldn't, and the Sapphire did not light up to help him. *Idiot!* Of course he would drop it!

"Fae?" a weak voice called out.

He straightened and turned towards the sound; somewhere close to the uhaan, their sides lathered in sweat. "Alysion?"

The prince slid from Sy-Sy's back and wobbled, putting a hand on the uhaan's heaving flank to steady himself.

"What's going on?" He sounded a bit out of it. "Where's Gale?"

"Gale is holding off the riders—you wouldn't wake up, so she told me to leave with you," he explained quickly. "I tried to wake you but dropped the Sapphire. It's around here somewhere." He went back to frantically searching for the blue crystal.

"It's there," Alysion pointed. "Its call pulled me back." Fae followed the tip of his finger.

Something glinted in the moonlight. Fae snatched it up with relief and gave it back to him.

"Let's get going. Gale's been keeping them busy for a while, but I doubt she'll hold out much longer." He looked back to where they'd left her, but a strange blackness obscured the area. "Can you ride?"

Another terrifying roar split the air.

Fae peered harder into the darkness. Some shapes broke out of it, moving towards them with unnatural speed.

A glance at their mounts told him that both were spent, especially Sy-Sy, who had carried them both so far. They could not outrun the dark force hurtling towards them.

"They're coming," Fae said, drawing his sword and feeling terribly useless.

Alysion nodded and clutched the pouch, the Sapphire safely tucked back inside. But he was in no condition to fight; his eyes were shadowed with exhaustion, and his body was worn thin—a slight breeze could knock him over.

The riders, to Fae's surprise, didn't immediately assault them once they were in range. Instead, they formed a circle, trapping the young elves inside. Their steeds were twisted versions of uhaan, thin skin clinging to skeletal bodies with hooves sharp as blades. Strange black mist wafted off of them, emphasizing their strange white or red eyes. Fae caught a glimpse of sharp teeth.

"You're coming with us," one rider said, staring down at Alysion. Was she their leader? She wore nothing that distinguished them from the others—no crests, no badges.

But Fae couldn't think about that now. Seeing his parents' murderers up close filled him not with fear but with overwhelming hatred.

"What did you do with my brother?" he demanded before he could stop himself.

The leader hardly spared him a glance.

All sense of caution flew away like the prairie winds had blown it out of him. With a savage snarl, he raised his sword and lunged.

"Fae, no!" Alysion cried.

His sword collided with something solid but unseen, pushing him back with such force he could barely remain on his feet. A faint red barrier separated him from the leader, who looked down at him from under her hood.

"Now, isn't this interesting. You survived all these years?" she said. "I'll never understand why your father saved the useless one."

Fae's breath caught, and he went cold. Had she been there?

"Shut up!" shouted Alysion. He glared at her with an intensity Fae had never seen before. "You have no right to speak to him like that!"

It was comforting to know Alysion was mad on his behalf.

Someone in the circle snorted.

"Capture the prince," the leader ordered.

Alysion grabbed Fae and pulled him close, creating a dome of earth around them. It shook as the riders' spells struck it with explosive force, but it did not break. For the moment, they were safe.

"This won't hold them for long," said Alysion, shaking. Save for the faint green glow coming from the crystal pouch, they were in pitch darkness.

"How many more spells do you think you can cast? Big ones."

"Maybe one or two, depending." He sounded weary. "I could try dropping fire on them, but it'd set the grass on fire too."

With the prairie grasses drying out as autumn approached, using fire wasn't something they wanted to risk. Not unless they were truly out of options. The dome shuddered harder, dirt and roots raining down upon them from the incessant barrage.

If only Gale were around to help. Could they do something with the Sapphire? There was no water nearby, and summoning or creating water would take more energy than Alysion had left. "Can the Emerald do anything else?"

"Its magic is defensive, but I might be able to do something."

"Could you bury them?"

"I could, but they'll get out eventually."

"That's not what I meant."

Alysion's eyes widened. "You mean *kill* them?"

Maybe he had overstepped a boundary. "They'll kill me if they catch us."

Alysion looked green, and it wasn't from the Emerald.

"Can you trap them like this?" Fae suggested, pointing to their shelter. "Just make the earth extra thick."

Something powerful hit the dome, and their knees buckled from the impact. A sliver of moonlight fell across Alysion's face. They were out of time.

"On my signal, I'm going to drop this dome and hit them. Ready?" Alysion said, holding out a hand to him.

Fae laced his fingers into his, their pulses beating against each other. "Do it."

The dome blasted outwards. Chunks of earth smashed into the unsuspecting riders, knocking them from their steeds. A few, including the leader, kept their seats, but maintaining their shields put a strain on their abilities.

Alysion took advantage of the confusion to call up the earth. But before he could entrap them, he let out a sudden gasp and fell to the ground, his spell dying.

"Alysion!" Fae called out, dropping to his knees beside him. "Alysion, wake up!" Panic consumed him as he shook the prince's shoulder, trying to rouse him. He couldn't let them take him away!

He hardly noticed the roar echoing across the prairies, nor the frightened shouts that followed. Awkwardly, Fae hauled him up; Alysion was as lifeless as a ragdoll. Another roar—this time from directly overhead—rang in his ears. Something was wrong.

He looked up, buffeted by a sudden gust of wind that nearly blew them over. He froze in terror.

A massive dragon circled above them.

"By the gods," he whispered.

The dragon's mouth opened and let loose a stream of white-hot flames, scorching the elves furthest away. Batting their great wings, the dragon landed heavily and roared again, golden eyes blazing in the moonlight.

Fae stood rooted to the spot.

"Look out, Fae!" the dragon said, their voice familiar.

Gale.

So many things about her suddenly made sense: her knowledge of the land and the creatures inhabiting it, her affinity for the wind.

"Idiot boy," a voice hissed behind him.

The leader raised a hand burning with magic. Magic that would instantly end him if he moved. Two others came around either side and roughly pulled Alysion away.

"Leave him alone!" Fae snarled, hand itching to draw his sword. He would *not* lose anyone else to these murderous elves!

The leader grabbed Alysion's face. "If you want him unharmed, I suggest you keep still," she said.

Fae's heart tore. He refused to let them take Alysion, but the threat stayed his hand. The elves—and Alysion—disappeared into the surrounding chaos.

"Good boy. Now, you die," said the leader, unleashing a bolt of purple lightning. Fae closed his eyes, wishing that he'd been able to save Alysion, that he'd been able to find his brother.

But the void of death never came.

Gale's fiery breath intercepted the spell, incinerating it. If his eyes hadn't been closed, the intensity of the flame would have blinded him. When he did dare to open them, the black riders had turned and fled, Alysion in their grasp.

"Gale!" he hollered. The dragon bounded towards him, the earth shaking with each massive step. It was difficult to see the colour of her scales in the silvery moonlight, but he suspected they were red like the streaks in her hair.

"They've got Alysion!" he shouted, pointing at the group making their way towards something bright—a gate. All the riders who could still move raced towards it, eager to escape the dragon.

"We can't let them take him through!"

"Climb on and hold tight," said Gale, her deep dragon's voice resonating with age and untold power. She knelt, and he climbed up her shoulder, settling between her wings and the base of her neck. There was nothing for him to hold onto, so he hugged her as tightly as he could with his arms and legs as she loped towards the gate, lacking the time or distance to get airborne.

The first few elves had already made it through, but Alysion's dead weight slowed the others.

We're going to make it! Fae thought, trying not to get too excited.

Gale opened her maw and let loose another burst of flame; the fleeing elves dispersed to avoid it.

"Careful, don't hit Alysion!"

He felt Gale huff, and he shut up. Who was he to tell a dragon what to do?

One of the elves carrying Alysion released him, clutching their flaming arm. But the leader took their place, snatching up the prince. All three glowed red for a moment, then shot toward the gate like a falling star, disappearing in the blink of an eye.

"No!" Fae screamed as the gate began fading.

"Hold on." Straining, Gale charged. But she wasn't going fast enough—they wouldn't make it.

"Gale!" he cried. "Faster!" He couldn't lose Alysion!

"Jump!"

Without a second thought, he lept from her back. Before he touched the ground, a blast of magical air shot him across the grass. And towards the gate.

"I'll catch up!" was all he could make out before he hurtled through.

Part Five

The ride back to Sylandris felt as if it took decades, but Tarathiel would not risk further damaging Illuven's arm.

"I'm fine. We can ride faster," Illuven insisted.

"You are *not* fine. I don't want any more deaths on this trip."

"I'm not going to die," said Illuven quietly.

"But your arm could be permanently injured." That was something Tarathiel would not stand for.

They reached Sylandris near sundown. As they passed through the wards, Tarathiel sent out a distress signal. It didn't take long for a patrol to find them and send his message up the chain of command.

Darkness had fallen when Captain Anaril met with them. "We're here to open a gate. It will take you directly into the palace where their Majesties are waiting," they said. Judging by the sizeable force the captain brought along, they were already on their way to investigate the corpses.

"Is there a healer with you?" Tarathiel asked. Illuven needed to be seen right away.

"One has been dispatched to the palace," replied the captain.

Tarathiel nodded to hide his annoyance, then dismounted. He went to help Illuven, but the other elf shook him off.

"Only my arm is injured; my legs are fine."

Try as he might to hide his pain, Tarathiel caught how Illuven winced as they walked through the gate, keeping space between them so as to not antagonize the princess.

The palace was an enormous multi-level structure carved within the hollowed trunk and sprawling branches of an ancient tree. Supposedly, the Ancestors had planted it millennia ago for their descendants. Tarathiel wasn't sure if he believed such a thing.

They found themselves in the Lunar Hall on the ground floor, where gatherings and celebrations were usually held. It was packed with nobles when Tarathiel and Illuven arrived, all of whom were listening intently to the queen and princess, seated on a dais facing the entrance.

Princess Lymsia looked bored on her wooden throne. The queen, clad in luxurious robes of embroidered light blue silk and a finely-wrought silver circlet inlaid with star-shaped stones, was harder to read. She'd married into the royal family. Her mate, King Othillion, had succumbed to injuries he'd sustained in the Syl-Raanian War while she had been pregnant. Othillion was a descendent of the Ancestors, passing down their divine lineage to his daughter, Princess Lymsia, who now eyed Tarathiel unpleasantly. The heir was always the opposite gender of the divine parent and never *aelim* like Captain Anaril. The Ancestors had done this to ensure equality throughout the kingdom. Tarathiel found this notion comical; he'd never trust the snooty princess to lead anyone, much less an entire kingdom. Perhaps if she'd grown up with a father, she wouldn't have turned out so bad.

"There they are," said the queen, tapping her staff on the polished wooden floor. It was a slender, twisted piece of wood with a clear, fist-sized crystal resting within the fork at its apex. The branch had come from the very tree containing the palace.

All turned to the newcomers. Tarathiel immediately dropped to one knee in a bow. Illuven awkwardly tried to follow, but the queen's hand stayed him. "You're injured. Let us tend to that first."

A noble stepped forward. Tarathiel recognized the court's most powerful healer, the *eranyl*, Silanniel.

"Let me inspect the injury." He had light blue eyes and golden hair typical of his lineage. Of course, his hair was still nothing compared to Illuven's. Besides, Illuven would one day surpass him in magical prowess if he hadn't already. Tarathiel was sure of it.

Illuven nodded, doing his best to hide his discomfort as Silanniel removed the sling, though perhaps Tarathiel alone could see his pain. No one else knew him that well, not even the princess.

Tch. Just seeing her annoyed him, and from the expression on her face, the feeling was mutual. She glared at him from her seat; it took everything he had to keep his face neutral. Antagonizing her in front of the queen and all these nosy nobles would not go over well.

"Certainly a break, but an easy fix," said Silanniel. As Tarathiel had done in the hills, he held a blue-limned hand over Illuven's arm, muttering as he worked. Within moments, Illuven was flexing and stretching it.

"Thank you, Eranyl."

"You are most welcome, Illuven-*sera*," replied Silanniel with a slight bow.

Tarathiel bristled. Sera was only used for the future royal consort.

"Now that your injury has been taken care of, please give us your account of the events that transpired," said the queen. "Illuven-sera?"

Illuven explained how the ride out to the cave had gone well, that they hadn't seen any signs of a dragon the first time they passed through the rocky hills. When it came to describing the fight and the deaths of their friends, his voice wavered, but Tarathiel believed he was the only one who noticed.

"If we'd had any warning, Tiriel and Ylana wouldn't have perished," Illuven said as he finished.

The court was utterly silent, shocked by the appearance of a dragon in forbidden lands.

"And you?" Princess Lymsia addressed Tarathiel, breaking the silence. Her rudeness didn't go unnoticed by the court, but her mother didn't stop her. "What is your report? How did you alone manage to return unscathed?"

Tarathiel could nearly *feel* the blame she was placing upon him. He was a threat to her; he would have to be careful.

"I was simply lucky. As Illuven explained, I didn't get too close to the dragon. Needless to say, I wish I'd been injured instead of Illuven."

The princess gave him a dark look, but it disappeared from her face before anyone apart from Tarathiel took notice.

"I don't have much to add to Illuven's account."

"If I may ask a question," said Panoma the *arlian*, the court's most powerful spellcaster.

"Granted," said the queen.

"What spell did you use to kill the dragon?" she asked him.

There was no point in lying. When the dragon's corpse was examined, they would discover his magic's shadowy aura.

Tarathiel cleared his throat. "It was a type of magic I've never used before, so I'm not entirely sure what it was. It felt like light magic, only," he took a small breath, "darker."

The nobles muttered amongst themselves. The queen and Panoma exchanged a look.

"That explains why your aura feels different," stated the princess.

Tarathiel stared at her, her tone and the strange gleam in her eye making him uneasy. His aura had changed? Was that even possible?

"Tarathiel Greyleaf, are you aware that shadow magic has been banned from this kingdom for centuries?" asked the queen.

"Of course, Your Majesty. I wasn't even aware that I could use it. The spell simply came out when I saw that Illuven had fallen."

Illuven nodded beside him.

"Why did you slay the dragon?" Princess Lymsia asked.

Tarathiel and Illuven looked at each other, thrown for a loop.

"The dragon attacked us without warning and killed two of our friends," said Illuven.

Lymsia narrowed her eyes. "Did you attempt to speak with them?"

Tarathiel's annoyance flared up like dry wood on a campfire. "Neither side made any attempts to communicate," he said. "There was no opportunity for it. Any stalling would have led to injury or death. The dragon—"

"That's rather convenient," she said.

Tarathiel blinked in shock. Convenient? What about all of this was *convenient*?

"You happen to come across a mad dragon, and of the four, *you* alone return unscathed. And you used a forbidden form of magic to accomplish it." She looked from him to Illuven and back. "I believe that this was all a plot—one that failed miserably, but a plot for you to run off with Illuven-sera."

Tarathiel and Illuven stared at her dumbfounded. How in the name of the Divine Ancestors had she come up with something as ludicrous as this? He glanced at the queen, a sinking feeling coming over him as she considered the nonsense her daughter was spouting.

"I beg your pardon, Princess," said Illuven, polite as always, "but we rode back as fast as we could. We were slowed by my injury, but I can assure you that we had no intention of running off into the wilderness. As for the spell Tarathiel used, I am grateful that it slew the dragon, regardless of what kind of magic it was."

His words warmed Tarathiel's heart.

"Of course, you were unaware of his plans," she said. "You never would have allowed him to lead a dragon into the region."

The floor swayed beneath his feet. What was she saying? Was this actually happening?

"I despise dragons," Tarathiel spat.

"Then why do you spend all your spare time researching them in the library? For someone who despises them, you certainly put a lot of energy into learning everything you can about them."

"That's—"

"Pardon me, my Princess," Illuven interrupted, "but I think you have the wrong impression of my friend. He has no love for dragons and would never conspire with one."

"It's about time that Illuven-sera be shown to his chambers. He needs rest after this ordeal," said the princess.

"I'm feeling quite fine," he replied sternly.

But the queen, by some unspoken agreement with her daughter, waved a hand and summoned attendants to escort Illuven from the hall. He went without protest, casting a concerned look at Tarathiel.

Tarathiel knew where this was going. The princess controlled the whole situation, warping it to suit her needs, and her mother was on her side. They wanted him out of the way.

"Tarathiel Greyleaf," said the queen, still standing. "There is reason to believe this incident was a plot devised between you and the dragons to stir up trouble for the royal family, and by extension, the entirety of Sylandris."

Tarathiel watched the nobles. None of them appeared shocked by the queen's statement, and they shot him disapproving looks.

By the Ancestors, they're all against me! All because she is jealous of my relationship with Illuven!

"What reason is that?" he asked sharply.

"You are the only one who returned unscathed, and you have a motive: to keep the future king from assuming his role in favour of your own desires," announced the queen.

"This is ridiculous!" he snapped, losing his composure. "I would never work with a dragon. Never! I've spent my entire—"

"Is there any way for you to prove that? Are there any witnesses or evidence you can provide?" Lymsia asked coldly. The crowd muttered.

Oh, how he wished the dragon had killed her instead! She was the only one their age who hadn't gone on the disastrous trip.

"Illuven gave you his account of the incident."

"But Illuven wasn't with you before the outing. He was here at the castle, training," she replied. "He cannot say whether or not you were meeting with dragons before this happened."

Tarathiel's vision went red. He took a few slow breaths to calm himself.

"It's unlikely that someone followed you around night and day. There were plenty of opportunities for you to slip away to plot with the dragons," she continued.

"If you knew anything about me, you'd know that I've spent my entire life studying how they were left unpunished for the crimes they committed against our people during the war."

Princess Lymsia shook her head. "You claim to study dragons; does that not only further prove your guilt?"

"I've been studying them so we can exact proper revenge upon them!" It felt strange to admit what he'd been doing the past few decades to the entire royal court; he'd only ever told Illuven.

"Ah, I understand," she said, a fake smile on her lips, her mind working against him to twist his words.

"So your plot was to kill one of the hated beasts to start a new war against them while also stealing away the future king. And now, my final question: how did you manage to get a dragon through the Sky Peak wards? Is that what you've illegally been practising shadow magic for? Or was the magic simply to flaunt your disregard for our royal decrees?"

Tarathiel couldn't believe what she was saying. And that no one was stopping her. The nobles whispered in hushed voices while the queen looked on in silence, agreeing with this nonsense. They would do anything to add Illuven to their royal line.

This is all to get rid of me, the threat to her relationship. Ridiculous.

The hall was quiet, waiting for him to answer the princess' questions.

"I have no idea how to get through the Sky Peak wards. I'd never left the forest until now. And as I explained earlier, I didn't even know I could use shadow magic. You said it yourself; my aura has changed. This is the only time I have ever used it, and had I been aware of what I was doing, I would not have. If we're going to get picky, I used it outside of our borders." But his words fell on deaf ears. "If you're so concerned about my relationship with Illuven, then why did you allow him to come on the outing? Why didn't you come yourself?"

"I had royal duties to attend to."

Tarathiel suppressed an eye roll, jaw clenched.

"Illuven-sera requested it," said the queen. "We didn't want to deny him one last adventure with his childhood companion."

Childhood companion, right. He frowned, slowly piecing things together. No, it couldn't be. Had they planted the dragon there to frame him, to tear him and Illuven apart?

Given the expression on the queen's face when Illuven had described the attack, he didn't believe she was aware of its existence. Princess Lymsia, on the other hand—he wouldn't put it past her, and it would account for the shoddy planning. It wouldn't be too difficult for her to learn how the Sky Peak wards worked; as a member of the royal family, she had access to safeguarded knowledge.

"Considering the danger you put him in to disrupt this court, perhaps you were using Illuven, too," the princess continued, "and your relationship with him is merely a ruse for your hateful goals."

"How dare you make these accusations! I would never use Illuven! I love him more than anything!" Tarathiel snarled. He was angry—at her, at admitting his feelings before the court. He was losing the last shred of his dignity, but he didn't care. He wouldn't let her slander their love.

"Enough!" said the queen, banging her staff on the polished wooden floor. "It is time to make a decision, one that will be carefully thought through," she said pointedly at her daughter. "Take him to one of the holding rooms."

Tarathiel wanted to fight back, but he couldn't afford to make the situation any worse. He shot a look of pure loathing towards the princess as he allowed Elithar to escort him out. They slapped a metal band over his wrist, suppressing his aura. Never before had his abilities been weakened like this; it was deeply unsettling. He hated feeling vulnerable.

His cell, like the Lunar hall, had been formed in the base of a tree. Once there, he flopped onto the bed and examined the band in a poor attempt to take his mind off everything: it was a simple strip of silver inlaid with bits of moonstone. If not for what it could do, it would have been lovely. *Whoever enchanted this must have been incredibly powerful, likely a Brightstar of the past.*

Anger flared up in him. He stood and paced the confines of his cell, needing an outlet.

"How dare they! They're the ones who defied their own treaty, and for that, they will pay." He resisted the urge to punch the wall, knowing it would bring him nothing but pain. "Damn her."

After what felt like forever, the door opened. Two elves approached; Captain Anaril and one of their lackeys. Wasn't the captain supposed to be examining the scene of the attack? Tarathiel narrowed his eyes.

"We're here to escort you," said the captain. "Your sentence has been decided."

When he returned to the Lunar hall, it was packed with elves, from the highest born to the lowest. Tarathiel steeled his expression and held his head high as he approached the throne, unwilling to allow the Elithar push or pull him along. If he was careful, he might be able to win the crowd's favour, making it difficult for the royals to exile him.

A quick scan of the hall showed him that Illuven was nowhere to be found. That did not bode well. As king-to-be and a victim of the incident, he should be there. *They don't want him around because the crowd will side with him.* Illuven had always been popular among their people, more so than Lymsia, despite her blood.

"Tarathiel Greyleaf," said the queen, standing to address the crowd. "You have been accused of conspiring with dragons in order to disrupt the court and bring chaos to our lands."

A quiet muttering passed throughout the crowd, and the queen paused, letting it sink in. Noble gossip would strengthen the case against him.

"After careful consideration, we have found you guilty of treason and using forbidden shadow magic," announced the queen to the now silent congregation.

Tarathiel glanced up in shock, white-hot rage boiling within. He shot a look of pure venom at the princess, but she ignored him, staring out into the clamouring crowd. One day, he would get revenge on her. One day.

"There is only one punishment for treason," continued the queen, tapping her staff to call for renewed silence. "Though you are still a child, you are near enough to adulthood to be treated as one. Due to the gravity of your crime, you are no longer considered one of our people. You, Tarathiel Greyleaf, will undergo the Silias and be henceforth exiled from Sylandris."

Tarathiel, seething, could only nod obediently. He longed to cause a scene, but the guard would be on him in an instant—his life was forfeit, after all. Until he underwent the Silias and passed through the wards, he was somewhat protected; if he ever dared set foot in Sylandris, he would be fair game. If he could rid himself of the exile's mark, that is.

"May I make one small request?" he asked.

The hall went dead silent again. A sentenced traitor making a request was highly unusual.

The queen motioned for him to speak.

"I would like to say farewell to Illuven before I depart."

The crowd held its breath as the queen exchanged a look with her daughter, who exercised tremendous effort to contain her anger. Good.

"We will have someone bring Illuven-sera to you," said the queen, standing. She banged the staff on the floor a final time, signalling the end of the gathering. The crowd lingered as they cast judgement on the scene, gossiping none too quietly about his sentence, giving Tarathiel a wide berth as the Elithar marched him from the hall. No one wanted to be associated with a traitor who conspired with dragons.

• • • ● • • •

Illuven never showed up.

Tarathiel ground his teeth as the Elithar escorted him through a gate in the forest, far from unwanted eyes. *That damn princess!*

His anger momentarily abated when the gate dropped him—not at the border, but onto the grounds of the Great Temple; a place elves only visited during times of strife or ceremony. The Striiya would be taking place here less than a moon from now, but he wouldn't be attending. Nor would Tiriel or Ylana. Illuven and the princess would be the only one receiving their tattoos.

His heart sank. How had things gone so wrong? His friends were dead, and he would never see Illuven again. All because of one jealous princess.

They approached a large wooden statue of the Ancestors in the middle of the temple grounds, surrounded by various twisting trees housing halls and towers. A plain wooden dais stood at the Ancestors' feet with several elves clothed in black, silver, and violet waiting upon it. Floating flames provided some light, illuminating their unnaturally white hair—a side effect of the initiation ceremony that strengthened their damai and spiritual connection to the Ancestors.

The isidyll was said to speak and act on behalf of the Ancestors, but Tarathiel didn't believe that for one moment. He'd never seen the Ancestors do anything for anyone. *It's all a sham.* But he didn't doubt the disciples' aural power; he'd seen it during the Solstice and Equinox festivals. These elves were not to be trifled with.

At a gesture from one of the ayel, the guards led him onto the dais and stepped back, leaving him with the temple's keepers. Rage blazed up again, obliterating his growing fear.

"Kneel," said one.

Tarathiel did as he was told, for what else could he do? He had no chance of fighting them off, and even if he did, there was still the Elithar. He had nowhere to go.

He bowed his head and closed his eyes, fury churning beneath his skin.

"We begin." He heard them move, forming a circle around him. The wind picked up, and light flared against his eyelids. Over the sound of rustling leaves, the elves chanted, but it wasn't a soothing festival chant that promised prosperity—it was something much more sombre, as if the Ancestors derived no pleasure in abandoning one of their own. Tarathiel ignored it, focusing instead on his vengeance, keeping his violent rage close to his heart.

Excruciating pain ripped through his chest. He threw back his head and screamed as his damis throbbed. Magical energies crushed against it, threatening to shatter his very being. How did anyone survive this?

Tarathiel was on the verge of blacking out when something inside him pulsed. Something familiar. Desperate to escape the agony, he embraced it, letting it consume him. The pain faded. The power grew within him with speed; it would kill him if he didn't release it. Unconcerned with the elves around him, he let loose the very magic that had contributed to his sentence. The disciples cried out in disbelief as their magical light was snuffed out.

Before he could make sense of it, darkness took him.

Twenty-Five

The Temple

Fae woke beneath an unfamiliar canopy of leaves. Dazed, he slowly sat up, taking stock of his new surroundings. Then it all came back with the force of a stampeding herd of nuu: Alysion, the elves, Gale hurling him through the gate.

He jumped to his feet and swayed, a wave of dizziness washing over him. He steadied himself against an enormous tree; it was far too large to be an Odenian tree. Sylrandris, he was in Sylandris. But as to where he was in the immense forest, he had no clue. If only he had a damis, he could track the Alysion and the crystals!

There was no sign of Alysion's captors, either; no footprints or disturbed plant life. Had he ended up somewhere else?

Great—just what he needed. Alysion was in danger, and now he had to wander around this gods-forsaken forest to find him.

This would be a lot easier if Gale were here. Fae still hadn't gotten over the shock of seeing her massive dragon form. Well, at least he'd been right to be suspicious of her. Questions buzzed in his head—why was a dragon in Odenia, and how had she gotten through the wards? He shook them away. *Focus.*

The portal had opened facing southeast, meaning he travelled northwest through it. He peered up through the trees to locate the rising sun. *There.* Having no better plan, he continued heading northwest.

The air shimmered before him. Given how large the trees were, Fae didn't think it was the Sylandrian ward; he would have seen the smaller Arrow Branch trees beyond it. Bracing himself, he stepped through. A bout of dizziness made the trees spin, but he shook it off. The bigger concern was whether or not the wards had alerted anyone to his presence.

At least they can't track my aura.

He picked up the pace, wanting to put as much distance between himself and the wards as possible.

Not long after passing through the barrier, Fae slowed, catching a glimpse of something through the thick undergrowth between the massive trunks. Cautiously he crept forward, trying to make as little noise as possible as he crouched down in the dense foliage to peek through the leaves.

Before him was a sprawling temple complex formed from living trees encircling a courtyard. A towering statue of two elf-like beings stood in its centre, facing the opening of the circle.

The tree towers were nothing like his childhood home. Somehow, the living trees had been hollowed out, allowing elves to occupy the entirety of the trunks and—in some cases—thicker branches, woven together to connect the silver-railed verandas spreading from tree to tree. The tallest of the towers stood directly across from the courtyard's opening; just by looking at it, Fae could tell it was important. His eyes flicked back to the statue, and a long-forgotten memory slowly resurfaced. He'd seen this place before; a drawing in a book. This was the Great Temple, and the tall tower was the Ancestral Hall, built to house the Ancestors when they ventured into this world. He remembered asking his dada when the Ancestors had last come, but Dada told him that no one had seen them for a long time.

His heart ached at the thought of his father.

Fae remained crouched in the bushes near the opening. Why would these Ancestor-worshipping elves want to help Drath, a known traitor to their people? Not only had they kidnapped the prince, but they'd murdered Fae's parents. Had the Ancestors sent their lackeys to his home to eliminate a blight—him, the damisri? As ill as it made him feel, he could see that connection. But why would the Ancestors want a traitor to disrupt the court? The mysterious hooded elves behaved more like cultists than worshippers. No, the Ancestors had nothing to do with this; Fae was sure of it. Something else was happening here.

All right, enough wasting time. Alysion needed his help *now*.

Fae scanned the courtyard, his sense of unease growing in the oppressive silence. Since they had Alysion, he figured the place would be a flurry of activity—he took the empty courtyard as a bad sign. It didn't help that the air felt wrong, similar to what he'd experienced in the canyon, a deeply unsettling sensation that struck to the very core of his being. He fingered the hilt of his sword. Is this what it was like to sense auras—minus the doom and gloom? He nearly laughed, for he found himself wishing he couldn't feel it.

The scent of sandalwood wafted through the air so intensely it was as if someone shoved incense up his nose. Fae stifled a cough, not sure if he'd been found out, and readied himself for an ambush.

Elves in sweeping robes of silver, black, and violet swarmed into the courtyard. They faced the gap in the circle, pointed towards Fae's hiding spot. Their hoods were down; all had the same short, unnaturally white hair the colour of bleached bone.

The back of his neck prickled uncomfortably. Despite his lack of damis, they must have known he was there. He had two options: flee and get shot at, or give himself up and hope he lived long enough to save Alysion. If he misstepped, he would surely be killed, and Alysion would have no hope of escaping. No one aside from himself and Gale knew he had been taken, and only Fae knew where.

Heart pounding, Fae slowly stood, revealing himself to the group, praying he was making the right decision.

The elves muttered as he approached but made no move to attack him. Instead, they parted, allowing him to step to the statue's base unhindered. As he neared, he saw a dark shape slumped on the wooden dais at the statue's feet. *Alysion!* It took everything he had to resist scrambling over and holding him tight, reassuring his prince that he was here and everything would be fine.

Fae tried to read their expressions, but the robed elves kept their faces devoid of emotion. Though the elves appeared calm, he could sense their murderous intent; it wasn't a feeling disciples of the Great Temple should invoke. *Which of them did it? Which of these elves attacked my home that day?*

They moved to fill space behind Fae, trapping him. As he made it up to the dais, Fae's eyes raked over Alysion's crumpled form, searching for signs of life. He had no visible injuries, nor blood or bruises, but that didn't mean much when magic was involved. His chest rose and fell in a reassuring rhythm; Alysion was still alive. Fae intended to keep it that way.

The eyes of every disciple bored into his back as he crouched beside Alysion and gently lay a hand on his shoulder. From this close, Fae noted how pale his skin had turned.

"Hey," Fae said quietly, every muscle tensed for a fight as the disciples whispered amongst themselves. Fae couldn't make it out.

Alysion cracked open an unfocused eye, staring at him unblinking for a few heartbeats. "...Fae?" he whispered, voice cracking.

"I'm here."

"—shouldn't have followed," Alysion mumbled, trying to sit up.

"Why not?" Fae helped him with a trembling hand.

"Not safe...for you." His voice rasped with exhaustion. What had they done to him?

Fae's anger flared, but he did his best to tamp it down. If he lost control, he was bound to do something unwise.

"How are you feeling?" He feared the prince had an internal injury that he couldn't ever hope to detect or treat.

"Fine, just tired," Alysion wearily replied. "I woke up when we came through the gate and tried to fight them off, but I wasn't successful. The isidyll took the crystals from me."

Fae surveyed their surroundings as Alysion spoke, searching for anything that might help them escape. The sea of robed elves was impossible, and they had the statue to their backs. If only Gale were here—but she was somewhere on the Manwan Plains, unaware of their location. They were alone.

He should tell Alysion about her. But he was nearly asleep in Fae's arms, too weak to sit upright by himself. That would have to come later.

"What are you doing to my captive?"

Fae looked up as the crowd of elves nearest the Ancestral Hall parted. A dark figure outfitted in light leather armour strode towards the dais. Their hair, unlike the others, was long and retained a hint of blond. Fae gasped in recognition, fear rooting him to the spot. *It's him!* This was the one who had caused so much misery and pain in his life, the one who had led the attack on his home, who had used him—a small child—as a shield against his father's attacks.

"Who are you?" Fae asked, fighting to keep his voice steady. He held Alysion close.

"Ah, so you did survive, Faeranduil. Interesting how fate brought you here."

"What do you mean by that?" Fae demanded.

"You'll soon find out." The elf stopped once he reached the dais. "Now, step away from the prince; we still require his assistance. If you behave, perhaps he'll be returned to you." The older elf's eyes flicked to Alysion for a heartbeat, a strange expression flashing briefly across his pale face.

"I won't let you have him!" snarled Fae, knowing how desperate he sounded.

"That's not your decision to make."

"It's time!" announced a voice, magically carrying across the courtyard. "It's time to bring forth the last crystal and claim the throne for ourselves!"

The gathering of elves broke into cheers.

Fae stood in front of Alysion, keeping the prince between the statue and himself. His hand wavered over the handle of his sword.

The crowd parted again to admit an elf in elaborate layered robes of white and silver, their face hidden beneath their low hood. The spiritual leader of the temple, Fae surmised. Was this Drath?

The isidyll stopped at the bottom of the dais, but the pale elf hopped up and stared down Fae. "Stand aside," he said, a wicked blade appearing in his hands like he'd pulled it out of thin air.

Glancing at the blade, Fae was surprised by his lack of fear despite knowing it guaranteed his death. Perhaps it was because Alysion's safety was on the line.

"I won't!" He drew his sword.

The older nelim struck fast and hard. Only Fae's reflexes, honed from sparring with Gale, saved him from being sliced in half. The elf struck again, and it was all Fae could do to block the bone-jarring attack. He was severely outmatched—landing strikes of his own would be impossible.

Don't give up! Protect Alysion!

The surge of attacks slowly pushed Fae from the prince, who, to his surprise, had made it to his feet. A sudden burning sensation bloomed across his upper arm as his opponent's thin blade tore through his skin. *Don't look at him, don't get distracted.*

But Fae was weak from their journey, already tiring as he gave everything he had to block the endless barrage. His reflexes slowed. The thin blade landed more frequently, each cut burning like fire. Fae's vision swam, hazy with the pain he tried and failed to ignore.

"You know," the elf said too quietly for anyone else to hear, "you're doing well for a damisri orphan. Though I am curious as to why you're interested in protecting a kingdom that doesn't tolerate your existence."

The elf slashed a final time, sending Fae's sword spinning out of his hands. It clattered on the dais beside him. A cold blade pressed against his neck.

"We didn't come for *you* that day," the older elf whispered in his ear. Fae suppressed a shudder. What was he talking about? What else could they have—? The blood suddenly drained from his face.

"Don't!" Alysion called out.

This was it. This was the end. He'd failed Alysion, and he'd failed Ash.

"Drath-ayel," said an unfamiliar voice. "Hold for now."

Out of the corner of his eye, something white moved. The isidyll ascended the steps and stood before the prince.

"If you give up the last crystal, the Kunzite, your companion will live," said the isidyll.

Alysion gave him a hard stare, his expression betraying no signs of exhaustion Fae knew burdened him. "Will you guarantee our safe passage out of here if I do?"

"No!" gasped Fae. Drath's blade pricked his skin, drawing a line of blood. *I'm not worth it!*

But Alysion said nothing else.

"I shall grant it," said the isidyll.

"Then you'll need to outfit me for this quest, as I don't know where the Kunzite is."

The isidyll laughed. "Oh, my prince, you have no idea, do you? The Kunzite is right here." He pressed the tip of his index finger to Alysion's chest, right where his damis resided.

Twenty-Six

Reunion

The prophecy's mark flared up, blazing on Alysion's wrist.

"What are you talking about?" he asked, eyes narrowing as he pushed the isidyll's hand away. Though standing was exhausting, he needed to buy them time to develop a plan.

The isidyll smirked, amused by Alysion's ignorance. "Don't you find it strange that the elves closest to the Ancestors are the ones plotting against you?"

Of course I find it strange! But Alysion remained silent. His eyes flicked to Fae. Damn, they needed to come up with something quickly.

"The Shadow Amethyst was given to me as a gift, and I will use it to facilitate my revenge!" the isidyll said.

Revenge? If Drath was the one holding Fae, then who was the isidyll? The strange dreamlike encounter on the plains hadn't revealed anything.

"I was told," continued the isidyll, "that if we collected the crystals—the artifacts used in the war to slay the vorais—then we would possess enough power to strike at the court for the hurt they have caused us."

Alysion nodded along. Using what little power he had, he touched the isidyll's aura but couldn't detect any lies. He went further and checked the elf holding the blade to Fae's neck. Alysion's gut churned, recognizing the aura he'd felt at the light crystal's hiding spot. This was the elf who was plotting against them, the one who wanted to turn their world upside down. And he was only one crystal away from accomplishing it.

"If you know how to get the Kunzite, then you may have it," said Alysion. "Don't forget that you've promised to let my companion and I go once it is in your possession." Except Alysion had no intention of giving it up—he would take it and use whatever power it granted to get himself and Fae out of here. And for once, he didn't care if he took lives doing it.

Alysion braced himself. If this crystal was indeed inside him, taking it out was bound to hurt.

"Careful, Isidyll Navir," said Drath, "We may still need him."

The isidyll didn't acknowledge Drath as he closed his eyes, chanting in a harsh language Alysion didn't recognize. He raised his hand, glowing with the power of the six crystals it held.

Agony tore through him, as if his damis were being cut away with a rusty knife. Fae shouted, but all sound morphed into incomprehensible noise amidst the pain. He had to fight, but how could he? He could hardly think.

Pain became everything: his thoughts, his aura, the very essence of his being. It was inescapable. All he could do was pray for its swift end. The last thing his mind registered before darkness took him was a pair of familiar brown eyes.

Fae.

• • • ● • • •

"Alysion!" Transfixed with horror, he watched Alysion crumple as the Kunzite emerged from his body. It blazed bright pink, floating to the isidyll's chest while the remaining six crystals drifted from his hand, hovering in a circle around him. Heeding the call of the rosy Kunzite, the crystals glowed, bathing him in a rainbow of light. They flickered, sending out a shockwave of energy that buffeted everything in its path.

The blast had blown back the isidyll's hood, revealing a face Fae would never forget.

"Ash?" he whispered, mouth dryer than a desert.

His brother didn't hear him. Beams of light shot out from the crystals, connecting with Ash's damis. Slowly, he rose into the air as if pulled by invisible strings. He shuddered and doubled over, clutching his chest just as Alysion did when bonding with the crystals.

"Ashmyr!" Fae called, the sword at his neck forgotten until it bit into his skin.

"You'll lose your head if you keep that up," said Drath.

Fae didn't care. There was no way Ash would survive this. The Ruby alone had knocked Alysion out for a good while; bonding with all seven at once was suicide. The crystals burned brighter, a sudden wind surrounding Ash in a swirling vortex of energy.

A horn echoed throughout the grounds as a flurry of spells burst from the trees towards the dais. The crowd scattered, figures in familiar armour dashing into the courtyard.

The sword at his neck disappeared. Fae dropped to the ground, legs giving out. Still, he clutched his sword, struggling to stand.

When he got back on his feet, Drath was gone, and Captain Anaril was charging towards them.

The captain knelt beside Alysion and held a glowing hand over him.

As they worked, Fae dared to glance up at Ash. His brother was still inside the rainbow vortex of magic, growing in intensity. What were they going to do? They had to get the crystals away from Ash. But why did he have them in the first place? Why was he working with these elves? They had killed their parents! Fae's wrist throbbed.

Alysion started to come around, mumbling incomprehensibly as he opened his eyes.

"Alysion?" Fae dropped to his knees beside him. "Are you all right?"

He grunted and tried to sit up, pushing away the captain's hands. "I'm fine," he croaked.

"I must get you to safety," said Captain Anaril, straightening up.

"But what about the crystals?" asked Alysion as Fae helped him to his feet. The captain's harsh eye followed, but he didn't care.

"Our warriors will take care of it. We must leave now." They stretched out a hand.

"We can't. We're bound to the prophecy." Alysion held up his wrist, the mark glowing clear as day upon it. Fae's own wrist did the same. "We have to—"

The swirling magic around Ash suddenly dissipated. Captain Anaril's head snapped towards him, cold eyes narrowing.

Fae stared up at Ash in horror. Ash's pure white hair was streaked through with the colour of each crystal, and his brown eyes had gone completely black.

Fae didn't need the ability to sense auras to know that something had gone very wrong.

"Ash?" Fae said.

"That's Ash? That's your *brother*?" asked Alysion incredulously.

Fae nodded, wrist burning like he'd stuck a red-hot brand to his skin. "Ash isn't—"

A blue barrier shot up, surrounding them just before a brilliant flash slammed into it with a thunderous crack, glancing off into the trees.

"Leave now!" urged the captain, one of their hands raised. "There's a gate to Lyrellis just outside the wards."

"We can't!" snapped Alysion. "We need to save Ash."

Fae's heart warmed.

"I just need a moment to think," he continued as another powerful spell hit the barrier, rattling their ear drums.

The captain frowned. "Then I will distract him." Energy cracked as they pushed through their own shield to confront Ash.

"I promise you, Fae, we're not leaving without him," said Alysion.

He nodded, unable to tear his eyes away from the battle building before them.

"I can still feel the crystals," Alysion continued. "My connection is weak, but it's there. If I can get control of them, it should free your brother."

They flinched as a flurry of green sparks struck the barrier.

"We'll save him," said Alysion, putting a hand on his shoulder.

• • • ● • • •

Drath felt the aural shift when Navir took control of the crystals. Pleased, he scanned the chaos before him, watching the Elithar clash with his followers from one of the verandas. But then he caught sight of something even better, something that brought a twisted smile to his face. Avoiding spell and steel alike, he leapt from the tree and snuck behind his target, sword aimed square at her back.

The belim fighter whirled to meet his blow. Sparks flew as their blades collided.

"Tarathiel," she said coldly. "I'd hoped never to see you again."

"It will take much more than your pathetic plots to end me, Princess Lymsia. Though I suppose it's Queen Lymsia now, isn't it?"

He'd planned on using Navir and the crystals to storm the palace and take it by force. *I should thank Anaril for alerting her the next time I see them.* Facing the queen one-on-one here and now made his plans much simpler. And much sweeter.

Lymsia narrowed her eyes and took a step back, disengaging her weapon. "I suppose you're here for revenge?"

"Naturally." He struck again, quick as a serpent, aiming for her heart. Oh, how he had longed for this day! All those centuries of plotting were finally about to pay off—soon, Queen Lymsia would be dead, and Illuven would be his once again!

Lymsia's sword flicked up to knock his strike away. Tarathiel quickly pulled back and slashed but again, her blade met his. Undaunted, he kept up his barrage of attacks.

"For some reason, I expected more from you," she said, throwing darts of fire at him as he leapt back.

He summoned a wall of water, but one dart slipped through, grazing his arm. Tarathiel didn't mind the stinging pain; he could afford to take a few hits if it meant outlasting her. And if Lymsia thought he was weakening, she would naturally lower her defences.

"For someone who claims to have slain a dragon, your performance is unimpressive. Though, I suppose Illuven did most of the work back then. You simply landed the final blow once he fell."

She was trying to get a rise out of him—it would have worked in the past, but now, Tarathiel felt nothing. His hatred had festered for decades as he'd plotted, awaiting the opportunity to channel his hurt into something useful. Her death was steadily approaching; anything she said was meaningless.

She came at him with her blade, her other hand hurling a sphere of water. "I won't let you ruin my kingdom!"

Tarathiel withheld a snort as he sharply turned, the spell flying past him. But her blade caught his hip, stinging through his armour. "*Your* kingdom? You may govern it, but it certainly doesn't belong to you. Just as Illuven doesn't belong to you."

That struck a chord, and she attacked with more ferocity—just as Tarathiel wanted.

"Illuven is *my* king. There is nothing you can do to change that!" She punctuated her last words with a flurry of razor-sharp ice.

"He's only king so long as you're alive. When you fall, he will be free!" Tarathiel sprang out of the way, the shards embedding in the ground near his feet. He didn't give the melting ice a second look as he retaliated with a spell of his own. Or tried to, but the Elithar had noticed their queen's assailant and rushed to her aid.

"No," he hissed between his teeth. He refused to let them ruin this moment! A swirling dome of dark mist formed around the two of them, preventing anyone from entering—or leaving. He severed his connection to the spell and anchored it there. Whenever an elf brushed against it, or a spell struck it, the mist absorbed their aura, using it as fuel to maintain itself. With all the fighting going on, he didn't have to worry about the wall failing, the necrotic energy flaring each time it sucked in more magical energy from friend and foe alike. It left him free to take on the queen with his aura intact.

"This is precisely why shadow magic is forbidden!" said the queen, coming at him with two swords; the one she had been holding before and another magically formed from ice.

Of the two, the iceblade was more troublesome, imbued with the power of her hatred; as she neared, her eyes burned with freezing rage.

His blade met her icy sword, wisely ignoring the feint from her metal one.

"Shadow magic saved Illuven's life all those suns ago! And it will do so again!" he retorted, not bothering to tell her that the dome was entirely different type of magic.

Her metal sword came around to lop off his head, his blade trapped and unable to block. He only managed to avoid it by disengaging with a great leap bolstered by his magic.

Queen Lymsia closed the gap and struck with everything she had. For someone who never had a reason to draw her weapons, she certainly had excellent stamina.

But even if she trained exclusively with Captain Anaril, it was nothing compared to what he'd put himself through during exile. He'd roamed the lands beyond Odenia before infiltrating the temple and learning spells the royal family could never even dream of—they were too pure for that. And when he hadn't been practising forgotten, darker forms of magic or executing his plans, he'd put all his time into honing his body, preparing for this very battle. And if all else failed, he had Navir and the crystals.

Tarathiel went on the defensive, only moving as he needed to block her attacks. She pushed back fiercely, expending more energy in her eagerness to finish him off.

"You know, I thought you'd be more worried about your prince," he said to get her to drop her guard.

"Captain Anaril is with him," she said tersely, throwing a blazing arrow of flame at him.

Tarathiel swung his blade, summoning a blast of cold air that snuffed out the arrow. Interesting—she wouldn't save her only heir?

"Didn't you feel it? The isidyll has already taken what we needed from your son. Your captain was too late to save him." Did she care about her son at all? Well, soon, it wouldn't matter.

Lymsia's eyes narrowed as she came at him again, dual blades moving faster than before. Finally, she was starting to take things seriously. Good—it would be all the sweeter when he felled her.

"Once you're out of the way, I will rule Sylandris with Illuven at my side," he said, goading her. "We will fix this dying kingdom, and at long last, give the dragons what they deserve!"

The queen snorted in an undignified manner, aggressively advancing on his solid defences. "I'm surprised you didn't run off to join those scaly beasts."

"You're well aware that I'm no friend of theirs. They will pay for what they did to our people, just as you will pay for your crimes. The truth about the rogue dragon—" He threw up a wall of rock, shielding himself from a torrent of water.

"No one will ever believe you!" Lymsia hissed, appearing beside him. Tarathiel sprang out of the way, barely avoiding being cut to ribbons by her swords. It took everything he had to keep her at bay.

"You don't deny it?" he asked, unable to suppress a grin. If the truth got out, her entire rule would unravel.

Lymsia responded by flicking her magical blade and sending out another barrage of ice shards. It appeared to be her favourite spell.

Tarathiel made quick work of them with a burst of flame. Some got through and sliced painfully along his arm. He hissed, red clouding his vision. How dare she! She who'd ruined his relationship! She who'd lied and ruined his life!

"You'll be held responsible for bringing a dragon through the wards! And for the deaths of Tiriel and Ylana!"

She shot out a white-hot dart of fire, but he easily deflected it.

"Were their lives worth taking Illuven from me?" he hissed, dark, twisted energy enveloping his raised blade. He closed the gap between them and struck.

She crossed her blades, catching his blow. But he pressed on, determined to break through and end this. They remained at a standstill, neither able to best the other, sweat beading up on their foreheads.

So Tarathiel let loose his forbidden magic.

Lymsia's eyes widened as the blade's shadows crept along hers. She tried to pull away, but the magic wouldn't let her.

"How could you sacrifice them? You're supposed to protect our people!" The slithering shadows thickened into a dark cloud. "Your selfishness is utterly revolting! *You* should be branded as a traitor!"

Lymsia struggled against the shadows enveloping her, but it was useless. She couldn't break free—not even her magic could pierce it. Tarathiel removed his sword and stepped back, admiring his handiwork.

"How dare you!" she cried, shooting him a look of pure loathing.

Tarathiel pressed the tip of his sword to her neck, drawing blood. "It's almost a shame that you won't see what becomes of your son, but you've made it clear that you care little for him. At least he will be with that damisri my scouts inform me he is so attached to. I wonder if he—"

The swirling dome around them suddenly vanished, dissipating into nothing as a familiar shape stepped through. Tarathiel froze.

Illuven.

Twenty-Seven

Revelations

Tarathiel couldn't help but stare, Lymsia momentarily forgotten as he took in the sight of his beloved Illuven. After all these years, he was here—really here. But of course he was, why wouldn't he be? The kingdom was in trouble and he was one of its rulers.

"Tarathiel?" Illuven said, aghast. "I thought...I thought you were dead." His eyes slowly wandered to Lymsia, still trapped in her prison of shadows. "You told me he perished during the Silias."

Tarathiel caught the accusation and hurt in his voice. It pained him to see Illuven distraught, but at the same time his heart soared.

"Consider him dead," she said, stone-faced. "What you see is nothing but an echo of the past that shall soon be wiped away. I thought I asked you to remain at the palace in case the intruders attacked there."

Illuven didn't seem to hear her, his eyes glued to Tarathiel. "What happened the day Tarathiel was banished?" he asked as he advanced. His blade was drawn, but held loosely at his side.

The queen pressed her mouth shut in a firm line.

"If you don't tell him, I will," Tarathiel hissed at her.

"He escaped the Silias," Lymsia said, a golden light suddenly outlining her head. "He used his forbidden magic to kill the ayel."

"Killing them was an accident," said Tarathiel, eyeing the strange glow. What was she up to? "But that's not what you need to tell him."

The queen vanished in a burst of light—a teleportation spell. Tarathiel hissed between his teeth and whirled around. Damn. He wouldn't make that mistake again.

"There is nothing else to tell him that he doesn't already know," she spat, reappearing a few steps away. Her iceblade shattered, its magic spent, though she pointed the other at his heart.

Tarathiel blinked. Did Illuven know who had sent the dragon? No, he couldn't; he would never have stayed with her if he did.

Lymsia lunged, eyes blazing, sword flashing. Caught up in his emotions, Tarathiel raised his sword a heartbeat too late.

Gold flashed before his eyes.

Clang!

Illuven's blade had stopped her.

"Stand aside," she said, trying to keep her voice level. "He's a liar and a traitor to our people. You can't defend him!" She stepped back, sword at the ready, looking past Illuven to Tarathiel.

Illuven shook his head. "Leave it, Lymsia. I learned the truth about the dragon a long time ago."

For the first time, she was shaken.

"It took some time, but eventually, I pieced it together." When Illuven spoke, his eyes were on Lymsia, but he placed a comforting hand on Tarathiel's shoulder. Tarathiel nearly melted. "It broke my heart to learn the truth. But..." He looked from one to the other. "I must ask you both to sheath your swords."

Neither obeyed.

"You would rather she live?" Tarathiel demanded, anger flaring. "She's the one who set me up!"

"I know, and I've never been able to forgive her for it." Illuven's hand left Tarathiel's shoulder.

How could Illuven become the queen's consort after learning what she had done? How could he have had a child with her? Hatred burned in his eyes. If only she would disappear...

"Please, Tarathiel. If you let this go, you may leave Sylandris whole and unharmed."

Whole. Illuven wouldn't let them perform the Silias. It was more than any criminal could ever hope for. But Tarathiel couldn't live in a world without Illuven, where Lymsia's crimes went unpunished.

"If I left, would you come with me?" he asked. "You're miserable here. Leave and be free." He held out a hand.

To his dismay, Illuven shook his head. "I can't. If I left now, it would throw the court into chaos and force Alysion to take the throne. He's too young for that. And I can't leave him. Because I've been so wrapped up in my own hurts, I've neglected him for too long."

The remaining pieces of Tarathiel's heart shattered.

• • • ● • • •

Alysion sat amidst the chaos, eyes closed, aura connecting with the powerful amalgam of energy that was Fae's brother. His *twin* brother; such a thing was unheard of for elves.

Tentatively, he brushed up against the aura, the mass a swirl of colour in his mind's eye. But the auras weren't as bright as they should have been. *By the Ancestors, it's just like Great Snapper! Ash can't properly bond with the crystals!* Which meant it wouldn't be long before Ash lost control. But Alysion would have to take it slow to keep his manoeuvring unnoticed. Hopefully, Anaril would keep Ash distracted.

A familiar aura flared up amongst the others, calling to him—the Ruby. Already the red stone was losing its lustre; it would come to him easily.

Working quickly, he let his aura mingle with it. The Ruby didn't reject him, but it couldn't free itself from Ash. Alysion carefully followed the connection—if Ash caught him in this whirlwind of aura, it would take nothing for the elf to crush him.

A hand shook his shoulder, startling him. His weak connection to the stone vanished.

"Alysion," Fae said, panicked. "Anaril's barrier is down. We need to move!"

Instantly, he was on his feet. They leapt from the dais, racing across the torn-up courtyard. The captain was still fighting. Alysion could feel their aura, but it was as insignificant as an insect before the combined power of the crystals.

"Gale! Gale!" Fae bellowed, waving frantically at something big, red, and loud diving out of the sky towards them.

Alysion couldn't believe what he was seeing.

The dragon roared and landed hard before them. She crouched, allowing Fae to drag him onto her back.

Alysion, in shock, grabbed onto one of the long spines extending from her scales. He nearly jumped out of his skin when he felt arms wrap around his waist.

"Sorry, nothing else for me to hold onto," came Fae's voice from behind him.

He nodded, ears heating up. His stomach lurched as Gale leapt into the air, her massive leathery wings straining as she quickly gained altitude.

"Ash—my brother—has the crystals, but Alysion thinks he can get them back under control," Fae explained once she had levelled out, circling above the chaos.

Alysion's focus was torn between learning the truth about Gale and the exhilaration of flying astride a dragon. He marvelled at how the world opened up below them—minus the carnage. The Elithar and Drath's followers had separated into smaller groups. It was hard to see which side was winning; there were just as many robed elves laying still as there were warriors.

He caught sight of Ash and reached out for the crystals. "We need to get closer!" he shouted above the rushing air.

Gale angled her wings, spiralling towards Ash. But it was difficult to get close; the temple elves threw spells to keep them at bay, which Alysion deflected, or Gale swooped to avoid, deviating from her path.

"I feel them!" he shouted once they were almost directly above Ash. Captain Anaril was still keeping Ash busy. They darted around, shooting all sorts of colourful spells at him. But judging by their dimming aura, they wouldn't last much longer. Alysion winced as the captain took a hard hit from a row of rocks bursting from the ground. They flew across the grass and didn't get up.

No!

Their still form disappeared from view as Gale angled her wings. Then, something just as chilling as Anaril's defeat caught his eye: Drath was squaring off against his parents. What were they doing here? All three were moving, the king and queen pursuing Drath across the clearing as he sprinted towards Ash. A dark cloud erupted, obscuring their vision, allowing Drath to escape. Alysion's stomach tied itself into a knot. It took everything he had not to leap from Gale's back to give pursuit, but his stinging wrist reminded him he had a job to do.

Alysion took a steady breath and closed his eyes. He reached out with his aura, seeking the Kunzite. He slipped past the Ruby and Sapphire as he wove his way through the mass of energies. The Emerald came not long after, followed by an orange aura that was light and playful—the Wind Citrine. Alysion ignored them all. A wall of light and shadows rose before him, blocking his path. The Topaz and Amethyst were protecting Ash.

Perhaps if he had some crystals to help him, he could get through the aural barrier, but he was on his own. An unpleasant feeling settled in his gut. He'd relied on the crystals for so much that he didn't know what his own magic was capable of anymore.

I have to do this. Fae is counting on me.

Steeling himself, he approached the mass of light and shadow, expecting Ash to discover him. Instead, the barrier pushed back, jolting him so hard he nearly lost his place in the mix of auras. Alysion only managed to hang on because he'd felt it—the Kunzite beyond the barrier.

• • • ● • • •

Gale kept close as she could to Ash, avoiding spells and arrows alike. Fae clung to Alysion's slim waist, eyes on his brother.

Ash cast spells indiscriminately, striking friend and foe alike. Elves scrambled away from him, fleeing into the trees. He shot a bolt of lightning at a group of combatants who leapt out of the way. It struck one of the trees with a thunderous *boom,* sending bits of wood flying through the air.

He'll destroy everything!

"Gale, I need to get down there!" Fae cried. "It's just like the lake spirit!"

Gale turned her head to look at him with one large, golden eye. "It's too dangerous."

"Please, Gale, I have to! When he realizes who I am, that I'm alive, he'll calm down!"

"You don't know that. The spirit didn't calm until the Sapphire was removed. I won't let you risk your life. Cane will tan my hide if something happens to you, remember?"

Fae grit his teeth. There had to be a way!

Gale suddenly dropped into a steep dive avoiding a blue fireball. This was his chance!

As she snapped open her wings to pull up, Fae slid from her back. "Don't let Alysion fall!" he hollered—the prince was alone now, completely unaware of the physical world.

Fae grunted as he hit the ground, rolling to soften the impact. Ignoring how everything hurt, he scrambled to his feet and sprinted towards his brother. "Ashmyr, stop!"

Ash paused.

"It's me, Fae! Your brother!"

Slowly, Ash turned his blackened eyes towards him, one hand cradling an crackling orb of dark energy.

"Come on, Ash, you know me!" Fae slowed. Out of the corner of his eye, something headed right for them.

"My brother died decades ago," said Ash, his tone devoid of emotion. "He was killed by the captain of the Elithar during an attack sanctioned by the court. They will pay for what they have done!"

Fae leapt to the side, barely escaping Ash's fury as he hurled the dark orb. It struck the ground behind him with the force of a cannonball, leaving a smoking crater in its wake.

"The royal family had nothing to do with it!" Fae cried.

"They ordered my brother's death and killed my parents in the process. All because my brother didn't have a damis!"

"I don't have a damis!" Fae shouted. "I know you can sense it. Who else could I possibly be? You should recognize your own face!"

A sharp pain flared in his side, and Fae hit the ground.

"Quiet, boy," a voice hissed.

Drath, the one who was truly responsible for their parents' deaths, stood over him.

"Isidyll Navir, this elf lies. He's suppressing his aura to trick you."

"He's the liar! He killed our parents!" Fae growled, fighting to stand. "Ash, look at me!"

Drath grabbed a fistful of Fae's hair and roughly forced his face to the ground.

"I won't let you ruin my plans," he hissed, his tone promising death. "But I will tell you a secret. Your lack of damis is your brother's doing."

Fae went still a stone. *What?*

"Of course, your brother has no idea what he did," said Drath, keeping his voice low. "Neither of you were born yet."

There was a loud *crack* as Ash, losing interest, threw another dark orb into the fray.

"When twins are in the womb, one absorbs the damis of the other, resulting in an extremely powerful sorcerer."

Fae's breath caught. This was why he had no damis? Because Ash had unknowingly taken it from him before they were born?

"Most damisri are stillborn. If they aren't, they're killed at birth to appease the Ancestors," Drath continued. "Even then, the courts will order the stronger child murdered as well, since their power rivals that of the royal family, threatening their *divine* position." He nearly spat the words.

"You attacked our home to take Ash," Fae said. "You believed he could be used in place of royal blood to control the crystals."

Drath grinned. "Very good."

Fae thought he was going to be sick. "You killed our parents because they wouldn't have given you Ash willingly."

"Fools. I tried bartering with them, offering to keep your wretched existence a secret in exchange for your brother, but they refused. Then, they had the audacity to threaten to expose me."

It was because of Drath that he had lost everything. It was because of Drath that Ash believed the Brightstars had killed his family. Fae's vision swam with his unbridled fury. Invigorated by his rage, he fought against Drath's hold, scrambling to his feet.

Fae drew his sword.

Twenty-Eight

The Crystals

In an instant, Drath was upon him. Fae knew he didn't stand a chance. But he was willing to fight for Ash.

Avoiding a blast of violet fire, he charged. Drath's wicked blade appeared out of nowhere, meeting his with a resounding *clang* that shook Fae to the marrow of his bones.

"One round wasn't enough for you?"

Fae responded by slashing at his wrist.

Drath effortlessly flicked the strike away. "Are you that eager to reunite with your parents?"

Fae ignored his taunting. Drath was trying to get under his skin; he wouldn't survive if he let that happen.

"Ash!" he called out, avoiding Drath's slim sword.

"Your brother can't hear you."

Fae shifted his grip and unleashed a series of blows. Drath flawlessly countered each one.

"Your swordsmanship isn't bad, but there's much room for improvement. If you had a damis, you would be quite powerful."

He wouldn't fall for this. Fae struck again; Drath dodged.

"You know, it may be possible for you to gain a damis of your own."

Fae nearly dropped his sword.

"Once your brother has mastered the crystals, I suspect he'll be able to grant you one."

His gaze met Drath's, heart pounding like a racing uhaan. Was he serious?

Drath made no move to attack. "Of course, that means you'll have to prove your worth and swear fealty to us. Having the Crown Prince of Sylandris on our side would be an asset. We would welcome both of you."

Having a damis of his own would be a dream come true. But not at the expense of Alysion's freedom. Or his own.

"Never," he spat, a sense of calm coming over him. He'd never be able to live with himself if he joined his parents' murderers—why had he doubted that?

"Well, I must applaud your loyalty." Drath sprang into action, swiping his blade horizontally across Fae's neck.

Fae ducked out of the way, a few pale strands of hair falling around him. Slashing at Drath's knees, Fae forced him to leap back, giving himself time to fall into a better stance.

But a shadowy arrow from Drath shot towards him in the same instant. Instinctively, Fae raised his blade to protect himself—the arrow connected, the force of the blow pushing him back before the magic glanced off into the surrounding chaos.

Fae didn't see the second one coming until it was too late.

Fire erupted between them, obliterating the arrow. Squeezing his eyes shut, Fae staggered away from the blaze. By the Ancestors, it was hot! Something landed nearby, shaking the earth with its size and intimidating growl. *Gale.* But when he cracked open an eye, he was met with a sea of shimmering silver.

"Go, my boy," said the dragon. "Get your brother. I'll take care of this one."

Shaking off his shock, Fae ran after Ash. Only one person called him that: Master Cane.

• • • ● • • •

Alysion had reconnected with his three crystals and bonded with the Wind Citrine before Ash detected his presence. Though he had to fight to regain complete control of them, the stones' loyalty to him and the prophecy couldn't be shaken. Ash tightened his grip on the Amethyst and Topaz, determined not to let them slip away.

Alysion growled, unable to master the dual auras pointed against him—under Ash's command, their defence was flawless. Every time he thought he saw an opening, a chance to bond with them, the other swooped in and blocked him.

Frustrated, he lashed out with a pulse of aura. The opposing crystals responded with a pulse of their own, sending his head spinning. *Wait a minute. If I can feel physical sensations here, then so can Ash.*

Praying his theory was correct, Alysion drew upon the combined power of his four crystals. When it became difficult to contain, he released it in a tsunami-like wave, sending it crashing into the barrier; it cracked but did not shatter.

But Alysion was fine with that. He'd fulfilled his true objective—Ash's presence had disappeared.

He cautiously sent out a pulse of aura, feeling for the two crystals. To his delight, they didn't push him away, allowing their auras to mingle with his. Alysion clutched his chest, crying out in pain as their auras bonded. Feeling his body so acutely while floating around in the aural plane was staggering.

Slowly—far too slowly, in his opinion—the aching subsided. Before him was the muddy pink aura of the Kunzite, accompanied by another powerful presence. Ash's aura was not a single colour: it was a strange mix of black and white as if it had once been two. *By the Ancestors, he has Fae's damis!*

Alysion reached out for the Kunzite as Ash struck.

• • • ● • • •

Fae had nearly closed the distance between them, but Ash had stopped his advance and shook his head as if bugs were buzzing around it.

"Ash?" Fae said, carefully approaching. The Elithar hovered in his periphery.

His twin didn't respond, but went still.

Breathing deeply, Fae stepped before him, praying he wasn't about to be blown to bits. "Ash, please look at me. I'm your brother, Fae."

Ash's black eyes met his, but there was no recognition in them. There was no emotion at all.

Hesitantly, Fae reached out to touch him. In a flash of violet, some invisible force threw him to the ground. Coughing, he got to his feet. "Stay back!" he hollered at the approaching warriors.

They ignored him. Ash shot magic in all directions, misshapen darts of light and shadow that blasted their targets across the courtyard.

Ducking and weaving, Fae scrambled over to him. "Ash, stop! They're not the ones responsible for Ama's and Dada's deaths!"

Ash paused.

"The royal family didn't do it! Please listen to me!" Fae stepped in front of him. "Drath lied; *he* killed them!"

"*You* lie," replied Ash, his voice deeper than before. It sent a shiver down Fae's spine. "Drath-ayel has always been loyal to me."

Ash cast a spell that knocked the wind from his lungs. Doubled over and coughing, Fae stood his ground. "It's an act!"

"Drath-ayel took me in after my parents and brother were killed." Ash raised a glowing hand, holding it between them. The veins around his eyes darkened, spider webbing across his face.

"I survived! Dada saved me by sending me away. He would have sent you away too if he could." Fae clasped his hands around Ash's glowing one, wincing as it burned. "Ashmyr." Ash's hand blazed hotter, the smell of burning flesh filling the air—Fae refused to let go. "Look at me. You know me."

Something flickered behind Ash's blank eyes. Recognition? Confusion?

"Remember how we used to play in the forest? How we'd eat lunaberries until we got sick? Ama would get so mad at us when we came home covered in purple juice."

Ash blinked, the darkness in his eyes receding. His hand slowly cooled. "Fae?" he said quietly.

"Yes, Ash, I'm here." He tried to pull his brother into a hug, but Ash stepped back, his mouth open in a cry of agony. His hand flew to his chest, clutching the spot where his damis resided.

The blood drained from Fae's face. "What's wrong?"

A rainbow glow clouded his vision.

• • • ● • • •

Success! Alysion pulled out of the swirling mass of aura, returning to his body. He felt like he'd been trampled by a herd of nuu, and the rocking of Gale's body as she flew wasn't helping.

"Gale, take me down there!" he hollered.

She dived into the courtyard below.

It was a mess: the ground was torn up and smoking in patches; massive chunks were blown out from the tree-towers, many of the verandas and raised walkways obliterated by magical blasts. Alysion tried not to look at the bodies scattered amongst the wreckage.

Gale touched down near Fae, kneeling over the prone form of his twin. The young isidyll was in bad shape; his face twisted with pain as he clawed at his chest. Alysion slid off Gale's back, legs buckling when he hit the ground.

"What's happening to him?" Fae asked, eyes glued to his glowing brother.

"I don't have full control of the crystals yet. I need to sever his bond with them." Alysion shut his eyes, holding a hand over Ash's chest. The rainbow light emanating from him separated into its six colours, becoming smoke-like before crystallizing into stones. Each flew to Alysion's outstretched hand, the mark on his wrist glowing white.

"Now for the Kunzite," he muttered.

The crystals flared, shining vibrantly. A pink glow arose from Ash's chest; slowly, the Kunzite came forth. Ash shuddered and went limp, the dark veins around his eyes fading. The pink stone joined the others.

Gale, who'd been chasing around robed elves, came over and pressed her scaley snout to Ash's side. "He'll be fine," she rumbled. "He just needs rest."

Ash's eyes fluttered open. "Fae? Is it really you? I thought...I thought..."

"Easy now, I'm here," Fae said to him, gentle and reassuring.

Alysion looked away, not wanting to intrude on their moment. One day, he hoped Fae would use that tone with him.

He scanned the courtyard for his parents, worry knotting his stomach. Where had they gone? Where was Drath?

There was a shuffling as Ash flung up a hand.

"Wha—?" Alysion started.

The world turned violet.

Twenty-Nine

Consequences

A dazzling flash blasted away the darkness. Ash went limp in Fae's arms, utterly spent.

Alysion stepped in front of them, the auras of all seven crystals coursing through him. It was exhilarating. Each was powerful on its own but all of them combined, with the Kunzite acting as an amplifier, was beyond anything he could have ever imagined. As Ash's light revealed Drath approaching, he felt no fear.

Gale growled.

Drath called forth a cloud of shadows that swiftly filled the area, obscuring their sight. With a simple flick of his wrist, Alysion swept it away. *Wow.*

When it cleared, he saw his parents running up behind the traitor. They looked haggard, as if their energy had been stolen away by a dark force.

"Tarathiel!" his father called out.

Drath turned.

"Enough, Tarathiel," said the king. "You can't win."

Alysion's glance shifted between Drath—Tarathiel—and his father, realizing who the familiar voice in his visions belonged to. His father had been friends with the traitor. Alysion spared a glimpse at his mother and flinched at her expression of pure loathing.

Tarathiel drew his sword. Everyone tensed.

"Please," his father begged, his voice strained like he was trying to keep himself together. Alysion had never seen him like this before. "Come with us and stand trial."

"No, Illuven," Tarathiel said far too tenderly for someone who had committed such atrocities. "I will not be tried again by a court who refuses to acknowledge their own treachery."

"Don't do this," said Illuven. "I can't—"

"And I can't live in a world as unjust as this."

The remaining combatants, noticing the exchange, paused. Master Cane, who'd been circling above, landed nearby. The courtyard fell into an uneasy silence.

His father regarded Drath for a long time before shaking his head. "Please, if you come with us, you'll get to live."

"If I go with you, then everything I have done will have been in vain." Drath raised the thin blade, pressing it against his neck. "May we meet again."

"Tarathiel!"

Alysion looked away.

• • • ● • • •

"Hey, wake up." Fae leaned over the sleeping prince, shaking his shoulder gently, trying to bring him back to the world of the living. "Wake up, sleepyhead."

Alysion mumbled something and sat up, rubbing his face. After the fight, they'd been sent to get some rest while the Elithar rounded up Tarathiel's followers. They'd passed out in the first room they'd found in the temple complex that had beds, Fae carrying Ash on his back the whole way.

"Everyone wants to talk to us," Fae said, handing Alysion a brush. He was covered in dirt, and Fae knew it would kill him to leave looking like that.

"Everyone?" asked Alysion, raising a brow.

"Gale, your parents, Ash, Captain Anaril, and Master Cane, oddly enough," he rattled off as Alysion quickly made himself presentable.

"The blacksmith? What's she doing here?"

"She's also a dragon. Come on. Ash already left to meet them." Knowing he'd gone ahead alone made Fae antsy. Though the queen and king had promised no harm would come to him, Fae was still on edge—he knew Ash would stand trial.

Everyone he'd listed plus a handful of high-ranking Elithar gathered in the Verdant Hall, filling a series of conjured benches. Three chairs had been set up to mimic the throne room, the queen in the centremost one, the king on her right. Both wore layered robes of silver embroidered with moons and stars.

"Come here," the queen addressed Alysion, motioning to the empty chair on her other side. Alysion looked to Fae, not wanting to be separated.

"Just go," he whispered, moving to sit beside Ash in the front row, relieved that he was unbound. Ash played with a lock of hair that had regained its pure white colouring. He nearly jumped out of his skin when Fae appeared.

Gale and Master Cane poked their large, scaley heads through the windows, apparently unable to reform their human disguises. The elves close by cast dark looks towards them; some shuffled away when Gale gave Fae a toothy grin.

Queen Lymsia tapped her staff—a twisted branch topped with a clear stone—on the floor, signalling for silence, then launched into a short congratulatory speech. "Though some of the elves responsible for recent events are no longer with us, there are others present who must give their accounts."

"We shall begin with Prince Alysion and his...companion."

Fae nearly snorted. His *companion*? Is that what the queen thought of him? Catching Alysion's eyes—the same green as the queen's—he stood, and the two recounted their tale.

Though they wanted to keep it short, Fae recounted the attack on his family as vividly as possible, impressing upon everyone that Ash had been a victim. He also relayed what Tarathiel had told him about the nature of twins and his lack of damis. Ash stiffened on the bench beside him. He and Alysion didn't leave much out aside from the nature of their relationship.

There was a long pause once they finished, so Fae sat back down.

"Next, we will hear from Ashmyr," announced the queen.

His twin went pale beside him and rose unsteadily. Fae took his hand and gave it a reassuring squeeze.

Ash took a calming breath and began with the attack on their home, further explaining how Tarathiel had carefully planned it out in order to steal him away, how he'd pinned the blame on the royal family to bend Ash to his will. He moved on to his training at the temple, how Tarathiel had taken an interest in him. Finally, he spoke of his rise to the position of isidyll, and the hunt for the crystals.

"Drath—Tarathiel has been secretly controlling the temple ever since he found out about the crystals. Because the Silias failed, he never received the traitor's mark that would have prevented him from passing through the Sylandrian wards. He infiltrated the temple decades ago and slowly gathered followers as he rose through the ranks. If I'd known the truth, that he'd killed my family just to get to me, I never would have done what I did." He fell silent, eyes downcast at the polished floor.

Fae's heart clenched. Seeing Ash in such a state tore at him. The brother he remembered had been so cheerful and energetic.

"Ashmyr, you shall be punished for the crimes you have committed against your people and your prince," said the queen. Ash didn't shrink before her, but Fae sensed his panic.

"Really? You're going to punish a child?" Gale snorted loudly from her window. "He was only a thelim when he was taken, and the elves that took him did nothing but abuse him."

"Quiet! It is not your place to pass judgement here, dragon!" said Lymsia, banging her staff. "If you do not remain silent, you will be escorted out until it is your time to speak!"

Gale rolled her massive golden eyes.

"He fought Drath, er, Tarathiel in the end," said Fae, on his feet again, meeting the queen's gaze. "Ash protected us from his last attack."

Lymsia narrowed her eyes, surveying him. "While I commend you for aiding Prince Alysion, a da—*you* have no say here."

"By the Ancestors, what are you talking about? Of course he does." It wasn't Alysion who had spoken out, but King Illuven. The king was pale, his expression strained. "He is one of our subjects and has just as much say as anyone else, perhaps more so, as he was chosen to collect the crystals."

The queen gave her mate a cool look before returning to Ash. "In light of recent evidence, you shall not undergo the Silias as originally planned. Instead, you are henceforth stripped of your title of isidyll. In penance to your kingdom, you will escort the dragons back to their homeland and aid with their report, conveying any messages from the vorais back to us."

Ash wasn't going to be exiled! But he'd just found him, and he didn't want to be separated so soon! Fae felt eyes on him and realized he'd spoken out loud.

"We won't keep him too long," said Gale. "And we'll make it easy for you to visit if we do. Besides, our work here isn't done. We're here to learn what happened to one of our own after they disappeared decades ago." She turned her gaze to the queen.

A strange expression crossed Queen Lymsia's face. "Go on," she said stiffly. The hall was deathly silent.

Master Cane spoke. "We followed their trail to the Sky Peak wards, surprised to discover that it continued past them. Even more intriguing was the elven aura also present. We know elves don't usually go near the barrier—we check it now and then. We could only conclude that some of your people let our friend through. Concerned, we created talismans that would allow a small group of us to take on human form, almost completely suppressing our auras."

"The talismans can only be used a few times. Their magic is now dried up," added Gale. "We passed through the wards undetected and have been looking for clues around your forest ever since. So far, we've found nothing." She huffed with annoyance, blowing a small burst of hot air into the hall. "Then all this crystal stuff started happening, and we feared whoever had triggered your stones might launch an attack on us since they had been used in the war to fight us. It seems our fear was correct."

The elves in the hall muttered amongst themselves, shooting glances at the dragons. Alysion's parents looked deeply unsettled by their account. Fae couldn't blame them; the Syl-Raanian War had been brutal, and now they'd learned their enemies could breach the wards.

Master Cane made a sound deep in her throat, and the hall slowly fell silent. Her being a dragon explained her skill with fire, her frequent trips, and why she'd found him so quickly as a child.

"As you know," Cane continued, "I found a young elf near the Sylandrian barrier not too long ago. The spell that sent him there was full of powerful light magic, so I couldn't ignore it. When I investigated, I found Faeranduil."

Fae fidgeted, sensing Alysion's eyes on him. Right, he'd never told Alysion his full name—the prince had first heard it from Tarathiel. He'd have to apologize later.

"At first, I thought he was dead; he was very still and had no aura of his own. But then he showed signs of life. When I checked the residual aura from the spell, I found a message hidden within the magic. It was from the boy's father, briefly explaining that they'd been attacked, asking that whoever found Faeranduil take good care of him."

Fae's throat tightened, and he blinked back tears. It was a good thing he was already sitting; otherwise, his legs would have given out. He had no idea Dada had left a message.

"Unfortunately, as a human, I couldn't pass through the Sylandrian wards to learn any more, but I trust a thorough investigation was made into the disappearance of two high-ranking nobles."

High-ranking nobles? What did she mean?

"When it became known Nylian and Imbryl Silvermoon were missing, we sent the Elithar out to their home, but nothing was found," King Illuven explained. "The attackers had covered their tracks well, and there were no signs of any remains, nor any auras to indicate that something strange had occurred. We were unaware they had a second child. They hid his existence well, something easily done when the child—when Fae—has no aura to mark his presence. Captain Anaril's team found some residual aura from the teleportation spell Imbryl had cast, thus concluding that the family had left of their own free will. All knew that Imbryl was one of the rare few with a natural affinity for light magic."

Master Cane nodded, and Gale huffed, blowing out a puff of smoke.

"I suppose you will be reporting all of this to the vorais?" the king asked.

"Of course," grumped Gale. "And we'll be coming back when we're done. We have yet to find the missing dragon."

Illuven's face hardened, and the hall immediately erupted into protest:

"You can't come and go as you please!"

"What's the point of having wards and treaties if the dragons break them whenever they wish?"

"The wards have to be recast!"

Queen Lymsia stood. "As per our treaties, you are strictly forbidden from returning to these lands."

"The vorais has determined this to be one of our most important missions due to the presence of Syandrian aid. They fear our companion was unwillingly lured across the border." Gale held the queen's cold gaze. "As we have yet to find any sign of them, your help would be appreciated. Otherwise, our vorais may see this as an act of war."

A chill struck Fae despite how hot the hall was becoming. Another war? Surely no one wanted that! From what Alysion had taught him about their people, they weren't prepared to handle a war; they were still recovering from the last one.

"Is that a threat?" Queen Lymsia said, emerald eyes narrowed.

"It's a warning," said Cane. "If you have *any* information about our companion, please give it to us before we depart."

"We will speak with you in private later," said the queen stiffly. "You shall depart for Fiiraania tomorrow morning."

Fae nearly slid off the bench. Tomorrow? That was too soon! He wanted more than a single evening with Ash! *It's not like it's forever,* he consoled himself. *He'll be back.*

• • • ● • • •

"How are you feeling?" Fae asked his brother as they made their way back to their room. A very unhappy Alysion was stuck in the hall with his parents. The lost looks flitting across Ashmyr's face were troubling.

He paused in the middle of the aerial walkway—one of the few still intact. Fae patiently stood beside him. "I don't know how I feel," he began. "My entire life has been a lie. Everything I've worked for was to fulfill someone else's selfish goals. I don't know who or what I am anymore." He was so distraught that Fae reached out to hug him. Ash instinctively stepped away.

"Ah, sorry," said Fae, dropping his arms.

"No, no, it's all right. As isidyll, no one was permitted to touch me. It's just habit." He stepped forward again, and Fae embraced him, holding him tight.

He closed his eyes and breathed in deep, never wanting to let go. Ash no longer smelled like the garden around their childhood home, but that was all right. He was here, he was alive, and that was enough.

"You're my brother. Nothing will ever change that. I missed you so much," Fae said, voice quivering. Ash fidgeted awkwardly, but still, Fae didn't let go.

"I knew you were alive. I thought about you every day. Once you're back from Fiiraania, nothing will separate us again."

Thirty

Coming Out

Fae was tucked away in the temple's vast library—engrossed in one of the many old scrolls in an attempt to distract him from Ash and the dragons' departure—when Alysion found him.

"Is something wrong?" he asked, noting the way Alysion played with a strand of hair.

"Well..." he said, leading Fae from the library to another tower across the courtyard. "It's my parents. They want to talk to us about, well, us."

"Oh," he said weakly, feet growing cold.

"I haven't spoken to them about our relationship yet, but..."

He nodded.

"My parents told me a bit about the crystals," Alysion explained in an attempt to settle their nerves as they made their way to the isidyll's chamber where his parents were staying. "They were used during the Syl-Raanian War to fight the dragons. By combining their powers and amplifying them via the Kunzite, the vorais was slain, ending the war. Afterwards, they were hidden away since the allure of their power is too tempting for many. The prophecy was created by select members of the court as a means of protecting them. Should a crystal be taken from its hiding place, the prophecy would be triggered, and the Kunzite would be transferred into the damis of the divine descendant most suited to the task."

Alysion had certainly measured up to that.

"Who created the crystals?" asked Fae.

Alysion frowned. "They didn't say, but I suspect some old ancestor of mine."

Fae just nodded.

All too soon, they reached the isidyll's chamber. The door was open.

He swallowed, throat dry. Alysion's story hadn't been enough to distract him from his nerves. The queen didn't like him; she'd made that very clear. The king, on the other hand, had stood up for him. But he knew they didn't approve of Alysion courting another nelim, especially a damisri. His guts twisted unpleasantly as a million thoughts raced through his mind. He almost wished he were fighting Tarathiel again. Almost.

• • • ● • • •

"You asked to see us?" Alysion said as they entered the room. His mother stood in the middle, arms crossed, watching Fae through narrowed eyes. His father sat in a chair off to the side, his expression strained. Clearly, they'd been arguing before he and Fae showed up. He'd heard his father whisper something about Tarathiel and 'the truth.'

He recalled how tense his father had been while his mother told the dragons how Tarathiel had lured the copper dragon across the border to stage an attack on Illuven and his friends. There had been a few instances where Alysion thought his father would speak, but he kept silent. Afterwards, the king had pulled him aside and told him about their history with Tarathiel. Alysion was still getting over the shock of learning that his father had once been with Tarathiel; it was partly why his mother was so averse to him courting nelim. It had been hard for his father to tell him this, but Alysion understood. What happened with Tarathiel was terrible, and he vowed not to let anyone get in the way of his budding relationship with Fae.

"You love him, don't you?" the queen said. It wasn't a question.

Alysion blinked, returning to the present. "Y-yes," he stammered.

"I've put much effort into trying to pair you with someone who would benefit the kingdom," she said, turning away from him and Fae to gaze out the window. "I've introduced you to every possible candidate in Sylandris, yet you've turned all of them down."

His breath caught. *Here it comes.* The rejection of Fae. Their outright refusal to accept him taking a nelim mate. Alysion, breaking out in a cold sweat, didn't say a word. Beside him, Fae did the same. There was some small comfort in knowing he wasn't alone. No, he wouldn't let his parents stand between them.

"I tried to tell you that I have no interest in belim," he said, voice cracking. His mother turned to face him, nostrils flaring. Not a good sign.

"Back then, you wouldn't hear of it, so I'm telling you again now," his voice steadily grew stronger. "I love Fae, and if you can't accept that, then there is nothing I can do for you." He grabbed Fae's hand. "If we will not be accepted here, then we will leave. *Both* of us."

He felt Fae's surprised gaze on him but didn't look away from his mother.

"I support you," said the king, rising from his seat.

"I beg your pardon?" snapped the queen.

"I will not allow another to go through what I have, least of all my own son," he said firmly, crossing his arms. "You and I bear just as much responsibility for recent events as Tarathiel does, Lymsia."

When his father had stood up for Fae the day before, Alysion had been surprised; this was something else entirely.

Queen Lymsia stared at Illuven, mouth hanging open in shock.

"I will not come between them," Illuven said, expression hardening. His father was having difficulty keeping it together; Alysion could see it reflected in his eyes. Despite all that had happened, the king still cared for Tarathiel.

The queen looked from her mate to her son. Then she furrowed her brow, crossed her arms, and sat on the bed.

"When you eventually assume the throne, whether it be tomorrow or centuries from now, this kingdom will be your responsibility. You may have stopped Tarathiel's plot, but that doesn't mean you have won over the hearts of our people. They are not used to change, and they will not easily accept you."

She paused.

"If you do not produce an heir, our lineage will end with you. Are you ready to accept that? Are you willing to be the last of the Ancestors' line?"

What did he care about the Ancestors' line? At this point, he wasn't even sure if the Ancestors existed. Not once had they shown themselves to him or tried to put a stop to Tarathiel's plot. Instead, they let their descendants scorn elves like Fae, who, despite lacking their gift, had proven time and time again that lineage didn't matter.

Fae gave his hand a gentle squeeze, and Alysion didn't need to think twice about his decision.

"I am."

His mother raked an assessing eye over both of them. Alysion bristled.

"You'll have to convince our people that he is worthy of their respect. He may have helped stop Tarathiel, but that does not mean our people will accept a dam—someone without a damis."

Alysion nodded, well aware it would take time for their people to warm up to the idea of their prince choosing a mate like Fae.

"And you," she said, addressing Fae. "Are you prepared to support him until the end of your days, regardless of what our people think? Of how they treat you?"

"Of course, Your Majesty. I love him," Fae replied.

Alysion's heart sang.

• • • ● • • •

Fae could hardly contain his joy as they hurried out of the room. He felt lighter than air, as if a giant weight had been lifted off his chest. Alysion's parents had accepted him! Perhaps begrudgingly, but it was acceptance nonetheless!

Back in the privacy of the library, he grabbed Alysion and spun him around. The prince's eyes shone like polished emeralds as their lips met, fire igniting between them through their kiss.

"Someone might see us," Alysion said when they broke apart, panting for air.

"Let them," Fae growled.

Alysion smiled. "I suppose they should know that you are their future king."

The floor jolted beneath his feet. Him? King? Not once had the thought ever crossed his mind. "Yes, they should," he said after a stunned moment, smiling as he buried his hands in Alysion's soft golden locks, pulling him close.

Alysion's face lit up, and their lips met again, both happy to be with the one he loved most.

Epilogue

The small smile on Illuven's lips died once the boys rounded a corner and disappeared. He turned and studied Lymsia as she gazed out the window, her back to him. He couldn't help but wonder if sending Ashmyr to Fiiraania had been a wise decision. If the boy knew the truth about the copper dragon's demise, had she put all of Sylandris in danger?

To Be Continued...

Uhaan Stallion

Mare

Acknowledgments

Thank you to everyone who helped make this book possible! First to Laura and Denae for being my main supporters. To my amazing editors Clare Marshall and Michaela Choi for all your hard work helping me shape this into something readable. A loud shoutout to my beta readers, Allie (who read it twice!), Erin, and Bee. To Chery for the stellar cover art, and for creating social media ads that are much nicer than my sad attempts. Thank you Anita Daher and T. D. Cloud for answering all my questions about traditional and self-publishing. And finally to my family who encouraged me to read.

About the Author

R. Dawnraven is a formless entity who enjoys collecting shiny rocks, flailing about with swords, and creating all kinds of art. They live on Treaty 1 territory. *The Hidden Crystals* is their first novel.

Instagram - Twitter - Tumblr

RDawnraven

Photo taken by Justin C. E. Penner

Made in the USA
Monee, IL
18 January 2023